AGAINST PEACE AND FREEDOM

AGAINST PEACE AND FREEDOM

by Mark Rosenfelder

≈8 ∂ YONAGU BOOKS

www.yonagu.com • Chicago • 2011

ISBN 978-0-9844700-4-4

Acknowledgements

Thanks to Christopher Livingston, John Cowan, Mark Irons, James Schuller, Mathieu Richir, Harry Rohde, and Alan Morgan for comments. James M. Li very kindly helped with the *wényán*. And special thanks to my wife Lida who read it and supported it, even though it was science fiction.

There's more about the Incatena universe (though nothing you need to know to read the book) here:
http://www.zompist.com/incatena.html

I

The Cardinal Principle of the Peace Movement is harmony. Is this not a beautiful aspiration? How misinformed one must be to rail against it!

—Planetary Marshal Jishuri Kumari

Atami

You're ready to take on Director Kumari, only you're a bag of bones.

It's normal; it's the defreezing process. Interstellar travel is expensive, even if the Incatena is picking up the bill. To save mass, they remove anything inessential: fat, hair, nails, epidermis, a large fraction of muscle and bone mass. A shuttle meets the ship a billion km from β Hydri with a cargo of diamond and ice, and they rebuild you during the approach to Okura. You stay asleep for most of it, but they have to wake you at intervals for a systems check.

It's glamorous, being an Agent.

You're soon well enough to stay awake, and you study the notes in your neurimplant and watch Okura through the windows of the lounge as the *Hydrogen Queen* gets closer. It's a homey looking planet, blue and green and white. Most of the green is native: Okura is one of the minority of planets with its own ecosphere, and the colonists have tried to cultivate native plants and animals rather than use Earth stock.

You locate Orindzai, the next planet in, as well. It's just a bright green point in the viewport, but like Okura, because of Okura, it's another headache, because it's a Dzebyet planet. The aliens got here first, six thousand years ago, but for some reason Kumari is stirring up trouble with them.

The quickship stays in orbit; another shuttle takes you down to Atami. You're expecting something brown and gloomy, with olive drab uniforms and steam engines. It's a dictatorship, after all. But as the shuttle lands you see that Atami is a little jewel of a city, bright white buildings located on a scatter of islands on the coast, nestled amid tall green mountains.

Spaceports are usually slow... it took you 24 years to get here, what's the hurry? But the officials are quick and polite, and they get you off the ship, reunite you with your luggage, and get you through customs in less than an hour. Kumari must be the type of dictator who makes the trains run on time, if he has any trains. *Are* there trains? It wasn't in the briefing, perhaps you should ask someone.

You're under cover, of course— you're an Indonesian business rep named Rimu Botaki. The officials check your documents thoroughly, they nanoscan you and your luggage, and soldiers walk around carefully giving the impression that though they haven't fired their plasmators in years they would really like to. But they do this to everyone, and everything is in order.

While you're at the spaceport, you adjust your inoculated watch. The term refers not to a timepiece that doesn't have to worry about the cruds, but one surgically implanted in the eye; it gets its power from the electric currents of your own nerves, and projects a digital display, adjusted to the ambient light-flow, directly on the retina. You've often been glad to have it, and the compass reading has come in handy too, although you've sometimes regretted choosing the model with the smiley face.

To readjust the clock, you simply place a finger in each ear and press the back of your palate with your tongue. A stream of travelers with both fingers in their ears is now a common sight in all major spaceports, and no longer frightens children. You click the hidden sense-spots until the display reads

13:15 20 Jul 185° ☺

and you're on your way.

You stride out of the spaceport. Still nothing brown and gloomy— the city is a mass of bright white buildings sparkling in the sunlight. Or β Hydri-light. Perhaps there's a better term.[1]

What should you do first? Check out the Commerce Association? Hunt out the dissidents, or the Oji— the underworld— or Ikkyū-shima? Maybe a good restaurant; you're still low on muscle mass.

-----

[1] The Peace Party has renamed β Hydri "Peace" (*Ewa*), so the approved term is Peacelight.

As you leave the spaceport, two men in business robes come up to you.

"Greetings, Botaki-san," says the first, in passable Indonesian of just a couple centuries back. He's a short, pale, nerdy, wiry fellow, as insinuating as a telemarketer, but not as pleasant to listen to.

How did he know you? Ah, through the passenger list, of course. The Directorate is very thorough.

"Greetings, o-san," you say, in Okurinese.

The second man, large, beefy, big, and with too many teeth, laughs. "Seems you've boned up on Okura." Something about the way the scar across his face reddens when he curls his lip induces an instant antipathy.

The first man, more suave, bows deeply. "We are honored to have visitors from the heart of humanity to our colonial planet. We are official minions of the Tourism Ministry, and our instructions are to assist you in any way which might prove necessary during your stay."

In other words, the Directorate has enough agents on hand to provide two to accompany visitors wherever they go in Okura and watch everything they do. You look them over. Pasty and Nasty, you name them.

"We've made reservations for you at the Hotel Soloy," Pasty tells you. "It is a very good, very modern tourist hotel."

Right. You have a feeling that the Hotel Soloy is going to be a kind of poster child for advanced cases of photonic surveillance.

There's a tourist kiosk nearby, with a list of hotels. You notice a hotel whose advertisement is entirely in Okurinese: the Yokan Otani; with a gesture from your neurimplant you grab its address. "I don't want to stay in a tourist hotel," you say. "I want to stay in a real Okurinese place."

Pasty's smile turns icy. "I'm afraid that's impossible."

"Is it illegal for foreigners to stay at anything but a tourist hotel?" you persist. "Is this some kind of dictatorship?"

"No, of course not," says Pasty, "but those are very bad hotels, not good for foreigners, and you have reservations at the Hotel Soloy."

"Thanks all the same, but I'll find my own lodgings," you insist.

Pasty mutters something in Nasty's ear. Nasty comes purposefully over to you, with his arm held straight out.

You are still deciding whether to shake hands or try a judo flip when Nasty grabs hold of your hand and, slowly but firmly, forces it around behind your back. It doesn't seem that your will has any effect either on him or on the trajectory of your arm. Nasty keeps twisting, rather beyond the point an arm is meant to bend, until you cry out in pain and annoyance. He leaves it there a moment, then lets go and steps back.

"I— I'm going to report this at Incatena House," you sputter.

"O-san, you are very far from Incatena, you play by our rules," hisses Nasty.

"You're pronouncing it wrong. In-*cat*-en-a. And Okura is a member," you insist. Nasty looks like he's going to cite the grammatical authority of his fists, but Pasty stops him with a raised hand.

"I most regret this unpleasant experience, o-san," says Pasty, silkily. "My colleague is most aggressive and patriotic, but we will care for you like deep brothers. Let us begin by moving in the direction of the Hotel Soloy."

Pasty hails a taxiboat.

You arrive at the Hotel Soloy, and your shadows check you in. The Hotel Soloy is a large, white, starkly geometric building, with all the modern conveniences the sophisticated traveler of today demands— room-scale holos, adjustable gravity, Vee connections, helper mecs. The price is C. 40 a night.

A minor problem is bugs— not the insect kind, but photonic ones. There's one hidden in the lamp, and the soft whir of recording devices occasionally keeps you up at night. It's reasonable to assume that the Directorate leaves these obvious anachronisms around so that you can destroy them, thus attaining a completely spurious sense of security.

You find that the care the Tourism Ministry invests in its guests is quite comprehensive. You eat with Pasty and Nasty; they have rooms on either side of you; they are there to make every arrangement for you. You need to get rid of them. That's an action item; you note it down in your data neurimplant.

At least there's that Vee connection. But it turns out to be laughable— the only scenes you can connect to are run by the government, and even those are shoddy, full of cheesy animated holograms and broken links.

You wish you had a good gun, or a good military implant, but that would never have got past the nanoscans. It's down to you and your wits and good looks.

At least you're able to confirm that Okura does not in fact have trains. Good, that's one action item crossed off. That leaves the big one: overthrowing the dictatorship.

Briefing

Just 24 years ago objective time, a few weeks subjective, you couldn't even spell Jishuri Kumari, and no one asked you to, really.

You were at your time-share in Areopolis, recovering from your mission to Novazema. The place was frankly a mess. People with an instinct for domestic happiness don't become quick-ship barnacles. For years on end you're on a mission, and then you've got six months or a year to crash, debauch, train, see if any of your old friends remember your last visit, and if so whether they're willing to overlook it— if not, cruise the Vee for new friends.

That, and certainly not (say) character flaws, is the explanation for the dirty clothes, music dots, obsolete weaponry, and datapacks littering the floor, the absolute nonexistence of food or vegetation in every room, the mail messages on the datanode dating back to the early 4800s. Besides, it's a time-share, and the furniture is only 1/20 yours.[1] It wouldn't seem like your place at all if it didn't have your mess in it.

And it wouldn't seem like home if it weren't for your pet. Iqizi is a trelentocynomorph, a creature native to ε Eridani IV, who has such a slowed metabolism that it takes him a week to cross the room. His food is a pile of iron shavings in a bowl; he eats the rust as it oxidizes. He is not exactly aware of you, but you always feel some affection for your old companion as you watch the small, solid, stubby creature shambling motionlessly across the floor.

---

[1] 1/19, technically, till they can track down the next of kin for Rodriguez, poor girl.

There were things to do, of course. Like laundry; that'd be on top of the list for weeks on end. You hate to do laundry, though you can't claim that it's hard work. Why is it you can't form the habit of dropping the stuff in the laundry hatch every night for the building to take care of? You wouldn't even have to check the pockets for guns or credit packs or anything; a house mec would bring them by in an hour or two, laid out neatly next to the clean and folded clothes. As it is, it takes about twenty minutes to gather up clothes from all parts of the house, not counting time spent trying to remember how some of this stuff got there, and in some cases who it belonged to and whether getting them out of it was a good time. Plus Iqizi always manages to pin down something with his feet, and then you'd might as well wait a day for him to shift position.

There's the Vee looming over you, too. You've got fifty years' worth of Solar history, science, and pop culture to catch up on. You have to recognize the new fashions, know the new slang, explore the new gameworlds. It's a tedious prospect, but it's part of your job, right? And you manfully take it on, between bouts of SimGalaxy, Zombies at Groombridge 1618, and Orc Rampage: Elfpocalypse.

You were bored, you had to admit. And yet the summons still seemed to come too early.

It's a short walk to headquarters: the Incatena Spire, the administrative hub of human space, housed in an imposing tower that breaks through the Tajima energy screen into the thin Martian atmosphere, dwarfing the more modest, ancient domes of Areopolis Center. From the upper floors there are marvelous views of the endless red Martian desert. Here and there are the remains of an abandoned terraforming project: a few stands of kudzu. Nothing else could be found that would grow up here in the highlands.

The Spire is a bustling place, with men and women and the occasional alien rushing past on their astoundingly important business. You can tell the colonials— they're the ones who say "Excuse me" when they run into you.

You get to the boss's office, late as usual. The boss looks out of sorts. He usually does. He's nursing a cup of Sihorian caf. He usually is. He looks like a man who's a little bit too awake. The cup has an animation of himself on it, scowling.

He nods at you, as if he'd seen you last night rather than six months ago, and jabs a thumb in the direction of his datanode.

"It's that damn Ormant," he says.

You've heard of Ormant. Interstellar tycoon. "What's he done now?" you ask.

"We don't know," confesses the boss. "That's just it."

"I see," you say, brightly.

"But what I want to know is, how does New Bharat get into this? And what do you think about the shit on the agg?"

You worry that not having heard the news hampers the effectiveness of your reply. "Sounds bad," you venture.

"Huh? What's bad?"

"Oh, well, you know, the news."

The boss seems to look at you for the first time, and give such an impression of seeing a pimple that you palpate your face anxiously. "What *are* you talking about?"

"You know, things are looking bad all over..."

The boss quickly loses interest in you. He's staring at a datascene hovering above his datanode. You manage to read the headline: KUMARI ANNOUNCES AMNESTY.

"You can trust that like a grant application," remarks the boss. He sips on his caf, mumbles something about the Dzebyet not cooperating, and focuses again on you, not for information, but to make sure he has your absolute attention.

He says, slowly, as if imparting a great truth: "The Incatena is a very delicate object."

This usually begins a speech. You relax. The boss's speeches don't require feedback, or even attention.

"I mean, it's *lasted* awhile," continues the boss. "Two thousand years. But *how* has it lasted two thousand years? What keeps fifty-odd systems sprinkled over a hundred-light-year sphere more or less together?"

"Restraint," you mutter, under your breath.

"Restraint, that's what," says the boss. "Everybody benefits if we accept a few simple rules. Like, no war."

He jabs into the air, bringing a holographic star map to life. That tenuous scatter of human colonies, the Human Incatena, appears.

He's droning on about war now. There haven't been any interstellar wars since Novorossiya, back in the 2600s— the one that showed how absurd it was in a universe where Einstein's speed limit applies. Even the most powerful human stellar system[1], if it wastes a huge fraction of its metal and energy resources to send a war fleet four light years away, can't defeat a system whose industrial complex is *right there*. And when you can't even tell whether your nukes hit anything till years or decades later, it can be questioned whether your expeditionary force is even yours any more.[2]

As everyone knows (but the boss is telling you anyway), the corollary is that you can't build an advantage any other way, because you can't back it up with force. You try your textbook economic imperialism on somebody, and they're going to get sick of it and confiscate your assets, and who are you going to complain to?

But we have a few common interests, so we have the Incatena, which facilitates commerce, research, cultural understanding, colonization, and police work. It talks to the aliens. It's a platform for sharing useful discoveries and currency algorithms and new anti-spam techniques.

"Everybody knows it's not a government, but we call it one, because it sounds better," the boss muses.

The smooth flow of his own words always calms the boss. He looks almost happy. But now a troubling thought seems to occur to him.

"Only once in a while some damn fool comes along who doesn't know what everybody knows. They've got some imbe-

---

[1] Sol back then; today it'd be ε Indi, almost entirely because of Sihor. Iemanjá doesn't contribute much except lovely ocean-front retirement condos for Sihorians.

[2] Once this was realized, the Douane's expeditionary force joined up with Euko, the next planet out, and the interstellar war became an interplanetary war, which is less stupid, barely. The war was over in a few years and the politics sorted out a few decades later, culminating in the Incatena Treaty.

cile idea about tactics, or the stock market, or God, and they try to turn the Incatena upside down.

"This time it looks like there's a whole load of damn fools out in the South Quadrant."

"Here's the bottom line, Morgan," says the boss. "You're going out there."

"Huh? Where?"

He stabs a finger at the little glowing dot of β Hydri, which glows a little brighter.

"Okura, of course. Kumari's mixed up in this somehow, and Ormant might be there."

He moves his finger out a bit, lighting up ζ Tucanae.

"Or here— New Bharat. Plan on both.

"Whatever Ormant's up to, stop it. Kumari too. Read the reports from the field before you go— you can trust Beloman, Hrvatski, and Xiang." He makes a UI gesture. "Bing. There's C. 15,000. In the worst case the whole Incatena's on the line, so don't fuck up. Now get out of here."

The boss swivels around on his levitating chair, taking his caf with him. You are dismissed.

Flatfootery

Before any major mission you like to do a little research. It helps to know your way around the planet you're going to, and you never know when some Agent might have solved the problem you're facing a few centuries back.

You settle into your office in the Spire. That means, of course, the generic office where they've installed your ergolounge and datanode and personal mementos, which are kept in storage while you're in the field. The workspace is covered with documents and printouts— in AD 4901 we're still awaiting the paperless office. Toys, souvenirs, weapons, commendations, and long outdated organizational charts crowd the shelves.

You turn on the datanode. A session of Undersea Destroyer is still going— the Blues have destroyed all the enemy submarines and are now working on the sharks. You exit it. The word processor is also up, showing an unfinished document:

Notes for half-century perf review

—What did I do?—
• negotiated treaty on Qeng
• Novazema— less said the better

—Strengths—
Experience, knowledge, savvy, languages, cool under fire, well-informed, compassionate, fit, loyal, courageous, hard-working, responsible, self-starter, communications skills, martial arts, socionomics, photonics, strategic thinker, weapons expertise, people person.

—Weaknesses—

> *—Plan for next 50 years—*
> • maximize strengths
> • minimize weaknesses

You can finish that later. You look in the Agent Reports for information on Okura. The last field report, Hrvatski's, is from 4878.

> Almost a hundred years ago, in 4790, the colony planet of Okura (β Hydri IV) was brought under a centralized totalitarian government, under the control of General Nobuto Nashimoto. He was deposed in 4821 by Col. Jishuri Kumari, his chief of staff.

"Jeez, don't start off with a joke or anything," you mutter to yourself. You keep reading:

> The Kumari regime, called the Directorate, has imposed on Okura (pop. 485 million) a paramount "Peace Party," a state-directed economy, a huge military budget, and a personality cult— all the trappings of ideological tyranny discarded in more evolved systems centuries ago. The Peace Party declares itself in possession of "the ultimate solutions which have eluded humankind for millennia," and exhorts the Okurinese to "lead the galaxy."

Hrvatski is an annotator. All the nouns have been linked to Vee resources, or festooned with popups; the eye tracker even brings up an animated helper if you focus too long on any one word. But you're a big picture person; you ignore it all.

> Kumari himself is an ascetic, with spiritual preoccupations. He lives modestly, but does not induce the Party elite to do so. Suspicious of plots, he never appears in public except virtually. He is said to have an actor's sense of translocation: his holo really seems to be looking at you. He is intelligent, cultured, an excellent metago player, in person alternately charming and domineering. He is not married.

> The existence of such a regime, with its disagreements with the Incatena, would be bad enough in any system; but the situation is

particularly grave in the β Hydri system, which we share with the Dzebyet.

Only a few intrepid dissenters have had the means and the energy to steal a scooter and escape to Orindzai. The Dzebyet have no wish to harbor a human refugee colony, but have allowed a few hundred humans to stay, and those who can have fled from Orindzai to other systems. This is a point of contention between the two planets; another is the anti-alien tone of some of Kumari's rhetoric.

The report goes on to analyze the prospects for resistance. It doesn't look good. It's a growing society, so general prosperity is enough to damp down resistance; and when that isn't enough the Home Ministry steps in. There are no legal avenues of protest, and Kumari keeps a close watch on plots within the Party and the army. He seized power himself, so he's never forgotten that others could do the same. And he's only 600, so relief isn't going to come soon by natural means.

The regional situation seems more promising:

Kumari faces one serious problem of internal dissent. Before Nashimoto's takeover, there were twelve nations on Okura, including his own, Gōsei. One of these nations, Ikkyū-shima— the largest, with a population of 90 million— was only incorporated into the union by force, during the Coalition War. Ikkyū-shima has regained its 48C prosperity, but to consolidate Party rule drastic measures were needed; the former elite was almost entirely replaced by Gōsei-jin. The Ikkyū-jin have been a security problem for the Party ever since.

There's a long section on conflicts with the Incatena; most of them sound infantile, but it's the closest Kumari has to an external threat. But this worries you:

On the official side, our Station Chief's policy has been to engage closely with the regime, though as a legal point dictatorships cannot be members.

In other words, Hrvatski thinks the Station Chief is an appeaser. Good to know. But perhaps things have changed? You

check the records; a new Station Chief, one Meillet, was sent out
about twenty years back. A political appointee; you recall that the
boss didn't name him as someone you could trust.

> I suspect that Kumari aims ultimately at secession from the In-
> catena. There are three thorns in his side: Ikkyū-shima, which is
> under control, and Orindzai and the Incatena, which are not.
> What power and prestige the Incatena commands is due largely to
> its inclusion of every human planet; Kumari can thus do us real
> damage. If it were possible he would certainly have external am-
> bitions, but Kumari is not rumored to be insane or stupid.

—Agent R. Hrvatski, Atami, Okura, July 4878. Received 4901/IC.

The Incatena's information on Jules Ormant and his disappearance is disappointing. Excellent at political analysis, the
Agents of the Incatena are typically hopeless when it comes to
high finance, and their reports on Ormant don't have much more
to say than "involved in numerous high-profile interstellar business operations" and "rich, unscrupulous, five times married,
three times divorced." If Incatena Agents understood making
money, they wouldn't be living on salary in messy time-shares.

Some research at the Mars Exchange seems to be in order.
The Mars Exchange is the hub of the Martian financial network,
and by extension that of the entire Incatena. Over C. 10^{14} worth of
shares, bonds, contracts, copyrights, and physical merchandise
change hands (or in some cases tentacles) here daily.

The actual trading floor is virtual; brokers all over the planet
plug in photonically, through the Vee. Their avatars tend to ap-
proximate one or another archetypal financier, from the jut-
jawed, aggressive young man to the trustworthy old uncle, from
the distractingly attractive young woman to the competent but
caring matron.

You check out the abstracted virtual trading floor, Xmes.[1]
There's fevered competition to be prominently featured in Xmes,

---

[1] There are scenes dedicated to each commodity, such as the
Copyrights Room or the Franchises Gallery. But the metaphor strained
and snapped once there were millions of traders, and developers abstracted them into packages. Then the packages were themselves ab-

and Jules Ormant is very well placed; his Ormant/Mars Enterprises is right on the home scene. Mining Xmes from a public datanode in the Exchange dome, you identify half a dozen other firms where Ormant is a major participant or stockholder. One of these, with the interesting name New Bharat Nice Trading, is listed in just one package, Venture! Outsystem Trading Aggregator.

You ask a buddy in a trading firm, Dinho Pereira, what this all means. "He's highly webbed, and near the door," he explains. "Ormant/Mars's got a spicy locus as a fat actor. Most of the deets you can ignore; it's just inkjet. The outlier's good bird-dogging, and I wouldn't be surprised if it's a sleeping slaver. VOTA's in-bed anyway."

"Thanks, that's what I thought," you say. You find another buddy, Antonia Chang/Nkruda, and ask her what the explanation of what it all means means.

"Ormant is one fuck of a presence on the Exchange," she translates. "There's not many companies that in themselves could have a serious effect on the market, but his is one of them. As for New Bharat Nice Trading, my guess is that it's the ultimate holding company for the bulk of Ormant/Mars itself. Probably set up so ordinary investors get a slow ride and no real power, while he can leverage his whole operation from there. And he owns the only package it's in, so he can even cut off access if he wants."

"Thanks, that's what I thought," you say. "By the way, what exactly is Ormant *in*? I mean, is he a bank, or an info provider, or what?"

"Oh, he doesn't *do* anything," Antonia explains. "He trades, he invests, he sells packages, he puts together deals, he breaks them up."

"So he's basically a useless parasite, who doesn't produce goods or information or services, a wood louse living in the interstices of our advanced but spiritually bankrupt civilization," you suggest.

---

stracted into a higher layer, the Exchange Meta Scenesuite (Xmes). It's said that the first abstraction level keeps you from knowing who you're trading with, and the second keeps you from knowing what you're trading.

"Well, yeah, but that that's basically what I do too, on an infinitely smaller scale, so I pretty much think he's God."

Kiboizing the Vee for mentions of Ormant, you come up with a few cryptic references. There's a lot of speculation on where he's disappeared to. He's from Sihor, he's probably gone back there. He's buying up most of the economy of New Bharat. He's joined a religious cult. He's hiding somewhere in a non-Douane nation.[1] He's out past Jupiter on his private liner, waiting for some crisis to blow over.

Someone who claims to know his oncosurgeon says he's been so genetically altered that his body rejects his own original DNA. This comment sparked a discussion on whether Ormant could disinherit his five sons, on the grounds that they were no longer genetically his offspring.

Ormant is said to be one of the only humans to have sold a franchise to the Garcheron, who normally don't buy anything but handcrafts from any species as primitive as ourselves.

He's said to have commissioned an AI with his own personality and knowledge. Building and training the AI took forty years; when it was done he had it copied and the copies now occupy all the number-two spots in his organizations.

A Sihorian businessman comments that all these stories are lies. He's gone yacht-racing with Ormant in the asteroids, and found him to be just a regular guy (a regular guy with the net worth of a small planet). He did seem a little severe with the help. When he lost the race he had his navigator's hand chopped off. Not very nice, but he could grow a new one as soon as they got back to port, right?

After these investigations, you feel you've formed a good picture of Ormant's character and commerce. You take notes in your data neurimplant:

ORMANT. *Involved in numerous high-profile interstellar business operations. Rich, unscrupulous, five times married, three times divorced.*

---

[1] The Douane and Luna are the Incatena members in Sol's system. A few Earth nations and space habitats never bothered to join, and thus are technically not Incatena territory.

Speed limit

As a frequent space traveler, you have a personal grudge against Albert Einstein. It's not so bad for civilians, groundnuts— people who only travel outsystem a couple times in a lifetime. Studying on Novorossiya (just four years from Sol), or migrating to Qeng (eleven years), can't even be called an extravagance, when lifespans approach a thousand years. But as a top Diplomatic Agent of the Human Incatena, you have a personal interest in this speed of light thing. It means you spend most of your days traveling, and not first class either— rather, frozen solid in a glorified bus in the dead of space. It doesn't eat up lifespan; it just screws up your life. Especially since trouble spots tend to be on the periphery of the Incatena.

You're supposed to keep the murders to a minimum, but you wouldn't answer for your actions if you ran into the cretins who write holofilms about Agents. They always show them falling in love with some beautiful local. Use some logic, you'd tell them, while dialing up the destruction level on your max gun to the highest setting. There's only three alternatives, each worse than the last: 1) Bring your civilian loved one along on all your missions— sure, two can live in harm's way as cheap as one. 2) Bring your S.O. back with you to Mars; hope the relationship bears up under twenty to fifty year absences. 3) Give up Agent work in favor of some other line where diplomatic skills and a lack of scruples pay. But who wants to be a politician?

Most Agents don't last more than a couple of centuries anyway. The deep-freeze, the crises, aliens, threats to life and limb, mind-numbing boredom, and the boss— two hundred years is enough for anyone.

Once again you wonder idly where Ormant's taken himself. It's not worth chasing after him; the chances are too good you'll guess wrong, and end up useless light-years away from the fireworks. The best guess is probably New Bharat; but that's 28 years away, and more or less in the direction of Okura, which is only 24 years away. You'd might as well head for Okura, see what Kumari's up to, and head out to New Bharat from there if it still seems advisable.

"And if you're still alive," the boss adds, encouragingly, when you tell him your plans.

With your destination set, you decide to acquire a cover. This is not, in an age of DNA reads, neuromapping, nanoscans, and mass subliminal surveillance, a matter of pasting on a false beard. Your new identity is sculpted by the best surgeons and psychotechnicians in the Incatena, over a period of two months. It involves giving you a new face, editing your DNA with viruses, and electrochemically altering your neural patterns. Plus there's a whole new past to learn, new ways of speaking, documents to acquire. With all this you just might pass the barrage of tests you can expect if your cover is suspected.

Thus your cover as Rimu Botaki, an Indonesian, travelling as an advance agent for a telephotonics firm, Tir Research, which is planning to expand into the South Quadrant. (Tir is a real firm, and these are real plans.) You thus have excellent reasons for viewing building sites, talking to government employees, making technical enquiries, and other activities which are clearly not espionage.

They're not going to rely on a patdown at the other end.[1] They'll be scanning every one of your personal molecules and rifling through your neurons— you'll have to leave your favorite gun at home, and your less favorite dozen guns too, and can't have any suspicious augmentations either, just your basic neurimplants.

You have a backup cover, too— an Okurinese named Nohashi. Same body, different documentation, one of several identities the Incatena has stockpiled just in case. Nohashi is a freelance writer, a cover that facilitates doing research; some rather vapid interviews have been published under the name.

The Incatena offices on Maraille, Sihor, New Bharat, and Orindzai (the Dzebyet planet in the β Hydri system), are sent descriptions of your new identity, but not the one on Okura, in case it's been compromised.

---

[1] They still *do* a patdown. They like doing that.

You pat Iqizi goodbye (he's been circling his bed for the last few weeks, getting ready for sleep) and head out to the spaceport.

Areopolis Spaceport is a relatively new complex, dating only to the 47C, but modernity cannot conceal its essential nature, which is a giant holding bin for nervous and tired people who are not yet where they want to be, who won't get where they want to be for many (subjective) weeks or months, and whom other people are delaying for incomprehensible reasons. The city government likes to call it the Gateway to the Galaxy. Those who use it know it as "Hell with a Snack Bar."

You arrive a little late at the *Hydrogen Queen*'s shuttle, and they don't want to let you on. Embarkation phase is over. You should have come on time, they tell you. Everybody else did. You argue for a long time, up and down the chain of command. The frustration is that one phone call to the Incatena Spire would clear everything up, but you're under cover.

Eventually they relent. You settle into a seat in the lounge, and they announce that departure will be delayed for five hours while cargo loading is completed.

You lift off, finally. This part of the job never stales— watching a landscape fall away, domes and monorails disappearing into the pale orange sands, Areopolis itself becoming a dot, the familiar map forming— there's Syrtis Major, there's Olympus Mons, with its awesome skiing— until the world becomes a mere planet, and recedes still. In only a few hours more, Mars is just a red dot in the sky, and you remember that you forgot to leave Iqizi's door to the garden open. That'll be one more bullet point in the nasty note the next Agent to use the time-share always sends you.

Finally you're on the *Hydrogen Queen* and can enjoy the amenities. When you're tired of the fine dining, the riskless gambling, the high-concept holofilms, and the company of businesspeople and Mormon missionaries, you get yourself reduced and frozen, a process which, despite all the technological advances of recent centuries, seems unnecessarily and offensively cold.

Minders

Most of the guests in the Hotel Soloy are offworlders plus their Tourism Ministry shadows. A few of them have been here for years, and have come to be close friends with their minders; a few even sleep with them. It's a dismal prospect, and it's not even like they got the really good thugs; they all pretty much look like Pasty and Nasty.

You mention that you need to visit the Commerce Association.

"We'll arrange a tour," says Pasty, at which Nasty unaccountably laughs. They sign you up for the 7 a.m. tour, which lasts all day. You and two other tourists, outnumbered by your Tourism Ministry shadows, are given an all-stops tour of the building. You start with a soporific talk from an official of the Association, then move through endless departments, statistics, and informational holos. You're invited to an official dinner, where another official tells you that due to the drive of the Okurinese people the Party's ambitious goals for the last year were exceeded in every category, and will be even higher this year, and that problems with shortages in basic goods are expected to be sorted out as soon as the responsible saboteurs are found and executed.

The day ends with a Peace Party parade, featuring a folkloristic dance by a small troupe of chubby, grinning teenagers, and a demonstration of a forward assault by the building's Peace Defense Unit.

You are so tired in the evening that you decline Pasty's invitation to attend the All-Gōsei Lawn Bowling Quarterfinals, which are going on tonight.

Maybe they'll loosen the reins if you get to know them. You can talk to anyone; it's your gift, or curse.

Encouraged to talk beyond platitudes, Pasty confides that he has a girlfriend, and her chief merit, so far as he's concerned, is that she'll do "anything" for him. He describes the anythings in lavish and demeaning detail— you feel sorry for the poor girl, but he goes on and on, till you have a headache and wish that one of the scenarios he describes would lead to his embarrassing death. And hers too; she shouldn't encourage him like that.

His only other passion is meta-go— an officially encouraged pastime, since Kumari plays. It sounds intensely dull.

As for Nasty, he likes sports of the kind that involve bruises, yelling, beer, and chances of death.

Now that they think you're interested, they bring up one of these subjects *all the time*. Nasty is even dropping hints about a threesome. Why is there no Undo gesture on life?

What can you do to get rid of these two? How about the Dzebyet Embassy? Even if they let your shadows in, they wouldn't be able to cause a scene if you attempt an escape.

"You don't want to go there," say Pasty and Nasty. "It's not very interesting for offworlders." Instead, they take you to the Peace Party Agricultural Fair. You see the latest in agricultural implements, happy farmers carrying small pigs, young women distributing fertilizer samples, small children doing a traditional dance in honor of agricultural productivity, a parade by veterans of the Okurinese Peace Army, and a very fat woman singing "Somewhere my Bonnie Lies Sleeping" with a male chorus.

Pasty and Nasty very kindly keep you from falling asleep during the fairly frequent moments when this might be a problem, and induce you to drink large quantities of *tanaki*, a weak Okurinese liquor that reminds you of liquid soap. You're too tired at the end of the day to do anything but sleep.

Pasty and Nasty, you decide, have got to go.

Meta-go à gogo

You consider attempting to escape the deadening duo in a crowd, but you decide that the odds (that would be two of them, one of you) are not good. The only time you're alone, away from Pasty and Nasty— and the only time the two of them are apart, as well— is at night. Nocturnal evasion it is then.

The obvious problems are that the door is locked and the windows have bars on them— to prevent injury, explains the hotel brochure; the bars themselves say the same if you touch them.

You could try breaking through the door by force, but it's a big door, and no doubt you're under video surveillance; most likely all you'd get for your trouble would be a bill for damages. Or maybe they'd call it even if Nasty did equal damage to you.

Instead, you decide to invite Pasty into your room for an after-dinner game of meta-go, and assault him. You don't tell him about the assault part. He readily accepts.

About ten at night, then, there's a knock on your door. There's Pasty, in his business robe without the outer cloak, and carrying what looks like a big black book under his arm. He doesn't seem to be armed— a pity, because you'd have liked to have his weapon.

"Shall we?" he asks, holding up the game set with what's meant to be an inviting smile.

He places the board on a table in your room and touches some controls. An array of ghostly bluish dots forming a three-dimensional grid appears above the black base. He demonstrates how you can move your hand to a particular coordinate and cause a brightly glowing spot to appear— red for you, gold for him. The rules seem simple; you alternate turns; surrounding a line of opposing pieces turns them to your color; whoever gets five pieces in a row wins.

The game moves quickly, and proves harder than you expected; you lose. He smiles and suggests another game. You have other ideas.

"Sure, but let me fix us something to drink," you say. You get up, with your back to the table. In one quick motion you pick up the lamp from the desk and swing it at his head. It smashes satisfyingly. He's not quite out; he struggles to get up out of his chair; but a couple quick punches and he's out, sprawled on the floor.

You straighten yourself up, breathe hard, and think about what to do next.

First, you escort the unfortunate Pasty back to his room and lay him out on the bed, tied to the bedposts. The room is set up with a plezh wire— nothing too good for our tourists— and you attach him to it, not because stimulating his pleasure center is high on your list of priorities, but because plezh, used while asleep, has a disordering effect on memory, and you'd like this boy's account of the night's events to be a little confused. There are chemicals that would do a better job, but you don't have any.

A search of the minion's room reveals recording equipment, a good supply of business robes, some interactive porno nodes, a datanode with risible security, and a max gun. You copy a bunch of documents from the datanode, take the gun, and head out into the hall.

You've almost reached the descent tubes when Nasty emerges like a bad dream from his room. Stuffed into a business outfit, he was no prize; but half-dressed and unshaven, in a sleep-robe a couple of sizes too small for him, he's enough to make you want to change your species. He's next to you like a bad dream, reaches out a hairy arm and places it on your shoulder with the evident intention of leaving it there for awhile. "Where you go-ing, o-san?" he growls.

"I'm, uh, just going to get a drink."

"We got room service in the hotel so nobody wanders out of their room where they might get hurt," he informs you, steering you back toward your room. They must pay this boy in raw meat, you think.

Then the gridfire of an outraged universe pierces through to your captivity like a knife through butter, and with a prolonged, terrified scream the big thug is melted like wax into pools of fleshy slag.

Actually, that doesn't happen. Damn.

You know a little Qengese gōngfū. Would this be the time to try it?

You concentrate your *ji* into your left elbow, mainly because Nasty has such a firm grip on your right shoulder that there's no room for any *ji* there. You shove your elbow violently back into Nasty's gut, then twist yourself free and knock Nasty into oblivion with a kick to the throat.

At least that's your plan, but it doesn't get much past the elbowing stage. Nasty doesn't have any particular reaction to your blow to his stomach, but he has one to your attempt to get away: he knocks you on the head with a flat slap of his ham-sized fist. You drop to the floor, and Nasty piles on top of you. There's something in the gōngfū manual about using an opponent's superior strength against him, but it's hard to remember the details when your opponent is using his superior strength to roll you up like a futon.

Either you didn't concentrate enough *ji* into your elbow, you decide, or Nasty has a hell of a lot more *ji* than you do.

The one thing on your side is that you have a max gun. You manage to abstract your consciousness from what's happening to your windpipe enough to get hold of it, aim at the nearest portion of Nasty's anatomy, and fire.

Nasty howls with pain, and relaxes his grip. You scramble away, with some difficulty. Nasty is writhing in pain, trying to slap himself in six places at once, as the multiple max gun projectiles wander through his body. You knock him out with the gun handle, before his cries wake somebody up. You drag him to a maintenance closet, and leave him among the towels, batteries, and cleaning mecs.

The front descent tubes and the main desk will no doubt be watched; the back exit is a little safer. On the ground floor you skulk around kitchens, garages, and storerooms for awhile before you hit upon a stroke of luck: some people are unloading a cargo volant. You manage to join in this process in such a way that the people with the volant think you belong to the hotel, and the hotel people think you're with the volant. After about fifteen minutes of this, you simply wander off down the street.

Cautious about violating curfew, you spend the night hiding in someone's back garden; then at the break of day saunter to the water's edge, hire a taxiboat, and have yourself taken down-town. A couple more random rides take you to the Yokan Otani.

Service for one at the Otani

The Yokan Otani is a traditional Okurinese guesthouse, set in a cozy garden patterned after the mountain glens of upper Gōsei. Your room is in blond native wood, with floors of tatami matting. A niche in the wall displays a vase with a single spray of flowers; sliding paper doors at one end of the room open onto a little balcony that overlooks the bay.

A young woman dressed in kimono (with an ancient design featuring wide-eyed children and electronic components) comes in at dinnertime with your meal, and sits with you on the floor while you eat. You can talk to her as you eat; it's very nice. She also helps you get ready for bed, and tidies up the room. You stretch out on the futon, fondle a row of music dots, which each briefly display their data and squeal a sample, and select one; koto music begins playing on the music node.

The experience is soothing, and charmingly colonial. This must be what ancient Japan was like (today it's a crowded, exhausted nightmare). As you sit by the little table working, with the smell of the sea in the air, the problems of Okura and the Incatena seem far away.

Pasty's documents do not contain any great state secrets. There is a fairly full dossier on you— description, claimed itinerary, a record of your excursions in Atami with the two of them. You're nodding over the summary of Rimu Botaki's activities on Earth— the invented life history so carefully fabricated back at the Incatena Spire— when it occurs to you, eerily, that it's impossible, that what you're holding in your hands cannot be. They couldn't possibly have a file on every businessperson in Indonesia; nor could they have gotten any information from Earth once you arrived.

Several panicky and physics-defying scenarios pass through your head before it comes to you: Kumari has agents on Mars, who got hold of the *Hydrogen Queen*'s passenger list and did a little investigation before it left. Or perhaps spies on board the ship itself commed the passenger list back to Kumari's Solar agents, who did their research and sent it by laser to Okura. Quickships don't reach the speed of light; they could have worked a few weeks and their report would still beat the ship to Okura.

Pasty's notes don't contain any hint that your cover is suspected. The Tourism Ministry obviously proceeds under the assumption that *any* traveler could be a lackey of the decadent offworld plutocrats. Still, Pasty himself didn't see any threat in you, which is all to the good— although his precise wording, "incompetent stinking zero person," is somewhat wounding.

More important is a missive from the Home Ministry giving a general warning about businessmen; some sort of dissidence is suspected in, of all places, the Commerce Association. That's good; that wasn't in Hrvatski's report.

There's also Pasty's picks for the office bēsubōru pool, some junk mail advertising a junk mail prevention service, and a certificate honoring Pasty's graduation from the in-house Tourism Ministry Chicanery and Harassment training program.

You also take the opportunity to scan the Okurinese Vee. You'd love to get at the Incatena's local records, of course, especially since New Bharat is just seven light years from Okura, almost two decades closer than it is from Earth. But the local Incatena office doesn't know who Rimu Botaki is, and you're not ready to blow your cover. You registered at the Otani as Nohashi, but you'd rather go easy on that identity too.

Okura's Vee is censored— "moderated" is the term the Home Ministry prefers. This is only to be expected, but it's still distasteful to encounter. In practice the censorship most heavily affects the political and socionomic sections of the Vee; scientific and cultural discussions are fairly lively. Of course there's no telling what would be said if the discussions were completely free; but you can get a picture, at least, of what doesn't disturb the "moderators": scientific research, linguistics, the history and culture of other planets, pop culture, philosophy, religion (if it avoids politics), sex in all versions and perversions, virtual worlds, sports.

Even in politics, complaints and criticisms can be found; the only thing obviously missing is any serious discussion of alternatives to Peace Party rule, or criticism of stated Party goals; and only government officials seem to be required to write unreadable polemic. The Peace Party doesn't seem to aspire to true totalitarianism, the control over its subjects' inner thoughts. Control over their actions seems to be satisfactory, and is no doubt facilitated by allowing fairly free, if monitored, conversation.

So far as you can gather (but you'd like to see Hrvatski's latest reports), nothing much has changed on Okura since you left Mars. Kumari has installed and dismissed two Beloved Premiers. There was a major campaign against "putrid nihilists"; one against "vulture opportunists", and one (fairly popular, it seems) against "malodorous sf-holoshow prequelizers." The banality and forced cheerfulness of news from Ikkyū-shima indicates a continuing heavy hand in that nation. Rhetoric continues to run heavily against the Dzebyet, who seem to be harboring a small number of Okurinese refugees on Orindzai; against the communities of Ogorodé on Okura; and against the Incatena, which is alternately described as seeking to crush the independent spirit of Okura by its brutish military might, and decadently cowering before the dynamic righteousness of the Peace Party.

More interestingly, the Peace Party claims that sister parties have been organized on New Bharat, Maraille, Qeng, and Sihor. In the case of Qeng and Maraille, the claim is belied by internal evidence alone: there's no hard news, just manifestos and pledges of support. It would be an impossibility on Maraille anyway; as you (but not the majority of Incatena citizens) know, Maraillais society— we are not speaking of Île de Maraille here— has no political parties and no outside political contacts. The news about Qeng was obviously fabricated to appeal to Okura's population, since the planet was largely settled from there; and the Maraille story out of astronomic plausibility, Maraille being only 6.7 light years from New Bharat.

However, some minor activity may really be happening on Sihor; and the news of the New Bharati Freedom Movement has the ring of reality: actual events, occasional setbacks, realistic electoral strategies, coalitions in the Inter-Colony Association. Kumari's long-term strategy isn't hard to see: split the Incatena, taking as big a piece with him as he can. And Jules Ormant, citizen of Sihor, strong investor on New Bharat, and fat actor in the Solar marketplace, must be a key player in the same game.

You look for news of Ormant on the Vee. There isn't that much; he doesn't seem to have any investments on Okura. He is mentioned, and always approvingly, in the stories on New Bharat and Sihor.

You're beginning to see what the boss was talking about. Indeed, the boss's mindset imposes itself on you so strongly that you experience a wild craving for Sihorian caf.

One night, feeling a certain homesickness, you go out to look at the stars. You are only 24 light years from home, a tiny step in the galaxy, but most of the constellations are appreciably distorted. Some are quite ruined, as nearby stars (Altair, Procyon, Sirius) have moved about, and stars that are unremarkable viewed from Earth have become unfamiliar brilliances here.

What you really want to see, of course, is Sol. You know roughly where it should be— opposite the apparent position of β Hydri in the Martian sky— and you load an Okurinese star chart from the Vee before heading to the hotel's garden for your observations. It turns out to be near the Little Dipper (itself recognizable, though slightly smaller than it should be), not far from β Ursae Minoris.

It's about magnitude 4.0, barely visible in the nighttime haze over Atami; indeed, even with the star chart pseudo-projected on your visual cortex, you're not even sure you're looking at the right star. Instead of feeling reassured, you feel small and lonely, and wander in to bed.

Explaining it to you

Because commerce is one of the Four Pillars of the Peace Party, the Commerce Association has one of the grandest buildings in Atami. The lobby is about the size of a spacecraft hangar, and in fact it contains a small spacecraft: the *We Are Speaking of Speed,* the pride of Gōsei during the Coalition War. The walls are faced with stone veneer shipped from Japan, a foolish ostentation in an age when any merely material object can be nanoduped at will. The people hurrying past you are ancient, haughty, humorless, and dressed to kill, and that's just the staff.

Kumari evidently likes to keep tabs on this favored class; the air hums with photonic bugs, and one can occasionally read in a misstep or a solecism the presence of the Home Ministry.

Running a 50th century corporation requires experience, ruthlessness, and intuition, to say nothing of an encyclopedic knowledge of the financial climate, socionomics, and law in jurisdictions ranging from the local to the galactic. It's tedious, thankless work; that's why it's left to AIs. Executives do instead what they do best: schmooze, make deals, give speeches, and have the occasional billion-C. inspiration. (It only takes one to get on the board; and to remain there it suffices to suppress all further insights, none of which are going to be as good as the first.)

In the person of Rimu Botaki, you are a member of this tribe, and you set out dutifully to network. You eat Kwaikok slamfish in the ornate Commerce Association dining room; you stand rounds of drinks in the Association's well-appointed bar; you go hunting. This last impresses some of the locals; few business reps from the delicate ecologies of the Solar System have the stomach for this barbaric pastime; but you are after all an Agent, trained to put aside cultural squeamishness. Why shouldn't you hunt the fat and plentiful Gōsei *waman,* especially after one of them flew up above your field volant and crapped on your hunting fatigues?

38

Hondo-san is typical of the businessmen you meet on these trips. He seems to like talking to you— and talk he does, at great length, especially after imbibing large quantities of *tanaki*.

"I would like to explain it to you" is his catch phrase, and he is as good as his word. He explains the proper use of your weapons: what instructions to give the auto-guns to track and bring down the prey; what to tell the cooks to prepare it to perfection. He tells you all about the Hondo Corporation, a maker of photonic relays and chips, which he founded two centuries ago and developed into one of Atami's largest manufacturers. He explains photonics to you, how one starts a business in Gōsei, how one should manage employees (you hire the best personnel managers money can buy), how one creates quality (hire top-quality statisticians, and make sure that they know that quality is truly important to you). He tells you where they keep the best restaurants in Atami (the Planetary Marshal district), where to find the best sex mecs (the Nakamichi district), and what exactly is wrong with young people today (lazy, can't do anything for themselves). He praises the prosperous business climate created by the Peace Party, free of labor strife.

"Perhaps you will come to my factory," he says. "I would like to explain everything to you."

You respectfully decline.

Another prospect introduces himself at the bar in the Commerce Association: Goro Tsuichi, head of AXI Ltd., a bank serving the agribusiness sector. He is young and voluble, and you get on well with him.

You remark that he seems young to be the head of such a large corporation.

"Oh, yes, o-san, I'm only 350," he says, with a chuckle. "AXI used to be an Ikkyū-jin outfit, you know. After the war the Better-Than-Could-Be-Dreamed-of Director named your humble servant to the position. It's a great honor for one so young, of course, but I suppose it was considered a reward for service to the Party."

"You're a Party man, then?" you ask.

"I was Minister for Propaganda," he admits, modestly. "Didn't know a thing about agriculture, banking, nothing. Of course, I've had years to learn, marvelous AIs, a loyal staff, and advice from the Most Wise and Honored Director himself whenever I needed it. Tops, huh?"

You allow as how these must be powerful advantages, and hope that none of the dissidents that are supposed to exist here has seen you talking to Tsuichi-san.

The Dzebyet

If you don't count the Ogorodé (and the Ogorodé make it their business to be overlooked), β Hydri is the only system in human space to be shared with aliens, a fact which adds to the trickiness of your mission and the frequency of your thoughts about retirement.

The Dzebyet are a much older civilization than ours; they were travelling through space when we were still cutting our fingers knapping flint. They have settled thirty planets in twenty systems, including four within fifty light years of Sol. They describe their political system alternately as aleatocratic, aristocratic, anarchic, or antibiotic, depending on their mood and how smart they think their listener is.

The Dzebyet are small and wiry; an early explorer untactfully described them as looking like little blue monkeys. Like ourselves, they are warm-blooded, social, omnivorous, nominally monogamous, and prefer yellow to white or red stars. They come in two sexes; the females bear the eggs and the males hatch them, an equitable arrangement which has been held to account for the many admirable features of Dzebyet society.

They have two sets of vocal cords and two sets of articulatory organs, and can thus pronounce two sounds at once. As a consequence an unenhanced human cannot speak any Dzebyet language (*two* humans can, but this is rarely done). The word 'Dzebyet' itself is actually $\mathrm{G\theta\,^{je}\,b\,^{y}\,a\Omega}$ $\mathrm{^{Dz}\,_{\cdot}\,^{r}\,_{ek}}$, and even that isn't quite right— the Dzebyet can open their mouths wider than we can, so their ɑ is lower than any human vowel.

AIs (who can generate waveforms to meet any phonetic challenge) occasionally learn Dzebyet languages, for the challenge of it; fortunately for the rest of us, Dzebyet pick up human languages with contemptuous ease. Though showing an irritating tendency to consider AIs the important members of Incatena society, they get along well with humans, so long as we behave defer-

41

entially, and avoid physical contact. The tragic events of First Contact, when a well-intentioned handshake precipitated the destruction of the *Enlightened Manifest Destiny*, have long since been smoothed over.

The Dzebyet have been fairly gracious about the human colony on Okura, considering that they've lived on Orindzai, the next planet in, for six thousand years, and might reasonably consider the β Hydri system to belong to them. Apparently they considered Okura too big, cold, and wet, and simply left it alone. (From what we know of galactic society as a whole, only cultures relatively new to space are eager colonizers; most develop other priorities after a few millennia. That's why a planet like Earth, suitable for at least ten different races in our neck of the galactic woods, was never colonized by any of them.[1])

Entering the Dzebyet Embassy in Atami, you feel a bit disoriented. Part of it is the reduced gravity; they've set it as low as possible, and it makes you feel somewhat light-headed. The colors don't help, either. The Dzebyet are tetrachromats, responding to four rather than three basic light frequencies; as a result colors that look harmonious to us look ghastly to them, and vice versa. The reception room is consequently garish, in a random, thorough way that goes far beyond mere human bad taste. Now you know why, besides to maintain a sense of cool, Agents visiting Dzebyet planets are advised to wear dark glasses.

You approach the front desk, where a rather shaggy and spidery looking Dzebyet, wrapped up in a painful-looking harness— or in Dzebyet terms, a very attractive female, in a sexy outfit— sits sharpening her teeth.

"I'd like to see the Ambassador," you say.

She finishes filing an incisor, then remarks, in casually perfect Okurinese, "I can't imagine why. He's old and kinda twisted up on one side. I wouldn't call him aesthetic at all."

"What I mean is, I want to talk to him," you specify, with some annoyance.

"Well, that makes more sense."

---

[1] It may also be relevant that, from Earth, the Coal Sack blocks access to the Galaxy's top-rated entertainment program, *Crucis Rocks*.

After a moment spent waiting for some more sensible statement, you say, "Can I talk to him, then?" Then, before she can comment on whether you're able to or not, you clarify, "Do I need an appointment or something?"

"No, 'course not."

"You mean, I should just go in and see him?"

"Take a peek if you like, but I say it's not worth it. We've been *over* this."

"How long have you been a secretary here?" you ask, trying to control yourself. It's never been determined whether the Dzebyet truly have trouble with human idioms, or just like to annoy us.

"If you mean one of those people who delay access to the people who can decide things, we don't got any, thank the Four. Atami is crawling with them; they're a complete hassle."

She's no slouch at delaying access herself, but it doesn't seem politic to point this out. "Listen, eyesore or not, I do want not only to see the Ambassador, but to talk to him. Would you point me the way, or do whatever it takes for me to do that?"

"Does he know you?"

"Well, no, but I—"

"It's OK," she assures you. "If he doesn't know you, he doesn't have any reason not to talk to you. I'm pretty sure he's not doing anything useful right now. Go through that blue door over there," she says, pointing at a green door behind her. "You gotta take a blood test first."

"A blood test?"

She pushes a small medical machine toward you. "Yeah— if you're carrying any diseases, we'll need the blood to extract antibodies."

The machine has a panel of inscrutable instruments and a little needle attached to a flexible hose; you're still trying to figure it out when it seems to come to life; the instruments flash, and the needle pounces like a snake, poking your arm.

"Ouch!" you say, and the machine apologizes.

The non-secretary at the desk returns to filing her teeth.

Going through the green door, you find yourself in a large office which thankfully avoids the clashing colors of the reception hall; instead, it's so insistently monochromatic that you have to squint to see anything. There's a desk and several chairs, but there seems to be no one in them. You begin to curse the non-secretary, in modern Bengali, a good language for cursing.

"Konishwa, hello, hujambo, díhǎo," comes a voice. You look around dumbly, before your peripheral vision catches a movement, and you see a blue figure scrambling down from the ceiling.

"Ambassador?"

The Dzebyet reaches the desk, sits down on top, and indicates a chair with one foot. It's fairly warm in the room, and the Ambassador is, as Dzebyet generally prefer to be, completely naked. The organs thus revealed are neither comprehensible nor attractive to a human eye.

"$K^{T_{a}y}{}_{ê}^{k}{}^{\int}_{qq}{}^{f}$ at your service, o-san," he remarks. "Sorry if I don't speak the first language you were jabbering. You're Okurinese then?"

"Er, no, Ambassador— er, Tkaiqesh," you stammer, as you perch uncomfortably in a chair that's too small for humans and too large for Dzebyet. You do not, of course, make the mistake of shaking hands. "I'm from Indonesia. That's a nation on Earth."

"I know that; there's some Indonesians here," says the Ambassador, brusquely.

"Of course. I'm sorry." You seem to be getting off on the wrong foot; and it occurs to you as well that your identity as an Indonesian entrepreneur is completely in the way here. "May I speak freely, Ambassador-san?"

"Charging for one's time is a human custom," he reminds you.

"I suppose it is. What I mean is, if I can be blunt— how are your counterphotonics here? Are we being overheard somewhere in one ministry or another?"

"Whenever they try to bug us, we send them back their own radio stations," the Ambassador assures you. "Don't sweat it. We're not exactly neophytes at interstellar diplomacy."

"Of course. Well, I'm not actually an Indonesian, and my name isn't really, er, the one I didn't mention yet. It's Morgan. I'm a Diplomatic Agent of the Human Incatena, and I'm here to see what can be done about the Peace Party."

"I see. Is it broken then? In what way?"

"Well, it's a dictatorship. We don't approve of dictatorships, you know."

"No? And why is that?"

"Well, they oppress people. We believe in liberty— letting people do what they want— without harming others of course. It's a principle— a sort of religious belief," you explain, inadequately, hoping that the reference to religion will work in your favor. The Dzebyet are religious, and in fact they have just one religion; they explain that after 100,000 years you find out what's right. Or is that the Skweeoo?

"So you plan to interfere with the people of Okura, who want a dictatorship, in order to give them the sort of liberty that people back on Earth like to have?" asks the Ambassador. "I'm just trying to understand."

"The people of Okura don't want a dictatorship," you explain, patiently. "It's been imposed by force. That's the problem."

"That's not what the government here says."

"Well, they're lying. Surely you can see that it's in their interest to lie about that."

"So far as we can see you humans never do what's in your interest," remarks Ambassador Tkaiqesh. "But aren't they constituent members of your own Incatena?"

"Well, yes, but it's against the Incatena Treaty to have a dictatorial government. I know, it probably doesn't seem that we do half the things in the Treaty, but they are important to us; it just takes us time to get to them sometimes. We believe that it's a crisis situation and should be stopped immediately."

You fancy that you're beginning to sound like a Dzebyet yourself; or at least you're contributing to making humans sound as odd to the Dzebyet as they seem to us.

"Have you asked the government of Okura to respect this emergency scruple?"

"We have, diplomatically. It's time for stronger measures to be taken."

"Force, for instance?"

"That may be necessary."

"Wasn't that your objection to the government of Okura?"

"Well, the Incatena does have certain police powers, and as a signatory to the Treaty, the Okurinese government is subject to those powers," you explain; but you feel that you're floundering. "I don't know if I'm making much sense to you, Ambassador Tkaiqesh. Consider it a matter of human justice, if you will. We consider the government here to be an oppressive regime, violating the rights of its own people. Even if you don't see it the same way—"

"We see *all* your governments, as well as your other institutions and artistic conventions, as unnecessarily heavy on all four feet," comments the Ambassador. Out of boredom, perhaps, he picks up some small objects on his desk (fruit, apparently), and begins to juggle. His movements are very quick; he can keep six or seven objects in the air at one time. "Except the Incatena itself; it's so ineffective that it's a move in the right direction. Still, we have noted that the Okurinese government is incrementally worse than the usual run of things human. I suppose you're here to ask for our help."

Things are looking up all of a sudden. You are quite an Agent, aren't you.

"That's exactly the case, Ambassador," you say, eagerly. "We will do all we can ourselves, of course, and in concert with the Okurinese people themselves. But we would be very grateful to have your assistance."

The Ambassador stops juggling, and places the items he was playing with back on the desk. Now that you can see them more clearly, you can see that most of them are indeed fruit; but one of them uncurls itself, gives itself a shake, and scampers out of reach on tiny feet.

"However, we don't like to interfere in alien affairs," he continues.

You begin to rue the day you told the boss you wanted assignments featuring more interaction with aliens.

"It could be advantageous to the Dzebyet," you point out. "For instance, you've been kind enough to harbor some refugees from the Okurinese regime..."

"I've repeatedly asked the Incatena to send ships to take them, and I know the Incatena *has* ships in orbit here. They've told me they couldn't offend Okura."

"Well, that was true then, and in fact it'll continue to be true for a few more months; it may even get more true before it becomes false," you explain, diplomatically. "But once we get rid of

Kumari, you won't have that problem. And the anti-alien rhetoric that the Peace Party has been indulging in must surely be causing you some worry..."

"Annoyance, yes, but not worry."

"Kumari might be more dangerous than you think," you suggest.

"I doubt it."

"Still, that annoyance would be removed if..."

"What we would like to see," continues the Ambassador, "is to have the proselytization problem addressed. I've requested this of the Incatena before."

"The Okurinese are sending you evangelists? I can see that that would be very annoying," you commiserate. "Of course we'll put a stop to that."

"You misunderstand," says the Ambassador. "I find it provoking; please increase your intelligence. We want more evangelists, not less. Let's say ten or twelve from each major belief system. All Okura was willing to send was representatives of Kumari Thought; we've had those, you don't need to send more. We will study their beliefs and incorporate any revelations or insights they may have, and send them back unharmed. Of course, we will send you Dzebyet evangelists in return."

You examine the Ambassador's face for signs of levity, and find none, though you do notice that the Ambassador's face is indeed kind of twisted up on one side. "That's an unusual request... but of course a very understandable and reasonable one," you add, quickly. "I'm sure that it will be quite easily arranged, however, once the Kumari dictatorship is removed. And in return...?"

"We will act with discretion," explains the Ambassador, vaguely. "Mind you, we will use no weapon systems against any Okurinese humans, unless we are attacked, and I trust you, Morgan-san, to keep your war civil. We will be pleased, however, to use our naval technology to render the Okurinese fleet unusable in space. Even this we will not do to begin with; you must get the action going yourself first. We should also be able to provide information. Coordinate that with $M_{o}^{P}wh^{ur}{}_{y}^{\int}k$; he enjoys that sort of thing."

"I'll be glad to," you say, attempting to record this explosion of phonemes. Ambassador Tkaiqesh, I can't tell you how satisfied I am personally, and how grateful the Incatena will be, with your help."

"Why can't you?" he asks. "Perhaps you need a new neur-implant?"

When you finally leave the Embassy, you have a throbbing headache. But you feel happy; by sharing intelligence and by grounding part of Okura's space navy, the Dzebyet will provide significant assistance to your anti-Kumari coalition. Now all you need is a coalition for them to significantly assist.

Interview with the Director

The Directoral Palace is— by city statute— the most imposing structure in Atami. It certainly is big and solid. There is no architectural ornament on it with a thickness of less than a meter. The esplanade in front is long enough to land a small planetary cruiser; heavy artillery is emplaced to make sure that no one tries it. Guards armed with plasmizers are there to coerce the trees and grass into growing correctly.

Inside, tours of this temple of the worship of Kumari are available, led by enthusiastic teenagers in red outfits. Those with official business are quietly ushered into an anteroom by efficient aides. You've decided that a bit of sizing up the enemy is in order; you ask about the possibility of seeing the Honored Director.

The aide purses his lips, consults a datanode, fills out a form, consults a superior. After about three-quarters of an hour, the word comes back: more consultation is necessary. You must come back tomorrow.

The next day, a higher-level aide is present, and you explain your request once more. You give the name of Botaki and immediately regret it, but nothing happens— the name hasn't yet percolated onto any general watchlist, it appears. More consultations. You are blood-tested, retina-scanned, and neuromapped.

Finally the verdict is in: the thing can be done.

Naturally, there will be a short wait first. You are taken to a small anteroom. The wait turns out to be about five hours. Fortunately, there's plenty of Peace Party propaganda to read. By the end of your wait, you can recite the birthplace of Jishuri Kumari (Niwa-ku, Shatsu, Gōsei), the Cardinal Principle of Kumari Thought (harmony), and the chief error exposed at the 16th Peace Party Congress (perverse factionalism).

At last you are ushered into a conference room. You are seated at one end of a long conference table, which almost fills this long and narrow room. Halfway down the table a Tajima energy screen stretches from wall to wall. At the other end of the table is an empty chair; behind it, a wall bearing a map of Okura, flanked by the flags of Okura and of Gōsei. The room is dark, except for a light shining dramatically at the head of the table.

A man enters and sits in the chair. He is a middle-aged man in military uniform, fit, tall, rigid. A trim, severe white moustache and goatee surround an unsmiling mouth. Grey hair, prominent nose, dark magnetic eyes. No surgery has been performed to remove a small scar on one cheek.

"Greetings, Botaki-san," says the Planetary Marshal. "Your voyage was uneventful? You were unfrozen without incident?"

"Indeed, Director."

"Where in the Douane are you from?"

"Indonesia."

"I have warm feelings for Indonesia. You are enjoying your stay on Okura?"

"Yes, Director."

But that's it for free and frank exchange. It soon becomes evident that the views to be expressed will be those of the Director.

"I agree to meet with many offworld visitors," the Director declaims, "in order to promote interstellar harmony. It broadens the spirit to be in touch with the larger human sphere. That is why the Directorate has always been an active, supporting member of the Incatena.

"Calumnies are sometimes told against us, by those who do not know us. In fact we desire nothing but harmony.[1] This is the message we have for offworlders, for our own people, for all the nations of Okura. The Directorate had its advent in struggle, but that is history. Now, our hands are extended to build; the password is peace. We offer the harmonious community of our own planet as a model for the galaxy: a world where no man raises his hand against a brother, nor does nation rise against nation."

The Director smiles photogenically, and continues. "I am a believer in the simple virtues. I believe in the family; I believe in harmony, order, hard work, education, and equal treatment for all.

---

[1] Cf. Kumari, Jishuri, Director, *Harmony: The Cardinal Principle of Kumari Thought*; Shatsu Publishing House, Atami, 4884.

"I myself was raised in a small town in the interior of Gōsei— a long time ago now— I remember my grandfather's stories of the days of colonization, six hundred years before. And there has always seemed to me to be something healthy in that kind of life. We didn't live like rich men, but we were comfortable— if there were hard times we shared them together. We were not as sophisticated as people are today, not as clever or preoccupied with novelties as people in the city. But we had a kind of happiness the bustling folk of the big city rarely know.[1]

"I have always tried to rule so that the people I grew up with, those people who are the real bedrock of this nation, could be proud of me— could say, 'Yes, he is one of us— his heart is in the right place.'"

The Director waves his hand vaguely in the direction of harsh reality. "Of course, not every aspect of the Director's job is as pleasant as sitting here conversing with you. It is also my responsibility to protect my people, to maintain harmony. For human nature is not such that prosperity may be enjoyed forever, unthreatened by jealousy, by strife, by dissension.

"Together, strong, we will endure forever," he says, urgently. "We believe in a strong community, strong families, a strong nation. We are something of an outpost here— at the edge of the expanding wave of human colonization. That is one thing. And there is also the threat of division, of revanchism. It is hardly credible, perhaps, that anyone should look at the harmonious life we have achieved here and wish to return to the squabbles and the wars— very grievous wars— which preceded it; but there are some such, and we must remain vigilant to resist them.

The Director spreads his hands before him, pointing toward the future, up on the ceiling behind you. "I believe in progress," he says. "I am not one of those who believe that humanity is condemned to alienation or to contention.[2] We have advanced from the caves to the stars. Who knows what glorious destiny is in store for us?"

---

[1] Also see Nezumi, Mizuo, *The Life of the Surprisingly Glorious Director, Jishuri Kumari*; Shatsu Publishing House, Atami, 4922.

[2] Cf. Kumari, Jishuri, Director, *Five Errors to Avoid, Including the Nihilistic Belief that Humanity Is Condemned to Alienation or Contention*; Shatsu Publishing House, Atami, 4920.

"But whatever that destiny is, I believe that Okura will play a significant role in it."

He stands; a mild electric current in your chair reminds you to stand as well. "It has been a pleasure meeting you, Botaki-san," he intones.

He pauses long enough for you to express your gratitude.

He produces a pen and a small hologram, signs his name below his smiling portrait, and drops it in a slot in the table. In a moment, with a pneumatic hiss, it pops up out of a similar slot on your end of the table. You pick up the portrait and thank him; he smiles in return— the little hologram smiles with him.

"I wish you well in your visit to Okura."

The Director leaves. A mec or an android, obviously. You feel a juvenile impulse to ask for another interview so when he asks where you're from you can reply "Your sister."

Art and hypersaline gravy

To get hold of dissidents, find the artists; this has been known for so long that there's a chapter devoted to it in the Agent Directives. An excellent first step, you decide, would be to spend an afternoon at the Atami Academy. You don't expect to find any actual dissidents there; but it will be a good place to start to get a picture of modern Okurinese art (disagreeably, it's necessary to scan acres of art if you want to talk to artists).

The countryside, according to Peace Party thought, is the backbone of the planet and the repository of all virtue. The Academy, therefore, is largely devoted to the art of rural Gōsei— textiles, old-fashioned dresses, paintings of children with big eyes and naked butts, rocking chairs, saw blades with rustic scenes painted on them, dolls carved from tree stumps or horseradish roots, simple music played on homemade electronic keyboards. And it does have a certain charm— the first gallery of it. The other ten or twelve, perhaps less so.

Of course, like any modern human nation, Gōsei is 98% urban, and the actual agricultural workforce— the humans supervising the mecs— dresses and lives pretty much like everybody else. All of the art you see here is cranked out in special factories attached to the Director's Birthplace Heritage Village.

There is also a Special Exhibit focusing on art representing the Honorable Director, Jishuri Kumari. The Director's Hall is mostly filled with statues and holograms; the Donors Of C. 10,000 Or Less Annex features prints and video work.

The effect can be fairly described as mind-numbing.

A catalogue is available offering critical appraisals, trends in the artistic depiction of the Director, and the full text of the Director's four-hour speech last fall opening the exhibit. There are also postcards, posters, reproductions, tote bags, trinkets, even Kumari dolls for the children.

You buy enough trinkets for all your officemates. They'll love it; nothing this tacky has been made in the Douane for a thousand years.

In the afternoon, you explore the galleries devoted to non-agricultural Gōsei art. About half are devoted to classic Okurinese art. Okura has never produced an artist known to the rest of the Incatena, but its pre-Peace Party art is really rather pleasing.

You start paying more attention when you come to the Contemporary Urban Art collection, almost the only department of the Academy which constitutes a market for living artists. ("Art" is notoriously hard to define, of course, but as a working definition of "artist" we may take "one who has never been tempted to paint rustic scenes on saws.") You note down some names in your data neurimplant.

Nothing is really revolutionary, but there are some artists with evident talent— a quirky imagination here, an eye for the watery vistas of Okura there. There is nothing directly rebellious, of course, not in the official academy and hardly to be found even hidden in garrets. A few artists come close: here an overpunctilious and arguably ironic rendering of the favored rural art; there an allusion to classic Ikkyū-shima stagecraft; elsewhere, works of an indescribable sadness.

After this you stroll through the offworld collections, which are sparse, almost grudging. This is a human planet, someone must have calculated, so we must have some pre-spaceflight art. It was founded by colonists from Qeng, so we've got to have a roomful of Qeng. It's the only human planet which shares a star with another race, so we'd better buy some of the little monkeys' artifacts.

With the exception of the Dzebyet collection, almost everything is a reproduction— you get the impression that the major tool of the Acquisitions Department was the mail-order catalogue of the Library of Man on Sihor.

To be fair, everything is well-labeled, and the curators' choices, though never daring, are not uninformed. It's also worth pointing out that these are the most popular galleries in the Academy. Even the children taken on field trips to see the Art of Rural Gōsei and the statues of Kumari sneak off when they can to gaze at the outsystem œuvre. Paltry as it is, it's something of a window looking out from the glad-handing claustrophobia of the Peace Party. Also, a lot of the offworld art features naked people.

One more stop: the three small galleries devoted to non-Gōsei Okurinese art.

According to Peace Party propaganda, all the nations of Okura are equal. There is no significance to the fact that the Okurinese Peace Forces are entirely officered by Gōsei-jin, or to the fact that the Academy treats art from the rest of Okura as if it harbored prions. Pay no attention to it. We said, pay no attention.

There is a fair amount of painting and sculpture here from Xinqeng and Shr, as well as painted scrolls from Bansa ng Angwang, engravings and computer graphics from Songdae, and prints from Phu Quoc. However, you find that the most pleasing items are the wood carvings from Kamandamaung, the exquisite lacquerware from Burusandaku, and the naïve handcrafts from the Pretty Islands.

You find yourself staring at a large black frame, into which a hidden datanode projects a loop of subtle, ever-shifting colors and shapes in three dimensions.

"What you think it means?" asks an old woman next to you, in a heavy accent— startling you; you hadn't seen her approach.

"I don't know, I was just admiring the technique," you say.

She laughs. "An honest answer, at least. So many people have such high-flying things to say about art, no? What you think about technique, then?"

"Well, I don't like rendered graphics as a rule," you venture. "There always seems to be too much computer and not enough artist, you know? But this one really isn't bad."

"Nice color choices," remarks the old woman.

"Yes, that's part of it. Earth tones, flesh tones, nothing flashy— and the shapes are evocative, raising questions without attempting banal answers."

"What you see in shapes?"

"Oh, I don't see *pictures*," you assure her. "I don't think the artist intended that easy and literal a reading. So much of art is implication, you know: the cloud of associations called forth in both the creator's and the observer's mind— the artist's intent, that old bugaboo, in the foreground, half-articulated ideas and longings behind that, shading off into the remotest perceptions, recollections and images, assisted by the entire cultural milieu of both parties— if disparate, so much the better. But what this particular piece is saying, I think, is that there *is* no 'literal' level, no 'intended' meaning; the lack of aboutness is what the piece is *about*— and if that's irony, it's not because it's intended *ironically*— no, I think it's an unforced statement, and yet utterly without naïveté."

The woman looks deep into the swirling shapes, and you share an aesthetic moment together.

"It *is* a good screen saver," she says at last.

"A screen saver?"

"Yes," she says, and demonstrates; she touches the screen lightly, and the subtle shapes disappear, dissolving into a holographic image of a chrome dinosaur.

"I should have realized," you say.

"No, no, all you said is true," she protests. "After all, do ancient philosopher, Zappa, not observe that art is only experience with a frame around it? We have provided the frame, and anyway, it is better screen saver than picture, I think too."

Your new friend, who turns out to be Dr. Zhou, Curator of the Okura Nations Galleries, invites you to have lunch in the Academy's restaurant. You offer, grandly, to pay— you're on an expense account. Of course, you'll only be reimbursed back on Mars, a quarter century or more from now, if the bureaucracy gets to it within a couple decades of your return. With lifetimes in the centuries, no one is in a hurry.

The restaurant ("Le Bistro Chic Artiste") resembles every other cafeteria in human space. You have a choice of patty-formed chicken, beef, or fish, drenched in hypersaline gravy, accompanied by soggy vegetables and a small, hard roll. Or you can have indeterminate sandwiches wrapped tightly in plastic, apples and oranges which seem to have been bought from a decorator rather than a farmer, and egg drop soup whose chief ingredients are grease and pepper. At least the tea is decent. It has an unfamiliar flavor, presumably that of some native herb.

While you're eating, you can contemplate the portrait of Kumari striding purposefully at the head of a brigade of peasants which occupies one wall. As a nod to the 50th century, there's one small, helpless-looking mec on the far left. Along the opposite wall are hung children's imitations of the mural, some of them quite hilarious.

You learn that Dr. Zhou is an immigrant to Okura; she comes from Qeng, the same world from which most of Okura's original settlers came. "A beautiful world," she sighs. "I wish Okura was more like Qeng."

"That doesn't seem in line with Peace Party doctrine," you remark.

"O-san should not be a fool," she says, so matter-of-factly that you look around involuntarily for Home Ministry bugs.

She laughs. "They don't listen," she says. "Who pays attention to an old crone in a museum, who talks about nothing but art?"

Dr. Zhou travels the planet in search of new art for the Academy, knows most of the major artists and dissident intellectuals of Okura, speaks five languages (all with an ineradicable accent), and detests the repressive Kumari regime. You place her name, in bold, in the file in your neurimplant named *The Plan*.

As you continue to talk, you perceive that she is feeling you out as well— asking questions about your business, about your impressions of Atami, about your artistic theories. This too is a sort of code, a probing of values and language, conducted with acute sensitivity to the telltales of the authoritarian mindset, and yet demanding more than mere progressive rhetoric as well: seeking the disagreements and even contradictions that distinguish convictions derived from thought and experience from the pose of the unthinking convert— or the provocateur.

She takes you back to her office, which seems to have been carved out of a broom closet, and is made even smaller by stacks of books, disks, journals, monographs, and printouts. She shows you some of her plans for the Okura Nations Galleries on the datanode, discusses a few more artists, shows you her Vee connections, her projects for exhibitions, benefits, outings, Artists' Union activities; you readily grasp what she is showing you: the outlines of a dissident network, idealistic and artistically inclined, but practical and organized as well.

This is as explicit as she can be, even as an unregarded old woman, here in an official outpost of the establishment. "It's very much of a pleasure to talk with you, o-san," she says, at last. "Some friends of mine get together for a little party at the end of the week. They also are very artistic, very smart. I think they like to meet you. Would you do me the honor of coming?"

"I'd be glad to," you say.

Smoke and manifestos

Although you are an Indonesian businessmen, it wouldn't do to show up at an artists' gathering in business drag; no one would talk to you. You are not quite sure how artists dress in Atami, however. The present style in Martian art classes and hip neighborhoods, for both sexes, consists of shapeless robes in deliberately unpleasant colors, with cutouts revealed by movement. Unfortunately you left yours at home. You search the department stores of Atami, electronically; the closest things you can find are Indian saris and a sort of superhero outfit sold by a costume shop. The effect would be risible in the lamest music spot in Areopolis, and probably utterly baffling here.

Use your head, you tell yourself. Find out what was in vogue fifty years ago; it's bound to be acceptable bohemian attire. This will require some in-person shopping; the resale shops don't have Vee scenes.

You soon face an *embarras de choix*: should you take the trousers laundered almost to translucence, the army uniforms that have lost more than one war, the frilly party outfits, or the shiny shirts of aggressively unnatural fiber and colors that could look good only to the Dzebyet?

You consider asking the shopkeeper, but he turns out to be an Ogorodé— a small, sad, grey, nondescript alien with big eyes, dressed (if that's the word) in dark grey rags; and although your opinions are enlightened and you believe that humans can learn many things from the Ogorodé, you don't think fashion sense is one of them. Almost every planet has its small community of Ogorodé, taking jobs no one else wants— menial laborers, small shopkeepers, mountain farmers, database access coders— asking for no rights, adopting the local religion, and seeking to be as unobtrusive as possible. It is not a proud niche, but it is a remarkably widespread and stable one— so long as any intelligent race can remember, the Ogorodé have always been around, in every part of the galaxy; some have speculated that there are more Ogorodé than any other intelligent race.[1]

"Have you got any more of these black cryptodenim things?" you ask.

"I'll check for you, o-san," says the Ogorodé. He speaks perfect Okurinese, of course; the Ogorodé have lived among humans for a very long time.

The ice, you decide, has been broken. "What do you guys think about Kumari and the Peace Party dictatorship?"

"We are supporters in every way, o-san."

This shouldn't surprise you, but it does; it's the first time you've heard anyone sincerely praise the Kumari regime.

"Why's that? You're completely exploited. Wouldn't you like to have better lives?"

The Ogorodé laughs— a sound resembling a high-pitched, discreet belch. "We have no complaints."

"But haven't you read the papers? Kumari's got a propaganda campaign going against you and the Dzebyet. Things could get dangerous."

"There is no danger, besides a brutal killing or two," the Ogorodé assures you. "The overall situation will not change. There is always a place for us. There's always room at the bottom."

"That's the worst kind of craven appeasement!" you exclaim, angrily. The Ogorodé looks at you calmly, with his large, harmless eyes. "But I respect that, of course. It's your cultural choice, after all. But you Ogorodé know a lot of people— perhaps you know some of the people who *do* want to change things around here."

"You're from the Home Ministry?" asks the Ogorodé.

"No, no, I'm from Mars."

"I have a remote cousin in my aunt-mother's moiety who lives there," remarks the little alien.

"Perhaps I can do something for your cousin," you suggest. "I know some of the Areopolis Ogorodé. They have full civil rights on Mars, you know."

"Yes, my cousin says it's very disturbing. I don't think I can help you, o-san."

---

[1] Counting Diphdean Swarms as single entities, of course.

"Oh, please," you say. "You name it— contacts, jobs— I have a friend who needs a pet companion, a lot of our Ogorodé do that— or some file format conversion work, very easy and routine, very well documented specs, almost. Or maybe photonics? Datanodes, music makers, children's lasers, I can get it for you..."

"No thank you, o-san," says the Ogorodé, embarrassed. "Please excuse me, I wish to look for your cryptodenim."

If you were prejudiced you would curse the little stick-in-the-muds.

Dr. Zhou's neighborhood, Kigushō, on the waterfront looking out over Atami's island-speckled bay, was fashionable several centuries back, declined into a slum, and now, though the industrial concerns, tenements, and warehouses remain, there is a sprinkling of coffeehouses, hole-in-the-wall art galleries, used-node stores, and gay bars. It's about as hip as Gōsei gets.

You make your way up an interminable wooden stairway to Dr. Zhou's door; Dr. Zhou herself answers your knock.

Her first words are, "Where do you get that outfit?"

"Uh, an Ogorodé store in Blue-Sky-shōme," you answer, looking down with sudden misgivings at your cryptodenim jacket and pants. "Do I look terrible?"

"No, no, quite interesting," she responds, diplomatically. You look around; the Gōsei bohemian, it turns out, favors clothes remarkably similar to Indonesian business attire. "Come in, you meet everybody."

The apartment (small, and made smaller by an incrustation of books, disks, and objets d'art) is crowded and noisy. There is an acrid smell in the air, a linear combination of aerosol drugs, sweat, old books, wine, and stale pizza. A wicked Skweeoo ensemble whines out from a music node that could use a new drive; every once in a while it attempts to read the documentation track as music, producing eerie, not-quite-random squeaks and stutters. You let the overlapping streams of conversation wash over you.

"Have you seen those little ceramic head doodads over at Masmoto's? It's absolutely a step backward, it's *so* 48th century."

"The shaman says my aura's contaminated with bad chakras. *Again*."

"No, they broke up. She's been seeing a dragon in the Vee, got tired of meat sex."

"It's not quit-the-day-job material, I told him. I think he was offended."

"At my mother's. Yeah, I know, I said I'd never speak to her again. But *her* laundry mecs *work*."

"I'm into interactive micromedia game-acting, but what I really want to do is direct."

"Why bother? Kumari's not going to let it happen."

"Kiri said she'd boot me out if she ever saw me on plezh again. But she doesn't see too well."

You back up one conversation.

"Ryoku, I'm telling you, you're going to miss out." The speaker is a small, plain-looking girl with the earnest look of a collie or an organizer. "Ten thousand students marching through the streets of Atami. What's he going to do, mow us all down with laser fire?"

"Something like that, yes." That was the original speaker, a reedy, astringent young man drinking cheap white wine.

"He won't massacre anyone in his own capital," insists a very fat man, who is munching something that looks like fluorescent green insulation. "We're ready this time. Everything'll be broadcast live; no one knows the routes except the off-Vee computers..."

"And you think the man is a step behind you all this time? Don't count on it, friends. He's ahead of you all the way. He's going to have moles in the news scenes, on your exec com, probably inside the goddamn off-Vee computers."

"That's why I've been trying to get you to come in with us," said the girl. "You're smart enough to outthink him."

"I'm smart enough to stay the hell out of it."

You listen a bit longer, but it soon becomes apparent that Ryoku's assessment of the organizers' prospects is pretty much right on the money. There won't be any demonstration; Kumari's agents will quietly derail it long before the appointed day; or perhaps they'll allow a small, blunted rally, with Peace Party officials on hand to offer an immediate rebuttal.

The thought depresses you; you wander off to find some food. It's laid out on a table in the hallway: non-starch chips deep-fried in non-fat, sheets of seaweed, rice cakes, a can of mixed nuts, lentils and brown rice (labeled "Macrobiotic!" and untouched), squirt foods for the hurried. All the good nuts are already taken, but you root up some oily walnuts and a handful of the sawdusty non-starch chips, and pour yourself something carbonated and of a color not found in fifty ecospheres.

You straighten up and knock somebody's plate over. Rice cakes spill to the floor and shatter; nuts bounce about like marbles. You apologize, bend down, collect what you can, and deliver a handful of fragments to—

A very striking set of eyes. Oriental in shape, but deep blue. Deep enough to fall into for hours, blue enough to swim away in. That would be enough right there, that would be heaven, but wait, there's more: a face, a perfect face, which could be a model's if it was just a little stupider, and which is now sporting the sort of puzzled smile that tells you that your stare is a bit too obvious. You put that thought aside: you *want* to stare.

Black hair, cut short, with an airbrushed orange streak on one temple— a tad unconventional for Okura, but not garish. You like to think that that applies to yourself as well. Clothes: entirely black, with glowing silver edging down the sides, very elegant. A single earring.

You probably have no chance at all with this person.

"Hi, I'm Ba." The voice is low and thrilling. It enters your ears, reverberates back and forth in your cranium, and sinks all the way down through you, leaving a tingly sensation behind.

"Uh, sorry, thanks, hello," you reply, suavely. "I mean, I'm sorry about your rice cakes. I'm Rimu."

"Friend of Zhou's?"

"Yeah. We met at the Academy. I've only been onplanet for a few weeks."

This revelation of your offworld status leads to a short but intense and thoroughly pleasant interrogation on the subject of Earth, Indonesia, business, and your impressions of Okura so far. If the Home Ministry had agents like this they wouldn't have to resort to pulling out fingernails.

"I work for the Incatena," Ba remarks.

"Ah yes, I've heard of it." Then, to cover the immense stupidity of this statement, and because you've detected the hint of an accent, you ask, "Are you offworld yourself? From Qeng, maybe?"

"Shr."

"Really. That's what I thought."

"No, I mean that's where I'm from— Shr, right here on Okura."

"Ah, right. That's really interesting."

"It's pretty dull, actually. I mean, the whole planet's got to be a yawner to someone from Mars, and the whole Kumari thing is a real black hole, but everything's relative. So for me what could be better than Atami?"

"Sure."

"Shr? I tell you, it's boring."

This is not conversation as you'd like it to scintillate. Too many questions are clogging your brain, making it impossible for any one of them to come out: Tell me about your childhood. What are your deepest dreams and aspirations? Do you think your mother would like me? And of course the number one question: you aren't attached, are you?

And then, before it's even properly started, it's over, Ba is gone. Has to leave early— no details on why, just the hint of a busy life, a heady change for a rube from Shr. You're left staring at a pool of rice cake crumbs, dreaming of blue almond eyes and a single earring.

You're still wondering around in a daze when Dr. Zhou collars you. "I have someone for you to meet."

"I've already met someone. Ba, that was the name, I think," you add, as if it weren't burned into your neurons. "Do you—"

"Not now, Botaki-san. I have important man for you to meet. Very big man in our circle. Here," she says, leading you into a bedroom. There, sitting on the bed, on top of a pile of coats, is Ryoku, watching a book's holo display.

"Botaki-san, it's an honor," he says, smoothly, turning off the book. "Don't worry, I won't probe. It'd be a waste of time— Dr. Zhou's vouched for you."

"Thank you. I'm a little surprised to see you, er, in the position you're in. I heard some of your conversation out there; you seemed disenchanted."

"Not disenchanted, just realistic."

"Well, what do you think can be done about... about the situation?"

"Precious little, actually," admits Ryoku. "Preliminary and educational work, I suppose. Contacts offplanet— that's where you come in, we hope. Eventually things will happen— if not this century, the next."

"I am less patient," says Dr. Zhou. "I don't have a sixth of a lifetime left to wait. I want to see again freedom." She only mouths the last word.

"And *I* want to *see* it," retorts Ryoku. "But premature action doesn't do any good; look at the Tandō Rising. We're too damn small. Now, if we had business on our side, and Ikkyū-shima, Army and Oji elements, and the Dzebyet and the Incatena, we'd be shuttling to orbit. But we don't."

Ryoku should be an Agent.

You talk some more, the three of you, but this is not the time or place for serious negotiations. There's too many people at the party, and for that matter you want to vet Ryoku and Zhou more before things get specific. However, you are satisfied; you feel that things are moving at last, or if not moving, twitching a little in their sleep.

Tea for two

For the capital of a totalitarian dictatorship, Atami is surprisingly pleasant to look at. Almost everywhere you are in sight of the harbor with its boats and islands, and away from the harbor the city is framed by low mountains. The city itself is clean, full of trees, and not too large. The major boulevards are blighted by the architectural eructations of the Peace Party regime, and by ubiquitous militiamen with laser rifles; but by sticking to the side streets you can have quite a nice walk, and fantasize about sharing it with a certain someone.

You're near the neighborhood where Incatena House is located. Ba could be anywhere around here, grabbing a bit of lunch or doing some noontime shopping. Not very likely, perhaps, but it makes you a little more alert, so that you're paying attention when you come up to the big glass shop window. Very close behind you is an odd couple, a small pale thin man and a huge beetle-browed one; it could be any one of a number of comedy teams, but it isn't. Quite the opposite: it's Pasty and Nasty.

You wonder if they've noticed you. Perhaps they haven't seen you yet. Or if they have, perhaps they don't remember their last encounter with you, in which one of them got smashed over the head with a lamp, and the other was shot with a max gun?

You sneak a glance back at them. Pasty grins at you, and waves with the truncheon he's carrying. Nasty makes a gesture that resembles a strangulation, cracking his knuckles for verisimilitude. That about wraps it up for the 'haven't seen you' and the 'don't remember' hypotheses.

Your Agent training kicks in like a new gear. There's no reason to panic. All you have to do is lose them. This would be easier if they were two blocks behind rather than twenty paces, but it can be done. First, get onto a bigger street— more people, that's what you need. You slip onto the nearest boulevard— Home Ministry Avenue, as it turns out. Perfect.

Don't panic. You've been in this situation before and got out of it easily enough. Of course, that time you were able to call in air support. You make your way past an enormously fat woman walking two dogs— you contemplate knocking her over and bowling your pursuers over like ninepins. Ahead of you is a pair of militiamen; Pasty seems to be signaling to them. The militiamen plant themselves in your path. You can smell Nasty's lunch, heavy on the kimchee.

You dash into the first door to your right, some sort of office building. Pasty and Nasty follow. You take the escalator up three floors in the atrium, then down one floor. Pasty and Nasty are right behind you. You walk into an office suite, wander into a maze of sleek ergolounges. Pasty and Nasty do too. It looks like Nasty's taken out his gun.

You see a secretary, glance at the door behind her. "I've got a confidential meeting with Jidori-san," you say. "Please don't let us be interrupted." And you go in, before the woman can say anything.

You keep your eye on the door, but, amazingly, it remains shut, long enough that it begins to feel like it has the intention of staying that way. You breathe a sigh of relief, and you hear laughter behind you.

You turn to see a middle-aged woman in executive robes, considering you with an amused expression. This must be Jidori-san. "I'm so sorry to barge in, o-san," you say. "I don't suppose you have a back door or anything...?"

"No, but there's no need," says the woman. "They won't come in here; I've already signaled Machiko."

"Very kind of you," you say, awkwardly.

"You're in a spot, I can see that."

"I suppose I am."

"Under the circumstances, perhaps you'd stay for tea?"

"Er, yes please."

Jidori-san serves the tea herself, from a pot on the sideboard. You sit down warily before her desk— a very large desk, and almost empty. On one side of the desk, a datanode projects a blizzard of holographic documents; more photonic office equipment occupies a wall behind her. The mementos of an executive life litter the room: by-the-yard art on the walls; rent-a-foliage; pictures of family and dog on the desk; a sailboat on a plaque; the sort of pen set, clock, and note dispensers that no one buys for themselves; a child's drawing, ostentatiously framed; a Daruma doll with both eyes filled in; some unidentifiable piece of machinery with her name engraved on it.

"I'm Tomiyo Jidori," she says.

"Rimu Botaki."

"I don't mean to pry, but I'm always curious why someone is running away from Tourism Ministry goons," she adds.

You swallow hard. "Uh, they get in my way."

"When they're tailing a visitor, they don't need to show metal," she points out. "More likely, *you've* been getting in *their* way."

"With all due respect, Jidori-san, I don't know if I can trust you."

"You really don't have any choice, do you, o-san?"

As an Agent, you thrive on ambiguity. You wish people would just learn some tact.

"Is it safe to talk here?"

She thinks about this. "If they're using the LX-10s it is. The photonic ratcatchers can find them easily enough. The net feed is clean; I b-checked it yesterday. We've got a tape-delay jabberer feeding them garbage, and to keep them happy when they crack that, we've got an AI sending them off a more plausible rap under that. If they've got the 14000 mites on us, there's not much we can do; but they've only got a dozen analyzers in the whole city, and they take up a hell of a lot of cycles. I think we're safe."

"How do you know all this?"

"It's my business. We sell taps and bugs."

"Man, what kind of luck is it to just drop in on someone in the surveillance industry?" you marvel.

"It's a pretty big industry here in Atami," she points out. "Now what can you tell me about yourself? Besides the fact that you're from Mars, you're selling telephotonics or pretending to, you recently fell in love, and Tourism drones are on your tail?"

"How did you know all that?"

"Deduction, Botaki-san. For instance, although you speak Okurinese with an Indonesian accent, which one can even localize to Jakarta, with the suggestion of an underlying Sundanese mother tongue, you can't hide your adaptation to a lower gravity than Earth's. Only a Sihorian or a Martian could dissimilate their origin with such pedantic precision; but the Sihorian Secret Service isn't very subtle— they'd have come in here with lasers blazing. Shall I continue?"

"That's not necessary," you assure her.

"My own guess is that you're an Incatena spy," she says, looking into her teacup.

"Look, how do I know you're not working for the Tourism Ministry yourself? I've been to the Commerce Association— it's riddled with Peace Party plants."

"Such as?"

"Goro Tsuichi, for example."

"That pustulent little twit? He's only a former Minister, for heaven's sake. They didn't exactly sneak him into our midst; more like putting him out to pasture. I thought you might be talking about someone like Hondo. They generally send the wart to check out the visitors."

"Oh, I tumbled to him right away," you say, pouring yourself more tea.

She leans back in her chair reflectively. "Botaki-san, or whatever your real name is, I don't have a zapper on your privates, but it's damn close. I have a pretty good idea what you are, and the Tourism Ministry is just a keystroke away. And of course you know almost nothing about me. You couldn't trust me in those circumstances, could you?"

"Certainly I couldn't," you say, affably.

"But you have something on me too, don't you? You know that I didn't turn you in to the thugs when I had a chance. You know that I keep this office surveillance-clean. You know that I'm pointing out Peace Party moles in the Commerce Association. All that's enough to get me in a smelly pile of trouble. So you can trust me."

"Of course I can," you agree.

"There are those of us who are enlightened enough to despise Jishuri Kumari and all his works. Now, Botaki-san, why do you think that is?"

"Because business chafes under the restraints of dictatorship as much as anyone else."

"No, that's not it," says Jidori-san. "We really don't have any problem with that. Managed competition, do-nothing unions, you know. Hell, I'd have to completely change my product

line if things ever opened up. So what do you think is the problem?"

"Well, I suppose it has to relate to money somewhere down
the line."

"Damn right it does. We do all right under these mopes.
But we could do a hell of a lot better without all this bureaucracy,
without the monopolies, without the corruption, without the cro-
nyism, without censorship hobbling the Vee. And without all this
militarism. It's a waste of resources that could go into developing
this planet."

"I couldn't agree with you more," you assure her. "However, I personally couldn't do without political liberalization—"

"Reform," she suggests. "I prefer that word— reform."

"At the least, free elections."

"Yes, yes, that's fine, I'm all for that," she says, without
much interest. "What I'm trying to get across is, we don't want
any radicalism. None of this up-against-the-wall nonsense, no
heads hung from lampposts, no attacks on property. Reform, yes,
but let's have continuity as well."

"Well, we have found that radicalism, as you say, isn't very
effective," you volunteer, reassuringly. "You lose control of the
reaction. For instance, on Euko, after the Reorganization—"

"Well, that was a completely artificial situation. They'd just
lost a war with their own orbitals— a poor excuse for a war, yes,
but it seemed serious enough at the time. But the Technocrats
were completely wet anyway. There were only two things worth
doing at that time— rapprochement with Novorossiya, and terraforming— and they didn't do either. They did come out of Belt
culture, of course, miscegenated with the European gridlocracy,
but the signs were already in the air."

"The technology wasn't there," you point out.

"Enough of it was. They had the atmospherics, and the soil
research was already underway. Now, on Noyvelt, in 2872..."

This goes on for awhile. You touch on several more subjects— sociometrics, sailing, genetic linguistics, telephotonics,
Peace Party politics, Army corruption. She does most of the talking; and yet by the end of the afternoon you feel that she's wrung
out as much real information about yourself as a Tourism torturer
could in a week.

You do not discuss details of your respective activities, and you never explicitly describe your real role; but you know how to get in touch with each other, and you will be in contact.

"Your Tourism friends are long gone; it's safe to leave." she says, when everything has been discussed and your stomach is full to bursting with tea. "I'll have my driver take you to your hotel."

You accept, but soon regret it; the driver turns out to be an aficionado of an Okurinese sport, sumō fū, in which half-naked 300-pounders ponderously fight in the styles of various animals— the Bear, the Hippopotamus, the Overfed Crane, and so on. He not only gives you a guided tour of his holo collection, which he keeps conveniently at hand in the limo, but stays an extra half hour in front of the Otani, explaining fine points of strategy.

"You must come and see a match," he tells you as you're leaving the volant. "It's the biggest thing on Okura."

"It's on my list," you say, escaping.

Too damn much tea

Ryoku looks you in the eye. "It's time to put our cards on the table," he says.

You do so. "A run of low spades and a pair of jacks."

"Seven, eight, nine of hearts," says Dr. Zhou, gamely.

Ryoku looks discomfited. "I knew that would be a bad choice of expression," he says. "What I mean is, it's time to be honest with each other. What exactly do you bring to us, Botaki-san? Who are you really?"

You look around at the wet, dilapidated planking of the back room, still not very certain that this old farmhouse outside the city is completely safe. But according to Dr. Zhou, it took two months to find this place, and it can be used safely— once.[1]

Well, misplaced caution never ended any dictatorships. You take a sip of tea— everybody on this damn planet serves tea, they're worse than the Brits— and speak.

"Let's just say that I represent some powerful interests in the Douane," you say. "We've been very alarmed at the way things have been going here on Okura."

"So are we, but perhaps we don't see things from the same angle," responds Ryoku, cautiously. "You want to get rid of Kumari?"

"Of course."

"To replace him with a man more to your liking, perhaps?"

"To throw out the entire Peace Party dictatorship."

At that, Ryoku gets up and looks out the window, as if this highly charged utterance might have shorted out the local ozone. "Democracy," he breathes.

---

[1] You're not worried about Ryoku and Dr. Zhou themselves; you checked them out with your own Vee hacks plus some of Jidori's. It's a huge part of your job and so tedious that even footnotes about it are boring.

"I told you, Ryoku," says Dr. Zhou, with a smile in your direction. "Botaki-san very sound. I know these things, I know people. Just by how they look at art." She pours herself more tea.

"That's not enough," says Ryoku, fiercely. "Some kind of bourgeois restoration, back to the way things were before the Coalition Defeat— I don't think so. We don't just want reform; we want revolution. We want a remaking of society at the most basic level."

"I couldn't agree with you more," you say. "A really progressive state, that's what we're after."

"You know, from Spartacus to the Cathari to Mao Zedong to the Allahu Commune, history has been about just one thing, and that's the struggle of the haves and the have-nots," Ryoku informs you. "Everything else— religion, sex, technology— is just camouflage and distraction. They make you think the enemy is immigrants or fucking or plezh or Ogorodé or whatever. But it's always just this: they want to stomp in our faces just a little while longer."

"You forget, Ryoku. There's also art," Dr. Zhou reminds him.

Ryoku looks like he's just gotten some bleed-through from a neighbor's music node. "Ah, yes, there is art. But the most radical artist is also the freest human being, don't you think so?"

"If free of ideology, then yes, I agree."

"Yes, of course, free of all ideological fetters," declares Ryoku. "Free, completely free! I want all the barriers to come down! Do you understand, Botaki-san?"

"Oh, yes," you assure him.

The three of you smile at each other, savoring the glow of the future.

"Of course, true freedom comes from only libertarianism," says Dr. Zhou.

"You are so deluded!" exclaims Ryoku. "Libertarianism would just be the fig-leaf for the most ruthless exploitation the cosmos has ever seen! Only community, the solidarity of all honest, laboring beings, can guarantee real freedom."

"I don't agree," says Dr. Zhou. "You can't have exploitation without the threat of government force. No government, no force."

Ryoku turns to you, shakes his head pointedly. "This is a *tactical* alliance," he remarks.

Ah, children, children, you think. These people are more cut off from Incatena civilization than you thought. Regressing to these freshman-dorm disputes! Libertarianism, communitarianism, they're nothing more than wishful thinking, astrology. In civilized space politics is no longer a matter of argument. Not even a politician can advance a policy proposal without running it through a battery of simulations on advanced AIs.

"It may be a little early to write the new constitution yet," you suggest. You consider pouring yourself more tea, and dismiss the idea. You're sick of tea. Another drop of tea and you think you might be violently ill. "Perhaps *after* we overthrow the dictatorship...?"

"That's right," says Ryoku. "We bicker, and Jishuri Kumari's buns are still weighing down the throne of Okura."

"What you say?" asks Dr. Zhou.

"Buns. Buttocks."

"*Pìgu*," you supply, since Zhou still looks confused.

"The *pìgu* of Okura? I still don't understand."

"Never mind," you say. "Let's move on, or up, to practical matters, if we may. As I was saying earlier, the interests I represent want to see change, and we're prepared to lend a hand."

"We've got plenty of hands ourselves," points out Ryoku. "What's in yours? New tactics? Money? Arms?"

Dr. Zhou giggles. "He's asking if you have arms in your hands. That's backwards. First *pìgu*, now arms on hands." You both look at her, and she sobers up.

You think a moment. Personally, of course, you have nothing but your powerful intellect to offer. You can commit the Incatena to certain courses of action; but not what the Agent Directives don't allow (which is always subject to debate), and you can't commit the resources of your coalition partners when you don't know who they all are yet.

"All three, to some extent," you respond, cautiously. "We have a good deal of socionomic experience. As for money, it depends of course on what it's needed for, but as a starting figure, I'm sure a hundred thousand credits could be made available quickly."

That's nothing for overthrowing a planetary government, of course, but it's probably several times the funds a dissident organization will have on hand, and you think you could raise it from Jidori-san if necessary. Your calculation pays off; there's a discernibly greater level of excitement in Ryoku's voice as he says, "That's fine, that's fine... and what about weapons?"

The Incatena does have two Interfleet cruisers in orbit over Okura— not enough to take over a city, much less a planet, but it's proved essential, across human space, not to depend on the locals for the enforcement of the Incatena Treaty. The cruisers have weapons available, of course, including some maintained for just such contingencies as this— but they're not an industrial complex. "It's not so easy," you murmur. "A few strategically distributed hand weapons, perhaps, but it's not exactly easy to smuggle them in from Sol..."

The news seems to depress Ryoku. "A sidearm or two is nice, but around here power flows out of the barrel of a pulse-plasma inter-urban tank."

"You don't think you're going to take Kumari with a frontal assault, do you?" you ask.

"It sure won't be with a frontal demonstration," he counters.

"You don't need an army," you insist.

"Well, that's good," he says. "Because we haven't got one."

"But *he's* got one," you point out, eagerly.

"Yes. So he does. It does sort of stand in the way."

Dr. Zhou smiles suddenly. "I think I see what Botaki-san is getting at. We don't need army to take on Kumari. We let his army do it himself."

"Exactly," you say. "There's a lot of ambitious men in the Army, and they know where Kumari came from as well as anybody. Get the Army fighting against itself, and the battle is half won."

"We've always thought so," says Ryoku, catching up. "But we don't have many contacts in the Army— I'm 4-F myself— bad lungs."

Dr. Zhou shakes her head sadly. "I don't know any military either. But it's obvious someone need to go there."

They look at you expectantly.

"I'll take care of it," you say, casually.

"Thank you so much," says Dr. Zhou.   "Your cup is empty— you must drink more tea."

Department, please?

The pride of the Peace Party is its army; the Peace Army headquarters, the Enneagon, occupies a square kilometer of choice real estate between Glorious Colonel Jishuri Kumari Boulevard and Helm of the Revolution Jishuri Kumari Prospect.

Visitors to Army headquarters— and there are many, from busloads of schoolchildren to job- or favor-seekers to visiting dignitaries from the subordinated nations— are given every opportunity to contemplate the power and discipline of the Peace Army. Guards toting laser rifles point them cheerfully in your direction; batteries of photonic cannon, nuclear missile silos, and a pair of heavily armed space cruisers tower over the walkway; statues and bronzed weapons commemorate famous victories and successful funding increases. Vendors hawk sandwiches, bureaucratic forms, and souvenir army toys to the crowd. The effect is tackily Third Millennium, or even Second.

The main lobby is surprisingly small; a bank of secretaries sits under a large sign:

WELCOME TO THE HEADQUARTERS OF THE
PEACE ARMY

"Enforcing the Peace with Force"

DEPARTMENT PASS REQUIRED
FOR ALL VISITORS

Inform the desk sergeant of the number of the department you wish to visit. No queries, including requests for department numbers, can be answered at this desk: all queries must be referred to Computer Services.

"Department number, please?"

"Uh— I'm not sure what I need, do you have a list or something?"

For answer, the clerk points at the sign overhead. You consider it, as you had hoped not to.

"Well, give me Computer Services, I guess."

"Department number?"

"I beg your pardon?"

"I can't give you a pass without a department number."

"Well, what's the number for Computer Services?"

"We can't give out department numbers here, o-san. Security. They can give out department numbers at Computer Services."

"And how do I get Computer Services' number?"

"Computer Services can get you that number, o-san."

"Tell me one thing," you say, with a disarming calmness. "Are you under the impression that this system works?"

"Sorry, o-san. Security."

There's already a line of people behind you; they shuffle at you impatiently. You try one last tack.

"Could I have the commaudio address for Computer Services?"

"We don't give out addresses here, o-san. Security. You need to ask at Communications Services."

"Where is that?"

"I'll be glad to direct you, if you can give me the department number."

You wonder how many clerks a week are lost to homicide.

It occurs to you that some of the vendors outside might be able to help. And indeed, you discover a vigorous black market in department numbers. For only C. 150 you acquire the number for Computer Services: 019. Your triumph survives another wait in line; you present this number to the desk clerk, and duly receive your pass.

Computer Services turns out to be a line of clerked windows on the top floor of the Enneagon; for security reasons, no actual computers are present in this office. Signs divide the clerks into QUERIES, JOBS, and SERVICES. There's a long line for QUERIES; the other two clerks are doing nothing. You approach one of them and state your business.

"That's a Query," says the clerk. "Get in the Queries line."

You take one look at the other do-nothing clerk; he focuses on you just long enough to incrementally nod his head toward Queries.

You sigh and move to the end of the Queries line. The line advances excruciatingly slowly, so that by the time you reach the front you're vaguely expecting to be presented with a driver's license.

"I understand that you have a department list available here," you say.

The clerk shakes her head. "Who referred you here? Office Services is what you need."

She is already turning to the next person in line; you rudely interrupt to ask for the department number. It's 983.

You go back down to the lobby.

"You sent me to the wrong office," you complain.

"We don't send anyone anywhere," points out the clerk, swattably. "All we do is send you to the department you ask for."

"Your sign is wrong," you persist, pointing upward. "It's Office Services you should send people to."

The clerk looks up at the sign, studies it. "Are you making a complaint about the sign?"

"That's right, Galileo."

"Complaints have to be addressed to the Complaints Department."

The hair on your head starts to sizzle. It's not worth it, you tell yourself. He'll be lynched by another visitor soon enough. "Just give me a pass for department 983," you mutter.

Office Services turns out to be next door to Computer Services. The staff is happy to give you a list of departments.

001 Enlistment
019 Computer Services
317 Public Relations
592 Conference Room
638 Appointments Office
730 Commissary
818 Liaison Office

983 Office Services
992 Services Office

Other departments have classified department numbers;
you must apply at the department to obtain its number.

The Public Relations department seems to consist of grins,
which invite you to take a tour of the Enneagon. You accept,
without much hope. Perhaps you can surreptitiously pick up a
department number or two.

You see many rooms full of clerical workers. You see meeting rooms full of bureaucrats. In other parts of the building you
gaze upon vast barn-like expanses of people working in pitiful
little ergolounges. Entire wings of the building seem to consist
mainly of offices.

Also featured on the tour are glimpses of doors leading to
research laboratories, doors concealing wind tunnels, and doors
to map rooms, communications rooms, and other interesting
places which for security reasons you can't actually see.

You are taken outside and shown the parade grounds,
where recruits are stepping smartly through a simulated ethnic
cleansing, and the decorations hall, filled with statues, plaques,
awards, and declarations of gratitude from conquered nations.

Finally, you are taken to watch an informational hologram,
intended to explain the purpose of the army, which is evidently to
take off in jets, to crowd round conference tables, and to turn the
knobs on long banks of equipment.

By this time you're hungry, so you decide to stop in at the
Commissary (department 730). It must be some sort of temporary
insanity.

An army travels on its stomach, especially after eating the
food at the Peace Army commissary. There are three choices of
hot entrée available today: red, brown, and white. Each comes
with rice and a choice of vegetables, okra, eggplant, or Brussels
sprouts, all of which have been rendered completely table-safe by
a week's continuous boiling. There is also a choice of beverage:
hot black stuff, syrupy brown stuff, and indescribable green stuff.

You look round at the recruits; with their close-shaved
heads they look almost exactly alike; you'd swear that the only

variation is in their noses. They look much like any soldiers eating army food: like people famished for pizza and beer.

You overhear someone at the next table explaining how Okurinese soldiers are provoked into blood-lust during battle: "They say, 'Son, imagine that son of a bitch over there is your cook.'"

Another table is running through the various racial epithets current on Okura. You hadn't even known that there was a racial epithet for the Yakut.[1]

Next to you, some sailors are discussing what sucks more, being sunk by nuclear-tipped torpedoes or having to wear those silly hats.

To your right, some grunts are talking about which generals are most likely to lead a coup against Planetary Marshal Kumari.

Behind you, a Space Forces colonel is telling about the time their C. 7,500 toilets failed and they had to fix them with the C. 950 screwdrivers.

Wait a minute.

You backtrack with the speed of a politician, sharpen your mental pencil, grab a piece of mental stationery, and start taking mental notes. The mental room is a little too warm; you turn down the mental thermostat.

"I say it'll be Gen. Yataka," says one soldier, with a big, wide nose. "He's never forgiven Kumari for giving Hiroshi the fucking top job. They say he's got a picture of Kumari in his office cabinet that he uses for fucking target practice."

"No way, Yataka couldn't organize a trip to the fucking john," says another recruit, whose nose is long and delicate. "It'll be Gen. Hitsumi. He's a dissident, he's got all sorts of fucking nihilistic literature in his quarters. They'd have shot him years ago if he wasn't their fucking star general."

"They watch him too closely," points out another, small-nosed soldier. "He can't fart without the fucking Home Ministry bursting into his office. Gen. Daishiyō is the one to watch. He's completely fucking loyal on the outside, his fucking *hobby* is going to Peace Party demos. That's exactly how Kumari was, when fucking Nashimoto was in charge."

---

[1] 'Yaks'.

"You're full of shit," says a small guy with a piggy nose. "It's Gen. Sukuru. He's a brutal fucking son of a bitch— just likes power. God help you if you ever have to serve in his fucking battalion. He'll fucking shoot you if he don't like the way you fucking piss."

"You're all fucking nuts," says a fifth soldier, bulbous-nosed. "If anyone's going to do something, it's Gen. Rieszkowyczyk. He's based on the other side of the fucking planet, he's set up a personality cult on his base, and he's crazy as a fucking Skweeoo."

A talk with some of these gentlemen seems to be in order. You are told that this requires a preliminary visit to the Appointments Office, department 638. You're told wrong; the Appointments Office, since a recent reorganization, no longer handles appointments. It's the Liaison Office you want.

The Liaison Office turns out to be a small cubicle where a secretary sits reading a static book, apparently a very engrossing one, because he is not at all interested in your presence. It is really charming, in this technological age, to see such devotion to the printed word.

You solicit his attention, by coughing and looking expectant. No response.

You try murmuring, and then shouting, "Excuse me." No response.

Pretending to have a massive coronary: nothing doing. That's one engrossing book he's engrossed in.

You pull his book away. That does it.

You ask for appointments with all five generals. This turns out to be impossible, unless you are the Planetary Marshal or God, and even God had better have a damn good reason. You can see one general.

This requires some quick but careful thought. Yataka sounds incompetent; Sukuru is too nasty; Rieszkowyczyk isn't in this hemisphere, and though Daishiyō's outward loyalty would be a good mask for dissidence, it could just as well be a good mask for hopeless conformism. You ask to see Gen. Hitsumi.

The secretary busies himself with his datanode, and informs you that you should report to Department 802 in precisely three months.

"*Three months?* Isn't he available sooner?"

"Sure, but it's policy to make people without an appointment wait for three months."

You consider this. "But I've *got* an appointment. You just gave it to me. So I'm not a person without an appointment— the policy doesn't apply."

He thinks a moment. "You're right. I'll give you one four weeks away."

"Great, thanks. Now that I've got two appointments, wouldn't you say that I'm a frequent visitor? If you could…"

"Don't push it," he advises.

You gesture with your UI neurimplant, and in a moment of photonic osculation the date and location are transferred to your calendar.

"Now can I have my book back?"

You give him the book, but not before taking a glance at its title: *Getting Ahead with Superior Customer Service.*

Leaving the Enneagon, you find yourself marveling that an organization as mind-bogglingly inefficient as the Peace Army was able to conquer an entire planet. You realize, however, that this analysis is naïve. It doesn't take efficiency to kill people. Brute force does the job just fine.

Ikkyū-shima

You are in Tandō, the capital of Ikkyū-shima, a nation scattered among the islands of a vast archipelago. Much more than in Atami, you are conscious of being in a police state: armed patrols, sullen stares, grim grey buildings, ruins left untouched since the Coalition War, random screams from the local branch of the Home Ministry. And yet this crowded, bullet-pocked city has a certain faded glamour, reminding you that before its takeover by the Peace Army it was the capital of a mighty independent power.

You spend a week cruising the bars of Tandō, talking up strangers, buying rounds, betting on pachinko, watching holographic porno, singing karaoke, and ingesting cheap *tanaki*. You listen to a lot of very relaxed, slow-talking men complaining about their jobs, their wives, or the miserable performance of the Tandō Giants.[1] A stream of dubious-looking individuals approach you for spare change, sympathy, or romance. More than once you watch a table of businessmen slowly get drunk enough to tell off the boss.

They say that there's no better way to get to know a people than to drink with them. If that's true, then it can be said of the Ikkyū-jin that they are red-faced, noisy, and unsteady on their feet. Also that they like to drink a lot.

It takes a lot of listening to hear anything about politics, and what you hear rarely goes beyond bemoaning the number of soldiers and bureaucrats— although you do hear a few political jokes. (Sample: "Hawaki is in bed with Kumari's wife, when Kumari comes in and surprises them. 'Somebody's going to hang for this,' he says. 'Director-san, we'll find the Ikkyū-jin who's responsible,' replies Hawaki.")

---

[1] Every year the team puts on a performance of *The Tale of Genji*, for charity, and this year's show was unusually awful.

The local Vee is even more heavily controlled than that of Atami. The major scenesuite, available in rent-a-pad form at every street corner even if you never see anyone reading it, is the Peace Party outlet, the *Progress Net Tandō*. *Tandō Connect* is not much more useful.

Perhaps the journalists themselves are better bets. You manage to talk to a few editors and reporters. The editors are all Gōsei-jin, and talking to them is like reading their news scenes— all praise of the Peace Party, diatribes against foreigners, and encomiums to the happiness and prosperity of the Ikkyū-jin. Too many of the reporters are the same way. Some, however, are willing to talk about the continuing resentment over the Gōsei conquest of Ikkyū-shima, the forced exportation of the country's highest-quality products to Gōsei, and the occasional shootings of Gōsei-jin soldiers or bureaucrats in lonely parts of the country.

But none of them seems to know about any organized resistance to the Directorate.

"How do you resist a dictatorship? That's one for the Zen Masters," says one reporter, shaking his head.

"Oh, yes, rumors of the repression of Ikkyū-shima are quite unfounded," explains Narayo Yamafuta, secretary of the Values Party, in a mild Atami accent. "The existence of our party is evidence of the untrammeled flourishing of democracy on Okura. In the last elections we won a very encouraging 17% of the vote."

"And how do you oppose the Peace Party?" you ask.

"We prefer to say *supplement*. Last year we successfully supplemented them on the location of the Tatai Highway," boasts Yamafuta. "We have also fought to raise the allocation for the Education and Propaganda Ministry from 5% to 7% of the budget. Education is very important to our constituents. And we have agitated for the raising of the status of Tandō-*fu* to the status of *to*, which it had before the Glorious Coalition War."

"What would be the program of the Values Party if it achieved power?" you ask.

The question seems to stun Yamafuta; he looks around quickly before replying,

"Er, perhaps I have given an improper impression— our political system is built upon harmony, not upon contention or alienation. It is altogether a more civilized approach to government, is it not?"

"Well, what's the point of having elections, then?"

"We are committed to democracy," he reminds you. "A healthy and vigorous opposition is an integral part of the Directoral system, so long as it works in complete harmony with it, of course."

The Secretary is eager to explain things further for you; he suggests dinner at the Tiaohe Club, said to be one of the finest Chinese restaurants in Tandō. It certainly has, as you can see for yourself several hours later, suitably arrogant waiters, splendid furnishings, and apoplectic prices.

Fortunately, Yamafuta is buying; only the wine is on you. As you dine, then, he explains to you, over three or four bottles of Gōsei's finest, that Okura is not a dictatorship, that Ikkyū-shima is much happier since the Glorious Coalition War, and that Jishuri Kumari is one of the most remarkable political figures in human space.

There is no hope for him, of course. Nonetheless, there are allusions to struggles in the party, to the difficulty he has with the headstrong and uncomprehending among his flock... would it not be worth attending the upcoming three-day party conference he is inviting you to (all expenses paid, in return for a small contribution)?

You attend, and soon regret the C. 500 contribution, not to mention the C. 250 bar tab from the Tiaohe Club. The Values Party sees no serious problems facing Ikkyū-shima, unless it is a need for more strength and harmony, and less alienation and contention. It's full of admiration for the leadership of the Peace Party; it's an honor to be in supplementation to such enlightenment. The most impassioned speech you hear is on the subject of spelling reform; the old rōmaji spelling was fine a thousand years ago, but it has diverged widely from the spoken language, and surely it is time for re-phoneticization. The speaker receives a standing ovation. You begin to wonder how it is that the Values Party racks up as much of the vote as it does.

You do meet the dissidents. Their proposal is as simple as it is radical: Why not simply merge with the Peace Party? Would they not accomplish more that way, would there not be greater harmony? Polite applause. Yamafuta addresses the convention with noble outrage. What, if the honorable delegates' proposal were accepted, would become of *democracy*? Harmony does not arise from mere *consolidation*; harmony arises from the subordination of *multiple elements*. Separate and free, the members of the Values Party perform a greater service to the Directorate than they could as part of the Peace Party. Standing ovation.

The Values Party is not all work and no play, of course. The conference takes place at a luxury resort, and the delegates indulge themselves as much as is humanly possible. Whenever there is an important speech to be endured or a resolution to be rubber-stamped, aides must comb the casinos, the beach, and the virtual golf arcades for delegates who have mislaid themselves.

Lazing on the beach, with a daiquiri on the Party's tab, browsing a history scene, you begin to understand what's going on. The Values Party turns out to predate the Coalition War; it used to alternate in power with the Popular Party. Even then it was seen as pro-Gōsei, and the instrument of big business. The Populars were in power at the time of the war, and indeed interned some Valuer bigwigs on charges of collusion with the enemy; this is still talked about as the worst of the many criminal actions of the old regime. When the war was over, the Populars were jailed, and the Valuers were welcomed into their present little-brother status.

In short, there is no historical dissidence for the party to wake to; toadyism to the powerful has always been the party's bread and butter. You have wasted your time.

You snap your fingers. You figure the Values Party owes you at least C. 750 worth of daiquiris.

For completeness' sake, you decide to check out the local branch of the Peace Party. You are received most cordially by the General Secretary, a woman named Mariko Hitori. She is brisk, businesslike, and formidably built, and it is obvious that at no time, now or in her schooldays, would she have had the nickname Giggles.

You ask about relations with Gōsei. "Naturally, after the Coalition War, there was suspicion as to the intentions of the Gōsei-jin," she responds. "I think it can be said that the people of Ikkyū-shima (of which I myself am a proud example) have come to know, as the Director says, what is the character of the Ikkyū-go Peace Party."

"But Gōsei keeps close tabs on you, no doubt."

"Strength through Voluntary Community is one of the by-words of the Peace Party," she says. "Within the context of the total unity of the Peace system, we run our own affairs here."

"Really. How much autonomy do you have then?"

"We run the civil administration according to Directoral principles, but adapted to local conditions, which are of course very different from Gōsei's. However, the Peace Army units here report directly to Atami, and the Home Ministry too."

"Really? So you have no enforcement services at all?"

"We have the police, the armed Youth Guards, and Peace Party members in every village of Ikkyū-shima and every block of Tandō. What is our responsibility we fulfill very thoroughly; and nothing happens here that we don't know about."

"You have to forgive me if I have an offworlder's skepticism," you say, disarmingly. "Things seem pretty tightly controlled to me— no wiggle room at all. I've even talked to the Values Party people; they could hardly be stronger supporters of the regime if they were members of the Gōsei Peace Party."

This brings a short laugh. "Some of them *are* members," she tells you. "Don't pay them any mind. The only supporters of that clown Yamafuta are his countrymen."

"They do get a sixth of the votes here," you point out.

"There's a lot of Gōsei-jin here. Let me put it this way, Bo-taki-san. The Peace Party of Ikkyū-shima is the true expression of the deepest will of our people. We've spent years gaining their trust and building an effective organization. I think you'll find that their allegiance is more than a matter of our name. Now, if you'll excuse me, o-san, I have some work to catch up on."

Two days later you are picked up by the police. You are escorted by laser-armed minions to the metallic presence of the Chief of Police, Commissioner Gorudun-3, who has the pleasant features and wide eyes typical of Okurinese mecs.

"Thank you, minions, you may go. Rimu Botaki, you are under arrest. We have reason to believe that you are a spy of the Douane."

In the slammer

You've been in worse jails— soggy lightless crevices carved from caves, nameless hideyholes beneath ruinous castles, a drafty palisade downwind of a manure factory. Brigs on spaceships; lockups in the colonies; quarantine pens on alien worlds. This cell is simply a plain room somewhere in the bowels of the main Tandō police station. There are no bars; instead, a Tajima energy screen makes up one wall of the room, giving it the feel of a mere extension of the corridor outside. You can see into the entire row of cells opposite, each occupied by a lone prisoner, forlorn, furious, or flaked out.

You'd better get yourself ready for an interrogation, and on a backward planet like this, probably torture. The Incatena has prepared you as best as it can, of course. For years Agents were given a neural shunt, allowing them to shut off pain from any part of the body. A shunt proved to have disadvantages, however. Too many Agents activated it absent-mindedly in the shower, leading to second-degree burns, or to kill a toothache, resulting in occasional enemy unmasking of Agents due to swollen, malodorous gums. R&D is now working on a more complicated neurimplant, involving an AI that intercepts pain and decides when to handle it itself and when to send it on to the conscious mind; but progress has been slow. AIs are sulky mindguests, who resent having to take care of minor injuries and swollen gums when their photonic colleagues are running megacorporations. In the meantime Agents are taught ancient Aisan mind control techniques. These work fine except in situations of extreme mental stress— as experienced in torture chambers, for instance.

There's always your tooth, of course. One of your teeth contains a powerful explosive, invisible to X-rays, p-detectors, and anything but the best nanoscans, and capable of annihilating a significant portion of your vicinity— yourself included, unless you've taken the pains to disengage yourself from the tooth. Unfortunately, yours was put in over a century ago, and you've forgotten which tooth it was. You're always worried that your dentist will blow you both sky-high.

You are left alone all night. In the early morning the minions reappear, cuff your wrists in numbcord, and escort you to an office. Your cuffs are removed, and you are left to wait. You brush the mental dust off those mind control techniques.

The door opens, and in walks Mariko Hitori.

"I'm so sorry for all this," she says. "It is not the most pleasant way to treat a guest to our nation."

"I hope you can get me out of it, Hitori-san," you respond.

"Considering that I got you into it, that shouldn't be difficult."

"You mean, our conversation was overheard by somebody, who found something suspicious about it and denounced me to the police?"

"No, I mean I messaged Gorudun-3 asking him to arrest you," she clarifies.

There doesn't seem to be much to say to that.

"So are you a Douane spy?" asks Hitori-san.

You muster as much outrage and bluster as possible. "Of course not, I'm an Indonesian business rep. And as soon as the Douane knows that you've arrested me, an innocent traveler, there'll be a serious diplomatic incident over this, I assure you."

She cocks her head critically. "Not bad, but you need to put a little more quiver in your voice. Or how about a slight stutter? 'An innocent t-traveler...' That would be more convincing, wouldn't it?"

"I assure you, o-san, I'm not joking."

"Neither am I," she says.

She paces around the little office for a few minutes, looking at you all the while. You try to look extremely innocent— saccharine even. Finally she stops, facing you.

"Item," she says. "Subject is observed asking questions of various persons around Tandō: bartenders, students, journalists, officials of the Values Party and of the Peace Party. None of the conversations broach the subject of business."

"I can explain," you offer.

"Item. Subject arrived in Atami two months ago; has been spotted entering the Dzebyet Embassy and at a party attended by known Peace Party dissidents."

"I'm shocked," you say. "They seemed like such nice people."

"Item. Subject evaded Tourism Ministry escort within a few days of arrival. Not so hard to do, of course, especially with those two— but the need to evade the escort is rare, and suspicious."

"I didn't know an escort was necessary," you suggest. "Perhaps they simply lost track of me. I hate to imply any sort of incompetence..."

"I believe the escorts, top of the line agents expert in martial arts, were separated by guile, and then disabled with weapons, one of them with his own max gun."

"Went off accidentally," you murmur. "Devilish tricky things."

"Item. Subject is posing as an Indonesian, a Douane nationality convenient for undercover work on Okura."

"That's rather begging the question, don't you think?"

"Item. Subject happens to speak fluent Okurinese, despite no previous visits to this planet."

"Okurinese roommate in college," you explain.

"Item. No Okurinese nation has the resources to send an agent to Sol and back to hide their origin; no other star system has the motivation. Sihor, yes, but one or both of us would be dead. That leaves the Douane, or— what amounts to the same thing— the Incatena."

Your heart leaps. "A simple application of Occam's Razor..."

"How many items was that?"

"Six."

"Great. That's about five more than we usually require to put someone away for a long, long time," she remarks. "It doesn't look good for you, Botaki— if that's your name."

"I want to speak to the Incatena Station Chief."

"Don't bother. He's a political appointee and a complete idiot, and he's in bed with the regime," she advises.

You don't say anything. You're worried, and cursing yourself for neglecting your business image. Who was watching you in Atami and why didn't you notice them? Still, you're alive and not presently being tortured; there's no reason to budge from your story yet.

"Now, this isn't to say that a Douane agent isn't *welcome*," she continues. "You can thank your stars that you're in our hands, not the Home Ministry's. They've been in the police state racket for too long— all they're interested in is a steady supply of dissidents, real or imagined, to justify their existence. Torture and anonymous denunciations produce that supply, so they don't even bother to look for real enemies of the state anymore.

"But we do... and you fit the profile like a molecule map."

"It could be a coincidence," you say.

She smiles, but keeps all the humor to herself. "It could be. And if it is— if you continue to insist that you're simply an innocent traveler— we'll turn you over to the Home Ministry. You'd be useless to us, but they'd like you just fine, and we'd get a little something for cooperating."

"What, brown-nosing points?"

"Surplus surveillance equipment plus frequent flyer miles," she explains. "So there you have it. You're an innocent traveler— fine, we're rid of you, the Home Ministry gets itself some business— and believe me, when they get your hands on you, it's not a matter of a nice clean jail cell, and out the next day. Or year. You're a Douane or Incatena spy— we have something to talk about.

"I'm sorry to do this to you, Botaki-san, but it was the only way. We could circle around each other for months otherwise, and I'd never know what you are. As it is— I'll leave you to think for awhile. I'll be back in an hour for your answer."

She exits; the minions return, and escort you to your cell.

There's no question of keeping to your cover— that part of Hitori-san's trap is foolproof enough. Insist on your innocence, and you end up in a cell or a concentration camp, perhaps under the personal care of Pasty and Nasty. The real decision to make is whether to use your tooth. (You can try every tooth, if necessary— you've got the time.)

The Agent Directives are clear, if unpalatable, in a situation like this: destroy yourself before compromising a mission of this magnitude. You can take your interrogator out with you, if you like, but no other concessions to your own pleasures are allowed.

That's *if* the mission is compromised. Perhaps you should take Hitori-san, as the French say, at the foot of the letter? Perhaps she would indeed find an Incatena spy welcome?

To make a monthly quota, perhaps, or to ingratiate herself with the authorities in Atami? But she's laid it out for you: if that was what she wanted, she'd hand you over to the Home Ministry soonest.

When Hitori returns, you tell her that you are an Agent of the Incatena.

Buddha nature

"Incatena, eh? So much the better. Are you hungry?"

When you think about it, you realize that you're famished. You haven't eaten since your arrest, the previous day. You assent eagerly.

"What would you like?" asks Hitori-san. "Crab? Bluefish? I wouldn't advise the sushi, not till you've developed a resistance."

"I'm kind of tired of seafood. Do you have pad thai?"

"Sure. What about a beverage? We have a very nice wasabi punch here in Ikkyū-shima. The local beer is excellent as well. The simulated hops are really convincing."

"Just some green tea, please."

"Green tea. Any appetizer?"

"No... wait, yes. Half an order of spring rolls. Wait. Make that a full order."

"OK, spring rolls, pad thai and green tea."

The Peace Party leader calls in your order, then sits on the edge of the desk facing you.

"So what's your report to your bosses back in Areopolis so far?" she asks, conversationally.

"That the Ikkyū-jin are boldly building a counter-revolutionary organization in the very interior of the local Peace Party apparatus," you say.

"'Boldly,'" she repeats. "Insanely, you might say. And you? What are your instructions?"

"Basically, to serve the people in their thirst for freedom," you answer. "I believe that Okura has had its fill of totalitarianism. I've seen that there's a hunger for change, a desire to enjoy the fruits of liberty, to drink deep from the red wine of prosperity, to savor the bagels and cream cheese of human solidarity..."

You hadn't realized you were quite this hungry. The pad thai arrives none too soon; for ten minutes Hitori-san can't get a word out of you.

She looks at you reflectively. "There's nothing I hate more than wasting time, but boldness and even insanity aren't enough in this game, Botaki-san; one also requires a surpassing and devious caution... I'm certain now that you *are* a spy, but what if you're not working for the Incatena, but for Kumari?"

"If I was working for Kumari, I'd have let you send me to the Home Ministry."

"Really? How so?"

You think a minute. "No, wait, you're right. I'd have stayed right here. I see your point."

"How do I know you're trustworthy? That's one for the Zen Masters, I think."

Your heart sinks. "You mean you can't think of any way out?"

"No, I mean I'm going to leave it to the Zen Masters. I trust their intuition."

You struggle toward comprehension. She senses this.

"Go to the Zen Temple tomorrow. Ask for the abbot." She smiles. "You might want to bone up on your Buddhism. There'll be a test."

She stands; you are evidently dismissed. You finish off the green tea, wondering for the thousandth time why green tea tastes so good when you're eating out, and like nothing at all when you make it at home. You get up yourself.

"If you are who I think you are," says Hitori-san, with a cool smile, "we'll see each other again."

You nod, in a way that indicates that you understand and can be trusted, that you are impressed with her discipline and respectful of her achievements, and also suggests what an unexpectedly powerful and useful ally she has gained. It's one hell of a nod. She nods back, in a way that indicates that she just thought you were saying goodbye, and you head out.

The Zen Temple in Tandō is build on a small island in the geometric center of the Ikkyū-shima archipelago. The temple is large and open to the air; it is built in curves and pillars that respect the contours of the land and showcase the native vegetation.

Inside, after making the required offering, you are taken on a tour of the grounds. You see pilgrims pasting prayers on a great central shrine; you see schoolchildren on outings, in their identical blue uniforms, running round the exquisite gardens; you see the garden of raked sand, disarming in its simplicity and lack of sentimentality; you see the torii on the seashore, just past the rocks of the shore, somehow making this rocky shore and the sea itself a part of the holy place, an intimation of the oneness of the cosmos.

Spirituality is also made accessible to the people in the form of a reading room, funeral chapel, gift shop, and restaurant.

When you ask to see the abbot, you are led to a bare room with tatami flooring, where a minor monk, dressed in orange, looks you over from head to toe.

"Howdy," you say.

The monk says nothing, but seems to subject your greeting to deep scrutiny.

"I'm supposed to see the abbot," you say, with an ingratiating chuckle. The monk looks at you, but does not respond.

There is a pause. It lengthens.

You consider saying something, but it seems like the moment has passed. You're not sure how you would begin, anyway: Are you testing me? How does this work anyway? What about those Giants?

After this, not much happens.

There is another pause, and after that, silence.

The monk is still looking at you, alertly. You find that you can't meet his gaze for long. Nor are you supposed to, perhaps. It isn't a staredown contest.

Perhaps you're supposed to meditate? But you're not a Zen Buddhist, dammit.

A long time passes. As soon as it seems like you can wait for no longer— you must speak, or jump up, or shout— you find that, after all, you can wait just a bit longer. This newfound patience comes in handy, for what comes next turns out to be: nothing.

You're beginning to get a bit bored. Obviously, you're pretty low on Buddha nature.

Finally the monk speaks.

"What is the sound of one hand clapping?"

Fortunately, you have had the benefits of a multicultural education. You remember the answer from an issue of *Koan Komics* you read as a child.

"Mu," you say.

The monk nods, rises, bows, and leaves the room. In a few minutes another monk comes in, identical in dress but a little older. He sits down on the tatami matting and gives you the same once-over.

You settle down for another long wait, but after only a few seconds he asks his question: "At the heart of matter I come in pairs and triads, but never alone. One would have expected strangeness from the professors, but charm? Name me."

"Quark," you say.

The monk nods, rises, bows, and leaves the room. In a few minutes a third, middle-aged monk comes in. He sits down on the tatami matting, and inspects you. Indeed, his eyes never leave your face, making you feel extremely uncomfortable.

He waits. You wait along with him. He gazes at you intently. You match his gaze. They can't out-gaze you, an Agent of the Incatena. He's watching your face; you focus on his eyes. He focuses on your left pupil. You concentrate your perception on the ciliary gland behind the fourth hair of his right eyelash.

This competitiveness, you reflect sadly, no doubt reflects an appalling lack of Buddha nature.

"Right views, right intention, right speech, right living, right effort, right mindfulness, right concentration," declaims the monk. "What is missing?"

"Right action."

The monk nods, rises and bids you to follow. You are taken to another room in the exact middle of the temple, identical to the first, except for a small shrine set in one wall. Sitting on the tatami matting is an incredibly ancient monk. He makes no greeting as you enter, but continues to look straight ahead. You suppose he is blind.

He speaks, in a creaky voice: "There comes to trouble our meditations one from the home sun, indeed a samurai of the Chain of Worlds. Because one link in the chain is too strong, the chain becomes weak. Because division exists, the Whole is undivided. Though randomness is at the heart of the atoms, it is good to plan."

He pauses, breathing with some effort, as if speaking, or delivering wisdom, was itself an exertion at his age. You try to look receptive. He continues:

"The days are grim; that is why there is hope. The calligra-phers are experts in the drawing of characters, but they do not read. The Market closes high one day, and opens low the next. The coder programs, but the bugs do not go away. Buddha nature cannot be bought or sold, but can it be rented?"

There is a pause, and for the first time the ancient abbot looks at you, with bright, deep eyes. You see now that he is not blind, only rude.

"My monks have tested you," he informs you. "It seems that you are not entirely ignorant of the Whole."

"Thank you," you say. "Did I pass?"

"You are still under examination." He produces a sheaf of papers. "Please fill out these psychological evaluations. Follow all directions carefully. Don't think too long about any one question. In many cases there is no one 'right' answer. Don't make any marks outside the little ovals; it drives the grading mec crazy. At 8:00 tonight, you are to be at this address," he adds, writing spidery characters on a small slip of paper. "A man will meet you, wearing a headband with the kanzi *strife*. Go with him. At the end of tonight, untrust will be no more, and uncertainty will turn to understanding. *Sainara*."

The address is of a dock on the outskirts of Tandō. The man with the headband is standing, as at attention, at the side of a boat. He looks you over, bows, and gestures toward the boat.

"Where are we going?" you ask.

In response he turns to you and opens his mouth. He has no tongue.

He places the headband round your own head, as a blind-fold. With a shudder, you get in the boat and are on your way.

You sit back in the boat and are taken to an unknown desti-nation. The journey is long, and the tongueless poleman makes no conversation.

The boat pulls up; you are transferred with some awkward-ness to the shore, and marched a long distance, for more than half an hour, on a route that twists about and doubles back on itself; there are also sections of the journey taken on moving walkways and elevators. As a result, though as an Incatena Agent you have an almost perfect sense of orientation, you have no idea where the boat is, or even whether it's far away or near. At least you know what direction you're facing, thanks to your inoculated watch:

21:08 11 Oct 312° ☺

Your blindfold is removed, and replaced with a mask.

You are in a vast, dark space, lit by torches. The nearest walls, the only ones you can see, are of roughly trimmed stone. The air feels cold and musty; perhaps you are underground. An indeterminate number of people are standing here— black, silent figures, all masked. There could be fifty of them or five hundred. Their shadows waver in the light of the flames.

"This way," says a voice near you. One of the black figures takes your arm and leads you further into the dark throng.

In front of a raging fire there stands what appears to be a demon. As you come nearer you see that the raging eyes and grinning fangs are those of a golden mask, glowing luridly in the firelight. Two swords are strapped to the man's back; on the front of his flowing red robes is embroidered the picture of a leaping tiger. The golden mask turns toward you.

"Master, this is the Incatena Agent," says your guide; and then, to you, "The Master of the Kagedō Shadowmen."

You bow to each other.

You sense that you are not yet to speak, and therefore try to look like someone who, once deemed worthy to speak, will say something worth saying. This requires care and skill: if it's done wrong it just looks like you have to go to the bathroom.

The Master of Shadowmen turns to the crowd, and raises both hands in a gesture of invocation. "Warriors, greeting!"

A shout from the multitude rings in your ears.

"The stars are still high in the sky, yet the sun is rising. We are hidden, but all eyes are on us. Warriors and guests, all who are bound like serfs to the cause of freedom for the Realm of Islands, I bid you welcome! Do you desire freedom?"

"Freedom!" shouts the crowd.

"Failing freedom, what?"

"Death!" comes the shout from a thousand throats.

"What is our watchword?"

"The Shadow!"

"What is our mission statement?"

"Enlightened nationalism, cultural resurgence, and a more evolved state of awareness!"

The Master gestures toward you, and every masked eye turns in your direction. You lick your lips and think of the Agent Directives.

He bends toward you and addresses you in a whisper. "You don't have to go to the bathroom, do you?"

"No, no," you assure him.

He turns once more to his followers. "Here is the messenger from the Mother of Worlds! Messenger, let us see with what blades you propose to fight. You do plan to fight, do you not?"

"Yes, of course," you reply. "I mean, not personally, I saw myself more in an administrative role..."

"Your coming may be propitious," says the Master, with a hint of skepticism. "Indeed, you may mediate a dispute for us. Some among us have force at our command and are ready to use it. Others believe in peace and harmony; they suggest that the means of resistance must be the informed, prayerful use of the present system. What say you?"

"Well, really, you're making a false dichotomy," you offer. "An ideological minority can't mount a successful revolution— though they can coopt one. You want a broad coalition. As for force, moral persuasion is fine when you're dealing with an uncensored press, though even there it's the threat of radicalism that makes the moderate elements effective. And of course it's surprising how much information you can disseminate in a closed society. But here you'll definitely need force at some stage— *disciplined* force, not just a revenge party. We can discuss some specific tactics, if you like, and perhaps review your training methods."

The Master of the Shadowmen stares at you a moment, seemingly nonplussed; then he collects himself and says, "Messenger, there is another dispute, between tradition and idealism, between those who wish simply to restore the world as it was, and those who desire fundamental reform. Who is right?"

"The Incatena is not always quick to act," you say, "but when we act, we don't just kludge. Obviously, the old order on Okura held the seeds of fascism. The underlying causes have to be corrected."

A murmur of agreement passes through the room. You see nodding heads, even hear a few shouted, defiant slogans. At a gesture from the Shadowmaster, however, there is silence.

"Dark times call for dark measures," he intones grimly. "We are the strongest of those who would resist the Directorate; we are armed, and we are united. We are best suited to exercise power in the new Okura. A temporary dictatorship may be required, with the Master of Shadows at its head, to undo the evil of those who speak peace but bring tyranny. Do you consent to this small demand?"

You look around; the room is tense, waiting for your reply, seemingly ready to break out in cheers or in cries for blood. Most of the Shadowmen, you notice, are indeed armed. The firelight gleams off sharpened blades and wicked gun muzzles.

The Agent Directives are clear: just say no to thugs. But perhaps you should dissemble a bit, under the circumstances? Nothing you say now couldn't be corrected later.

On the other hand, there is justice and morality to consider. Also, your upcoming half-century performance review.

"A temporary dictatorship might be a good idea," you say, tactfully, "but it probably isn't. Either it tends to become permanent, or it's the dictator who ends up as temporary... I don't think we can get behind it."

The demon mask of the Master of Shadowmen comes near your face. "You will not elevate me to this lordship? And you make this pronouncement before my followers?"

"Er, sorry, no..."

He laughs. "Know you that the Kagedō Shadowmen do not seek their own liberation, but that of a planet. We will not become the new dictators of Okura, nor would we ally ourselves with one for whom dictatorship was congenial. Force, but only to beget freedom. Messenger, we will be allies."

The crowd erupts into shouts and cheers.

An hour later, in a back room, you sit with the Master of Shadowmen, the leader of the Ikkyū-shima Peace Party, and the Abbot of the Zen Temple, plotting strategy, devising codewords, and exploring contingencies. You work far into the night, but you are all satisfied with the scheme you come up with.

"You realize, of course, that this scheme requires that we have an inside man in the Peace Army," Hitori-san reminds you.

"It's in the bag," you say, exaggerating slightly.

You take the shuttle back to Atami, feeling almost light-headed. At last things seem to be moving. Then comes the message from Ryoku.

A disturbing picture

Ryoku's messages are always terse and restrained; he writes as if the secret police were mulling over every word. His sense of caution may be admirable, but the results can be frustratingly mysterious. This one merely gives a time and place and the annotation *Just us.*

He wants you to come alone, but why? You are about to message Dr. Zhou for clarification, when it occurs to you that perhaps he suspects her of something. His paranoia is infectious; you review your interactions with the curator in your mind.

Nothing stands out. It's probably something new. All you can do is go find out what's on his mind. You wait impatiently for the appointed time, then take a water taxi to the location, which turns out to be a yoga studio. You're not allowed in with street clothes; you change into an exercise outfit provided by the studio.

You find Ryoku upstairs in a large, bare room with several other students, putting himself into convoluted and painful-looking asanas and holding them for minutes on end. He is entirely naked.

"Um... Ryoku-san," you murmur. "I'm not sure if this is appropriate..."

"Botaki-san," he grunts, bent into a circle in a *Laghu Vajrasana* pose. He looks agitated, angry; the yoga certainly isn't calming him down much.

You perceive a UI message: *Security measure.*

You look around the room for machines before realizing that it's Ryoku. He's using his neurimplant to communicate. Basic espionage, usually compromised by the suspiciousness of sitting next to someone *not* talking. Unless you're in a context where not talking is normal— doing yoga, for instance.[1]

Left a picture on front desk datanode. Password Monkey_827.

---

[1] It's also slow— it's *typing*, albeit in your mind, so it's not as quick as speech. Besides, it's unutterably geeky.

"Fine," you say out loud. He says nothing, moving to the *Parsva Bakasana* pose, holding his body up on extended forearms.

Baffled and a little annoyed, you walk back to the front desk and access the datanode. There's a file with your name on it; when you give the password you see a 2-D photo. It's askew and a little blurry, as if it was taken quickly and surreptitiously with an imagizing neurimplant. It shows someone in a hospital bed, full of bruises, connected to machines and nursing mecs, one arm and one leg immobilized in refetalizing jackets. You grimace in sympathy. The face is distorted, and half-hidden by an artificial breathing apparatus, so that it takes some moments to even detect the general characteristics— it's an old woman. And then, with a shudder, you recognize her. It's Dr. Zhou.

Ryoku's precautions seem a little less absurd now. You go back upstairs and find him in the exercise room. He's bent back like a croquet hoop, in the *Urdhva Dhanurasana* pose. You adopt a simple *Vrksasana*, arms up, one leg pressed against the other.

What the hell? you message.

Home Ministry picked her up. Beaten, violated, left in a back alley. An Ogorodé street cleaner found her or she'd be dead.

But why? What'd she do?

Fucking nothing, Botaki-san. I talked to her. It was those student assholes and their fucking street demo. They went ahead with it, and the goons have been picking up anyone who knows them. She's close to a lot of them.

I want to see her. Where is she?

NO! Ryoku's protest is so vehement that he loses his concentration and his pose. He recovers himself and curls back into the *Eka Pada Rajakapotasana*, hand extended behind his head to meet one foot. You bend over into the neat diagonal of the *Utthita Parsvakonasana*.

Anyone who sees her goes on their list, he explains. *I'm already on it, doesn't matter.*

When will she be back at the museum?

Maybe, maybe not. Job status uncertain, but travel restricted. You don't understand yet, Botaki? They're bastards.

I know, you reassure him. *It's just... of anyone they could pick on...*

Welcome to Okura, he messages, grimly.

So— I'm sorry to ask, but how compromised are we?

The pickups seem to be over. Like I say, it was the demo, not anything real. But be paranoid.

How are you holding up?

Fuck, he explains. *Let's just get on with it. Just do it right.*

He relaxes into a sitting position, then bends up one leg behind his head in the *Parivrtta Surya Yantrasana.* It looks like it hurts; perhaps right now he wants it to.

It's strange to walk out into a sunny street filled with busy, unbruised pedestrians. You can still see that photo of Dr. Zhou— literally, as you've got a copy in your data neurimplant.

That's what you're up against; that's what the Peace Party comes down to. It's a regime where an art curator can get raped and beaten half to death because she wouldn't think Kumari Thoughts. That's why you're here.

Getting to know the General

It's time for your appointment with Gen. Hitsumi. Department 802 turns out to be an enormous waiting room; to save space, the Peace Army has decided that everyone who has to wait for anyone in the Enneagon can wait in one place. Messengers appear in a steady stream summoning people whose wait is over. When they are deposited at their destination, of course, the person they are supposed to see is not quite ready, and they must wait in a corridor or lean against a wall. Their host doesn't have chairs or a waiting area, because those are provided in Dept. 802.

You only have to lean against the wall outside Gen. Hitsumi's office for about an hour before you are summoned inside.

The General's office is no bigger than a sports arena. A trophy tank is parked along one wall, its turret pointed jauntily toward approaching visitors. It looks a bit lost in the huge room.

The General is seated at what looks like the control module for an interstellar cruiser. He's a short man, balding, with an imposing moustache and an astonishing contraption astride his face: transparent pieces of glass are held suspended before his eyes by metal frames, which reach back to wrap around his ears.

You suppress the urge to ask what they are. Some sort of personal adornment, you suppose; perhaps the frames are wired to his head like earrings. You wonder how such idiosyncrasy is permitted in the high reaches of the Peace Army.

"I'm a busy man, what is it?" asks the General. His voice is surprisingly thin and reedy.

"I'm a reporter for the *East Asian Scenesuite*," you say. "I was wondering—"

"Hate reporters," mutters Gen. Hitsumi.

"More of a researcher, really," you clarify.

"Well, what is it?"

"We're doing a series on prominent persons of East Asian descent, and we'd like to do a profile of you."

The General seems to look at you closely for the first time. "A profile of me? Why me?"

106

"Well, you are the star general of the Peace Army..."

The General nods. "Have you done Planetary Marshal Kumari?"

"Not yet. We intend to, of course. He's a very important figure."

"Yes, yes, very important," mutters Hitsumi. He looks at you a moment, and then smiles. He looks you over slowly, savoringly, like a rich man checking out his new volant.

"What would you like to know?" he asks.

You produce a portable transcriber. "Why don't we start at the beginning? You're from Gōsei?"

"Yes, certainly. Little town called K'sonoroba, in Ikeda-*ken*. Mostly agricultural— rice, soybeans, wheat, and *kōra*— that's a native grain, makes a sort of porridge. Not as good as wheat porridge, maybe, but filling, very filling. Ikeda-*ken* makes a lot of *kōra*— 65 million tonnes a year, I believe it is— but the best comes from K'sonoroba. I've had agronomists out there, they think it's something in the combination of the soil and the microclimate— can't be duplicated elsewhere. Some industry: a bicycle factory, a spindlemaker, and of course there was the old quarry out on the Ishagi Road. We lived on a little farm a kilometer out of town. A little more than a kilometer, actually— one kilometer would take you to about where the water station was. That was just down the road from us. We grew rice, *kōra*, soybeans— everything, actually. Wheat, too. I was the fifth of six brothers. The first, Toshiro, was big and round and not too bright. Once, when he was three years old..."

β Hydri slowly sinks in the sky; the room becomes dark. Night falls. Weeks pass. The Galaxy rotates; stars go nova, and the heat death of the universe approaches, and still the General hasn't got up to his tenth year.

Still, as a Diplomatic Agent of the Terran Incatena, you have patience— patience, and the ability to sleep with your eyes open. The General invites you out to dinner; and later, much later, when the cooks have marched out and the waiters have put the chairs upside down on top of all the tables, and the manager has been standing over your table for an hour with an empty coffee pot, the General invites you to his weekend retreat to continue the interview.

Slowly (that's the key word, slowly) you build up a picture of the General's life. The General's own favorite period seems to have been the carefree days at the Gōsei military academy, but you are most interested in his stories of the Coalition War and its aftermath, the first days of Peace Party rule.

"Oh, we were idealistic back then," says the General, sitting in his solarium nursing a tall *tanaki*, looking out at a lawn large enough to need its own forestry service. "We wanted to change the world... and we did, of course! Not as much as we thought we would, but..."

"What did you want to accomplish?"

"We wanted to shake things up. Nothing less than a return to neoteny, youngster! A return to neoteny!"

"A return to what?"

"You *are* aware of how humans differ from apes, aren't you?"

This seems like a bit of a non sequitur, but you play along. "Smarter and less hairy?"

"Not *smarter* exactly," he corrects; and, thinking of the average fraternity member, you have to agree. "Our DNA is over 98% identical to chimps', and don't think the 2% that remains is all added intelligence. Very little of it is. No, the major difference is *neoteny*. Arrested adolescence is what it is. We basically look like baby chimps, and keep their curiosity all through our lives."

"And the Peace Party?" You really want to hear this connection.

"How old are you, youngster?"

"Well, let's see— discounting time in the freezer, I'm 134— no, 135."

He chuckles. "Really a chicken. I'm over 400. Not young, by no means, but not what you'd call middle-aged, either. In the prime of life."

He stares at you with that particularly provoking look that some of your elders have, a look that invites you to throw away that consarned book-larnin' of yours and feast on some real wisdom for once.

"Now, what's the problem with old folks, youngster?"

"They think they know it all," you answer, immediately.

"Exactly," he says, rather to your surprise. "By the time you get to my age, you think you know how the world works. How to find jobs, how to get lovers, how to get rid of them, where to eat, which datascenes to enter and which will scar you for life, how to dress, how to handle the in-laws, how to run a planet." He chuckles. "We get to be pretty insufferable."

"Quite insufferable," you agree, filling your drink.

The General frowns at you, but continues. "The chimps are the same way."

"They never do get the hang of running a planet."

"Of course not! They haven't advanced! They sit around in trees going ook-ook! And why?"

You have to think about that. Something about having too much hair? Weren't in the right place at the right time? No stick-to-it-iveness?

"Neoteny," you suggest.

"Exactly. We're neotenous and they're not. Their brains are just too rigid. Ours are more flexible. Or were."

"Were?"

The General looks crafty. "You put your finger on it. We *were* less rigid. And still are— for a hundred years or two. Almost all real creativity, all new ideas, come from people under 200— or younger. You're likely already too old. Just a few exceptions. The rest— complete, utter stagnation. We realized this."

"We did? Where?"

"In the Gōsei Army, of course," snaps Hitsumi. "It was obvious. A young world, as promising as any place in human space, but completely sclerotic! Nothing had changed in two hundred years. Till Nashimoto came along! Now there was a man for you!"

"Neotenous?"

"Neotenous as hell, youngster! A man who dreamed of new things, a man who shattered things as they were! You talked with him for an hour and you thought your mind would burst. We were intoxicated!"

The General, seeking perhaps to relive that experience, refills his glass, then drains it.

"What kind of ideas did he have?"

"What kind didn't he have?" counters Hitsumi. "Ideas for Gōsei and Okura— you know how that turned out! A new way of organizing society for maximum efficiency. Putting the better people in charge. Ways to get rid of decadence, corruption— improve people's lives. New gadgets— a combination hat and hair-cutter— no more putting off a trim, you always look good! Philosophical ideas: the equation of time and inertia! So simple, and yet it explains everything. Solutions to historical dilemmas: Who wrote Shakespeare's plays! When did Jesus come to Japan! Why Zhū Dì burned the Ming fleet!"

Something clicks for you. "That device you wear— perhaps it was Nashimoto's invention?"

Gen. Hitsumi beams at you. "Good on you, youngster! He got the idea from ancient times. Right eye, adjustable telescope—" He seems to be twisting something on one side of the device, and his eye, seen through the lens, grows grotesquely larger. "Left eye, night vision. Plus, you can change them without getting surgery!"

The same thing can be done with neurimplants, but you decide not to bring it up.

"So where did Kumari come in?"

The General seems to sober up. "Planetary Marshal Kumari. Yes. Well, at that time he was Nashimoto's chief of staff. At a point some of us began to realize that the Director was getting— well, perhaps *feverish* would be the word. He was convinced that aliens were talking to him."

"Ah," you say. "And they weren't?"

"Well, of course they were. Excellent relations with the Dzebyet in those days. I mean, he thought aliens were talking to him *through his appliances.*"

"A tricky situation," you agree.

"Then he started to come to Cabinet meetings in the nude."

"Ah. And that was wrong?"

"Wrong? It was completely perverse!" shudders Gen. Hitsumi, and you file a mental note under *Prudery, colonial.* "And then he named Gen. Sukuru on a diplomatic mission to the wildlife of Okura, and had him studying birdsong... When Col. Kumari suggested that it was time for a change, in accordance with Peace Party principles, we could only agree."

He falls silent. You nod consolingly. "You must have felt—"

"But he didn't have to *eliminate* him," exclaims the General, slamming his glass against the table hard enough that it spills.

You nod some more, like one of those folkloric dolls with a wobbly head, and wait for more. But the General seems to be finished.

"General?"

"Yes, what is it?"

"When you organized the Peace Party— it was dedicated to *change*?"

"Yes. Certainly. Change, and neoteny."

"Do you think it's accomplished that? Some people might say that it's— well, settled down. It's been over a century since Kumari took over, after all..."

"Yes, yes," mutters Gen. Hitsumi. His face is very red; you suspect that he's relived the intoxication of the revolutionary era a little more than is good for him. He pours himself another glass.

"Do you want to die, youngster?" he asks.

You open your mouth, close it. You wonder if he's a loyalist after all.

"Well?"

"Uh, no, sir."

He laughs. "And who does? That's why we keep advancing human lifespan— no one wants to die! So why do we die?"

"Massive systemic failure, mostly," you say. "Cruiser crashes. Duels."

"Not *how*, simpleton, *why*? It's because nature is smarter than we are. We get too rigid. It's like a massive computer program: you can maintain it only so long; after awhile the architecture just can't be adapted any further— even Ogorodé won't work on it— and you have to start over. Unless you can come up with a more flexible architecture."

"Neotenous," you suggest.

"Neotenous, hell yes! At every level. Society: that's the job of our social engineers. Genetics: we're working on increasing human neoteny. And the race as a whole, why not? That same atherosclerosis afflicts the whole damn Incatena! Run by old men, 800, 900 years old— old men and AIs. And it doesn't help that almost everyone's raised alone, like firstborns. Makes us too adult, too conservative— too *old*."

You ponder. People back in civilization do talk about this— long lives slow down radical change, though they usually conclude that that's a plus. "That's what Kumari has in mind?"

"That's what *we* have in mind," the General corrects you. "Kumari... Well. Yes. The Planetary Marshal is certainly the heir of the old dreams, but..."

"Is perhaps interested mostly in personal power?"

He shakes his head— in perplexity, not disagreement, it seems. "Personal power," he repeats, and falls into silence.

You nod, to yourself this time. Your intuitions were right; Gen. Hitsumi is dissatisfied with the regime— and there's no one better placed to express his dissatisfaction using, say, tanks and plasma bombers. He helped put Kumari in power, and he can help take him out.

You are a bit worried about this neoteny rap of his. Others— the Shadowmen, Ryoku, Dr. Zhou if she recovers— would welcome radical change, but not, perhaps, a eugenic program to produce super-neotenous humans.

On the other hand, why not give the old boy a genetics lab and a stock of DNA? Breeding supermen is like promoting an artificial language: it never gets very far, because people start arguing over the target, and the whole effort collapses into mutually antagonistic factions. Let him find out the hard way.

It's time to start serious negotiations. You put down your drink, shake your head to clear it, and think a moment how to begin.

A loud snore erupts from the General's chair.

The Chain of Worlds

There are three places on Okura, which if compacted together with modern antigravity equipment would amount to about two city blocks, that are not subject to the authority of the Peace Party: the Dzebyet Embassy; the Skweeoo Embassy; and Incatena House.

The latter, representing the tradition and authority of fifty human worlds, is a sprawling compound on top of Ikebura Hill, a mostly residential area overlooking Atami Bay. Its tiled California-style roofs and anti-space artillery emplacements subtly clash with the staid apartment houses nearby.

When you walk in the door, you feel that a decision point has been reached; you seem to feel the weight of worlds on your shoulders.

Actually it's just the increased gravity field. You approach the receptionist, and are not quite prepared to see—

"Hello, Rimu-san," says Ba.

Ba's smile is enough to entirely counteract the increased gravity.

"Hello, hello!" you say, in a winning and seductive way, as you press down your hair, brush crumbs off your clothes, and try to ignore a newly developed tic in your left upper lip. "Fancy meeting you here! I mean it's not *so* amazing, since you work here, but it is kind of amazing that I dropped by, isn't it? No, *that's* not amazing really, but..."

Ba laughs. "I was thinking about you after that party."

You lean casually against the desk. This sets off an electronic alarm, so you stand up straight again. "You were? What were you thinking?"

"You were really cute the way you knocked over my plate."

That *is* a charming memory of you, isn't it?

"I'm glad that's the adjective that comes to mind, rather than 'preternaturally maladroit.'"

"I thought of that too, but 'cute' seemed like the better choice overall, so I went with it."

113

Wait a sec: Is *Ba* interested in *you*? This seems unlikely, but you are trying to think of a good way to probe for the possibility ("What are the five or ten things you find cutest about me?") when you hear a cough behind you. Three or four people are now waiting behind you, their ears lightly steaming. If they had horns they'd be honking.

"'Cute'— yes, well, I shouldn't take any more of your time." you say, casually. "I just wanted to see the Chief."

"Meillet-san? Sorry, Rimu-san, he's not here right now."

"Ah. How about Hrvatski?"

"Third door on the right."

"You take a lunch break?" you ask. You are so smooth you're aerodynamic.

"No, I usually don't. It's cheaper that way, you know?"

"What time do you get off work?"

"Oh, six. Maybe seven."

"I could—"

"Sometimes I work till ten. It's unpredictable. I never know."

"This weekend—"

"Wouldn't you know it, my grand-uncle is coming in."

"Sure."

"No, actually, he's not from Shr, he's from Phu Quoc."

"Is he."

"Yeah."

The sound of shuffling can be heard behind you. You remember suddenly that frontier societies often have a fixation with firearms.

"I should be going," you say, to a chorus of nodding heads. "But the week after next—"

"Sumō practice," sighs Ba.

"Haven't you got the message?" asks the old lady behind you. "*Not interested.*"

"Yes, yes, I got it," you say.

"See you later," says Ba, brightly. You dredge yourself away, trying without much success to chivvy up the will to live.

You tap on the frame of Hrvatski's ergolounge. He turns out to be a short, dumpy man a century or two older than you.

You take a deep breath; you're about to blow your cover. Again. Well, hell, why *not* do something reckless?

"Agent Hrvatski, do we have a 214[1]?"

He looks at you in surprise, thinks for a moment, and nods. "The whole building is a 214. We have a secure room, but I can't take you there unless..." You understand: you are still an unknown entity.

"80[2]," you say, sitting on the little guest chair built into the ergolounge. "So let's 1077[3]."

"1077?"

"80. Agent Morgan."

"80. What's your 1038[4]?"

"40."

He whistles. "Mine's 32," he says, with a touch of admiration or envy. "Of course, you understand we need a 680[5]."

"80. We can get it through Orindzai."

So as not to waste any time, Hrvatski immediately sends a message with your picture, retina scan, and neuromap to the Incatena Embassy on Orindzai, the Dzebyet world one orbit in toward β Hydri.

"That'll take 1 or 2 hours. We'll move into the 214, unless we get a -680. Want some 102[6]?"

"80."

He pours you a cup of 102. The smell makes you feel at home; it reminds you of the boss.

"So in a nutshell," says Hrvatski, "what's the 717[7]?"

"Extreme 172[28]," you say, gravely.

"-88[9]?"

---

[1] Secure speaking environment.

[2] Acknowledge.

[3] Agent identification protocol.

[4] Agent ranking.

[5] Confirmation of identity.

[6] Sihorian caf.

[7] Situation.

[8] Political interference. That actually is 172 squared. Sorry for any confusion.

[9] No shit?

"-88. What's the 717 with the 405^1?"

"Meillet? Kind of an 010^2."

"What's his 1038?"

"39."

That's good; you outrank him. When the 88 starts flying, you'll be the acting head of operations on the planet. The boss would have foreseen that, of course. You expect there may be problems with Meillet, however. The boss didn't seem to trust him.

"An 010, huh?" you say. "I hope he doesn't cause any 88 for the 172^2."

"Don't give in to 1312^3 over the 717," Hrvatski advises.

"The higher your 1038 the higher the 1312, that's the 88 of it— at least if you're not a total 010," you muse. "We would have -1312 if the cosmic 405 would give us a 680..."

Hrvatski shakes his head. "-80. I don't need any 263^4 doing a 172^2 on me. You've got to deal with the 717 as it is." •

"-80, -263," you insist. "It's just nostalgia— don't you get tired of 2909^5?"

"I get too much of the 405 to worry about any 2909," says Hrvatski, sadly. "Listen, it'll be at least 1300 before we get your 680, and it's almost 1200 now; what do you say to a 34^6?"

"Sure."

"What?"

"80."

Your identity is confirmed by the embassy on Orindzai, and you spend some time catching up on field reports— thanks to Einstein, that old spoilsport, the last one you read, back on Mars, dates from 48 years ago.

---

[1] Station chief.

[2] Prick.

[3] Existential despair.

[4] Atavistic tribal deity.

[5] Moral ambiguity caused by relativistic ethical standards, exacerbated by petty politics and all-too-frequent compromises for narrow political ends.

[6] Deep-dish pizza with pepperoni and mushrooms.

Internally, Kumari is only more entrenched in power. The security organs have been refined; constant vigilance is exercised over top officials in the Army and the Peace Party. Hrvatski's opinion is that the Party's ideology has devolved into a mere facade; but the facade is still rigidly maintained, and departing from it in any way still leads to an unfriendly visit from the Home Ministry.

According to official figures, the economy is booming, and general prosperity is just around the corner, if everyone will just make a few sacrifices. Most of the economy's growth, however, is due to increases in population— colonized only in the 3600s, Okura is still only lightly settled. The Incatena's best estimate is that per capita income is barely rising, and that the only people doing well are the Peace Party elite in Gōsei itself— plus the Oji, the Okurinese underworld.

This is not the Second Millennium; the laws of socionomics are well known, even in the backwaters of human space. The Directorate must itself be generating economic distress as a means of controlling the population. A pinched populace is a conservative and distrustful one. Working hard, and fearful of losing their jobs, the Okurinese will not be quick to become activists. The regime is careful, however, not to let the economy shrink; if it let things get worse, the desperation for change would become dangerous.

The Peace Party has also stepped up its campaign against various scapegoats: dissidents, slackers, VR addicts, the Incatena, the Dzebyet, the Ogorodé. The propaganda against the aliens has become horrific— the Dzebyet are said to be secretly trying to take control of Okura, while riots against the Ogorodé, led by Home Ministry provocateurs, have resulted in the deaths of several of the pacific little underachievers.

As for the Incatena, the latest trick of the official media is to talk about it as a foreign entity, one with which the Peace Party deals as an equal. School textbooks don't even mention that Okura is a member of the Incatena. This can hardly fool the older generation, which remembers the days before the Coalition War, but it probably creates some confusion. Hrvatski thinks Kumari is preparing the ground for some contrived dustup with the Incatena that can provide a pretext for secession.

You also take the opportunity to read the latest field report from New Bharat, from one Agent Beloman:

> The New Bharat colony, founded 150 years ago, now has a population of almost 3 million, concentrated on the eastern coast of the continent of Lālistan. The major cities are the capital, Colony Base (pop. 120,000), Jaipur, Nayadelhi, and Mumbai. There are bases and incipient colonies elsewhere on the planet, linked by the original colony ship's shuttles, which serve as the planet's spacelines. Agriculture, industry, and the information sector are developing as planned.
>
> Responsibility for planetary development is in the hands of the New Bharat Colonisation Corporation (NBCC), the entity organized two centuries ago to undertake the colonization effort. NBCC is a co-venture of a consortium of Indian companies, the government of India, and Ormant/Mars.

"Uh oh," you think. It's easy to turn a one-third stake into effective control, especially if one of your partners is highly divided and the other is busy, well, governing India.

> The corporation's board includes two representatives from each of the three co-venture partners, plus a member elected by the colony's residents. The current chairman is Rajiv Bhajari, an Indian (now New Bharati) industrialist.
>
> Although this arrangement has given the colony efficient development and sound finances, the Incatena has expressed concern over a corporation (even a non-profit one) being the *de facto* government and the largest economic entity on the planet. Incatena law also requires that all Incatena members have elected heads of government. To meet this requirement, a *de jure* planetary government has been put in place, the Inter-Colony Association (ICA). Limited in power and funds, it can be regarded as a creature of the NBCC. Its current president (elected 4910) is Sandeep V. J. Rai of Mumbai, a holo producer.
>
> As is to be expected, the major concerns of the New Bharatis are trade and development. The economy is growing at over 12% per year, a rate which attracts a healthy number of both immigrants

and investors. Immigrants come from several planets, although there is strong pressure to assimilate to the predominant Hindu culture. The chief trading partners are the Douane, Sihor, Maraille, and Okura.

The planet has attracted a certain number of Hindu-oriented fundamentalists and idealists; the most important of these groups is the utopian colony of Satyampur (pop. 40,000), the largest settlement outside the Lālistan continent. There is no significant planetary political movement, inasmuch as real power remains in the hands of the NBCC, but an unusual ideological organization has recently arisen, the Freedom Movement. Its aims, according to its literature, are "freedom, decency, and spiritual awakening," and it arose out of "sincere admiration for the achievements of the Peace Party of Okura." In fact the Okura party provides both funding and leadership. The reasons for this are obscure, and the movement bears watching, although its effective strength is no more than about 1,000.

Areas of concern for the Incatena are the evolution to a representative planetary government in effective control of its own territory and development, and the occasional lawlessness of what is still a frontier society. One Interfleet cruiser is assigned permanently to New Bharat, and assists the ICA police and the (larger) NBCC security services. A particular point of friction is the Maraille colony; Île de Maraille has complained more than once of attempts by New Bharati traders to evade the restriction of outside contact to the Island.

"Idiots," you think. Restrictions fascinate, and many people are convinced that the prominence of the Maraillais must derive from some hidden supercivilization in the restricted areas. If only they knew.

Although there is much hard work and little luxury by Douane standards, New Bharatis are land-rich, and advancement to a comfortable prosperity is fast; visitors and even Incatena Agents "go native" with ease. Agents sent to New Bharat should be equipped with particular integrity, or substantial holdings on another colony planet.

—Agent K. Beloman, Colony Base, New Bharat, February 4917.

All of this sounds disquieting in an obscure sort of way, but what really strikes your eye is the warning against going native. "Equipped with particular integrity"— that's you, of course, although substantial holdings on a colony planet wouldn't exactly disgust you. You picture yourself on a horse or the picturesque local equivalent, patrolling your substantial holdings— better yet, two horses, with Ba on one of them. You ride for hours, laughing and talking, till you come to a quiet lagoon, where you dismount and then mount— You have to stop this fantasy before you start hyperventilating in front of Agent Hrvatski.

You're still huddled over an old datanode not far from Hrvatski's ergolounge, running some exploratory socionomic simulations, when Ba comes over.

"I'm going home."

"Good for you."

Ba stands there a moment, then comes over and puts a hand on your shoulder. "I'm sorry if I seemed... cold, earlier. My mind was just on something else, you know? Would you still like to go out this weekend?"

"Really? What about your grand-uncle?"

"We'll double-date."

"Uh, I—"

"Oh, I'm just kidding. He can fend for himself. What do you say? I know a great Qengese place near here."

Your heart bobs up like a beach ball. "I'd love to."

"Great. See ya."

That smile again, so dazzling it imprints itself on your retina.

Rendez-vous

The soup is delivered. You stare through the steaming mist at Ba, admiring those startling, slanting, lively, intelligent blue eyes, that sensuous mouth, that trim, orange-streaked black hair. The restaurant is invitingly dark, you have a private alcove, the table is candle-lit, there's music in the air (a gamelan orchestra with a modern Sihorian beat)— you dare to hope that thoughts of romance stir in both your hearts.

Ba's first question almost makes you spit out your soup: "So why do you want to overthrow the Directorate?"

"I, er, the Indonesian government, I mean Tir Research has no intention of giving credence to no such allegation regarding no such inimical activity," you say, and for emphasis send the UI gesture *WTF?*

Ba laughs, produces a small photonic device, and attaches it to the candleholder in the middle of the table. You recognize it; it's a standard-issue Incatena photonic scrambler. Any photonic recording devices trained on this table will pick up only an innocuous AI-generated conversation.

But you have been in the other side's scuffed and unfashionable shoes. If you can't use photonics, you simply point a laser at the nearest wineglass and read the conversation from the vibrations of the crystal. To remind Ba of this, you point at the wineglass and wiggle your hand.

Ba merely smiles, and directs your hand under the table. The touch of Ba's hand on yours is electric.

"What, the gum?"

"No, no." Ba guides your hand to another device attached to the underside of the table: a countervibrator. "You see?" At the sound, the device springs into action: it shivers and rolls like an escaping bat, strong enough to make the whole table soundlessly vibrate. Any vibrational analysis of the immediate vicinity would retrieve only chaos.

You point to your eye, then at the walls. A nanotech recorder, or a dozen of them, might be ensconced anywhere, recording your conversation to be lip-read later. Ba smiles once more, and invites you to look at the soy and fish sauce dispensers more carefully. They are actually a pair of twin quantum-path retracers— in effect, devices which seek out every possible photon path in a room and zero in on the peculiar interference effects due to lenses of even molecule size, which can then be destroyed with a burst of laser light. Set down in a bugged room, a light show ensues. And they still dispense condiments, too.

An ordinary Agent would be satisfied with that; but you are no ordinary Agent. Where high-tech methods are stymied, there are the ancient alternatives. You gesture round at the other diners. Which of them might not be a minion of the Home Ministry?

"It will impede us not," says Ba.

You stare stupidly for a moment, before realizing why the words sound so strange: Ba is speaking, not any modern Okurinese or terrestrial language, but ancient Classical Chinese, *wényán*— a language which would be known by only a few Okurinese scholars, and only in written form at that... certainly not by any Home Ministry thugs. Moreover, even in the reconstructed form Ba is using, its phonology is so full of homonyms, its grammar so bafflingly succinct, and the preferred style so permeated by ambiguity, ellipsis, and allusion, that only one steeped for years in its nuances can hope to decipher it. Indeed, Ba's own utterance could equally well have been interpreted, *No problem is unthinkable*, or even *The pandas murmur threateningly*.

Fortunately, high-level Incatena Agents are encouraged to learn *wényán*; not only does it serve as a code, but the ancient Chinese writings on diplomacy and war are considered excellent training for Agents, and *wényán* style also comes in useful in writing policy memos.

"So," says Ba. (The word could also mean *consider*, or *usurpation*.) "Why dost thou wish to overthrow the Directorate[1]?"

"When we made acquaintance at the home of honored Dr. Zhou, thy mind seemed set against it," you say; or at least you hope that's what you said; you might instead have said "Under the autumn moon, frisky are the concubines."

"What sayest thou about concubines?"

---

[1] 衙門 *ŋa mən* 'court gate'

"*Mind*," you say, getting the word right this time. "Not concubines, *mind*. Was thy wit not opposed to the Director?"

"I have no policy, but I am Okurinese," says Ba, obscurely. "I wish to understand thee— what thou dost— whether thou *knowest* what thou dost. Thou appointest thyself an examiner of whole worlds..."

"What blatherest thou? Who is appointing examiners?"[1]

"Be not a barbarian's donkey. Didst thou not come to judge our circumstances, to take action against the empire?"

"Not I, but the Incatena[2]. Okura is a signatory of the Incatena; it covenanted to abide by its Treaty."

"Thou speakest so abstractly," says Ba, looking into your eyes.

"'Tis hard to do aught else in this cursed language."

"No, I ask, dost thou hide always behind pedantry?"

"When no other cover affords."

"Hey, can I take that?"

You both look over at the waiter.

"You're done with the soup? So how was that? The hot and sour chuma-egg is better, if you ask me, but we're all out. It's really popular! How are you kids doing? Can I bring you anything? More Xiaolin tea?"

"We cavil not," you assure him in *wényán,* and when that doesn't register, you say "We're fine" in Okurinese.

"I'll check on your meal. Should be ready in two shakes, and then I'll bring it out, OK?"

"Thank you," says Ba, in a voice that could freeze a geyser.

"Oh, no problem. No problem at all. Be back soon," the waiter promises, and finally ambles away.

"How pleasant and efficient is a robot waiter," says Ba.

"Oh, but the human touch bringeth such elegance," you say.

Ba seems to be studying you, and finally murmurs, "An entire world lieth under thy gaze. From four-and-twenty years as the radiance of heaven traveleth, the glorious Incatena proclaimeth Okura unfit to administer its own province, and it sendeth *thee*... I wish but to know what kind of person thou art."

---

[1] 按察使 *ʔân tshrât srəʔ* 'examining envoy'

[2] 開天聯盟 *khəˆi thîn ran mraŋ* 'Union that Opens the Skies', a term chosen for its sound as much as for its meaning

"I am a... a vassal? A functionary of the Incatena."

Ba sighs. "Behold my fears. That besides thy function, there is nought..."

"Say not so," you say, staring into Ba's eyes. "Besides my function, there is much. Things deep and beautiful..."

"I hope thou speakest the truth."

Ba smiles, which is a good sign at least. But something is bothering you. "Thou speakest as one loyal to Okura," you say. "But canst thou support the Directorate? Rule by one faction, constant surveillance, campaigns of re-education, camps holding prisoners?"

"These things do I detest. Yet the Peace Party might have been something else, something better... it seemed a new thing under heaven, and now we will never know. Ye will re-order us along socionomic lines[1]..."

"What dost thou want instead?"

"Thou confidest in devices, in socionomics... Hast thou no vision?"

"The lives of the people cannot be left to cranks suffering visions," you declare.

"Is there nought better? Thinkest thou that thy devices are cognizant of all, that there is no new wisdom under heaven?"

"If novelties thou hast, by all means let them be assayed. Let them be tried by simulation[2]— if it be efficacious, it shall not escape us. But the experimentation of a mad emperor, in that way wisdom abideth not."

You become aware that Ba's foot is touching yours— and, following Gōsei custom, you both left your shoes at the door.

"Er, uh, of what did we speak last?"

"Of novelty," suggests Ba.

"Ah, yes. I assure thee, I welcome new developments."

Ba laughs. "How old art thou?"

It seems to be a popular question. You give your age. "Why dost thou ask?"

"Some things I expect thou hast experienced already in that span. Many times, perchance."

---

[1] 經世之道 *kêŋ lhats tə lûʔ* 'Tao of world management'

[2] 電腦模擬 *lîns nâuʔ mâʔ ŋə* 'electric-brain imitation'

Ba's foot is now covering your toes. It's hard to think about anything else, especially in a complicated and deservedly dead language, but you make the effort.

"Yes, well, but in harmony with the Tao, some things are old, yet seem new with each recurrence."

"I wonder if our ancestors would make such statements if their lives spanned centuries," wonders Ba. "Doth the length of years never bore?"

"Never have I understood how our ancestors accomplished aught in seventy years."

"Seventy years... yes, that seemeth but little; I remember what a fool I was at seventy. But to be seven hundred, who desireth it?"

"'Tis said that the secret is to move past youth's foolishness without losing its spirit."

Ba's foot is now caressing your own. "Dost look with disdain upon foolishness?"

"In the right company, surely it is good."

"Art thou the right company, mayhap?"

You blush; the *wényán* phrase 'mayhap'[1] sounds exactly like Okurinese 'in bed'.

"*Thou* art in truth the right company."

"Thou findest me so, mayhap?"

"I find it, yes." You let your other foot explore Ba's ankle.

"The spirit of youth— that is important, mayhap," muses Ba.

"Yet the most important thing, mayhap, is a concern for others," you insist.

"Thou speakest of love, mayhap?"

"Well, 'tis said, nought but love bringeth happiness when we are seven hundred, mayhap."

"Speak not of old age," flashes Ba. "'Twas an error to mention it. 'Twere better we keep our thoughts on tonight, mayhap."

This isn't hard advice to take. One of Ba's hands is only a few centimeters from yours. You take it in your hands, and you look deep into those enigmatic blue eyes.

"Heads up, folks! Food's here."

You both look over at the waiter, audibly sighing.

---

[1] 豈其然乎 *khəʔ gə nan hâ* 'is it so?'

"Some of it, at least. I brought the slamfish bisque, but they're all out of the filet of leporid. What do you want instead? Do you want to see the menu again? Whoops! Oh dear, oh dear. The fish is really slippery, you know? No harm done— the table linen here is clean enough to eat off of! If you'll just let me help you... Whoops! I'm so sorry. I'll bring you a new glass, do you want the same thing? Napkins, too, of course. I'll get you that menu."

"Why don't you do that," you suggest, in a tone that you hope conveys menace not only to the waiter but to his posterity to the seventh generation. He skips off, a demonstration that harsh looks do not actually kill.

"We should talk about thy methods for overthrowing the Directorate," says Ba, when he's gone.

"Mayhap," you say.

"No, not mayhap, right now."

"One who acts for the celestial bureaucracy cannot be indiscreet," you insist. "Mayhap would really be better."

"Very well," says Ba.

You take Ba's hands again. You savor the moment: sharing a meal, looking into each other's eyes over candlelight, the feel of hands and wandering toes, the promise of more to come, mayhap...

"Hey, kids, here's that menu. Want to hear the specials again?"

The waiter is long forgotten. You and Ba are on the balcony of your room at the Yokan Otani, sitting side by side on a low bench, looking out over the bay. Okura's small yellow moon shines brightly in the sky, casting a golden glow over the sleeping city. A fresh grassy smell wafts up from the garden.

"I don't think I've told you how beautiful you are," you say.

"You have," Ba points out. "About six times already. You're pretty cute yourself."

"I always thought my nose was too big."

"Not at all."

"It's not goofy looking?"

"It's a fine nose."

"Those eyes of yours," you marvel. "They're from birth, or genofixed? ...I'm sorry, that's really rude."

"It's all right," says Ba. "Blue eyes are actually pretty common in Shr. I hope that's not all you like about me."

"I like everything about you."

You kiss. Ba's lips are as soft as they look. You kiss some more, holding each other in your arms. After that, you spend some time kissing.

Your hands, at first content just to hold, start to caress. First, some slow, safe touching: the back, the arms, the back of the head. Then you start to explore each other's bodies. The caresses become intimate; your breathing starts to become deeper. Your clothes become disarranged; and then there's the electric moment when a hand strays inside a loosened fold of cotton, and touches bare skin— it's just your lower back, but it feels like a new erogenous zone.

It *is* new each time, you decide. You may be a sophisticated sapient from a star-spanning race; but you are also an animal not far removed from the savannah, and powerful sensations can still be called up by the sight of a well-formed bare foot, or the smell of hair, or the warm cool feeling of skin.

And also, it's been a long time. Twenty-four years objective time. Subjectively, excluding cryostasis— hell, subjectively it feels like twenty-four years too.

Sex scene instructions

Words referring to male parts or persons (yours or your partner's) are *italicized*; those referring to females are in **boldface**.

Read according to your choice of gender for each participant.

In neurimplant-enabled editions of this book, the direction gestures may be used instead.

Ba draws back, smiles, and removes *his*/**her** *shirt*/**sweater**. **She**/*he*'s wearing nothing underneath. You gaze in awe at **her**/*his* **breasts**/*pecs*: not too large, but perfectly **formed**/*sculpted*. There's a tiny, tasteful tattoo of a **lotus**/*dragon* just above *his*/**her** left nipple.

"You're gorgeous," you murmur.

"I **don't** know **about that**," **she**/*he* says.

You touch *him*/**her**, tentatively at first, and then hungrily. **She**/*he* gasps with pleasure. You continue the treatment, with hands and tongue, while *his*/**her** hands fondly caress your **hair**/*butt*, and then the rest of your body.

She/*he* unbuttons your *shirt*/**blouse** and slips it off. You shudder in delight as **she**/*he* swirls *his*/**her** fingertips *through*/**around** your *chest hairs*/**nipples**. Then you come together, pressing your bodies against each other, feeling **breast**/*chest* against *chest*/**breast**, hands caressing naked backs. The cool night air breathes against both of you.

He/**she** runs **her**/*his* own hands along your *abdomen*/**breasts**, moves back to admire the *firm*/**round** outline of your *butt*/**derriere**, and moans, "I want you **in**/*around* me."

She/*he* reaches down to remove **her**/*his* pants. The *hard*/**wet** *pressure*/**insistence** of your own *man*/**woman**hood impels you to do likewise.

Now you're both naked. Your eyes and hands and tongue explore every part of *his*/**her** body— the short black hair with its vivid orange streaks, the inviting **breasts**/*rectus abdominis*, the long **athletic**/*muscular* limbs, the *firm*/**rounded** stomach, and, above all, that magnetic, newly revealed thatch of black, and the sex biding its time below it. And **she**/*he* reciprocates, caressing, kissing, biting, grasping, till the two of you are sweaty and panting.

Your lovemaking grows in passion. Even the **jazz**/*metal* from the music node grows more intense. Ba is a willing, uninhibited lover, a feast for body and soul; animal passion and the craving for emotional contact are both satisfied. Under the stars, overlooking the garden, it's like a rite of nature. Orgasm, when it finally comes, is *epochal*/**multiple**.

> Finally, read the dénouement corresponding to your orientation:

Straight male: Happy and satisfied, you go to sleep.

Straight female: The two of you process the experience together, then fall asleep in each other's arms.

Lesbian: You enjoy a cup of Galactic Seasonings together, then get into a heated debate on whether radical feminism or queer activism should be the community's first priority.

Gay male: Then you do it all over again, this time changing roles.

When you awaken in the morning, with Ba still nestled asleep next to you, legs intertwined with yours, you check the room datanode for mail. You have a message from Incatena House:

"Must call off 172^2 without fail. See me immediately. Meillet."

Pulling rank

Meillet can't see you immediately. This is impertinent, since you outrank him, but it's only to be expected— your relations, so far, have been arctic. You pass the time by checking out the Incatena's scenes on the Vee. The home scene has links like *Let's Learn the Planets of the Incatena, Your visa application, Interstellar money transfers*[1], *Tax tips for dual-planet nationals,* and *What does cryostasis feel like?*

Finally the station chief is ready to see you. Be cool, you remind yourself. You're not a supplicant, you're an Agent. Exude confidence. Show that you're used to being in control, so much so that you don't even need to be arrogant about it. You should really walk in with a dry martini in one hand.

You walk in, a suave half-smile on your lips, and promptly trip over a cleaning robot, which squeals and moves aside as you flail about to regain your balance.

Meillet is large and sour; his stomach is too large and his moustache too small. He looks at you like something in juvenile detention, and indicates an uncomfortable chair in front of his desk, short enough that it seems to be made for Dzebyet. A pathetic way of gaining a little psychological advantage, you think, contemptuously. It works.

"What's up?" you ask.

"Morgan, right?"

"Right."

Meillet looks at you, scowling, for some time. Then he spits out, "What's gotten *into* you?"

"Beg your pardon?"

"This 172[2]. Whose idea was it? Yours?"

---

[1] Things don't have prices; they have pricing algorithms, and these get hairy when the other end of the transaction is light years away. Software insulates us from all of that; all you have to worry about at any one time is the cost in C. the algorithm spits out, and the hopefully larger number issued by your funds algorithm.

"The boss's."

He shakes his head. "You veks holed up in that tower on Mars... Lose the whole lot of you, it'd be an improvement. Listen, I want it *stopped*. Right now."

"What? The 172²?"

"That's right. Terminated. 80?"

"Why?"

Meillet grimaces and grunts, as if your question has an unpleasant effect on some bodily function. "You're kidding, right? I suppose you're not. There's no *need* for it. Perfectly good planet. None of our business."

"It's a dictatorship."

"Dictatorship. It's *tough*, that's all it is— *tough*. What you *need* these days. Discipline, morality, *values*. They believe in God here. Wish we had a man like Kumari back on Earth. Completely gone to hell."

"Values?"

"Hard work. Discipline. Place where you can do business. The Peace Party has been very, very good for business, Morgan."

"I have some contacts in the Commerce Association who'd say otherwise."

Meillet waves away your objection like a mosquito. "Local types. Jealous. I'm talking Incatena business. Franchises, money markets, software. All of *that's* done very well here, very well indeed. Don't need some well-meaning *idiot* from outsystem— no offense— to come and play spy games here."

Ah. You understand now: Meillet is not a career diplomat; he's a businessman. The Incatena Station Chief is principally a commercial liaison, after all. Meillet is probably a heavy investor himself, in both the interstellar and Okurinese markets.

"Well, the Party does seem superficially to be pro-trade, but Hrvatski and I—" A snort indicates that the mention of Hrvatski doesn't add much authority to your statement. "And the analysts back at the Spire, well, we think that won't last."

"Don't believe it."

"Look, Meillet, we want business to prosper— a healthy business sector is good for everything else. But you can't use 'good for business' as a mantra; it becomes counter-productive. Look at the Collapse. They had a bunch of problems in the 21st century—hydrocarbon depletion, mismanagement, unequal development, runaway climatic warming— and they did *nothing*, because any proposal would be 'bad for business.'

"And when everything went bad at once, they turned on all their imagined enemies and created some of the worst dictatorships in history, both in the US and China. Borked progress for the whole planet for a century, and how is *that* good for business?"

"Yes, yes, collapse *bad*, -88," scoffs Meillet. "But let's not get carried away by our own rhetoric, 80? You seriously think Kumari is that bad? You see him starving the poor, degrading the ecosphere, terrorizing the middle class, repressing people based on biological trivialities? This isn't the middle *ages*. You veks still want to bring on the revolution, man the barricades, like it was 2115... What's *that* accomplish?"

"We're very good at revolutions these days," you assure him. "No reigns of terror, no cultural revolutions, no shots in the head, hardly even any working days lost."

"Not really the point," mutters Meillet. "It's the *principle* of the thing."

"That's just it," you say. "It's in the Treaty. We have to have an elected head of state."

"You don't *have* to," explains Meillet, with exaggerated patience. "When the government is doing what the people *want*, you don't *need* elections. Served here for thirty years—*here*, not in a tower twenty-four years away. Know what I'm talking about. And I'm telling you, the Party is doing what people here have wanted for a long time. Not just people *here*, either."

"Not everybody feels that way," you point out.

"Griefers and arcos."

Ah. You understand now. *Arcos* is a code word, a jibe at Earth's high-density arcologies and the campaigns at the time they were built against the ecological consequences of sprawl. Sprawl was ardently defended, especially by those who felt that everything in modern life was an affront to the perfect society, which happened to be that of their own childhoods. In mainstream circles the dispute is about as relevant as the Guelphs and the Ghibellines. But space is big; some people still seethe over the mad schemes of the arcos, and you've just met one of them.

"What exactly is it about modern society you don't like?" you venture.

Meillet has the satisfied smile of one who is about to rant, so you've hit home. "One, the Incatena, which is nothing but an arco plot to get in the way of businessmen and decent people. Two, the Ogorodé, intruding into planets where they don't belong and making demands. Three—"

"The only demands I've heard them make is to be left alone."

"Just what I mean. They used to be *docile*. Three, galacticism. It may be *out of fashion* to prefer human culture, but I happen not to hate the human species, thank you. Four, *sex* changes— that is *completely* indecent."

"Do you object to genofixing?"

"Of course not, what's that got to do with anything? Five, neurimplants. God made man and man made AIs— he sure as hell didn't tell us to *mix* 'em. Six, so-called *augments*. Hope I never see another arco with wings and fur. Seven, mechawombs. Eight, modern art. You can't understand it, and when you *can* understand it it's indecent. Nine, the while damn Solar System. Can't live free there and can't live decent. Ten, it's anti-God."

"Anti-God?"

"What do you think? Does the Incatena *encourage* you to worship Jesus and respect Muhammad? Hardly. The Incatena *hates* God. Frankly it's a pleasure to live on a planet that's *hospitable* to religion, and led by a religious man."

Ah. You understand now: Meillet is not just a conservative, but a fundamentalist, probably a Tunisian. The Tunisians are the ones who still hope to convert the rest of humanity to their way of thinking; the Anti-Tunisians prefer to leave the modern world on its way to hell, and join a colony somewhere in human space that's stopped the clock at the particular stage they approve of.

You think about Satyampur, the Hindu fundamentalist colony on New Bharat, and wonder, idly, if it's tied in with all this. Whatever's happening on these two planets already has two faces— the Peace Party and Ormant— why not three?

"You're not religious *yourself*, I suppose," says Meillet, with a predatory smirk.

"Oh, very much so," you lie. You're not an Agent for nothing. It's in the Agent Directives: *Always agree with fundamentalists; it disarms them.* "I'm a Reformed Marian Mormon, myself. I understand what you're saying very well."

"Wouldn't have guessed it," allows Meillet. "Good, though. Damn good. So you'll call it off?"

"Well, no."

"But why not, damn it all? If you *disapprove* of modern godless society—"

"Reformed Marian Mormonism is *very* strict on authority. And I *am* an Incatena Agent, you know. I'm sorry, but you see how it is."

"Yes, I see," says Meillet, sadly. "I can't tell you to disobey your *conscience*, I really can't." Then he brightens. "But see, I *am* the Incatena authority on this planet. Simple matter, really. Don't *like* to countermand Mars, of course, but as the man actually on the *scene...*"

"Say, what is your 1038?" you say, casually.

"My 1038? It's 40."

Your heart stops. It starts up again a moment later, but so far as you're concerned that only replaces one problem with a worse one.

"That's funny," you say, although it isn't. "Hrvatski said it was 39."

"He's a little out of date," Meillet says. He hands you a document, dated last week: his promotion announcement. The advancement process for station chiefs is complicated, but comes down to a combination of self and peer recommendation, the local AI's judgment, anything the local Agents or insystem Incatena offices have to say about it, and not being so outrageous that Mars rescinds the advancement when it gets word of it.

"Mine is 40 too," you say, unnecessarily.

"Well, you know the Directives," Meillet says, with annoying calm. "Except in certain emergencies, the 405 takes priority."

"I might consider the situation an emergency," you point out.

"Can't be considered an emergency until you get some *action* going," he counters. "And precisely what I'm telling you is *not* to get any action going. It's not needed, it's not advisable, and, my friend, it's *my* decision."

There isn't much to say after that. Meillet invites you to his Bible/Koran study, but you decline.

You need to get rid of this man.

Portrait of the Station Chief as a middle-aged bore

You hit the books— specifically, the Agent Directives. You've committed most of them to memory, of course; but the cross-references on the Vee are useful, and besides, there's something comforting in physically handling that small blue book, the distillation of so many centuries of intrigue, covert operations, and occasional rubouts in the service of the Incatena.

You find the right section quickly— *Removals.* You scan the headers: *Elected leaders. Unelected leaders. Generals. Bureaucrats. Cleaning personnel. AIs. Underlings. Overlings.* Subsection: *Station chiefs. Incompetent; Compromised; Insane; Ideologically extreme.* You read through the recommendations, check out the cross-references, and contemplate the big warning at the head of the *Removals* section. *Removal is a serious measure, and will be closely examined at the Agent's half-century performance review. Make sure you have three good reasons, no more than one of them personal, for any removal.*

Well, let's see. Meillet is standing in the way of the liberation of Okura from a brutal dictatorship. That's one— impersonal. He annoys the hell out of you. That's two— personal. He's no longer acting for the good of the Incatena, but only on behalf of narrow business and partisan interests. Bingo.

You study the available methods. Many of them are disquieting, even when a personal grudge is involved. You don't think assassination, maiming, or a neurovirus is in order. It's a pity Meillet isn't an AI; there's some good methods for getting rid of them. (*Psychotize by attachment to virtual reality. Poke a pinhole in the bottom of the main photonics maze. Form personal attachment; monopolize processor time solving personal problems.*)

Under *Ideologically extreme* there are basically three strategies: *Dislodge through intrigue; Outmaneuver by adopting a stricter position; Reveal ideological misdeeds.* You quickly come to the conclusion that only the third of these is practical. It's not a very pretty option— it's distasteful stuff, turning a man in to his fellow fanatics, and it requires a good deal of tedious, unappetizing work— and you briefly reconsider neuroviruses and maiming before settling on it.

You set up some photonic surveillance, without much hope; even if his guard is down, a station chief will routinely take measures against such efforts. (You use some equipment lent by Jidori-san; at this point it's a risk using anything from the Incatena office.) You scan the Vee for clues, too, but the burden of work will be on your own shoulders. Most likely you'll be bringing down your man with some old-fashioned footwork.

Two weeks later you know Augustin Meillet better than his own wife, and have no higher an opinion of him than she does.

Work: Spends most of the day hanging out with friends (all expats or local businessmen), browsing the Vee, or napping. Relies on his secretary to keep abreast of official business. For the most part lets the station run itself; when something serious comes up, however, or there's a potential question about his own conduct, reads all the documentation he can get his hands on, and deals with the problem in high-pressure one-on-one sessions (you've experienced one of those yourself). Has never shown any initiative in data gathering, political analysis, or the development of unofficial contacts.

Business: Meillet is a bulk franchise importer. Owns his own firm, incorporated on Homeland. Doesn't handle anything risky or innovative; merely the routine transfer of minor service and software improvements between Incatena planets. It's a business that accumulates billions in credits in dribs and drabs. Rich; owns estates on three planets, plus a private yacht now in orbit around Okura. Well-connected in the Commerce Association as well as in the Incatena-Okura Business Circle, of which he is a past president. Socializes with top members of the Peace Party. He probably couldn't have got where he is today without a fair amount of bribery and tax evasion. However, bribery is legal under Homeland law, which means the Incatena can't go after him on that charge; and his books are too well hidden; it'd take six months to build up a case against him. As for Okurinese law, it's purposely vague enough that the regime can build a case against anyone if need be; but his contacts would insulate him from anything you could come up with.

Home life: Married, children long grown, and running the family firm back on Homeland. Unusually, has been married to the same wife since before you were born. (You grimace on her behalf, thinking about her bearing those children personally, without a mechawomb.) They pretty much ignore each other. Ms. Meillet is heavily involved in charity and church events.

Religious activities: Church on Sunday, mosque on Friday, Bible/Koran study on Wednesday nights, volunteers at the church office on Thursday nights, business committee meetings on alternate Saturdays, teaches new members' classes on Monday and Tuesday nights every other month. Tunisians are big on damping down nonconformism by not leaving any time for it. The church is strict evangelical Tunisian, sniffy about anything newer than the 40th century, and conventional in every way. Good friends with the pastor and his husband.

Relaxations: Bolor, a Sihorian game in which two persons attempt to knock two balls from basket to basket in a specialized fieldhouse (the ball itself is self-powered and semi-intelligent, and attempts to escape by any means necessary). Space yachting. Writing: for the last fifty years, apparently, Meillet has been developing a magnum opus explaining the apostasy of the modern world against God, and calculating the probable date of the Second Or Third Coming.[1]

It's not that the man doesn't have vices. The problem is finding one that can cause him trouble within his church. His political opinions are conservative even for Tunisians, and this leads to arguments with the pastor, but the arguments are friendly, and he stops short of any real theological error. He drinks with his business associates, which is considered a sin, but it would neither surprise nor scandalize anyone if it were revealed in his church— a fervent apology would take care of it. About the same can be said for his not fasting during Ramadan. He's emotionally inert, suspicious, judgmental, has a failed marriage, disdains the poor, and supports the Kumari dictatorship, but the church won't have any problem with that.

---

[1] Some Tunisians believe that the advent of Muhammad was the Second Coming.

The traditional way to entrap Tunisians is through sex. There's still an occasional scandal over a wayward leader, but thanks to unamorodine, the Second Or Third Coming will likely be upon you before you catch Meillet so much as browsing a lascivious datascene. Some Anti-Tunisians consider unamorodine a 'drug' rather than 'medicine', and prefer to overmaster libido by willpower and prayer alone. The Tunisians, however, consider it the greatest assistance to the spiritual life since the invention of the electronic concordance, and with it Meillet can contemplate his once-a-year sex life not with whimpering frustration but with quiet satisfaction.

You keep up your tail, however, pursuing Meillet from work to restaurant to church to home and back, in an endless, mind-deadening cycle. Your very dates with Ba are scheduled for times when you know Meillet will be tied up for awhile, such as the four-hour Friday night revival meeting. Something is bound to come up. If it doesn't, there's always neuroviruses and maiming. Or perhaps you could replace his unamorodine supply with erotomegatol?

Where the believer sees an ordered cosmos created by God, the atheist, based on almost identical experience, perceives only a meaningless whirl of unconscious atoms. It's curious, or exasperating, how obstinately the universe has refused to definitively confirm or deny either vision.

First contact seemed to solve the problem: the Skweeoo had no God, no gods, no religion, no stories of the supernatural, now or ever. Although some believers took the news in stride, praising God for the opportunity for evangelism, most observers found it strictly inconceivable that a cosmic deity could simply overlook an entire intelligent race, while taking a passionate interest in the daily bread and the sex lives of human beings. The observer also couldn't help noticing the evident order and harmony of life among the atheistic, if large and rubbery, aliens.

Second contact reintroduced the old muddle: the Dzebyet believed in God— if *belief* is the right word; the Dzebyet make no distinction between religion and science, and consider God (or rather The Four) to be as well-established and empirically evident as the laws of physics. And the convictions of a race far older than humans or Skweeoo couldn't be easily dismissed as superstition.

To be sure, the old forms of earthly religions could be maintained only by denial. Fundamentalists explained that the worship of The Four confirmed the existence of God, but that the Dzebyet were sadly mistaken on many important points, and had better come to know the living Jehovah and/or Allah. Fortunately for the intellectual reputation of humanity in the galaxy, these opinions are mostly exchanged among believers on isolated space habitats, far from the corruptions of the outside universe.

The Dzebyet Four are emphatically not concerned with all beings, but only with the élite, those creatures whose spiritual evolution is sufficiently advanced to warrant divine attention. The universe, in Dzebyet eyes, is something like a cellular automaton left running by its programmer, who keeps an eye out for any interesting patterns that develop, and ignores the rest. They cheerfully concede that even the spiritual level of the Dzebyet themselves is barely of interest to the Four.

This is not to say that spiritual power (*tkeigh*) is unimaginably remote for the Dzebyet. On the contrary, it is as omnipresent and as useful as electricity. It cannot be exploited mechanically, however, like a material reality; it can only be encountered, in action, by an evolving spiritual consciousness. The first error of earthly religion, say the Dzebyet, is that it tries to turn enlightenment into law, which tends to destroy the enlightenment without fulfilling the law.

The second error of earthly religion is its war with science.[1] The Dzebyet explain, a bit condescendingly, that superstition and rationalism are both simply early, mistaken phases in a species' development. Superstition is the reification of the unknown, while rationalism is the exhilarating illusion that everything can be explained. The paradox of science is that it constantly accu-

---

[1] The next eight errors of earthly religion are: 3) filling voids in our knowledge of God by confabulation; 4) paying leaders to be religious for us; 5) the matter/spirit dichotomy, in place of the tripartite distinction of *dzan, tkeigh, pboéll*; 6) plaid suits; 7) a perverse obesssion with sex; 8) foolish metaphors based on primate society; 9) logorrheic moralizing; and 10) can't take a joke.

mulates more knowledge, constantly promises a Theory of Everything, and never attains it.

Dzebyet theology is not the last word on God. The Garcheron, for instance, maintain that different portions of the universe have different cosmologies— in effect, that gods are local, not cosmic. Tunisian theology, though influenced by what we know of The Four, retains as much as possible of the historical understanding of Jehovah/Allah (and continues the war with science by castigating neurimplants and nootech). And the Quelg, a fantastically old race who make the Dzebyet look like Neanderthals, like to declare that God is of no account at all, and add that the same is true of the entire material cosmos. It is difficult to say much more about Quelg philosophy, as further questions are brushed aside with the comment that creatures made of atoms couldn't understand the mathematics.

One Friday morning you're woken up by some urgent reports from your trail drones: Meillet's called in sick, called his wife from his volant, explaining that his presence is required at a Commerce Association conference and that he won't be back till Monday; and is now scooting out of town at high speed. You cancel your own weekend plans, which involve Ba— this is painful, but fortunately your weeknight plans had involved Ba as well, and you are in fact receiving the report in Ba's bed— and scramble to your own rented volant.

Where the élite meet

You follow Meillet up into the mountains, away from the city. There's a moment when Atami is spread out before you, the city glistening like a jewel set against the sparkling water of the bay; quite beautiful if you face away from the enormous statue of Jishuri Kumari set on a mountaintop overlooking the city. Then a curve of the hills hides the city, and you are in the highlands of Gōsei. For the first half-hour the mountainsides are dotted with resorts, temples, antimissile defenses, and the dachas of important officials. Then signs of civilization cease; you are flying over unspoiled wilderness, with not even a road to break up the mountain vistas. It's rather nice— it's the next best thing to being on one of the Investigation Teams that first explore an uncharted planet.

Meillet flies at top speed, quickly, tirelessly. You can see that he's the sort of driver who advises all passengers, whatever their age, to go before they leave, because there aren't going to be any stops till we get there; who refuses to count farm animals and exotic license plates; and who declares that it's the driver who controls the car's thermostat and music node.

You travel about twenty kilometers behind him— or more precisely not right behind, but on a parallel path about five kilometers to the side and three hundred meters higher. It's a textbook[1] method for staying in a volant's blind spot. You vary your position and distance from time to time, just in case he's using radar and might begin to recognize a dot in a particular location on the screen. But he shows no sign of having noticed you.

Hour after hour he flies on. And he had one thing right: you *should* have gone before you left. You cross your legs, and try to distract yourself by thinking about where Meillet is heading. Is

---

[1] *Surveillance and Tracking for Dummies*, Incatena Media, Areopolis, 4815.

he planning to leave Gōsei entirely? He's heading south, along the mountain chain that leads into Kamandamaung.

However, about four hours out, over a thousand kilometers from Atami, he slows and glides to a landing. It happens so suddenly that for several minutes, the time it takes to catch up, you fear you've lost him. Fortunately, the volant's heat signature still registers on infrared, at the fuzzy edge of a much larger infrared source.

You wonder what it is. You're still flying above trackless mountain country. The mountains are higher here, bursting above the treeline in sharp rocky peaks. The sea is out of sight. You still can't see Meillet's destination, though you should be just over it. You circle around, looking anxiously from infrared monitor to window and back.

Then you see it. Nestled high on a mountainside, just under the last straggling trees, is a log cabin. Or more precisely, you realize as you come closer, a log mansion, large enough to host the convention of a moderately popular cult holocast, or an alternative comics expo.

A crowd of volants is parked on the meadow facing this structure; you park in the middle of the pack (where it's a bit harder for security cameras to get a good look at you), conceal some imagizers about your person, and think for a moment about strategy. It basically comes down to two options: brazen, or sneak, your way in.

You've just about decided on 'sneak' when it comes to you that you are not alone: a volant is landing every few minutes. The visitors are mostly well-dressed middle-aged men, some in the company of elegantly dressed young women. You decide to give 'brazen' a try.

You walk in, half-expecting to be jumped by armed guards. After the bright mountain sunlight, all seems darkness. A mec approaches, one manipulator extended. You reach for the laser you left in the volant, and idly wonder whether the robot is armed with projectile or radiation weapons and whether you'd prefer to be shot in the front or the back.

"Take your jacket, o-san?" asks the mec.

"Oh, er, yes," you say. It takes your jacket, registers the claim number with your neurimplant, and holds out its manipulator expectantly. You tap it a credit, then, as the hand makes no move to retire, two more.

"That's right," says the mec. "Thank you, o-san."

As your eyes adjust to the darkness, you notice that the robot is dressed in a tie, white shirt, and elegant black dinner jacket. Its smart appearance contrasts tellingly with the casual clothes you threw on (your own pants, and one of Ba's shirts) back in Atami. It bustles off to some hidden outerwear repository.

"Welcome to Roshi's, o-san. What's your pleasure tonight?"

There's nothing robotic about that voice, although there's plenty artificial in the exaggerated figure of the young woman now facing you, dressed, where she *is* dressed, in black velvet and chains of iridescent gemstones.

"I think I'd just like to look around," you say.

"Your first time here, o-san?"

"Er, well, yes."

"Why don't you follow me?"

It's not hard to do even in the dark, what with the fluorescent jewelry. Her outfit is low-cut in the back to the point of apparent impossibility.

She stops at a set of double doors, faces you with a smile.

"Drinks straight ahead, games of chance on the main floor. Whatever else you want, and I do mean *whatever*, just ask one of us."

"I'll do that."

You walk in the double doors. Several hundred people have gone in before you, not to mention legions of inspired or at least busy decorators. Their budget and sense of scale were obviously at the robber-baronial level; and as for their taste, they seemed to have operated on the principle that shiny = elegant, and that where one color, texture, or light bulb is good, two are better. Flashing lights, blaring music, excited beeps and bangs, and the acrid smell of aerosol intoxicants combine to pretty much knock out the hypothesis that Meillet has come here for a church retreat.

The enormous room is by no means full; obviously it's early yet. The customers, though not decked out as elegantly as the service robots, can at least be described as dressed; the hosts and hostesses, by contrast, look like the floor show at a fetish convention. You wander around, taking stock. The main floor is filled with gambling tables. Balconies on three sides of the room feature bars, serving every sort of legal and illegal alcoholic, chemical, or aerosol intoxicant, and even forbidden electronics to tickle cybernetic implants; the fourth opens into a restaurant.

Nor is that all; Roshi's turns out to be a veritable palace of sin. Sexual services, from the obvious to the exotic to the inexplicable, are available in one wing of the mansion; banned neurostimulants and virtual realities can be administered, to say nothing of genofixes, neurimplants, cosmetic surgery, and every sort of body decoration and modification. There are roomsful of pornography and censored materials, including such highly dangerous materials as the last constitution of Ikkyū-shima and news scenes from offworld. It's even possible to indulge the most vulgar and destructive of ancient vices: cockfighting, gladiatorial combat, and smoking.

Roshi's is almost certainly an Oji operation. The only other possibility is that it's run by the Peace Party, which is known to run pleasure palaces for its members and favorites. But the Party's establishments are smaller, closer to population centers, and less imaginative— it would never occur to Party operatives to program bondage scenarios featuring Kumari, for instance— especially the ones where he bottoms. Not that Roshi's is hidden from the authorities; the customers obviously *are* the authorities. The remote location serves to hide it, not from the regime, but from the citizenry.

The time for speculation is later, however. Now you've got to find Meillet, and find out exactly how he's disgracing himself. You spend a tiresome hour walking the length and breadth of the place, scanning tables and gambling machines, peeking into cubicles like a voyeur, glancing under tables and behind bushes. You accumulate about twenty propositions for six indecent or illegal activities, but find no sign of the Station Chief.

All at once there is a diversion: a band of barbarians invades. Hairy and half-naked, swinging swords and maces, laughing maniacally, they dash down the hallways, jump on tables, whoop out war-cries. People run out of their way; women scream; security agents draw their lasers and max guns. Others are more level-headed, and simply laugh. Their reaction proves to be well-informed; the barbarians are rowdy, but not murderous. Indeed, scrutinizing the way they swing their weapons, you guess that any serious injuries will be accidental and self-inflicted.

It's common enough on most Incatena worlds, purposeful anachronism; the only surprise is that it's illegal on Okura. If he prohibits this kind of thing, how does Kumari expect to keep his computer programmers happy?

You look over the barbarians as they settle onto tables with some distaste (you've seen real barbarians on Maraille, and don't have much patience with imitations). And there— second table from the left, in fur and gold, slamming a beer stein rhythmically on the table— is the church deacon, the bulk franchise importer, the Station Chief of the Human Incatena, Augustin Meillet.

You laugh, loud enough to attract the attention of a few nearby gamblers and drinkers. You start snapping pictures like a paparazzo (invisibly, of course; the imagizers respond to signals from your UI neurimplant). When the barbarians leave, as noisily as they came, you follow.

In the two hours that you follow him, before he disappears in the woods for some iron-man under-the-stars barbarian action, Meillet does nothing that offends you— if anything, your estimation of the boy has gone up— but he's basically trampled the Covenant of the Evangelical Muttaḥid Tunisian Church of Gōsei backwards, forwards, and sideways. Play-acting, drinking to excess, gluttony, fornication, participation in pseudo-pagan rituals, fighting, dancing, card-playing, gambling, ungodly language, lodging in a house of ill repute, lying, failing to set an example of sobriety and righteousness for the younger brethren— all that was bad, very bad. But those were merely sins; they paled before the real, unforgiveable offense: *making an utter ass of himself.*

You smile to yourself, and wander back into the main room, wondering vaguely whether you should head back to Atami and resurrect your date with Ba, or try to find a room here.

A man places a hand on your shoulder. He's a big man, a very big and muscular man— he's built like a warthog, basically, but seems less friendly. He's wearing business robes, which makes him look about as elegant as a rock with a monocle. The people who hired him were obviously looking for muscle, and their attitude was, you can't have too much, heap it on— and if it makes his face look like a transport volant, so much the better.

"You follow me," he says. "Head wants to talk to you."

"I think you've got the wrong person," you suggest, helpfully.

"You Rimu Botaki?"

You admit to answering to that name, though nothing good ever seems to come of doing so.

"I got the right one. You come along."

You go along. As *he's* going, and he hasn't seen any need to let go of your shoulder, you might as well.

A talk with the Head

"By the way," says the thug, a bit nervously, "you don't want to *say* anything to the Head."

"I don't?" Something that makes this apeman nervous can't be a good thing.

"About— about his looks, see?"

"Of course not."

"He's sensitive about it."

"I understand."

The thug looks dissatisfied. He seems to be still searching for the words that convey the seriousness of his concern. He finds them.

"You say anything to upset him, I'll rip out your throat."

He illustrates his thought by making a fist and ripping out some imaginary stuffing.

"Got it," you assure him.

You're taken to a luxury suite, not yours of course, but the Head's. It looks about as you expected; the tastes of gangsters have always been predictable. There's a well-stocked bar with a mec attendant, a music node that could double as a power plant, a full-wall holochamber, his and hers gravity controls, a combination hot tub and autogym. For ambience, objets d'art (the style is Kamandamaungese, as if that mattered), overstuffed chairs, wilting imported Novorossiyan jungle plants, and a New Bharati rug. The scene wouldn't be complete without an assortment of dark suits on the furniture, most of them occupied by gangsters, and there they are. Bottles, drug containers, half-eaten plates of food, a pox of music dots, discarded rent-a-pads, and assorted weaponry litter every available surface. A partially clad blonde sulks in one corner. She looks at you disdainfully: one more thing standing between her and fun.

Your own personal thug, the walking talking side of beef, propels you into the center of the room, head to head with the Head.

"Here he is," intones the man-mountain.

147

You look over the Head. You are taken aback to see that this appellation is not a mere metaphor, but literal fact: the Head is a disembodied human head, the neck protruding from a metal box no larger than an accordion, although there's no keyboard. The box is hovering in the air, not quite two meters up, so that the Head is about where a head should be. If this arrangement is meant to be reassuring, it can't be said to succeed.

The Head is bald, and glowers at you beneath thick eyebrows. The nose is large and curved; the eyes dark, and accustomed to command; the mouth is sour.

"Botaki," it growls.

"That's right. Rimu Botaki." You extend your hand, before collecting yourself and dropping it quickly to your side. "And who do I have the pleasure—"

"Quiet! Yukio, give him a little tap."

The little tap turns out to be a blow to the ears that makes your head ring like a firehouse.

"You'll speak when I ask you a question," the Head tells you, coldly. "Understand? *Understand*?"

You nod in an understanding way.

The Head's got a lot of unprocessed anger to deal with. You wonder if it has something to do with his handicap. You have to admit he's done pretty well for himself, considering.

"An Indonesian business rep," continues the Head, with a rather wounding disdain. He turns to his companions— he still has neck muscles, it seems. "Now what do you suppose this Earthling was doing so far from home?"

"Likes looking at trees," suggests one thug, with one of those back-in-the-throat laughs fostered by excessively butch environments.

"Sex," says another, looking over your ass with excessive interest. "It's always sex."

"Just looking for a drink, really," you offer. "You know how crowded the good bars are in Atami. When I head— I mean heard about Roshi's—"

"I think it's got more to do with the presence of one Augustin Meillet in the joint," says the Head. "Isn't that the case, *Morgan-san*?"

You sigh. You wonder if anyone on Okura hasn't cracked your assumed identity.

"I also think Morgan-san is up to something, something bad for the Party, with our friend Meillet-san," continues the Head. "What do you say, guys?"

The assembled thuggery is in agreement.

"This is how rumors get started," you point out, cajolingly. "Actually I'm just here to look after Meillet-san. We do worry, with these extracurricular activities of his..."

"Yukio, make him stop that," says the Head.

Yukio has several options available: quiet persuasion, brotherly admonition, brute force. He opts for the latter, in the form of a fist pounded down on your head. You feel like something in a whack-a-mole game.

"Thank you, Yukio. Not that it'll do much good— these Agents all got neural shunts to take away the pain. You can knock scum like this around all you want, they don't feel a thing."

"Lemme see," says Yukio, raising a fist bigger than his head.

"Later, Yukio. Now, Morgan-san. Don't act any dumber than you are. We got guys in the Shadowmen— heard all about it. And I tell you, I got no problem with whatever you rabbits are up to."

He smiles in a way that completely fails to convey benignity. There's a condition coming; you look skeptical and wait for him to state it.

"But all this good will don't come for nothing."

You stare in disbelief. "You're kidding. You're trying to *shake* us *down*? The Incatena?"

"Naw, naw," says the Head, sarcastically. "We wouldn't do that. We just want some cooperation, that's all."

This is tricky. You'd considered approaching the Oji, but had decided against it. The Agent Directives are clear on this. The underworld can be fantastically useful in executing covert actions; but they tend to ask too much in return. And fixing a society where corruption has become entrenched is not easy.

"What kind of cooperation do you want?"

"Oh, not much. Not much at all. We want a little non-interference, is all. During your little action and afterwards. Then once you veks are in power, you come to us, you see what we need. You *consult* with us. That's the word, isn't it, boys? *Consult*."

"And why should we do that?"

"I like this vek," declares the Head. "You hear me, guys? I like this vek. Straight and to the point, I like that. Why should you do that. You do it 'cause I'm asking, that's why. 'Cause so far I like you, but I don't like people what aren't agreeable to a little cooperation. Tarō, what happens to people I don't like?"

"They get into accidents," answers Tarō, who looks small and vicious.

"Yeah, accidents. Morgan-san, you think a lot of people turn me down when I ask, real nice, for cooperation like this?"

"I'm sure nobody does— I mean, no *one*. No one does," you say.

"Now you're kind of a special case," continues the Head. "Normally about now I like to give a practical demonstration. Yukio, show the vek what I mean."

Yukio shows you what the Head means. The Head means a punch to the solar plexus. You double over in pain, gasping for breath.

"But, see, that's the problem," says the Head. "That stuff don't affect veks like you any. They don't feel it. You can shoot 'em, blow 'em up— it don't even put 'em off their lunch. But they got a weak spot. You know what it is, boys?"

"What is it, boss?"

"Their organization, boys. Meillet-san. Ranking rep of the Incatena, and a frequent visitor to our little palace of indulgences... You see what I'm getting at, Morgan? You cooperate with us, and your boss is safe. You try to play any tricks, though, and there won't be anything left of him bigger than his own balls, and those are pretty small, if you get my drift."

You think about this. This could be even better than disgracing Meillet in front of his church. It has to be played right, however.

"Let me get this straight," you say. "If we don't give you a free hand— I mean, a sphere of influence, and bring you into the new government, you'll—what's the idiom— 'rub out' Meillet-san?"

"You're not so dim, you figured it out," says the Head.

"There's a flaw in your plan," you point out.

The Head frowns, his face reddening. "What's that?"

"Well, so long as Meillet-san is out here in your log cabin drinking beer in a leather harness, you've got some leverage. But once we're in power he's going to be untouchable— like Kumari is now. If you even think about laying a finger— I mean, causing him any trouble, troops are going to be pointing battlefield nukes at your head."

"You little shit," snarls the Head.

Yukio raises his fist in anticipation.

"You got a point, though," continues the Head.

Yukio lowers his fist.

The Head has made up his mind. "Okay, we kill him now. You don't have no revolution without him, eh? What do you think of that?"

"That's better," you say, brightly. "Only, that won't *stop* the revolution. We don't need him for that, that's mostly a matter of arms— I mean, firepower. We need him for afterwards, the period of reconstruction. That's when he'd really be doing us a disservice by being dead."

The Head thinks a moment; then a baleful grin spreads across his face, and he pilots himself forward till he's eye to eye with you. "I got it now," he says. His breath is bad, but not in any ordinary way; it's some kind of chemical smell. "We're going to keep Meillet-san right here— right here in the log cabin, as you call it. All the way through the revolution. You play any tricks on us, he has an accident, permanent-like. Then, afterward, when you're setting up your government, you *consult* with us, like I say. If we like what we hear, you get him back *with* all the bodily organs he came in with. You understand?"

"Yes. Good plan, very scary."

He zips back, turns to an associate. "Give me a beer," he commands.

You watch with interest as one of the thugs grabs a beer, opens an access panel in the Head's tray, and pours in the beer. A flexible nozzle snakes its way out from the base of the tray, aims itself, and pours a stream of beer into the Head's mouth. You'd like to see the Head enjoying a bowl of ramen noodles; it must be quite a show.

"Are you done yet?" comes the querulous voice of the moll in the corner.

"Yeah, yeah, we're done, doll," says the Head. This must be an interesting relationship, you think. "Yukio...?"

Yukio nods, grips your shoulder again, and leads you out. It's your other shoulder this time. Great; you'll have matching bruises.

Your escort doesn't seem any more approachable than before— he looks like someone looking for a dog to kick—but something is on your mind. "How does that work?" you ask. "I mean, the girlfriend. How does he..."

Yukio stops and looks around carefully before answering. "The docs saved... one other part of his body," he confides in what is, for him, a whisper.

"Ah."

You decide you don't need to know more.

From the first curse on

In coming years historians will argue over the event that marked the start of the second Okurinese revolution. Was it the moment Gen. Hitsumi climbed aboard a corvair-volant at the Tesuto Space Forces Center and began his famous five-hour oration on the Sclerosis of the Neotenic Ideal? Was it the Mass Inaction instigated by the pop singer Wei Meilin? Was it the momentous events in Ikkyū-shima?

Historians have to argue over such things. They've watched what happened to the social sciences: as fact replaced speculation, the flamboyant sociologists of old disappeared, replaced by engineers— always in agreement, or disagreeing about things outsiders can't fathom; never interesting, never featured on talk shows, their lives never made into holodramas. Historians learned their lesson. They take care to provide good entertainment: bold counterintuitive theories; colorful personalities with tragic failings and powerful sex drives; tears and stabbings at the quadrennial awards ceremonies; lifelong feuds; the occasional armed rout of an opposing theorist's department.

For the record, in your view the hostilities began with a curse— a targeted photonic virus, launched with a wave of your hand in the view region of Hrvatski's ergolounge. The curse multiplied itself in the planetary photonic network, seeking out certain precise junctions in the Party news-distribution mechanism. The junctions were not undefended; but the company that programmed them was a plant of the Incatena, and there was a back door. The curse subtly modified the programming of the junctions, then deleted itself.

The effect of the curse was simple enough: it deleted or redirected certain transmissions, but continued to send forged acknowledgments back to the sender. The cursed junction would also detect tests and probes, and behave faultlessly whenever it was under scrutiny. The result was to slightly impair the Party's main propaganda channel, and to bollix up the daily work of the people responsible for Kumari's mass communications. Some

154 • Against Peace

missed news articles here, a private e-mail made public there, a directive lost over there, or perhaps the word "not" inserted into a crucial decree: the increased levels of mistrust and annoyance were as important as the actual inefficiencies introduced.

It wouldn't bring down the regime, but it would help— it and a dozen more curses, with different targets and different behaviors— long before the regime even knew that it was under attack.

Not long after this, you bring Dr. Zhou to Incatena House and have a long talk. She's just out of the hospital, and looks it. She's happy to see you, and she's as anti-Kumari as ever, but it's evident that something has changed. There's a tiredness that doesn't leave her eyes.

Carefully, you explain that you don't expect her to do more for the revolution. But she doesn't object; she looks relieved.

You discuss options— there's time to get her off-planet if she wants. But she has relatives in Xinqeng who can keep her safe.

"You go and give them hell, Botaki-san," she tells you. "If I were feeling a little better I would..."

"You were there at the beginning," you assure her. "We're doing this for you. If we were launching a ship it'd have your name on it."

She holds your hand a long time, and then changes the subject and talks about the newest artists from Xinqeng.

Over the next few months you rarely leave Incatena House— not such a deprivation, as Ba is there too. As the 11-405 (Acting Station Chief), you must spend your days building good relations between the Incatena and the Kumari regime, leaving you the evenings to undermine them.

The first thing is to engineer a minor depression. For this you rely chiefly on Jidori-san and her friends in the Commerce Association. The businesses involved slow down their ordering, freeze their hiring, put off expansion plans. Forms, visa applications, guarantees, and approvals that must go through Incatena House also slow down to a trickle. A few banks raise their interest rates; as these include the Bank of Atami and the Hong Kong Bank, two of the banks that maintain the Okurinese money supply, other banks soon follow their lead. The stock market obligingly collapses, and that in turn spreads the retrenchment further, to most of the private sector. People need to feel that the system isn't working as well as it used to.

Another source of slowdowns and snafus is the artistic community, organized by Ryoku. All of the artists in the dissident community have day jobs, often with the government, and there they undertake a slowdown, coupled with minor acts of sabotage— erasing important files; shredding originals left in the copier; messing with the boss's e-mail.

This is where the pop singer, Wei Meilin, comes in. She's a friend of Dr. Zhou's, a native of Xinqeng, no more than 25 years old, and immensely popular across Okura. Her songs, sung in three languages, are mostly about love and everyday life[1]; the regime has occasionally denounced them as frivolous, but as it hasn't detected any political content, it's allowed her music to be freely sold. Her latest album, however, is pure dynamite. It doesn't take much to read "Free From Him", for instance, as about Kumari rather than an abusive boyfriend; and "Why Work Hard for a Boss Who's a Bully", though bouncy and sung in a lolita voice, is widely credited with spreading the notion of a workers' slowdown— the Mass Inaction— across Okurinese society.

This puts the Kumari regime in a disagreeable bind. Left alone, Wei would surely move on to even more provocative actions, and perhaps cause some serious trouble. But imprisoning her would cause resentment among people immune to most political appeals. In the end the regime manages to have the worst of both worlds. It mounts a propaganda campaign against her, as a "corrupt and cynical self-promoting decadent, imbued with Incatena virtues", which of course only cements Wei's popularity and gives her time to release the even more flagrant single, "When My Land Was Free," which, thanks to the curses in the propaganda network, receives an award from the government of Xinqeng. Then she's arrested by the Home Ministry, and the planetary Vee is full of unprecedented outrage.

---

[1] Top hits: "Blue Over You", "Deep Blue", "Not So Blue Any More— Kind of Reddish Pink", "Will I Still Know You After Your Genofix?", "Playing At Love On Company Time", "Why Did I Get Your Name Neurimplanted on My Retina?"

You take the opportunity to issue a formal censure of the Okurinese government for human rights violations, as well as for not moving quickly enough to solve the mystery of the disappearance of the Incatena Station Chief. You estimate, correctly, that the government, in the midst of its furious denials and countercharges, will publicize the Incatena's complaints across the planet, thus sending an important message to the population: The Incatena is no longer silent.

"What's next?" asks Ba, in between bites of chocolate. You're in the back yard of Ba's house, a cottage in a rustic neighborhood in the wooded foothills of the mountains looking down on Atami. The nearest neighbors are a half-kilometer away, and you're lounging by the pool in your pajamas, eating homemade brownies and playing one of Wei Meilin's albums too loud on the music node.

"More subversive activity," you answer. "The alternative net is almost in place, so we've got a whole comm system outside of Kumari's control; we've got some labor confrontations to work up, and then Ryoku's Student Movement will start its anti-corruption campaign."

"An anti-corruption campaign? Won't that just get co-opted by the Peace Party?"

"No, that's the beauty part," you explain, excitedly. "A campaign for democracy or something would just get suppressed. But the Party will have a hard time working against a movement ostensibly fighting for its own ideals."

"You don't know the Peace Party. They'll do something about it anyway."

"I *do* know them. I did my dissertation on retrogressive social movements.[1] The point is that it'll take them time to decide what to do, and by the time they decide it'll be too late; another popular organization outside their control will be in place— and *they'll* have helped put it there."

---

[1] Indeed you did, and a masterful and ambitous analysis it was, too— unfortunately curtailed by an insufficient allocation of research time, so that the study ended up being called *Retrogressive Social Movements from A to H.*

"That is clever," says Ba, gratifyingly, "but I still don't see how that's going to get rid of Kumari."

"The art of revolution consists of waiting till outmoded structures can be blown down with a puff of air," you say, quoting the Agent Directives. "Of course it'll be a pretty powerful puff, what with Gen. Hitsumi, the Shadowmen, and the Incatena forces. But the important phase is really what's going on right now. The longer we can fight without them even realizing what's at stake, the better our chances."

"And then? Afterward?"

"The revolution. Dancing in the streets. Statues of Kumari toppled. Lasers fired in the air. Fortunately that's pretty harmless— it's worse with projectile weapons."

"And after that?"

"Socionomic reconstruction. Normalization. Muddling through. That's kind of the boring stuff. That's when I like to take off, myself."

"Take off?"

Ba looks at you, and there is a hint of inconsolable sadness in those deep blue eyes.

"Get out of the revolution business, I mean," you clarify, quickly. "Settle down, perhaps. Are there any more brownies?"

"That's what you like to do, isn't it?" asks Ba. "Save the poor colonials from the evil oppressor, and then step back into the next quickship and leave... Off to new adventures. And the people you've left behind..."

"Well, let's talk about this," you say, with concern. "Are you saying that you want..."

"I'm not saying anything about what I want. We're talking about what you want."

"Oh, come on. This is about both of us; I could see it in those beautiful slanted eyes of yours."

"Your eyes are slanted too," Ba points out. "Were they always?"

"A little. I'm a bit of a mongrel."

Ba seems to be lost in contemplation of the flickering shadows at the bottom of the pool. "There you go. What do I really know about you?"

"What do I really know about *you*?"

"There's nothing *to* know," Ba insists. "Rube from Shr; lives a life that seems glamorous in comparison, except it's nothing but a small town on a sick backward planet; falls in love with an Incatena Agent who's here to fix the place and who's going to do it and then go fix some other place... What else is there to know? Who cares?"

"None of that is coded yet," you protest. "I— we— haven't decided what happens after the revolution."

"I know what *you* want," says Ba, with a devastated look.

You go over and take Ba in your arms, and you hold each other tight.

"What I want is you," you say. "Don't worry. We'll think of something. Just a couple more missions and I'll have my pension, that's just a hundred years or so... you can even be in stasis if you want..." That doesn't seem to be working; you try again. "Or I can stay here and work for Jidori-san or something. Or you can come with me to Mars. You'd like Areopolis; it's a beautiful city, spires and domes piercing through the energy screen into the pink sky— the greatest cultural scene in the Incatena— great alien restaurants— infinite holo channels[1]. We could get a little house in one of the terraformed valleys, it's almost as unspoiled as this... I love you, Ba."

"And I love you," says Ba, smiling again. "I just don't want to lose you. Are you sure you'd want to settle down with me?"

Not sure at all, you want to say. Could you give up this life of interstellar intrigue for just one person? The boss's Sihorian caf, padding around your time-share in slippers, alone; long journeys spent frozen in a cask; encounters with alien ambassadors who juggle small animals, prisons on twenty planets, long hours spent dodging laserfire or designing targeted photonic curses?

Or could you possibly settle for this: the pool, the homemade brownies, Ba's warm body intertwined with your own, already half out of its flimsy coverings. You help the process along with some close, purposeful caresses.

"Sure," you say.

---

[1] They're literally infinite. To avoid competing on number of channels, the holo companies use AIs to generate new channels and content if anyone tries to surf off the end of the dial. Some people claim that this is the only stuff worth rezzing.

"No," says Ba. "Anywhere but Shr."
"Just kiss me, silly," you say.

Shadowboxing with Kumari

The regime's first countermoves are somewhat pathetic: a publicity campaign against "ruinous apathy" and "destructive carelessness"; distribution of an improved internal mail program which, with no help from your curses, immediately breaks down; protocols requiring central government approval of all provincial music awards.

Then the Peace Party sends official notice to Incatena House that the presence of the two Incatena police cruisers in orbit round Okura is "no longer compatible with the development of the Directorate". You have to laugh at this; although it's a treaty violation, equivalent to secession from the Incatena, Kumari knows as well as you do that the cruisers aren't leaving orbit. The regime is simply escalating its provocations.

Official communications, of course, are not couched at the level of *realpolitik*. Your response is to remind the Peace Party of its commitments under the Incatena Treaty. The regime then declares that it is time to renegotiate elements of the Treaty which "do not harmonize with planetary sovereignty." You invite the government to bring the matter up with the Council back in Areopolis; the regime complains that your response is "frivolous".

A few days later a satellite explodes in orbit. News coverage is brief, mentioning only "coding difficulties" and promising the execution of the engineers involved. But bad code rarely blows up satellites, especially these days when almost all BASIC has finally been eradicated— it's clear that the satellite was deliberately destroyed as a warning to you.

The first thing you learn at the Academy is that the influence of the Incatena is entirely based on the shrewd use of laughably insufficient resources. You and the station AI soon find a pretext for a spectacular use of the Incatena cruisers: in cooperation with a local police operation that had requested high-level backup, a raid is staged on Roshi's mountain resort. The raid nabs three Kamandamaungese black marketeers, six women forced into prostitution, and two Sihorian smugglers for which

160

the government of Qeng had submitted an extradition request fifty years back. In addition, Roshi's is cited for a number of health department violations. (It's not yet in your interest to rescue Meillet; but it's just as well to plant a seed of doubt in the Head's mind about his own strong-arm tactics, if that's the word.)

In effect you're daring the Peace Army to attack your cruisers. You're betting that Kumari is not quite ready to take this step, and for the moment you seem to be right.

The regime's next move is irritating: the continuing depression is blamed on the bad influence of the Ogorodé, who are given one year to leave the planet.

A week later you get a grim commaudio from Hitori-san in Ikkyū-shima. Infiltration into the Ikkyū-go Peace Party is suspected.

"How bad is it?" you ask, fearing the worst— the moment of tooth, as Agents say.

"Excrementally bad," she assures you. "We've got an office pool going on when the Home Ministry troops arrive."

"That's bad," you say. "What's the smart money saying?"

"Two hours from now. Of course, the payout then is low, because everybody's taking that slot. I picked tomorrow morning— if I'm right I'll pick up C. 2,000. Don't think I'll get it, though."

"So who sang?"

"Our own AI," says Hitori-san, sadly. "I still can't understand it. It had always been so enthusiastic... we even gave it an upgrade."

"Your AI turned on you? That's unusual.... Wait a moment. What kind of an upgrade?"

"A memory rearchitecting. Raised it a whole class. Cost us a hell of a bundle, too."

You sigh. "It also would have completely restructured its pseudopsyche."

"That's what it said. Never quite understood that. What's it mean?"

"Imagine having your entire mind scrubbed clean, then getting about half of it back, entirely reorganized. You might not really look forward to it, even they told you your new personality would really be an improvement."

162 • Against Peace

Hitori is silent for a minute. "I guess I wouldn't," she says. "The new personality was nicer... didn't really realize it was a new person."

"Gen. Hitsumi might go for it, I suppose."

"What?"

"Never mind. What're we going to do?"

"There's only one thing *to* do," she says, decisively. "Proceed, drives full on. *Now.*"

You think about this. You don't like it. "It's too early. We didn't want to play our hand for at least another month."

"We don't have a choice. In two hours we've either got a revolution or we're in jail."

You nod, a completely useless gesture on commaudio. "All right, let's do it."

"Right. I'll see you over Kumari's dead body in thirty days. Or in Hell."

You put down the comm unit and sigh. You've got a busy night ahead of you; better send out for pizza.

The next day, Ikkyū-shima erupts into civil war, which soon spreads to Xinqeng and Phu Quoc, where garrisons of Ikkyū-jin soldiers mutiny in support of their countrymen. Kumari's armies pour into all three countries, where they meet fierce resistance from the police and the Shadowmen. At about five in the morning the conflict goes nuclear.

Mold and grandmothers

Humans cannot enter most Ogorodé homes. It's not a matter of protocol; we're too big. We'd crash through the floor, or our heads would burst the ceiling. Or the Ogorodé shantytown may simply be inaccessible: perched on hillsides, floating on marshes, strung between skyscrapers, hanging from the ceiling of abandoned warehouses.

The Ogorodé community in Atami is at the edge of the spaceport, an area made unsuitable for human habitation by noise, fumes, chemical leaks, and tremors. Ogorodé shacks are always made of material abundant and useless in the local economy; here, that means mud reinforced with sticks, pebbles, packing waste, industrial detritus, broken surveillance tools, and plastic sheeting. On some planets, such as Mars, the wood would be valuable, the plastic and metal recyclable, and mud available only as an expensive luxury; the Martian Ogorodé build their houses with bricks baked from terraforming refuse.

Inside their houses, the Ogorodé live at a virtually medieval level— they have only simple possessions, without photonics or running water. Piles of rags serve as beds; the walls are generally covered with mold. The latter detail shocks and disarms those human visitors who come close enough to the shacks to stick a head in; but it's really just theater. The mold is edible and indeed nutritious— to Ogorodé; in effect it lives in humble symbiosis with the Ogorodé, as the Ogorodé live in symbiosis with a thousand races across the galaxy.

On the edge of the community are larger shacks— places for doing business with the outside world. You sit inside one now, sitting at a low table across from three of the little grey aliens, which have been introduced to you as the leaders of the planetary community of Ogorodé. Their names— at least, the names they give to humans; it's said that they have secret names of their own as well— are Tarō, Miyako, and Chen. Others, a dozen or more, cluster against the walls behind them, giving you The Look— the image of complete inoffensiveness, the air of not mattering, of blending into the landscape, that's their ticket onto planets across the galaxy.

Your surroundings are austere: a dirt floor; walls bare but for a portrait of Kumari on one wall; one bare lighting field, casting a dim light with black shadows over the room.

"Please, have some more *tanaki*," says Tarō.

"O-san is not Okurinese," Chen points out. "O-san would prefer something from Sol system. Rustle up something," he tells a retainer, behind him. "Earth drinks aren't cheap— sell someone into slavery."

"It's really not necessary," you insist. "*Tanaki* is just fine."

"It's no trouble. Hiroko here has an aged grandmother who's doing nobody any good."

You shudder. "Do you really sell yourselves into slavery?"

"Being a slave's not so bad. You live in a human house. You get meat, sometimes. If you're agreeable, they don't beat you much. It beats database access coding."

"But it's against the Incatena Treaty," you protest.

"At our level of society," Miyako reminds you, "treaties and laws have nothing to do with how things work."

"Yes. Well. What can I do for you?" You have an idea, but you want to hear what they'll say. You've tried to recruit the Ogorodé before, but till now you've always been rebuffed.

All three Ogorodé screw up their faces. "*Do* for us," repeats Chen, shocked.

"*We* want to serve *you*," Tarō assures you.

"We hope to be of much benefit," says Miyako.

"Yes, yes. But you want something in return, don't you?"

"We're in a bit of a bind," admits Tarō.

"We have our sources," says Chen. "We believe Glorious Marshal Kumari is serious. He wants us off this planet. He's already deported two communities in Kwaikok."

"Deported? How? I can't believe he's going to use valuable spaceships to ship Ogorodé outsystem."

"They're not actually offplanet," clarifies Miyako. "They're in concentration camps. Those who can pay their way are allowed to leave the planet. Those who can't will be destroyed."

You haven't heard about this. That's not very surprising— no one, official or unofficial, pays much attention to what happens to the Ogorodé. You make a mental note to check, anyhow; it's a hole in your intelligence gathering.

"You see why we are eager to cooperate, in order to topple the Twice Glorious Director," says Tarō.

"You don't have to call him that here," hisses Miyako.

"Sorry, o-san. Force of habit. I mean the despised and tyrannical Director, of course, the defier of the justice of the Incatena," says Tarō, smoothly.

"Would you like more *tanaki*? I would also be glad to order chips," offers Chen.

"You're laying it on a little thick," you say. "Listen, I'm inclined to help, I really am— though the Agent Directives kind of discourage the idea, and usually the Ogorodé do too. But what do you have in mind?"

"We are in every part of Okura," suggests Tarō. "We are cleaning people in government offices, programmers and radioactive waste handlers in army compounds, training victims in Home Ministry offices. We hear many things, we will tell them to you. We relay messages."

"We are in the houses of the top officials, top generals," says Miyako. "We know their scandals— who is sleeping with whom, who says bad words against the dictatorial tyrant Kumari in their beds."

"We pilfer documents," offers Chen. "We put curses on computers. We make important equipment fail."

"Yes, yes," you say. "I think I can square it on my half-century performance review. But let's talk about what you want. Money? Weapons? Materials? I can't offer you much..."

"Our lives are at stake," says Chen. "We are not *selling* our services. But we do have— well, they are not *conditions*..."

"Prayers," suggests Tarō. "Groveling beseechments."

"Without certain assurances, it is better for us to die," says Miyako, simply.

"Boot-licking supplications," offers Tarō.

"Yes, yes. What have you got in mind?"

"First, we must remain on the bottom," says Chen.

"We don't want social advancement," explains Tarō. "No new rights, no citizenship, nothing better than the least human on Okura receives— *after* the war.

"Second, what we have done for you must remain secret. Our role must *not* be mentioned in news reports, or history books, or official files."

"This is very important," says Miyako. "If it became known that the Ogorodé might take part in a revolution, might act in any way against our host societies, for no matter what reason— our situation would become perilous on a thousand worlds."

"We'd be dead beef," clarifies Tarō.

"I understand," you say.

"Please, have more *tanaki*," Chen urges you.

"No thanks. All right: no social mobility and no publicity. It's against all policy, but since you make a point of it... what else?"

There is some hemming and hawing. The three spokesbeings give each other The Look, each hoping the others will speak. The spectators (you can't call it a crowd— a group of Ogorodé never looks like a crowd, only like a random assemblage, seemingly surprised to find so much of itself in one place) mutter a bit and grimace encouragingly at their leaders.

At last Chen manages to speak. "There would also be the desire for certain material goods," he confides.

You nod, and slowly the list emerges: tools, medical supplies, Vee nodes and other photonic devices, a kilometer of ceramic tubing, yeast, and six toy volants.

"Toy volants?"

"The big kind, the ones for children," says Miyako.

"It's for setting up a transportation service in the ghetto," explains Chen.

"Ah. Well, I don't think any of that will be a problem," you say, as you finish writing down the list.

"Atomizers, not anodizers," says Tarō, bending over to inspect.

"Right, right."

Miyako points out another error. "Photo, not porno."

"My handwriting," you explain. "Anything else?"

"Our business is done," says Chen. "But you are not in a hurry, are you? It's time to celebrate. We liquidated two grandfathers in order to save money for this night."

"I wouldn't dream of missing it," you say, truthfully enough. You've never been to an Ogorodé party, and— what is more striking, in this age of total information, you've never heard of any other human having attended one. What secrets might now be revealed? Are you about to witness rituals long hidden from human eyes, or reckless depravities, or parliaments of poetic fancy, or merely the unusual sight of the somber Ogorodé getting drunk and funky?

Your hosts bustle about. A feast is laid out before you: mold, rice, and insect delicacies for the Ogorodé; for you, more *tanaki* and what looks like Chinese take-out. Dinner conversation centers around the health problems, character flaws, and troubles with authorities (document problems, unpursued crimes, death squad persecution) endured by various members of the community, whose family histories and relationships with those present are politely explained to you. And when it seems the depths of tedium could not be further plumbed, it gets worse: the talk turns to intramural sports— games you've never heard of (but whose rules are patiently explained), played with no particular brilliance by beings you don't know.

You are sitting in a half-stupor, watching mold slowly spread from a serving plate to your own half-eaten mu shu pork, when you are aroused by a feathery touch on your arm.

"O-san," says Chen, urgently. "Please wake up; dinner is over."

"So soon?" you mutter. "Well, it's been delightful. So glad we could have this little get-together. Now if you could point me toward my volant—"

"Oh, no," says Chen. "You must not leave now, o-san. We are less than halfway through our fun, and it is all in honor of you!"

"Ah yes," you say. "What's next?"

"Games! In your honor, we will play games from your solar system tonight. We will start with Pictionary! Would you like more *tanaki*?"

"A couple buckets of it," you specify.

No more than half a dozen Ikkyū-shima cities have been destroyed before the Dzebyet, citing environmental agreements signed in the first days of the colony, demand that the warring forces henceforth contain their struggle to the stratosphere and below. The Kumari regime hardly knows what to do with this declaration. The official press is alternately mocking and threatening (except where your photonic curses have been effective, and press releases are issued praising the Dzebyet interference as in accordance with the highest ideals of Kumari Thought); an official request is made of the Incatena to stand and fight the alien menace together in the name of humankind; and the Space Forces prepare to carry on as usual. The Dzebyet then proceed to blast twelve space cruisers and two hundred nuclear missiles out of the sky.

The rage of the Kumari regime is apoplectic; but the technological edge of the Dzebyet is absolute, and the only countermeasure the regime can command is to order all Dzebyet on planet confined to their embassy and consulates, "whose extraterritoriality, in accordance with the rules of warfare, we respect," as the official communiqué notes. What it avoids mentioning is that the Dzebyet energy screens surrounding these enclaves are impervious to anything short of a nuclear attack (and destroying Atami in order to level the Dzebyet Embassy strikes even the Peace Army as inadvisable).

Nonetheless the Space Forces are grounded. The war proceeds furiously at all levels under the stratosphere, however, both in Ikkyū-shima and in Xinqeng, where the revolt of the Ikkyū-jin army units has been joined by local irregulars, and where even areas free of armed rebellion seethe with civil unrest, apparently precipitated by rumors that Wei Meilin has been murdered by her Home Ministry captors.

In Gōsei, Ryoku's new Student Movement is suppressed. It has as yet done nothing subversive— indeed, the plan was for it to support the Peace Party at an indecent level of enthusiasm— but in a climate of war, the Party's policy is to imprison first and ask questions later. Ryoku himself escapes, but the crackdown is the first major setback for the revolution.

You've virtually been living at Incatena House lately; Ba is getting more insistent about getting together for a date.

"We're constantly together at work," you point out.

"Except when you're in meetings, or on the Vee, or holed up with Hrvatski or the AI or both, or on commaudio with the Dzebyet..."

"We still spend a lot of time together. I mean, we eat together, I stop by to see you, you drop by to see me..."

"Yes, you come by to have me file this, and send that, and get that guy on commaudio, and then we relax by talking about strategy and tactics. I give you a massage to relax, and you want to talk about Gen. Hitsumi the whole time..."

"That wasn't so bad. It ended in sex, didn't it?"

"Yeah, sex on the briefing room floor, and you kept the datanode on."

"I have to keep in touch," you explain. "Besides, it was kind of pretty, making love in a sea of holographic images..."

"And immediately after orgasm you run off to Hrvatski, shouting 'Now I know what to do about Roshi!'"

"The timing could have been better," you admit.

"So either you get ideas about tactics from screwing, which is pretty disturbing, or else you're thinking about tactics *instead* of screwing, which pisses me off."

This isn't a line of thought you want to prolong, so you give in; you agree to go out for a change, and to spend the night at Ba's cottage. And in fact it turns out to be a very nice evening. You have dinner in a little Zhuang restaurant, and remember how to have a conversation that doesn't touch once on politics. You do a little dancing in a Burusandakuan bistro, swaying to the ethereal music of gamelans and theremins. You retire to Ba's bed, and discover anew why beds are more popular than briefing rooms.

Early in the morning you get up and take a long walk in the hills, seeing no one, looking down at the awakening city, at β Hydri peeking like a curious giant over the horizon, filling the sea with sparkling facets of light. From here the capital of the Kumari regime has nothing ominous about it; it is simply beautiful, a work of crystalline perfection nestled between mountains and sea.

You see a couple of men coming toward you, and nod to them. Facing into the sun, you notice only too late that they're not gesturing to their Vee nodes; they're training max guns on you. You look back; two more agents fall into place behind you. Your mind races. Did you pay that last parking ticket?

"If you could accompany us," says one of the men, quietly. "You're under arrest, for espionage."

On ice

That's the way it goes. One minute you're at the helm of the Revolution; now you're languishing in a prison cell, taming spiders.

Someone five or six hundred years ago was provident enough to erect a heavy stone building and let it fall into decrepitude, so that the present regime has a perfect place to stash prisoners, the ones it doesn't plan to return to circulation any time soon. The walls are rough, and glisten with greenish moisture. On the floor is a pile of polyester and bedbugs that deduction but not perception can call a mattress; as a place for sleeping it is preferable only to the floor, a mass of grime, sand, sawdust, mold, and less attractive substances encrusting a layer of cracked flagstones. There is a hole in the floor which you use for defecation, although the first time you used it for that purpose you are sure you heard a moan of complaint from far below. Now you courteously shout a warning before using the facilities, and wonder what sort of hideous crimes could land a poor wretch in the unimaginable netherland below.

Between you and the outside world stands a thick wooden door, whose barred window is the only source of light in the cell, letting pass a few desultory photons from a weak bulb down the hall. At the base of the door is a slot through which, once a day, a thin pan of yellow, overcooked rice is passed. For water, there is an ancient faucet which can occasionally be coaxed to yield a cup or so of tepid, untrustworthy water into the tin cup which is your sole and precious possession.

At night a hidden speaker system plays the eerie sounds of human beings being tortured: screams, moans, tears, pitiful pleading, an occasional sick thud. The first night, you are terrified; the second night, anxious and outraged; the third night you realize that the sounds are exactly the same each night; you are listening to a recording. It doesn't much lessen the air of foreboding, but at least now you can sleep.

170

It's no way to treat the acting Station Chief of the Human Incatena; you make a mental note to protest stiffly at the first interrogation.

However, those who are detaining you (The Home Ministry? The Peace Army? The secret police?) don't seem to be in any hurry; you've been here for over a week, and no one's come by to give you so much as a cigarette burn. (There's no need to scratch a calendar into the slime on the walls; you have your inoculated clock.)

Escape seems like a remote possibility, but you check the cell carefully. What the hell else is there to do?

The ancient rock of the walls is as hard as rock. The flagstones are more fragile— they chip when attacked savagely with the bottom of the tin cup— but it would be a long, long process to work all the way through, and most likely all you'd do is reach another layer of stone and ruin your cup. At best you'd reach the deeper cellar below, which is almost certainly a dead end. Only in the holodramas do these places lead to caves or underground passageways.

Generations of prisoners have worked on the door, which is scraped and gouged in various places. There are some deep indentations near one hinge, evidently made by the teeth of something inhuman. In another century or two, you judge, some lucky prisoner might break his way through.

You could live out that century and several more, but not here. Fed on nothing but rice and water, you'll be lucky to last six months.

You recite poetry— all the poetry you know. Nursery rhymes, ancient epics, Sihorian space chanties, Qengese love poems, the ballads of the asteroid miners. Your range is impressive; it's just a pity you can't recall more than six lines of any one poem.

You recall the plots of holodramas to yourself. You design new VR scenarios. You write revengeful short stories based on experiences with ex-lovers. You do a dramatic reading of the Agent Directives. You practice your Modern Hindi and your Ancient French. You think about working on your half-century performance review. You may have thought of something to put under *Weaknesses*.

Would it have killed them to put a music node in here?

Ten days into your incarceration you're served a thin beef gruel instead of rice. It almost annoys you, because it requires changing your plans, which had involved writing an epic novel on your neurimplant, then dying of scurvy and malnutrition in six months. That has to be put off, now.

Plus you have to decide: should you make the novel a trilogy, or proceed directly to the musical comedy adaptation?

The next day— diarrhea. You cancel your writing plans for the day, so as to devote your full attention to being completely miserable.

What the world really needs, you decide, is not another novel, but a searing exposé of the utter foolishness of being a so-called Agent of the so-called Incatena. If there's anything more putrid and nauseating than the boss and his insufferable Sihorian caf, it's those twice-damned holo producers that metastasized from somewhere in the drug-addled wrecks of their cerebra the laughable idea that the life of an Incatena Agent was glamorous and meaningful.

On the sixth day after that you're given a cellmate. You could kiss him; only he's having none of it. He sulks in a corner, emerging only when the food arrives, whereupon he makes a pitiable grab for both plates of food. Fortunately, you're stronger than he is, at least for now.

You try speaking to him— first in Okurinese, then in Qengese, then in every modern language you can muster, all to no avail. He only scowls at you.

Half a day later, he collapses into sobs. Ever the soul of compassion, you move over to him and put an arm around his emaciated shoulders.

"[gɑdæm aɪwɪʃjukœdspikɪŋglɪʃ]," he enunciates.

This has to bounce around in your brain for more than a minute before a meaning tumbles out. "Goddamn, I wish you could speak English."

He speaks Ancient American English, a language dead for three thousand years. Fortunately you've studied it; it's a necessity for proper understanding of the most important literature of the 20th century— *Peanuts, Calvin and Hobbes, Pogo, Mad, Brenda Starr, Love & Rockets*, and all the rest.

The amazing truth dawns on you: he's a frozener.

Freezing started in the 20th century, but due to failures of technique the pioneers are all irretrievably dead. Successful thawing is only possible with those frozen after about 2050. For a few decades in the 2100s freezing was popular among the newly or nearly dead. Maintenance, and presumably one's eventual unfreezing, were to be covered by interest-bearing bank accounts. Times were lean, however, and public opinion rebelled against the idea that the fruits of the productivity of the living should be handed over to people who were not only dead but didn't have the decency to rot peacefully in their own era, leaving their wealth to console their bereaved, but insisted on taking it with them into the indefinite future.

The bereaved could think of better uses for the money, and so could the government. The frozen, being dead, had little to say on their own behalf. Inevitably, then, cryogenic trusts were prohibited, and the funds in them confiscated.

Thrown on the mercy of their heirs or on that of the state, the fate of the frozeners varied. Those who had actually died were generally transferred to less optimistic forms of after-death care, such as cremation. Thousands who had been frozen in their last days in the hope of a cure for what ailed them were thawed out less than fifty years later. Some found their cures; most did not. Those who survived generally adapted badly to the post-Collapse world, already much changed from the one they had left: poorer, less Western, less tolerant of rich people's eccentricities, and generally rewarding very different skills from those they possessed.

The Douane preserved several hundred frozeners for anthropological research. A number of them were eventually sold to research institutions outsystem, notably the Library of Man on

Sihor. And evidently at least one was purchased by an Okurinese university. But how did he end up in this unnamed prison?

Eventually, your frozener thaws. His name is Ben Cramer, and he was a "CEO", that is, a sort of shaman employed by the early corporations in the pre-AI era. Like tribal shamans who believed in their power over the sun and the rain, the CEOs took the credit for their firms' success, if any. If the company did well, they were granted a life of hedonistic indulgence. If not, they were expected to jump from the ledges outside their offices.

"So how did you end up here?" you ask him.

"Goddamnest screwup you ever heard of in your life," he explains. "Complete comedy of errors. Be out soon as I talk to a good shylock, though. If they'd just let me get a phone call in. Just have them buzz the American Embassy, that should do it."

"The what?"

"American Embassy. Don't tell me you don't know what it is; you speak American."

"We haven't got one."

"That I find hard to believe," says the frozener, coldly. "How far in the future is this anyway?"

"4924," you say. You don't bother to point out that it is, in fact, the present.

"What? No shit. I really got to get to a phone. Gotta call a bank and see how rich I am. Fifty million dollars at compound interest for over 2800 years... you don't suppose they're trying to steal it, do you?"

"Did it three millennia ago," you say, shaking your head.

"Of course I did. Not sorry I did it, either— it was a piss of a time to be alive in. Things had got out of hand, I could see that. Environment shot to hell— anarchists— people shot in the streets— in New York! Should be better now, though, right?"

"It's definitely better," you assure him.

"Except *here*," he says, with a certain heavy irony.

The appearance of the frozener takes some getting used to. They've cleaned him up as well as they can, of course— got rid of the harmful bacteria that produce that distinctive early-man smell; cured his gum disease and inflamed liver; irradiated away a multitude of dangerous viruses. Nonetheless he retains a powerful air of wildness and squalor. At first glance this might be blamed on prison; but a closer look shows that his condition is not one of mere deprivation. His skin is mottled with little spots, bumps, and wrinkles; he's shorter than any normal human being; he has the remains of a paunch; he's hairy, especially in places that don't strike you as needing hair at all: his ears, the back of his hands, his nostrils.

Only some sort of fantastic degenerative disease could have such effects today. And that's exactly what it is: a disease called old age, long since eradicated. The very old today, those approaching their eighth century, look very different— glossy skin, watery eyes, a tendency toward fat chests and arms— and generally die of sudden, massive system failure.

You can diagnose the disease, but you find that you can't estimate its seriousness— that is, you don't know how old he is, except that he's decades younger than yourself.

"I'm aiming to steal a plane or something," says Cramer, conspiratorially. "What I'm chiefly after is a way to get back to America."

"That's a long way from here," you say, indulgently.

"I've got to get out of this Jap country," he continues. "You can't trust these people. Polite on the surface and all, but they're not *like* us. Life is cheap to these people."

"They're not Japanese, really," you say, determined to move the man a little of the way into the present. "They're Gōsei-jin. They don't even come from Japan; they come from Qeng."

"Whatever. Orientals, all of them. We beat the hell out of them once, but then we let 'em beat us *economically*. I never bought any of that Chinese software, always bought American. If everybody else had done the same, we wouldn't be in the state we're in. Had a Jap car and TV, though— they didn't even make 'em in America anymore."

Your brain is running overtime trying to relate this to memories of old history books. There was a war— yes, a nuclear one, one that unleashed mutant monsters on the Japanese archipelago for decades. 'Cars' were ground transports, yes, but what were TVs? Something to do with religion?

"So what are you? You look kinda Jap yourself."

"Uh, no— I was born on Mars."

"Huh. I guess it *is* the future. You got a colony there, huh? Always seemed like a hell of a waste of money to me."

"There's about four billion Martians who'd disagree."

"No shit? I guess I'm out of touch. Well, I should have a few thousand descendants these days. Think they'll be glad to have the old man back? It'll be like fucking Abraham Lincoln coming back to life. By way of some kind of ersatz Japan."

"I'm still not sure how you ended up here."

"Shit, don't ask. I gave 'em hell, that's for sure. Landed a beaut of a right hook on one of those Japs— looked like he was about to pull some of that kung fu, but not after I socked him one, I'll tell you that. I might not look like I'm in shape, but appearances are deceiving— you don't want to get into it with me. But if I could just see a lawyer who speaks American, I'd be out of here in a flash. The money isn't a problem, I'm good for it."

"You were rich in your time?"

"Fifty million bucks a year. *Base,*" he tells you. "You could use a man like me in your time."

"We could?"

"Man from the past. You folks have it too easy— too soft. Guy trained in the business jungle could clean up here. Business is war under another name. Examine the enemy, identify weak points, and annihilate. Bet you I'll be the richest guy in the solar system in one year. If I can just get out of here. One call to the American Embassy..."

"There's no American Embassy," you explain, once more. "The closest thing to it is the Incatena Embassy."

"The Catena? What's that?"

You try to explain.

"Kind of a UN, huh? I hope it's less useless than ours was. But I'll talk to their Ambassador, if that's what it takes."

"You're doing that," you say, gloomily.

"Damn straight I'm doing that. What the hell is he doing while an American citizen is locked up in this hole? Damn Japs— we should nuke 'em back to the Stone Age."

You never do piece together his story, but you can pretty well fill in the outlines. It's certainly barbaric of the regime to incarcerate this poor frozener, but at least it's clear why they don't let him go. Paranoid delusions, megalomania, violent episodes, general incoherence and inadaptability— he's crazy as a loon.

Interrogation

You've killed yourself eight times already— or you would have, if you'd found the right tooth. As it is, all you have to show for your efforts are several loose molars and a toothache. Six times, your hopeless prospects impelled you to this desperate act; twice, it was Cramer's attempts to cheer you up. His last try was the worst.

"You know what we need? *Sex*," he suggests.

"Don't I know it," you sigh, thinking of Ba.

"Well, what about it?"

"*What* about it? Are you suggesting we call room service?"

"*You* know what I mean," he says, and, horribly, you do. "I mean, we may not be each other's precise type, and the ambience could be better, but hell, it's been three thousand years, I'll stick it in anything that moves."

"How romantic."

"It's not *love*," he assures you. "It's just expediency. It's a basic human need, after all, just like eating and excreting."

"It's hard to turn down an offer like that," you say, and then, fearing that subtlety may be lost on the mentally unmoored, "What I mean is, Cramer, I'd rather be disemboweled. Nothing personal."

Cramer thinks a moment. "Wrong orientation, huh? I guess I should've known. You look it."

"It's not that," you inform him. "I know sexual orientation was a big deal in your day, but not nowadays... no, it's just revulsion."

"I thought people would be less hung up in the future," says Cramer, with a hint of bitterness.

"Just look around you, man," you say, angrily. "If I wanted to have sex with a frozener at all, not that I'm prejudiced, do you think it would be *here*?"

Cramer looks around the cell. There's a pause.

"You don't like me," he says.

You say nothing.

"You don't say it directly, but I can tell. You don't like me."

One good bite should do it. You could be out of here, and take Cramer with you. It'll be all over.

"It's not like I'm asking for sympathy. In the deep freeze for three thousand years, then taken out in some Jap country, deprived of my rights, thrown into some nameless, forgotten hellhole with someone who doesn't even *like* me— no, I don't expect *sympathy*."

But what if it just worsens your toothache?

"I just think a friendly attitude would be more in order. I mean, here we are, trapped together, without hope of escape. You'd think we'd be *buddies*. Us against the world, you know? It's not that *I've* been unwilling..."

To hell with the toothache.

The door opens. A booted foot kicks you in the shins.

"Get the fuck up and come with us," says the guard. "Interrogation slash torture session."

"Thank God," you say.

According to your inoculated watch, this particular long fraction of eternity has been just two weeks:

15:46 19 Jan 359° ☺

You're sitting in a small dark room, whose walls have apparently been sculpted out of the rock with blast plasmizers. The chair faces the inevitable cheap metal desk; the only furnishings are the inevitable bright light shining in your eyes, the inevitable portrait of Kumari hanging on the wall behind the desk, and the somewhat more evitable sofa and matching loveseat in the corner.

Sitting at the desk is a clean-cut, uniformed young man with a long nose and a small thin moustache, idly tapping at a datanode. Two guards, judging from the heavy breathing and the odor of cheap *tanaki*, are right behind your chair.

"I'm sure you know why you've been brought here," says the young man.

"It's those parking tickets," you offer. "I can explain."

"I don't think so. Try again."

"The arresting officers said something about espionage. I'm sure you've discovered by now what a complete mistake that was."

"Why, yes," says the officer, looking up at you. "A regrettable mistake, that's all it was. You're free to go."

"Really?"

"Just kidding," he says, with a laugh. "No, you were right the second time— it's espionage."

"But that's completely absurd," you protest. "You can't pick up the acting Station Chief for the Incatena on an espionage charge. It's completely against protocol."

"True enough. That's why we've added charges of abuse of diplomatic privilege, incitement to treason, and fomenting revolution."

"Well, that doesn't get you out of your pickle," you say. "I mean really, er— what was your name again?"

"I hadn't given it yet, but it's Tanaga."

"Tanaga. Nice to meet you, Tanaga-san; my name is Morgan."

"I know."

"As I was saying, Tanaga-san, this is going to be a bugger of an interstellar snafu. It's a black eye for the regime, as I'm sure you realize. Detain a few garden variety spies, sure, it's all in a day's work, but the Incatena Station Chief— it's not going to win you any friends back on Mars *or* Sihor, and there's the Incatena cruisers orbiting Okura to worry about..."

"The Incatena cruisers that *were* orbiting Okura."

"That *were* orbiting Okura? What the hell did you do with them?"

"You should have figured it out," he says. "Your side: two ships. Can't nuke the whole planet even if your Agent Directives allowed it. Our side: one entire planet. Can we nuke two spaceships seven light years from their nearest reinforcements? We can."

This is not good news. "But—" you say, and stop; if Tanaga doesn't know what you're going to say next, you're certainly not going to help out.

"But the Dzebyet," he says, filling in expertly. "That was a miscalculation as well, wasn't it, Morgan? Once we've decapitated your revolution and blown up your ships, the little monkeys won't feel any need to do you a favor, no? They have nothing to gain from you, and a good deal to fear from us."

"But then—" you say, and stop.

"But the Ikkyū-jin," he supplies. "Fucked, without the Dzebyet air support. Did you really think you were a step ahead of us, all this time, instead of a step behind? We'd had our suspicions of the local Peace Party for some time. Now, thanks to you, the traitors have revealed themselves, and have been dealt with."

"I don't think—"

"Gen. Hitsumi? A sad case, to be sure. One of the founding fathers of the Glorious Revolution— one of those who prepared the way for our More than Adequate Leader. But you don't maintain absolute power for a hundred years by allowing sentiment to overwhelm vigilance. He's been dealt with as well."

"You—"

"Haven't mentioned the virus or the dissidents, I know. Fizzled. Must be disappointing for you— I know it is for us. We expected more from your side, really—more than one rather unimaginative Agent."

"Well, I suppose I should congratulate you," you say, bitterly. "You're free to oppress your own people for another decade or two, till the next Agent comes along, or till the Dzebyet decide to lob a black hole at you once and for all. I just have one question..."

"What's that?"

"Well, since you're going to kill me anyway—"

"Or let you rot here forever."

"Or let me rot here forever, you'd might as well tell me what Ormant and Kumari are up to. Starting their own empire, was what we figured— four star systems to begin with, and with the Incatena in disrepute, and reeling from whatever financial shenanigans Ormant can whip up, perhaps more..."

Tanaga laughs. "You don't think I'm going to fall for that one, do you? I never could swallow those bad-guy-reveals-plans-to-hero-who-then-escapes scenes in the holos. Being in the business and all."

"Aw, you just don't *know* what they're doing."

"You don't think so?"

"Yeah, that's what I think."

"Well, I do know, but I'm not telling you."

"Because you don't know. But don't worry, you've told me something already. And that should worry you, because you don't know that I have a biophotonic signaler operating right now..."

The officer suddenly scowls. "We did a nanoscan when you came in, and all we found was a cheap inoculated watch and an explosive device wired to your #15 molar, which we removed."

"The decoy," you suggest, weakly.

"You're still here, aren't you?" he counters, unassailably.

"So what do you want from me?"

"The full story, of course. From the beginning."

"I'd love to help you," you lie, "but I can't. Inserted blocks, you know. I get epileptic attacks just thinking about it."

Tanaga sighs. "This isn't a bad job, Morgan-san. Good benefits, nice people to work with, excellent channeling of aggressive instincts. But I frankly find this part tedious. The breaking of the will part, I mean. If you don't mind, I think I'm going to leave it to my assistants here. You know them already, I believe."

You hadn't paid much attention to the guards. You turn around slowly. They smile at you. Their smiles are not what you'd call friendly, but they are familiar, terribly familiar. It's Pasty and Nasty.

"So good to see you again in these circumstances which are less pleasant than before," says Pasty.

"What he said," says Nasty, cracking his knuckles.

Next time, you decide, the boss can execute his own damn missions.

Bad news

"I've got a plan," Cramer confides.

"Oooooohhhhhaaaarrrgh," you say.

"I think we can get out of here through the hole in the floor. Bet you wish you'd thought of that earlier, eh?"

"Nnnnhhaaarrggghhh."

"I made a little discovery. You know what it is?"

"Mmmnnnnnmmmnnnnmmmnnnhh."

"We can use our tin cups to chip away at the floor near the hole. It's made of soft stone— it chips. Kind of a damn big hole in the security arrangements, huh? It may take us a few days, but we're gonna get out of here."

"Oooooohhhhhhrrrrrrrggghhh," you say, bitterly.

An interrogation can be conceived as a chess game— to be sure, a chess game in which one player can cause the other enormous pain at will. Organizers of chess tournaments have in fact tried such improvements, in an attempt to make the game more hologenic; but they generally consider it more sporting to arm both sides. Interrogators are aware that their own practice may err on the side of injustice, but they are a conservative lot and prefer doing things the old way.

Being predictable, they are subject to study, and Interrogation Survival was one of your best subjects at the Incatena Academy, right after Psychopathology of Aliens. You can still remember kindly old Dr. Ieoua-Czyrnczyk— V^5C^{10} as the students called him— explaining the principles of Obfuscation, Pseudo-Revelation, and Biofeedback, and demonstrating various brutal attacks and psycho-technic intimidation techniques on the terrorized students. "Not to worry— if there is anything left of you alive, we can patch you up," he promised. What fun years those were!

As in other areas of diplomacy, the technological edge has moved back and forth over the millennia. The invention of the neural shunt, which allowed an Agent to smile pleasantly and even hum a tune as limbs were chopped off and plasma was applied to valuable areas, unbalanced things considerably. The other side soon had a countermeasure in its large and meaty hands: neuroscanning, in which neural structure is duplicated photonically and analyzed by AIs specially trained to rivet out every secret you have, from plans for world domination to the taradiddles you whispered to your kindergarten deskmate. There were side effects, such as the destruction of the brain being analyzed, but this was not always considered a minus.

The eventual response was neurimplants that would blow up the brain before it could be scanned— not much consolation to the brain in question, of course. Neuromapping came along to detect the neurimplants; genofixing stepped in to provide biological defenses undetectable by nanodevices. And so it went, for centuries.

The present time is something of an impasse, and both sides have been thrown back upon earlier resources. Fortunately, Dr. Ieoua-Czyrnczyk had insisted for centuries on teaching the old techniques. Too many Agents protected by the latest neuro- and nanotechnology had been caught up by a simple lie detector, or by tricks interrogators learned in the first week of Effective Interrogation (sometimes from Dr. Ieoua-Czyrnczyk, who taught the course in alternate years).

It seems like the questions are without end. Who were your principal contacts in Atami? Who were your principal contacts in Ikkyū-shima? Who did you talk to at the Commerce Association? What were the sources of the Incatena's information on Okura? Why did you move to the Hotel Otani? How many warriors were in the illegal meeting of the Shadowmen? How many pop singers had the Incatena corrupted? Was Meillet part of the plot? Was the Oji part of the plot? How much Incatena money has been diverted to the Okurinese revolution? What are the chief exports of Ikkyū-shima? What is the capital of Shr?

You respond with a mixture of arrogant refusals, prepared lies, evasions, meaningless but confirmable truths, and bits of simulated insanity— V^5C^{10}'s best conventional defense against a conventional interrogation. The best way to hide information— certainly a lot easier and leading to less frequent beatings than attempting to maintain a noble silence— is to submerge it in drivel. It's a lesson taught every day by the Vee.

Tanaga listens, asks thousands of questions, treats you badly one day and courteously the next, awakens you in the middle of the night for extended sessions, makes promises and threats, harangues you with political diatribes, consoles you, drinks with you, slaps you. In a word, he carries out all the standard methods for shaking you up and information out. And, at never quite predictable moments, he turns you over to Pasty and Nasty for persuasion of a more hands-on style.

There are methods for inflicting pain without leaving a bruise. Pasty and Nasty do not bother with these. Bruises, wounds, and missing digits are, obviously, not counted against them; or if they are, they're not the kind of people who obsess over a performance review. They enjoy their work, these boys, it's easy to see that.

And yet you persevere, pulling yourself up after the bloody beatings, mustering the strength to keep up the war of nerves with Tanaga, sleeping like a hog in the filth of the cell in between times, or fighting with Cramer over the nameless broth and thin rice gruel you're given.

Something is wrong in all of this, you realize. It's not easy to resist— but it should be harder. You've scarcely spilled anything of significance, even counting only your true statements, and you've only had to fake three shamefaced revelations and one bout of dementia. And Tanaga's tricks, though they've been expertly executed and would perhaps fool a civilian, have all been easy to see through.

Tanaga is only going through the motions. The regime doesn't really expect to learn anything from you. Why is that? Has its victory really been as total as Tanaga claims?

You soon learn.

Tanaga's voice is low and hypnotic. "There's no use in resisting us any further. We have all the information we need. All we want from you is confirmation of a few details."

"Yes, of course," you say, in as bright an impersonation of a cheeky upper class officer as a bruised sack of scurvied bones can muster.

"You've played your part very well, I don't mind telling you. Your masters would be proud of you. But there's no point in playing the game any longer. You'll just get yourself killed—you'll waste away if nothing else. You do see that, don't you?"

"An irrational hope sustains me," you mutter. "One day, all the peoples of the Galaxy will be free. One day..."

"One day you're going to bore me to death," confesses Tanaga. "There's no need for pretenses on my end either, Morgan. We have all the information we need because we have agents of our own, Morgan. Very accomplished agents."

"Like these?" you say, contemptuously, pointing at Pasty and Nasty. They scowl at you. It's one of life's little pleasures.

"One of them has been a key player in your own case," continues Tanaga, imperturbably. "Allow me to introduce the two of you, and you can judge the level of accomplishment for yourself."

He presses a switch on his desk, the door opens, and the betrayer enters, with a smile that seems cruel and oddly warm.

"Not that you haven't met Lt. Col. Ba already."

Can we still be friends?

"Ba?" you say.

"The same." The voice is as thrilling, the eyes are as deep and as blue, the short black hair is as fetching as ever; but now the body is packed into the uniform of the Okurinese secret police. Ba, Ba, black sheep— who would have believed it?

"I don't understand," you say, not understanding.

"Don't you really?" asks Ba.

"I can't believe it. I *trusted* you, like an idiot..."

You shake your head, disgusted by the betrayal and by yourself. It was Ba's fierce questioning of your motives on your first date that lulled you, you decide. It seemed like too risky a move for a spy.

Ba looks you over. "I'm sorry to see you like this, baby. I did care for you, you know. I *do* care for you."

"I know, maybe we could be friends," you say, bitterly.

Ba laughs. The laugh is the same as ever, too. Come to think of it, you never really liked Ba's laugh. Too cold, somehow. An agent of the secret police might have a laugh like that.

A wonderful thought occurs to you. "I'm sure this is a trick, Ba," you say. "You've been captured as well, and forced to play this shameful charade, but no matter what you say I'll believe in you, as I came to know you, as you really are..."

"You know how I turned you down the first time you asked me out?"

"Yeah," you allow.

"Then I came back and accepted?"

"Yeah."

"I was ordered to."

"Ba, how could you do this? How can you sleep at night? How can you look yourself in the mirror?"

"I *am* sorry about it, from the moral point of view and all," says Ba. "But it was too good to pass up, really. This way I can

187

get a promotion from Trainee/Footpad all the way up to Senior Espionneur/Backstabber."

"They must have threatened your family," you say.

"No, not really. It was my mother that suggested I send my résumé to the Home Ministry. Everything else, it comes and goes, big risk, but there's always work there, she said."

"I'm glad your career is going so well," you say.

"You're bitter, aren't you?"

"Of course I'm bitter. Why wouldn't I be?"

"You have every right to be," says Ba. "Would you like to talk about your feelings?"

"I'm sorry, Ba, I don't think this relationship can work out."

"Why's that?"

"Because you betrayed me to the secret police!"

Too late you remember another Agent Directive, even if it's the technically ignorable section called *Heuristics*: Keep the inevitable local romance out of the job, even if the subject is really beautiful. *Especially* if they're really beautiful.

"Tanaga, I think you've done enough for the day," you say. "How about letting me go back to my cell and stew for awhile?"

Tanaga looks at you with a slight smile, whether of triumph or commiseration, it's hard to say. "Sure," he shrugs.

Now, the bitter, witty comment to throw in Ba's face as you pass. "Feeling proud of yourself?" No, no, too obvious. "I don't know how you pass a mirror without spitting." Too melodramatic. "How many other people have you slept with for your job?" Too vulgar. "The Agent Directives have a word for people like you." Too bureaucratic. "A thousand autumn moons will pass, but the traitor finds no peace." Too esoteric.

You're halfway back to your cell.

That evening, on the off chance that Tanaga was lying about having had your bomb removed, you bite down so hard on a molar that it comes out.

Not one of your better moments

They make Agents out of stern stuff. You have been betrayed, but you hardly show it, not beyond the tantrum— you couldn't really call it that, it was more of a demonstration— in the interrogation room. Lying inert for hours on end on the soggy pile of stuffing you call your bed, collapsing into mournful wails, raging at the heavens, all you were really doing was mustering the courage to go on, to face whatever other cruel tragedies a heartless cosmos might next send to afflict you.

It's not like it's the first relationship you've ever had. Oh, you've had plenty— you're quite the heartbreaker. You have that intriguing smile, those rueful eyes, that tell that your heart has been broken, in your short hundred-thirty-odd years, more times than any human being can be expected to bear. You'll get over it. There's other fish in the sea. There's other pips in the pomegranate. There's other gumdrops in the candy store. It's a setback, yes, but you'll take it in your stride. Didn't mean anything to you, really.

That no-good, rotten, lying, seductive, blue-eyed piece of colonial crap! What did Ba take you for anyway? Besides a sap and a sucker, that is?

How can anyone sleep with someone because their superiors ordered them to, anyway? It's just not something you can understand. You've never slept with someone just because it was part of your job— you had to enjoy it, as well.

"I *do* care for you." It's like a broken data recorder is feeding it to you on an endless loop, till your brain echoes with it. The sorry story started in a directive and ended in betrayal, but perhaps there was love in between. It couldn't have *all* been an act. Even now Ba might be alone in a room, crying like a broken child. "Why did I do it? I should be in that stinking prison cell in Morgan's place... Still, I *am* a lieutenant colonel now; I'd better make the best of it. This is a big city; I'll find someone else."

189

You've never been that good at revenge fantasies. You try again; you imagine Ba at your knees, begging for forgiveness, apologizing for the shameful act which not only betrayed you but condemned an entire planet to untold years of dictatorial misery. "It's all right," you say, magnanimously, drawing the sobbing Ba into your arms. "It was just a stupid mistake, that's all. Just a stupendously bad error of judgment. You're really not the kind of person to cold-bloodedly betray a lover." "I am, actually," says Ba. "I mean, I didn't exactly enjoy it, but it wasn't anything like as hard to do as I'd thought. All my friends told me I wouldn't be able to sleep nights, but that really hasn't been a problem, not with the pills. I've been working for the Home Ministry for years, after all. It's like your first killing; at first you think you'll never be able to do it, but after your fifth or sixth time it's nothing."

At last your Ancient French will be of some use; Cardinal Richelieu, the Éminence Rouge of France, is here in your cell. You recognize him instantly from his portraits: the voluminous red robes, lifted fastidiously above the muck of the floor; the narrow, handsome face, with its large piercing eyes and neat goatee; the decorations awarded by his master, Louis XIII; the striking beretta, sitting like a red loaf of bread atop his head.

You bow, and welcome the Cardinal-Duc to your humble abode, and apologize for being unable to offer the King's chief minister a welcome worthy of his position.

The cardinal waves aside your declarations with some impatience. "I am not simply a man of the church but also a soldier, and as such unfazed by conditions of the utmost squalor," he reminds you.

"Certainly, Monseigneur; but I nonetheless regret my inability to offer Your Eminence so much as a bottle of *vin ordinaire*. Nonetheless I am at your service, body and soul, though the former is weak and with bad teeth, and the latter is somewhat unhinged, as a result of an unfortunate reverse in the field of love."

"Many a gentleman of good will and noble heart has found that particular field to be treacherous," comments the great man. "Was I not myself spurned, to great personal chagrin, by Anne of Austria?"

"Were you? I thought the historians had largely discredited that rumor."

The Cardinal dismisses the subject with a wave of his hand. "It is of no account. To business," he says. "Now, I know you are not of my party, and it is to be regretted, for I do not consider you an enemy. You are a worthy and courageous soul, of fine intelligence, obedient to your superiors, and skilled in the arts of war, and I would be glad to have such a one as you in my service."

"Leaving my native Mars, my father recommended to me to earn my living with wit and valor, and to stand for no insult, except at the hand of the boss, and Your Eminence. I would be sorry indeed if, in my service of the former, I showed any lack of devotion to the latter, especially inasmuch as I have been chiefly active against the Director of Okura, and not the *ancien régime*."

The cardinal smiles weakly, as if tiring of everyday hypocrisy. "Did you not conspire with outwardly loyal but inwardly rebellious provinces of the realm? Did you not have dealings with foreign military powers, and with those who owe much to the sovereign but rewarded his patronage with treachery, and also with defenders of liberties of thought unrecognized by the laws of the King?"

When you still seem to hesitate, he hisses, "Don't get hung up on the French angle, kid; it's an analogy."

"Oh, *right*," you say. "You *would* be for absolute power, and Machiavellian intrigue, and all that."

"That charge is but a calumny of my detractors," frowns the cardinal. "I have always worked for the good of the state, and not simply that of the monarch. The people prosper when there is order, when the state is powerful, respected by its enemies at home and abroad, when the church (or the Party in this case) is of the highest morality, when there is freedom of thought but not freedom of agitation against authority. The Peace Party has pursued no tyranny, except in the service of these virtues. I pray also that you will weigh in my favor my founding of the Academy, and the volumes of plays, theology, memoirs, and political science I have submitted for the consideration of posterity."

"And are there no higher authorities?" you counter. "France, er, Okura belongs to the Incatena, as well as to the galactic community at large."

"I commend your idealism, which is becoming in the young; but let us not exaggerate the real importance of these institutions, which is scarcely greater than, say, the Papacy, or the Holy Roman Empire, both of which I respect, but have not hesitated to oppose (despite the advice of many well-meaning ideologues on my own right wing) when the interests of the State called for it."

"Really? I thought it was mostly just a personal vendetta against the Duke of Buckingham."

"He was a nothing," sniffs the Cardinal-Duc. "I do not even boast of his defeat; he defeated himself. Did he not most dishonorably break his promises to the Rochellais?"

"I believe Your Eminence threatened to expose his liaisons with the Queen," you point out.

"Oh come on, Dumas just had it in for me," says Richelieu. "These tawdry bits of gossip have nothing to do with how affairs of state proceed."

"Your Eminence has to admit that such tawdriness proved useful in disposing of the former Station Chief of the Incatena."

The *Éminence Rouge* laughs in the friendly way of a man whose opponent has just set himself up for a knight fork. "I would think you would not be quick to bring up the memory of this Station Chief," he says. "The representative of the interstellar order you would have me respect— a puppet to his own appetites, and by no means hostile to the ideology of a state supposedly in violation of the *Traité de l'Incatène*."

"An aberration, as I'm sure Your Eminence will admit."

"Actually he was pretty much of a piece with the last four Station Chiefs."

"A fairly common aberration," you allow.

"Perhaps like Ormant?" enquires the cardinal, ironically.

"He's on *your* side," you protest.

"But he is a product of yours," counters Richelieu. "The most powerful men of the Incatena seem not to be very loyal to it."

"With the utmost of respect, Monseigneur, that's completely lame. It's no argument against freedom that some poltroons make use of it."

"Yes it is," snaps the cardinal.

"No it isn't."

"Yes it is."

"Are there not abuses of authority among authoritarians? Those who sacked the Huguenot cities, despite Your Eminence's own example of clemency in La Rochelle?"

"I see what you mean," concedes the leader of the *Conseil d'en haut*, and adds, mumbling into his beard, "Truly this one must be mine."

He turns to you with a smile. "Some wine?"

"I would be most pleased."

He produces a bottle, fills your tin cup, and pours himself a glass as well. You watch him... were his eyes that large in the paintings?

"My dear Morgan, you must have noticed the lenient treatment you have so far received."

"I am alive," you concede. "In prison and hallucinating a conversation with a 17th century French cardinal, but alive."

"You must not blame me for choosing to negotiate from a superior position," says the protégé of Marie de' Medici, smoothly. "If you have been spared torture and death, it is due to my intercession and my favor, and I have not been unopposed within the Party."

"I'm grateful, Monseigneur," you say. "Where's this wine from? Anjou? Dijon?"

"Yomiuri supermarket. To continue, it has been and remained my conviction that you may yet be of great use to us. Your own cause being lost, will you not join with us, incurring pardon for your actions on behalf of a godless and unbridled individualism by placing your considerable talents at the service of order, piety, and realism?"

"Certainly not," you declare. "How could I betray my principles and the Human Incatena for a mere— how much did you say you were offering?"

"Two hundred thousand *pistoles d'or*, or roughly C. 1 million at the current rate of exchange, plus titles of nobility, a late-model volant, and a competitive benefits package."

"You do me too great an honor. Rather, observe with what effect I acquit myself in the coming siege of La Rochelle— oh bloody hell, is that coming or already passed?"

"What *are* you talking about?"

"I don't think I can do it," you clarify. "Previous commitments, and all."

"Did I mention that you would be working with a certain Lt. Col. Ba, of whom I believe you have already made the acquaintance?"

Your heart churns. You look closely at the terror of Huguenot and Habsburg. Details swim before your eyes— the Maltese
cross hanging from an enormous blue ribbon round the prelate's
neck, the long brown boots, the emblem of the Peace Party— but
they refuse to coalesce into a stable picture, and you can't seem to
find the controls. You feel light-headed and weak in the feet.

"That changes everything," you mutter.

"I'm pleased to hear it," says the Cardinal-Duc.

"Completely treacherous and untrustworthy, of course,"
you add.

"Morgan, you idiot, take it," says Cramer.

"What? What are you doing here, Cramer?"

"I live here."

"You're completely out of period," you complain, glaring at
the frozener. You look at the cardinal almost apologetically, but
he only smiles indulgently. Doesn't it bother either of them that
the floor won't settle down?

"You're in bad shape, Morgan." says Cramer. "Whatever
these Japs are offering, *take* it. Live to fight another day, right?"

"He's *French*," you object.

"This is what I know, this is what I fucking *do*, Morgan,"
says Cramer. "Negotiations. You've got the short end of the
stick, being in this fucking prison, but the fact that they're dealing
at *all* means you *got* something."

"But..."

"Your companion is *astucieux*," smiles the cardinal, offering
his hand. You can't see anything but that hand; you reach for it
before it disappears. But you are left in darkness anyway.

Someone is shaking you awake, bringing into consciousness
a heavy tongue, a wooly head, an empty yet turbulent stomach,
and aches in every muscle in your body.

"Cramer, get the hell away," you murmur. "I was better off
asleep."

"Sorry to wake you, o-san," says the doctor. "It'll just be a
moment."

Hospital

Your body is a public place. You have the sensation of one doctor after another cutting into it, injecting chemicals and nanocures, reconstructing and rearranging like the new owners of a particularly tacky house. You see yourself among them, bending heads together, consulting AIs, trying to piece together this shattered wreck of a human being. You feel yourself hovering above your own body, feeling nothing, hearing music with lots of schmaltz and strings, and at the same time experiencing a background of pain that is infinite.

Surely this is more pain than a person can be expected to bear. A certain amount of pain to warn you of danger or damage, fine; but what demon designed the human body to respond so exquisitely to the spectrum of physical pain, when there's nothing to be done about it? You call feverishly for more painkillers. A nursing mec shows up, consults its computer overlords, and announces you that you are on the maximum allowable dose.

You wake up one day without internal organs. Your chest looks like a large machine has been driven through it, and there's no internal sensations at all— no heart, no lungs, no stomach, no bladder. In place of a heartbeat, there's a soft gushy whir. You aren't breathing, but there's no sensation of holding your breath, or needing air— there's no sensation at all. You try breathing in, and you can, but there's no feeling of your chest rising, although a bag attached to one of the machines surrounding you deflates momentarily.

A nursing mec turns an optic toward you. "You're awake, are you? Don't worry. We'll be done here shortly."

"What the hell are you doing? Where's my organs?" You have to talk in short bursts, using and re-using the air in the little plastic bag.

"Over there," says the mec, waving a manipulator. You look; there's a row of transparent tubs along the side of the room, sprouting tubes and monitors— modern canopic jars, life support systems for detached organs.

"But what are you *doing*?" you ask. You try to get up, but you're stuck like a bug; all you can do is jiggle your arms and legs a little.

"You were in bad shape, we're doing an overhaul," explains the mec. "Can we do anything to make you comfortable? You want to watch a holo or anything?"

"We're getting high adrenaline readings back here," says a mechanical voice behind your head, quickened almost to the point of incomprehensibility, the way mecs speak when they address one another.

"The patient's awake, that's why," chirps the nursing mec.

"I'm panicking, that's why," you clarify. "Are those my *organs* over there?"

"Dose in some opiates, would you," comes the loud, deep voice of the main surgical mec, who seems to be near— no, who *is* the machine merged with your midsection. "I can't work with all this quivering."

"Okay," chirps a voice behind you.

"Wait a—"

The next time you're aware of anything, your basic allotment of guts has been restored, and it's all hurting, as if trying to make up for lost time.

You feel warm and well, healed and healthy, and then you wake up. It's cold and once more your body is a quilt of sharp pains and dull aches. You'd never noticed before that you could dream temperatures.

You ache; but the hot rush of fever and delirium is gone; now you are merely a sick person convalescing. Your previous existence seems less than a memory; reality now is an endless succession of tests, nursing mecs, plastic food, and pathetic weakness.

But they cure you, of course. A little malnutrition, torture, and disease is nothing to modern medicine, if modern medicine is allowed to get its hands and probes on you. You have a new set of teeth now, new lungs and kidneys, new skin on most of your body, all built from your own phenotype (itself a confused mixture of your own genetic heritage and alterations acquired by genofixing over the course of a subjective century). Nanocures have scrubbed out your insides, and a sophisticated AI has even checked over your neural structure, patching up signs of incipient dementia. There is a precise etiquette for this; trauma caused by the interrogation, for instance, can be removed; but your feelings at Ba's betrayal are considered natural, and left untouched.

A young man is sitting by the side of your bed, observing. You've seen him several time now; you don't know if he's a doctor, an interrogator, a guard. He's handsome and smiling, in the way of a Peace Party functionary or a Mormon doctor. He sports a neat goatee, and carries a pocket datanode, which he uses to take notes. He greets you politely when he enters, or when you wake up while he's watching, but makes no conversation.

When you're well enough to get out of bed, he accompanies you in your walks down the hospital corridor, guiding you and supporting your arm with his.

"That's it. Our job is done," the surgical mec says one day. It barely slows its words down for the humans present; it's obviously one of those AIs that deeply resent having to operate at biological speed. "Doesn't need anything but some good rest. Right as rain."

Right as rain? Run through a tornado is more like what you feel.

The young man is there, along with an older man you've never seen before, and a menacing-looking gaggle of mecs.

"How much rest?" asks the young man.

"It hardly matters, does it?" growls the older man. "We've got all the time in the world."

"That's true."

"A few weeks," says the surgical mec. AIs tend not to be quick on the uptake when it comes to noticing when their information is no longer needed.

"We'll take it from here," the young man informs it. "Thanks very much for your services," he adds, and bows.

"Pleasure," says the surgeon. "Bill to the Peace Party, as usual?"

"That's right."

"Pleasure," says the surgeon again, and bustles off immediately on its small wheels. The old man leaves with him.

The young man looks at you a moment. His eyes are gen-ofixed to be extra large, somewhere between disturbing and freakish. There's a perpetual half-smile on his face, as if there were no more amusing place to be than a hospital.

"Time for a walk," he tells you.

"I don't feel up to it," you say.

"You've got to build up your muscles," he points out.

"The surgical mecs can do that."

"It doesn't last. The brain doesn't build the right paths if you don't do it yourself."

You sigh, get out of bed, and follow him out the room. You don't need his arm for support any more.

"I suppose you're only doing this to get me ready for some more interrogations," you say, bitterly.

"Interrogations, no," he says, with a chuckle. "We've got other plans for you."

"Yeah, keep me on ice."

"In a sense. Shall we walk outside the ward a bit?"

You're interested, despite your bad attitude. He's leading you through a set of doors you've never been taken through before. The corridor beyond is as bland and institutional as those inside what your host or guard calls the ward; it could be the upper floors of your former prison. You take an elevator to another level, and now you're in a carpeted hallway, with indirect lighting and bulk-discounted prints on the walls; this could be a corporate office or a hotel, though it's strangely cramped.

You come to a lounge. It's night; the stars are a spectacular sight in the wraparound windows.

You recognize the constellations, not only because of your Agent training, but because you've often sought out these particular stars, to gaze thoughtfully at the dim little point that is Sol.

There's a bright point of light in an unaccustomed position. A planet, perhaps? You ask the young man, though you don't expect Peace Party drones to have much interest in astronomy.

"That? That's β Hydri," he replies.

You stare at him, then back at the star. It's much too bright to be a planet, you now realize.

You're not in any sort of office building; you're on a shuttle, heading for a quickship.

II

The people of New Bharat are pleased to welcome non-indigent travelers who wish contribution to the project of building free and wealthy New Bharat!

Visitors are reminded to attune their neurimplants to New Bharat Colony Corporation algorithms for correct life support billing.

—Display node, Colony Base spaceport site

The Duress Faction

"We do intend to build a spaceport," Chattanji assures you. "However, it's still a young world, although completely modern and self-sufficient, and such a thing is not being possible."

Your new acquaintance, and captor, emphasizes his words with emphatic gestures; as he's also brandishing a small laser the effect is a bit alarming.

You look around; it wouldn't be inaccurate to describe the view as a desolated field of rocks plus a shuttle and a cabstand. The ground is blasted and scarred by plasma exhaust. On three sides of you there are low, distant, rocky hills; in one direction (thanks to your inoculated clock, you know that if you were on Okura it'd be east) the valley empties out into a vast, flat desert, empty except for a few dismal clumps of blue-green vegetation.

"They could have built a snack bar or something," you comment.

"There are not so many flights," says Chattanji. "One every two weeks, perhaps. Whoever needs to meet a shuttle takes a taxi; there's really no need for anything here. We are a young world, Morganji. You shall find that efficiency is the key, here. No wasted effort. Here, you! Lazy bum!"

One of the taxi drivers looks up, puts his hands together and bows.

Chattanji remembers he's holding a gun, and puts it away. "How much to the Congress Hotel?"

"Two credits, babaji."

"Seventh son of a bandit! Do you take me for a heathen, or a rich man, or a donkey? I'll give you a half credit."

"I have a family to support, babaji, six children, and barely two hectares of land. Don't jeopardize your salvation with stinginess; give at least a credit and a half."

201

"Contemptible low-caste scum, you shouldn't have so many brats if you can't support them, it isn't my problem. Three quarters of a credit."

"Begging the pardon of a selfish oppressor like yourself, babaji, but I came to this planet so that I could hold my head high, and let God give me all the children I want, and I won't accept less than C. 1.25."

"Damn me, this sort of cockroach should be squashed with a boot, and not allowed to molest innocent travelers. Do you think for a moment I'd let you extort more than one credit from myself, an honest person?"

"For one credit you can hike over that hill there and walk to town, if your stinking feet were up to honest work, which I doubt. For one-ten, however, you are welcome in my taxi, which moreover is air-conditioned."

"Scavenger jackal, you'll start your next life as a parasite in an unholy river," exclaims your host, opening the back door of the taxi. The two of you get in.

"Congress Hotel, was it, babaji?" asks the driver, amiably.

"Yes, yes."

The volant lifts off, and speeds away from the makeshift spaceport at a reckless pace.

Chattanji hunts through his pockets. "You don't have any spare change, do you?"

"Sorry, they took all my personal effects back on Okura."

"That's damned typical of them," complains Chattanji, excavating some coins out of a pocket of his suit. "We are supposed to take care of their problems, no? They send us a prisoner, but in what conditions? Completely indigent. We are self-sufficient, but we are not a rich planet, we are not a Sihor here."

"It doesn't seem fair," you offer.

"They're just lucky it was our faction to which you were entrusted," mutters your captor.

"Which faction is that?" you ask, smoothly.

"The Duress Faction."

"You're the Duress Faction of the Freedom Movement? What's the other faction?"

"The Static Faction."

"What's the difference?"

Chattanji sighs. "It all started with Bannerji. He and Bakhtiar were co-directors of the Movement— directors as a terminological nicety, you understand; the Political Council was organized along purely democratic lines. Bakhtiar was really the *primus inter pares*, due to his ideological abilities, but Bannerji was receiving a good deal of respect as well. He was in charge of the street thugs."

"I take it he's in the Duress Faction," you suggest.

"This was before the factions— the present factions, I mean. When Chakko was arrested by the damned NBCC fascists—"

"Who was Chakko?"

"Operations commissioner. As I am saying, once Chakko was arrested there was a hole in the structure, and Bannerji and Bakhtiar both wanted to fill it. We reorganized instead, and Ganesh was put in as a kind of buffer zone."

"Ah yes. The elephant-headed god," you say.

"*Named* for him, yes," Chattanji specifies. "However, we are entirely rejecting antiquated superstition; the Freedom ideology is science-based."

"You don't support the Satyampur folks, then?" you ask, with some surprise.

"What do you know about Satyampur?" Chattanji asks, with sudden suspicion. "Damn me, you're not a spy, are you? What were you arrested for anyway?"

"You don't know?"

"That part of Haikoa's transmission got jumbled."

"Ideological errors," you say.

Chattanji looks at you with a sour expression. "Yes, yes. So that's *our* problem, naturally. They could deal with their own damned ideological antisepsis, especially in a civil war situation."

For some minutes you've been in a city, if that's the word for it— Colony Base, as a few signs confirm, the premier city of New Bharat. It's not much less empty than the spaceport, though the ground is now littered with buildings and clumps of buildings— huge red solid-looking things, evidently made from the same rock the plain is made of; but each one is the solitary occupant of a huge square of land. The city sprawls on for kilometers, but so sparsely that the total population is barely over a hundred thousand. No city center or any particular high-density sector is visible. You peer down with interest at the anachronisms: small farms; ground vehicles and roads for them to move on; stone fences; a small oil refinery.

The taxi swoops down and lands in front of a large brick building, which looks like it's been hit by a bomb. Closer inspection shows that it's a case of construction rather than destruction. Judging from its unfinished framework, the Congress Hotel was intended to be twenty storeys high and house several thousand guests; perhaps a tenth of it is complete. There are cranes and building materials scattered about, but they're rusted and sandblown; it doesn't look like there's been any construction activity for the last decade.

Chattanji pays the driver and leads you inside, complaining all the while of the Peace Party.

"*They* have *jails*— damned nasty and effective ones, I've seen them. So they no doubt imagine that the Freedom Movement has its own damned jails too. Damn me, I wish it did! Failing that, however, Morganji, we must house you here, in a hotel. A hotel! You must wonder what sort of political movement we are."

"I quite understand," you assure him. "No need to apologize."

"Thank you. You at least are understanding," says Chattanji, signing the register. "*They're* going to pick up the tab, damn me, if I have to personally beat that tight-fisted goat, Akamura-ji, to the consistency of wood pulp. I don't care if the datamoot is coming up. Do you want to see the room?"

"I'm not in any hurry."

"Let's have a drink," he suggests.

You settle yourselves in the bar, which is large, dark, and almost empty. The decor is an imitation of New Delhi knockoffs of 47th century Sihor. Chattanji orders a local liqueur, made from one of the desert plants; it's a little bitter, but good. There's a row of outsystem intoxicants above the bar, but the prices are as astronomical as their origins, and they are coated with a layer of dust.

"So, where was I...."

"The elephant man."

"Yes, yes. Ganesh made a little too much of the propaganda department, and took the whole council in the direction of collaborationist interventionism. Akamura-ji was furious, and although of course she has no official place in the council at all, not even observer status, she does have influence."

"Naturally."

"We had another reorganization, and then the Union Faction broke off— that's the Freedom Movement (U) you've probably heard of, you absolutely must not confuse those cockroaches with us— with *either* of us. Bannerji was in charge of the propaganda division for some time, then."

"Who got the street thugs?"

"They were divided between Bakhtiar and Kapur, which was a big mistake, of course— the two gangs immediately started fighting each other. Then when Bannerji was found in the university garbage dump with a bullet hole between his eyes..."

The story goes on and on, and you start to have trouble following the details. You never do understand how the factions arose, or what their relationship was to Bannerji and Bakhtiar, both of whom are long gone. The Duress Faction is, as its name indicates, in favor of coercive provocation— guerrilla actions to create a political presence, kidnapping and bank theft to bring in cash— tax revenue, as it's called in anticipation of the eventual accession to power. The Static Faction of the Movement trusts more in infiltration and propaganda, with the aim of building a popular base and dominating the ideological climate.

Amateurs, you think. Probably got their strategy and tactics from watching the holos.

The two factions were hardly speaking before, but since the Okurinese civil war started, the Movement has been effectively divided in two; each faction disowns the other, has its own Political Council, and claims to be the sole representative of the Freedom Movement on New Bharat.

The Okurinese Party knows nothing about the division, of course— the news will only reach Okura in five years— but both sides nonetheless feverishly monitor news and secret communications from Okura, attempting to divine clues which would indicate Okurinese support for one faction or the other. It's more or less an accident that you're in the hands of the Duress Faction— the Party representatives on the ship, comming ahead from the quickship as it approached the planet, happened to use codewords in the Duress Faction's hands. Chattanji makes the most of the opportunity; he grills you on what you know of the situation on Okura and the ideological currents of the Peace Party.

Finally he takes you to your room, which is well furnished in New Bharat's primitive style; no gravity controls or Tajima bed, of course, but a datanode, music node, and the scriptures of six major religions.

Chattanji apologizes once more for not having a proper jail, or even a proper guard; the planet is self-sufficient, but it is a young world and certainly doesn't have the resources to supply guards for whatever damned outsystem political parties are wanting it to guard their damned prisoners for them. He locks you in and leaves you to your own devices, which are limited, for the moment, to the machines in the room and your own inoculated clock.

News at five

The first thing you do, once you're alone, is to head for the Vee. The first thing, that is, after taking a long shower, ordering an expensive meal (mulligatawny soup, nan, tandoori chicken, eggplant curry, and vanilla ice cream) and charging it to the Duress Faction, watching a holo on New Bharat's animal life (which runs largely to insects and lizards) and taking a long, well-deserved nap.

The first thing you do on the Vee is research— the first thing, that is, after a few hours spent cruising students' home scenes looking for embarrassing pictures and gushy tributes to second-rate bands. There's also a review of the next version of SimGalaxy to check out.

Finally, you're ready to do some research. First, you turn to the news from Okura. Since light (including comm lasers) travels only a little faster than a Lepantine quickship, the news, though seven years old, dates from just a few months past the time you were spirited off the planet.

You'd suspected that Tanaga was exaggerating the success of the Peace Party's counteroffensive, but you're surprised at how much. Okura is in the midst of a three- or four-way civil war. Ikkyū-shima and Xinqeng are still in open rebellion, though both have been counter-invaded and have themselves invaded Gōsei and Muaŋ Sai. Gen. Hitsumi has declared himself the true leader of the Peace Party, and as much as a third of the Peace Army is behind him. And all the combat has been ground-based, which means the Dzebyet are still interdicting air and space attacks.

Kumari's forces did try to destroy the Incatena cruisers, but only succeeded in crippling one of them; the other dropped a couple of nukes on the Peace Army's main spaceport (presumably unnecessary in view of the Dzebyet interdict, but prudent) and on Kumari's home village (the Peace Party denies this— good confirmation that the bomb hit home in more ways than one).

208 • Against Freedom

There have been setbacks— Tandō, the capital of Ikkyū-shima is currently under occupation, and Ryoku's been arrested (you remember with a shudder talking to Ba about Ryoku and Dr. Zhou, who were friends of Ba's, after all)— but also unexpected successes. For instance, the entire Vee in the Peace Party sector, bar Atami, is down. That was certainly not in your plan, but it should add nicely to the chaos, and cripple the military and Party communications.

The official media made much of your capture and subsequent "confession" and "trial"; there's no hint of your trip here. The Peace Party— Kumari's part of it— now considers itself "the victim of an invidious war of aggression launched by the Martian Incatena against its sacred sovereignty", and Gen. Hitsumi, though he criticizes the "traitor to neoteny, former Col. Kumari" in every other respect, has been dismayingly silent when it comes to Okura's Incatena responsibilities.

Your side, or sides, had better win. If it doesn't, you hate to think of the devastation which will be visited upon the age-old, if modest, institution of human unity. Even worse, what's it going to look like on your half-century performance appraisal?

As for New Bharat, the planet is seething with constitutional unrest. The relationship between the NBCC (the commercial consortium which founded the colony) and the ICA (the de jure planetary government), as well as the future political structure of the colony, are up for grabs. Debate fills the Vee and any group of three or more New Bharatis turns into a discussion group on the topic.

The obvious progression, one that the Incatena has pushed for years, is for the ICA to develop into a true planetary administration, with the NBCC subject to its laws, or even broken up into smaller firms. However, it's the ICA that's widely portrayed as the villain of the moment, and would be dissolved if majority opinion had its way. And the Incatena, widely perceived as the sponsor or controller of the ICA, is reviled along with it.

The shoe had not long ago been on the other foot, nor were the stockings producing such an odor. Two years ago the ICA acquired a dynamic young leader, one Rama Khunarg, who had a plan for planetary progress. The first step, the election of a Planetary Parliament, was uproariously popular. The second, the long overdue creation of a planetary court system and trade commission, was a disaster.

There are more than a hundred individual colonies on New Bharat, some with only a few hundred citizens, plus thousands of villages and homesteads that don't consider themselves to be part of any larger entity. Each colony has its own courts and trade bureaucracies, and considers itself entirely sovereign. The system has worked as long as it has only because all the colonies inherited a common legal system, that of India, and because most planetary and interstellar commerce is under the control of the NBCC anyway, and thus effectively outside the cities' jurisdiction. But planetary commerce is expanding, and legal systems and trade regimes are diverging; the old system is rapidly becoming cumbersome.

Khunarg's courts would require some surrender of local autonomy to do their job, and this was intolerable. The ICA produced simulations showing that the status quo would lead to rampant protectionism and economic shrinkage in ten years or less, but no one was convinced (except the legislators in the new Planetary Parliament, who wanted something to legislate about). As a Colony Base alderman proclaimed, "We do not need any court system. Here on New Bharat a man's word is his bond; if his word is not enough he has his fists, and if his fists are not enough he has his laser." (Despite these noble sentiments, the colony courts are always snowed under with cases.)

Then came the shadowy incident known as the Shadowy Incident, in which three ICA representatives were killed in a laserfight at the fundamentalist Satyampur colony. The Satyampuris' explanation of the incident, an odd mixture of apology and diatribe, was never very clear, and the ICA, with no living eyewitnesses of its own, could add little to the story. The sympathy of New Bharat was naturally with the Satyampuris. If the ICA reps got themselves shot, it must have been because they were sticking their noses where they didn't belong, or plotting some new governmental intrusion. (In fact the representatives had been in Satyampur to discuss the founding of an agricultural college.)

It was about this time that the Freedom Movement noisily quit the Planetary Parliament, claiming that the ICA was a "proto-dictatorial organization" seeking, under dire Incatena directives, to ban the Movement as a first step to "suppressing all dissent on New Bharat."

You feel a twinge of professional admiration; you couldn't have timed it better yourself. A year previously, such a move would have been seen as a smokescreen erected by a radical organization which was itself in the pay of an outsystem dictator. Now, people shook their heads and talked about civil liberties.

Khunarg's reaction makes it clear, to you at least, that no Incatena Agents are whispering advice in his ear, or if they are, that that ear is unusually waxy. He first ignored the provocation, then invited the Movement to return and "openly discuss the future of New Bharat without prejudice," then ordered a police investigation of the finances and control structure of the Movement— "Let's see just who the terrorists report to."

Finally, just two months ago, some contracts between the NBCC and the ICA came up for renewal, and Khunarg, desperate to find a planet-pleasing issue, demanded, as part of his conditions, ICA regulation of certain NBCC activities. The New Bharatis were suspicious and somewhat shocked. Regulation is not the New Bharati way. Some of the locals try to explain it to you on the Vee.

J. Khrishnamurti from Mumbai (whose Vee avatar is an animated self-portrait— he's a handsome man with a big black moustache): "It is not like Mars here— you don't rely on some pasty office wallah to safeguard your rights. It is up to you. If you come to do business with me and you screw me— well, the next time me and my laser see you, you're going to pass a difficult quarter hour. Everyone knows this here."

"How does that apply to an interstellar business that controls half the heavy industry on New Bharat and two-thirds of the planetary product?" you ask.

R. Bhagvan, Colony Base (avatar: pink Ganesh): "If you don't like their shuttles and volants, don't get inside them. You can walk around on your own two feet here."

"And their air purifying engines, and machine shops, and infectious disease labs, and AIs, and genofixes, and comsats, and weather simulations, and the comm network we're talking over? Can you get by without those too?"

There are many vociferous responses to this; the consensus is more or less that they *could* get by without these things if they *had* to, at least till local technology catches up, but they *choose* not to, and because of this distinction the seeming total dependence of New Bharat on the NBCC is illusory.

"Doesn't it bother you that the NBCC is charging roughly twice the Incatena average for its technology, and taking millions of credits of profit outsystem?"

J. Subbia, Mumbai (avatar: small black duck): "It is balanced by the millions that get skimmed off the cash flow here."

B. Bose, Nayadelhi (avatar: a Dzebyet): "That is very likely what Khunarg's after. Did you know he tried to get a job with NBCC once, twenty years ago? He couldn't get a paw inside the biggest credit-skimming operation on New Bharat; so he is trying to build up the second biggest."

R. Bhagvan: "It will blow up in his face at the datamoot. He'll be lucky if there's anything left you could mistake for a planetary government in the dark at sixty paces."

"You need a planetary government to have Incatena membership," you point out.

J. Subbia: "Bugger the Incatena."

"So, it's all right with you if New Bharat becomes the private fief of Ormant instead?"

N. Vikam, Jaipur (avatar: image of a soap opera actress): "You haven't been on New Bharat long. This isn't anybody's fief, and if Ormant thinks it is, he is going to end up in a small horizontal fief six feet under!"

T. Rai, Gangamipur (avatar: blue and green striped tiger): "It will not be so quick as that. He has a massive estate in Pashchim Pahar and a private army."

You press for more details, but that's about all T. Rai knows (or cares to reveal). Reference datascenes provide little more: the 2600-km^2 estate, called Jaimunda, is at the other end of the continent from Colony Base, and is said to be almost entirely wilderness. No word on whether Ormant is living there, or indeed if he's ever even visited it.

You make a note of it, before remembering that you're a prisoner and shouldn't leave evidence of your preoccupations. You manage to set your notes on fire by abusing the room's cooker, and entrust the information instead to your data neurimplant.

On a whim, you look up Cardinal Richelieu in the *Ancient Times* datascene. He's described as a "political alchemist"— doing the best he could to rationalize his country's administration, but defeated by the unbelievable inefficiency of an aristocratic system, by inappropriate moralism, and by being born a millennium before the birth of socionomic theory.

The gilded cage

Fortunately, revolutionaries keep late hours too; it's nearly noon when Chattanji knocks on your door.

"Lunch?"

"Sure, I'm starved."

"How does Okurinese sound?"

"I don't know, I just spent half a year on Okura. How about Indian? I've only had one New Bharati meal so far, and it was just room service."

"I have it every day at home, but if you are insisting... The scarbeetle vindaloo is very good."

"Scarbeetle?"

"Or the riddlewasp with eggplant. I shall also recommend the giant frightwing for offworlders. They're kept in a cage in the dining room; you can pick the one you want prepared. Astonishing damned things— almost half a meter long, with a wingspan of—"

"You know, I wouldn't mind something less arthropodic."

"Eftlizard tandoori, now that is a treat," says Chattanji, without missing a beat.

"We could do Italian," you suggest.

"Let's."

Chattanji leads you to a ground transport vehicle— a sorry-looking jalopy that looks like it's held together with wire and hope.

Your host notices your look. "It's a young world, you can't expect to ride around in a damned volant."

"Oh, no, I wasn't thinking anything like that," you lie. "I take it this was made here?"

"Indeed. We are entirely self-sufficient in transport. Now, let's go. The restaurant is in the ship."

"You mean, another ship's landed?"

"The ship *neighborhood*," explains Chattanji, with some annoyance.

You don't understand, but you'll find out soon enough, you decide.

You look out the windows at the heavy stone buildings passing by on their great parcels of land, and try not to think about the unfamiliar and objectionable sensations of ground transport— the vibrations, the slight swerves and dips, the sudden starts and stops, to say nothing of the stuffy air. The windows are shut tight to allow the air processor to run. New Bharat's air is breathable, but only barely; you don't want too much exposure to it. In addition to all this, there are insect curries and eftlizard tandoori not to think about, too.

There's no doubt about when you're getting near the ship: you see it looming ahead of you, a huge, grounded space liner, more than two kilometers long. As you get closer, you realize that the ship is a ruin; huge sections have decayed or been dismantled; newer structures branch out of its bowels; portions of it are reduced to nothing but its enormous metal ribs. A railroad line passes right through the ship.

Chattanji leaves the ground transport near a port— that's one thing that can be said for New Bharati urban design, there's always parking— and you enter a section of the ship whose structure is mostly intact. The decks here are occupied by offices, industrial concerns, and shops; the restaurant is located on the highest remaining deck. It's still known as Deck 15; so fourteen decks that were once above it have vanished, leaving behind a superstructure of girders, wires, and conduits. Far above you, you can even see an array of solar panels— twisted, burned and blasted by the descent through the planet's atmosphere.

"It's the largest of the colony ships, the *Atman is Brahman*," says Chattanji. "Beautiful old thing, isn't it?"

It looks like it's gone through a war, and lost; but of course it's only the normal process of colonization. No solar system, even one as rich and quirky as Sol, can afford an unending hemorrhage of iron and other high-atomic-weight elements. Interstellar trade does not deal in bulk items, but only in items whose value far surpasses their weight: datastores (which can include anything from novels to symphonies, franchises to patents, stocks to scientific formulas to nanodupe patterns), AI cores, gene samples, seeds, nanotech devices, veneer, a few luxury goods— and human beings.[1]

The colony ship itself, then, is the colony's single largest import, a precious shipment of bulk asteroid metal, processed chemicals, heavy machinery, and other manufactures the colony will be unable to build on its own for centuries, and which will not be shipped again. The ship's facilities— medical clinic, machine shops, chemical labs, instrumentation, datanodes, and weaponry— become the high technology of the new colony; and even the fittings of the ship are designed with a second, land-bound life in mind. The cryogenic units in which the colonists sleep become refrigerators; the Lepantine drive turns into a power plant; the attitude jets are made into airplane engines.

The restaurant offers a good view of the sprawling cityscape of Colony Base. You order gnocchi in Alfredo sauce, which turns out to have a strange acidic taste. Something about the soil, Chattanji explains.

You ask your host, or jailer, if he was born on New Bharat.

"Born on a little homestead near Purijanda," he boasts. "The colony was just a few decades old then— damned primitive it was. The kids today don't know what it's like to live like that— no ground cars, no datanodes, no supermarkets, no police. Whatever we needed we made, or did without."

Some discreet questions establish that the settlement's electric system, medical supplies, pesticides, datanodes, commaudios, lasers, earthmover, and rail connection were not exactly built by hand out of rubble and spit.

Still, it must have been a difficult life. Why did his parents immigrate?

"Why? Damn me, what do you think? Back in Kolkata they had a twenty square meter apartment on the ninetieth floor of an apartment monolith, fifteen years of college and no prospect of anything but a clerkship, *if* one opened up in a hundred years; one child allowed *if* they were judged healthy enough, and meat

---

[1] For some centuries the technology has existed to send only frozen heads between star systems. When you arrive, you get a new body, whose original head is itself travelling elsewhere. Despite the service's lower cost and catchy slogan— "Head for the Stars!"— the business has never taken off, so to speak.

still too expensive for weekdays... Here, they have ten hectares of land, no restrictions on fertility, and no one to tell them what to do."

"It sounds idyllic all right, except maybe for the giant frightwings," you allow. "But still, if I may ask, if it's that wonderful here, why are you advocating violent revolution and the establishment of a Peace Party dictatorship?"

"Dictatorship? Damn me, I see why they jailed you," remarks Chattanji.

"Dictatorship by New Bharati standards," you say, a little edgily, as if any idiot should have known that's what you meant.

"New Bharat is not Okura," says Chattanji, waving his finger at you. "I have this argument with Akamura all the time. The unified ideology of the Freedom Movement may lead to differing results in different situations— for instance, an authoritarian state on Okura; on New Bharat, perhaps no state at all."

"No state at all? How do you figure?"

"On a party-theoretical level, there's no doubt about it. New Bharat is a young world, and does not need the *remaking* that Okura does," explains Chattanji. "Naturally, whilst there is resistance to the Freedom Movement, the pure ideal is not obtaining, and we will retain a firm leading role."

"But you will lead forcefully in a democratic spirit no doubt?"

"Great Krishna, no. You see with Khunarg and his gang what sort of damned foolishness happens when you have a democratic government. Modern society is too complex to be run by the masses— or the jackals who have tricked the masses into supporting them."

"That's why most societies are run by AIs," you remark.

"That's just where most societies have gone wrong," counters Chattanji. "My parents' country, India, is run by AIs; it is no advertisement for the system. They keep people from starving, but what else can be said for them? Only a human being can know what a human being needs; but most human beings are as brainless as scatterbugs. But instead of giving up control over human life to AIs, let us be creating humans as intelligent and as large-spirited as AIs. Damn you, get over here, you cockroach!"

He's addressing the waiter, ordering some dessert. They have an insect fixation, these New Bharatis, you decide.

"Now, what should we do with you?" Chattanji wonders aloud, once the tiramisù has arrived.

"Well, what are the attractions in Colony Base? I'd like to see everything."

"Colony Base is a completely modern city," Chattanji assures you. "Aqua-disco, performance malls, neurojams, Dzebyet opera, sitar polka... we have it all."

That takes you back— these were the hot entertainment options from your childhood, nearly four hundred objective years ago on Mars. "Sounds delightful," you say. "But perhaps something with more local color?"

"There's a dance troupe from Satyampur in town."

"Sounds interesting."

"Dance may not be the right word— *meditation with movement*, I think they call it. Swathed in layers of thick cloth, representing illusion, chanting and swaying back and forth for four hours— it has a cumulative power, they say."

"I've always enjoyed aqua-disco," you confess.

"Yes, yes... what I'm really thinking of is what to do with you tomorrow, and the next day..."

"Dzebyet opera," you suggest.

"And the months after that... I can't shepherd you around all the time, but it's a damned pity to leave you locked in your room. You don't seem dangerous..."

"Not at all," you agree.

Chattanji sighs. "I don't know what I was thinking. Orders are orders, damn me. We must keep you on ice until we hear from Okura. Of course, the situation there is very different by now— I shall have to ask what they consider your status to be."

Oh, good, he's going to *consult* with them. He'll get an answer in a mere fourteen years.

"Surely you could decide for yourself," you say.

"Damn me, I should! That's just what we're always being told— take more initiative. Easy for them to say, of course. Take initiative in *what*, I commed back to them. Haven't heard back yet."

Oh, good. He's going to consult with Okura, get an answer in fourteen years, and then ask for a *clarification*. And this is the *active* faction of the movement.

"Which faction in the civil war do you favor?" you ask.

"We have no clear direction on that," admits Chattanji. "We didn't know there *were* factions in the home movement till the war started. It has been a shock, really— they seemed so strong, so confident... Of course, the Incatena is strong as well."

"That's true."

"Clever and devious as demons, too."

"*Awfully* cunning," you agree, modestly.

"It seems that their chief Agent on Okura has been captured. Must have been unusually incompetent."

"*Utterly*— er, I guess you could say that."

"The real pity is that all this happened when we were so close to victory..."

"Now that Ormant's arrived?" you hazard.

"Now that he's *operating*," clarifies Chattanji.

You think about this. It seems to fit; if Ormant was indeed headed for New Bharat, he would have arrived about four years ago.

"Now, you're not behind this thing with Khunarg, though you've handled it very adroitly," you insinuate. "But Satyampur, perhaps?"

"We were *involved*, yes, damn me," says Chattanji, proudly. "Now the Pandit was—"

An alarm goes off. Chattanji nods, assumes a vague look, and begins speaking intermittently in Neo-Tamil, a language you unfortunately don't speak. Evidently he has a neurimplant that links him directly to the commaudio net, without a datanode. Convenient, but geeky, you think. Business people, teenagers, and holo producers favor them— people who like to be able to stay connected even as they take a swim in the aqua-disco, hike in the woods, or space-walk a million kilometers from the nearest mammal. It makes it fairly excruciating to spend any time in their actual physical presence.

When Chattanji hangs up, with another nod, you ask about the Pandit; but your host is now in a hurry to get to his office. Something's come up, obviously. He leads you distractedly down to the ground transport.

He brightens up in the car, and tells you anecdotes about his college days on Okura; pleasant tales of ideological indoctrination, self-criticism sessions, neoteny drills, paramilitary training, and late nights lubricated with *tanaki*. He has a terrible accent in Okurinese.

As you arrive at the hotel, however, he receives another call. He listens, then his face turns ashen. He parks disastrously, swerving into a waste can, knocking it over; it rolls and rolls on the red barren ground. He pays it no mind. He speaks only in short, shocked monosyllables.

He hangs up, but he might as well still be on the commaudio; he simply repeats at intervals (but at least in modern Hindi):

"No... no... no..."

Enter the Static Faction

When Chattanji isn't stuttering, he's staring into space like a man whose favorite band has decided to hawk hygiene products. You perceive immediately— your mind *is* like a steel trap— that something is wrong.

"Something wrong?" you inquire. But Chattanji merely waves his hand at you, as if trying to clear a fog. Scarcely paying you any attention, he stumbles into the hotel bar, orders a bottle of whiskey, and collapses into a booth.

"Now we wait," he says, as you slide in across from him.

"Wait for what?"

"The vengeance of fate."

And you can't get another word out of him.

About half an hour later, the vengeance of fate arrives, in the form of a strapping woman in a lizardskin jacket and pants. It's an outfit designed for life in the New Bharati outback; the material is strong and yet cool, and it's festooned with pockets and metal reinforcements. The wearer is large and muscular, with short hair, no makeup, and a general air of not responding well to being called "dollface". As for accessories, her feeling seems to be that if it's silver it's good and if it can be used to impale it's better.

She picks up a chair, swings it into the air to clear another table, and bangs it to the floor in front of your booth. She straddles it, rests one arm on the chair back, and draws a laser from a side holster. She twirls it ostentatiously in one hand, then spits on the floor. The spit, and her teeth, are bright red in color.

"Harma," says Chattanji, who's paled as if someone added cream to him.

"That's Rakashri-ji to you," remarks the newcomer. "Especially now."

"I just got the call," admits Chattanji. "I'm not sure whether to believe it. The interpretation of the Okurinese situation can be damned difficult; it should be studied fully before..."

"As of this minute," Harma informs him, "all leadership cadres in the Duress Faction are, under orders of the Peace Party, under arrest."

"That's absurd. You know that as well as I do, damn me. The present divisions of the Freedom Movement won't even be known to Okura before—"

"Contingency directives."

"What?"

"Latest contingency directives describe the current situation perfectly. There isn't any doubt. Not that it wasn't pretty damn clear from previous messages..."

"You snaky slime-covered opportunist! Akamura-ji is going to have your head for this."

"Akamura-ji issued the arrest orders."

Chattanji thinks about that. Harma takes the opportunity to spit more betel juice on the floor. Fortunately the pattern of the carpet has plenty of red in it.

Chattanji swallows hard, holding onto his whiskey bottle for support. "You realize that I'm armed," he says, rather weakly.

"Yeah? With what?"

"M38X auto-broiler."

Harma laughs. "That coffeemaker? You've got to be joking. I mean, look at this, a Kshatriya K44..."

She shows him the label on the base of the handle; he immediately slaps her hand with his whiskey bottle. The laser flies through the air and lands in another booth. There's a splash and a curse. Before Harma can react, Chattanji is covering her with his miniature laser.

"The tables are turned, Harma-ji."

"Individual acts of lawlessness won't save you and your faction," says Harma, seemingly unfazed.

"If you could place both hands face down on the table..."

"Chattanji, get this through your thick, useless skull. You're still under arrest, and I'm still armed."

Chattanji looks at her empty hands, distrustfully, then shakes his head.

"I've had a buccal plasmator installed," she clarifies.

"Damn me!" exclaims Chattanji.

Then, after a moment's thought: "I don't believe you."

For answer Harma turns her head and shapes her mouth into an O. A bright flash seems to explode from her mouth with a roar. A few feet away a small table bursts into flames, spilling a tray of silverware with a clatter and leaving a smoking crater in the wall beyond.

Chattanji watches open-mouthed. "Damn me!" he says again. "I must get me one of those!"

Harma spits out another wad of betel juice, singed black this time, and relieves Chattanji of his laser.

The table is surrounded. Three waiters in formal tan, the bartender, and a desk clerk, all pointing lasers and max guns at your party, accost you politely.

"We do not mean to disturb your entertainment," says one of the waiters. "But we cannot have gunplay in the establishment. It is against the rules and not good business."

"We were just leaving," says Harma, rising. She looks meaningfully at the two of you.

"Yes, yes," says Chattanji. The three of you file out.

"Could have taken them," mutters Harma as you leave.

"What do you plan to do with us? You cannot be keeping an entire damned faction locked up, especially when we are not in power yet."

"It's a problem," admits Harma. "If we'd had just a few weeks' more notice, the concentration camp would be finished. As it is we've got a personnel crunch— and look at you, adding to the problem! Who is this person, a recruit?" She glares at you, as if seeing you for the first time.

"Morgan-ji is a prisoner, not a recruit. An ideological exile."

"From Okura," you add.

"Ideological exile?"

"A prisoner of the Party, sent to us for safekeeping— babysitting— as if we are doing nothing but sitting on our hands here! I have been wracking my brains thinking what to do—"

"You don't have brains to wrack, Chattanji. Prisoner of *what* Party? There's a civil war on, you know." She spits on the ground disdainfully. Tiny black insects immediately swarm over the spot, gathering up the precious moisture.

"The— the Party. Straight from Atami. The Home Ministry— Tanaga was the contact, I believe."

"And *those* wallahs have been purged now," muses Harma, leaning against the wall of the hotel. "Fine, that's it then. You two switch. Morgan-ji— that was the name, right?— you guard Chattanji." She hands you Chattanji's laser.

"I protest," says Chattanji. "This is against all the regulations of the Freedom Movement. With all due respect, Morgan-ji is a political prisoner, entrusted to our faction, which..."

"Which is under arrest for political crimes," points out Harma.

"I protest that as well. This is nothing but an illegal seizure of power within the Movement, intended to distract attention from the chief goal of the Movement, which is to seize power. I demand to speak to Akamura-ji. I also insist on my right to a show trial. Do you hear me?"

"Hard not to," sighs Harma. "Morgan-ji, I almost have to apologize. I forgot what Chattanji is like." She spits on the ground, contemplatively.

"He's been keeping me in a room upstairs. It can be locked from outside."

She looks at you, nods. "Good. We're stretched tight; we can use another hand. Can you pilot?"

"If it moves I can fly it."

"Speak Okurinese?"

"*Ruchona.*"

"Maraillais?"

"*Assurément.* Also Qengese, Sihorian Franca, and the major Martian languages."

"Firearms?"

"Crack shot with anything human or Dzebyet from this millennium."

"Military rations?"

"I can hold 'em down."

"I'll swing by tomorrow for you," Harma tells you. "In the meantime, watch over this jackal. If he tries anything, remember that an inopportune death would save us all the bother of a show trial." She presses her hands together and bows; then she's off.

"Interesting lady," you say.

"A she-bandit, red-spitted follower of Kali, stinking blister on the foot of every decent person," agrees Chattanji. "You still want to catch the Dzebyet opera? It seems my schedule has opened up..."

With the factioneers

After months of idleness, it feels good to be busy, even if it's just scutwork for the Static Faction. You chauffeur party cadres; you deliver messages, packages, and threats; you escort prisoners and outsiders; you're one of the somber figures with dark glasses and barely concealed max guns the leaders use to remind everyone that they are leaders. Few questions are asked; the Static Faction, simultaneously fighting the outside world and its sister faction, is seriously understaffed.

Your chief concern is to find out what the faction is up to. To this end you talk to all the faction members you can. Disciplined and driven, they're the sort of people you want for a Party, but not for a party, at least not the kind of party where you have dancing, flirting, and high-fat snacks, rather than arguments on whether studying for free at a state college is making the state pay for its own undermining, and thus a revolutionary act, or an exercise in self-indoctrination, and thus pitifully anti-revolutionary.

The faction members talk easily; they have plenty of grievances, mostly against each other, and they're eager to rehearse them with a new face. It seems that Lakshmi, for instance, likes to steal other members' boyfriends. Narin, cultivating a true guerrilla image, strives to sleep with as many of the women as possible while never bathing. Sanjiv never has any cash on hand when the pizza comes. Rahesh has managed to alienate almost everyone with his moods and his complaints about anti-Dravidian prejudice. People are sick of Rama's endless quotations from Kumari. Mina's girlish looks have helped divert suspicion from her three successful assassinations carried out for the Movement. Ajav is missing one arm, the result of a shooting incident: his four-year-old neighbor got hold of a max gun and shot him with it. The quick-thinking Ajav managed to draw his own gun with his bad arm and down the toddler before he could escape.

From hints interspersed in the gossip you begin to form a picture of how things work. The Static Faction is small, with less than a hundred members in Colony Base, but enough titles for a planetary government, which of course the faction conceives itself to be. The Political Council has sixty members— roughly, those who can be counted on to attend meetings where food is not served— and these in turn elect the Supreme Policy Group of fifteen, which determines and promulgates faction policy.

Now you feel you're getting somewhere. You slip a photonic mic— the faction has a box of them in a storeroom— into the conference room and record a few meetings. The results are soporific. Obviously some canny strategist has succeeded in packing the Policy Group with the movement's most contrarian and eristic individuals, who spend their time arguing with each other, hardly realizing that real power rests elsewhere.

Another approach is needed. What do the members actually spend time *doing*? Chattanji's story was that the Static Faction believed in working through the system. The members do devote a good deal of energy to conventional politics and to the Freedom Movement datascene; but the goal is not acquiring power but achieving a public presence. So far as you can see, the faction succeeds in gaining attention through inflammatory tricks (such as the two Planetary Legislators from the Movement, Mehta and Amin, publicly burning their paychecks), and then dissipates it with manifestos and policy statements produced by the Supreme Policy Group.

On a deeper level, the strategy of the faction is infiltration: the idea is for faction members to insinuate themselves into positions of power, which can then be manipulated in the movement's favor. This would never work on an established planet, where advancement (thanks to lifespans that reach a millennium) is glacial. Here, it's had some results: there are Freedom Movement members in the ICA, in various NBCC offices, in several influential datascenes, in the city police, and on the New Bharat University faculty. The faction's star operative is a policy advisor to the NBCC's deputy legal counsel; but perhaps the most admired member is a woman who's penetrated the secretive Satyampur religious colony. When she can, she breaks away and attends Political Council meetings in the colony's trademark topless sari and heavy veil.

Time to go deeper. Might as well do something with that box of mics. You start slipping them into people's shoes, their watchbands, their datanodes, their hair; you sprinkle them around like a bad uncle with a supply of sneezing powder. Then you sit back and collect the secrets.

—Four members are of a different sexual orientation than you'd suspected. One is of a different sex. Three more actually belong to the Duress Faction.

—The woman who complains the most about Lakshmi stealing other members' boyfriends is a former lover of hers.

—Sanjiv, who has access to the treasury, has been skimming off money for himself.

—When he's with his closest friends, Rama makes endless jokes about Kumari. None of them are very funny, except the one about the sheep and the alarm clock.

—If Party activism doesn't pay off, Mina plans to go into accounting.

—Somebody is planting photonic mics on people— probably the ICA. You wonder why they bother.

—To finance its operations the faction runs contraband. You're a bit surprised to discover that there are any restrictions on trade at all on New Bharat. Weapons from nanocaps to anti-volant batteries are readily available; stimulants from neurodetonators to absinthe to jigglebrain are sold in pharmacies without a prescription, and even multi-level marketing is permitted. However, there are a few things which even New Bharati traders find beneath them— distributing left-wing magazines, selling surveillance equipment to government agencies, hawking address books to bulk e-mailers— and these the Freedom Movement is happy to take on, for a fee.

—Only three members strike you as having a real political consciousness and the strategic know-how to do something with it: Harma, who has the title of Security Minister; the odoriferous Narin, who directs the smuggling and assassination teams; and Amin, one of the movement's Planetary Legislators.

It's Narin, in fact, who brings a couple of quantum-path retracers to the next Political Council meeting. A spectacular burst of laserfire ensues, and your entire array of mics is destroyed, bar a few left in people's volants, closets, and shower drains.

"Now that I have your attention," says Narin, drily.

"What the hell was that?" says Sanjiv. "I almost pissed my pants."

"*Almost?*" joke a few people.

Narin explains about the photonic mics. "We've been under surveillance. Of course I've told you a thousand times to assume you are *always* under surveillance, but maybe this will help some of you believe it."

"So who're the bastards responsible?" asks Mina, looking round the room. You do your best to look puzzled, indignant, and a bit sheepish, like most of the crowd. You also, like most of the crowd, periodically rub the little burned spot where your own mic was vaporized.

"It's stinking Khunarg," says Mehta, the other Planetary Legislator— a self-important zero, according to everything you've heard.

"Khunarg? More like the NBCC," says Lakshmi.

"Don't be a bunch of damn fools," says Harma, planted like a monolith at the front of the room. "It's Ormant."

"You and your Ormant," says Rama, disgustedly.

There's more discussion, but it leads nowhere; nothing important is going to be decided in a general meeting. Most of the meeting, rather, is spent making preparations for the Planetary Datamoot, which seems to be some sort of political demonstration in the Vee.

When it's over you find Harma and ask, "Why Ormant?"

"Stands to reason," she says. "He knows we're his only serious enemies on this planet."

"We are?"

"Yeah. Some of us," she responds, phlegmatically.

"I thought Kumari was pretty friendly with Ormant," you venture.

"It doesn't much matter what Kumari thinks any more," she says.

You're not sure what she means, and she disappears before you can ask. Has there been some secret communication with Okura? Or for that matter has there been some open communication? You search around frantically for a datanode. The only one you can find was harboring a few photonic mics, and came out of the laserfire barrage a little worse for wear. Still, the day's main story is mostly readable:

KUMARI THRXWN XUT XF PXWER XN XKURA

Embattled Planetary Marfhal Jifhuri Kimuri waf relieved xf hif dutief txday, accxrding tx xfficial Peace Party (Lxyalift) media.

The difmiffal, figned jxintly by the Central Cxmmand xf the Peace Army and by the Peace Party Emergency Cxmmittee— a previxufly unknxwn bxdy— waf brxadcaft at 6:58 a.m. Atami time. Nx reafxn fxr the difmiffal waf given, and nx replacement waf named. "Nx change in pxlicy xr in the cxnduct xf the war will enfue," the annxuncement cxncluded.

Rebel reactixnf were varied, but mxftly xptimiftic. All ftreffed that the military ftruggle wxuld cxntinue unabated.

Bad news for an Okurinese teenager

Narin bursts into the faction office. "Hey, Harma, are you using Morgan?"

"Not really, we're just chatting about Okura."

Having a little interrogation is more like it, you think. She's just spent half an hour grilling you on Peace Party politics.

"Talking about the K-man? Well, I'm heading over to Akamura-ji now and I need a little protection."

"A little protection? You could use the whole stick," comments Harma.

Narin pays her no attention; he's looking you over. In a well-ventilated room, he's attractive enough: long, wild black hair, classic features, strong nose, a trim black beard and moustache. He's bisexual— or more accurately, as Mina puts it, checksexual— everyone, male or female, is a potential checkmark in his little black book. "'Course I don't know who's going to protect *you*," he confides.

You select a pulse plasmator from the faction's array of weaponry, and wave it in his face. "Don't worry about me, Jack."

He laughs. "I have to keep remembering— not *everyone* finds me overwhelming."

In a small ground car they do. Within a few blocks you're wondering if exposure to a partially poisonous planetary atmosphere can be all that bad.

In hopes that some intellectual input will interfere with that from the olfactory bulb, you ask Narin if he thinks Ormant was behind the photonic mics.

"Ormant? Nah," says Narin. "Harma's got a riddlewasp in her panties about Ormant. Always thinks he's trying to take over the planet. I keep explaining: you don't have to take something over that's in your back pocket."

"So who do you think it was, then?"

"That's kind of a puzzler, really." He scratches his head; the air in the car, you swear, becomes perceptibly foggier. "I mean, who the fuck doesn't know everything they could possibly want to know about us? It's the kind of stupid-ass gesture I'd expect of the Duress Faction if they weren't neutralized. A new element of some kind, gotta be."

This isn't a chain of thought you want to encourage. "Lakshmi says it's because of the datamoot," you say.

"If you can't fuck it, Lakshmi doesn't know anything about it," Narin advises you.

"What *is* going to happen at the datamoot?" you ask.

"We get rid of Khunarg, most likely."

"And seize power?"

"'We' as in New Bharat, not 'we' as in the faction," explains Narin. "Listen, Morgan, I don't want to fuck with your idealism or anything, but the movement as you see it right now couldn't seize its own ass, OK? Five years from now, we might have something."

Narin should be an Incatena Agent, you think. Not only could the Incatena use someone with his brains; if he was an Agent he'd be on another planet right now, instead of ten centimeters away.

Namiko Akamura is tall and rather severe looking, at least 500, with purple hair pulled back into a bun. She glances at Narin, curls her nose, and then fixes you with a sharp stare.

"That's Morgan-ji," says Narin, noticing. "Harma's recruit. Ideological exile from Okura."

"Which country?" asks Akamura, in Okurinese.

No one's thought to ask you that before. You think quickly. Akamura's accent is Gōsei; you'll never pull off a claim to be from there. Ikkyū-shima would invite too many questions. You probably know enough about Shr, from what Ba told you, to fool a Gōsei-jin— except you don't look Chinese; you'd have to have a damn good story. You'd better stick to the one ethnically plausible country.

"Burusandaku," you answer.

"Kamaunday is one of my favorite cities," she remarks.

"It *is* one of the most beautiful cities of Muaŋ Sai," you parry.

"The news was very shocking, wasn't it? Were you one of Kumari's Peace Scouts, perhaps?"

"Nashimoto was Director in those days, o-san."

232 • Against Freedom

"His people back in Anatokkawa must be so disappointed, don't you think?"

"Perhaps o-san is thinking of Niwa-ku? Anatokkawa was where the last battle in the Coalition War took place."

She gives you a smile of great brightness and little warmth, and turns back to Narin. "Harma's recruit, did you say? Harma-san has such excellent discernment. Now, what can I do for you, Narin-san?"

"I think you were appointed by Col. Kumari himself, weren't you?"

She frowns at him. "Certainly not," she says. "I was named by the Political Council of the Peace Party. I'm surprised at your question, Narin. We've always worked so well together."

"We have, baby. But it's a new world today."

"The entire gist of the revolutionary message to the Peace Party and its affiliates," says Akamura, speaking as if to a kinder-gartener, "is that there is no change in policy. Everything is as it was before."

"What about the personality cult?"

"We will re-erect it when a new personality is chosen."

That's the way of the world. You get yourself named dicta-tor, with your thumb on an entire planet, your mug is posted on every wall, your every idle word is published, with a concor-dance; your birthplace is a museum, with sound-and-light shows and re-enactments of key events from your childhood; you chuckle in your sleep and a million people shudder— and then, in a single day, you're out, denied, denounced, unmourned, except perhaps by the fourteen-year-old who played you in the re-enactments, and who doesn't look like any of your replacements. All anyone cares about is making their tongues forget the taste of your boots, and placing them in the path of whatever leather looks like it's coming their way.

You pour yourself some tea from the pot on Akamura's side table, and listen to Narin and Akamura, but they're not even speculating on what happened, only making sure that, so far, it hasn't threatened their own plans or positions.

What should your own position be? Based on a news report from a planet seven light years away, it could be argued that your mission is over. You could pack your bags and head back home to Mars. Kumari is gone; Okura is in no position to sabotage the

Incatena; you have the admission of the Freedom Movement's top operative that it has the same potential for trouble as a water balloon in a swimming pool; and you know where Ormant is, don't you?

You imagine yourself explaining this to the boss. It'd be worth it to see him choke on his caf, and that would about exhaust the pleasure potential. You'd be tossed into a desk job so fast it'd dent the desk.

You turn your attention back to Akamura and Narin. They're bent over a datanode, examining the list of names in the Emergency Committee, which was released today. All twenty of the names are familiar, and clues can be divined from the order of the list; the two of them are pointing out things and arguing like boys fighting over whose holo-hero is strongest. But they eventually come to a consensus.

"In short, Narin-san," says Akamura, "there's no essential change in the situation."

"That's about the size of it."

"How did the meeting go last night? Smoothly, I hope?"

"Had a little light show." Narin explains about the photonic mics, and his counter-measure. "Not sure who'd pull such a stunt. Somebody's trying something new."

Akamura laughs. "I must try that myself sometime. I'd know a lot more about why you never accomplish anything."

"If we had ten operatives half as competent as myself, instead of three," says Narin, unperturbedly and probably correctly, "we'd show you something. As it is..."

"Something new," muses Akamura, staring in your direction.

Uh oh.

The door opens behind you; you almost spill your tea all over yourself. It's Chattanji and his Static Faction watchdog— a nervous little guy who looks like he's barely shaving.

"Pramavi, what the hell are you doing here?" asks Narin.

"Narin, dear, it's my office," says Akamura.

"Oh, sorry. They do work for—"

"What is it, Pramavi-san?"

The young man steps forward, virtually forgetting his prisoner in his excitement. "We just discovered something, Akamura-ji, and— sorry to interrupt, I should say— I was guarding

234 • Against Freedom

him here and we heard on the commaudio, I mean it was me of course, but Chattanji reminded me of the code, and I thought we should tell you and all. I mean it was Chattanji who said— except I would have thought the same thing— sorry to burst in like that, but..."

"What *is* it?"

He thrusts a piece of paper forward— the printout from a commaudio transmission, with the decipherment scribbled over it.

Akamura reads, then looks up, her brow creased. "It's the same transmission from a few weeks ago. The contingency directives. We acted on these already— I authorized the arrest of the entire Duress Faction."

"With one emendation, Akamura-ji," says Chattanji. "It's a correction."

"Shut up, you," hisses Narin.

"Oh, he's right," says Akamura. "One word inserted— the word 'not'."

Your heart sinks.

"No big deal," says Narin. "The meaning was clear enough. There's no reason to—"

"I'd say it reverses the meaning entirely," says Akamura.

Freedom Movement decisionmaking

There's a good deal of grabbing the paper and reading and re-reading it. Pramavi could have brought copies for everybody. Young people can be so thoughtless. And then everybody is talking at once.

Akamura raises her voice like a schoolteacher, cutting through the din. "There's no room for argument. We are an autonomous Peace organization under orders from outside agitators, and when our parent organization speaks we must autonomously and zealously agree."

"But in this case—"

"*Autonomously and zealously agree,*" says Akamura. She has a real gift for increasing the volume without sounding like she's shouting. "Our previous response was in error; we have to reverse it."

There's a pause.

"You don't mean you're going to have *them* arrest *us*?" says Narin.

Akamura holds her hand out; someone passes her the commaudio printout. She studies it one more time.

"No, I don't see how you get *that* from it," she says. "It's perfectly evident that the subject is a hypothetical faction which matches exactly the characteristics of the Duress Faction; the only change is that this section which used to be 'entirely clear' is now 'not entirely clear'."

"Well, that's a relief," says Pramavi. "Here I thought I'd have to hand my laser over to Chattanji! Ha ha ha!"

You all look at him in embarrassment till he stops laughing and pretends to be coughing.

"I'm not questioning your interpretation of the directive," says Narin. "But—"

"If you're not questioning—"

"But in the present circumstances—"

"*If you're not questioning my interpretation,*" says Akamura, commandingly, "then there is nothing to discuss, is there?"

There's a silence for a moment. Narin looks furious.

"Very good," says Akamura. "Have the Duress Faction released. And tomorrow I want to see the top cadres from both sides here. In view of the new situation on Okura, and the delicacy of the situation on New Bharat, with the datamoot coming up, the present factionalization of the Freedom Movement is no longer acceptable."

"We will come with happiness," says Chattanji. "I am sure that with minor rectifications on both sides—"

Narin towers over Akamura, shaking his finger. "The situation *hasn't* changed on Okura— that's what we just spent half an hour deciding."

"It hasn't changed on *Okura*," agrees Akamura, looking up at him, unmoved. "But the cataclysmic events there have thoroughly changed the situation *here*."

"That's absurd. If things haven't changed there they haven't changed here."

"Here is not there. As I say, there is no room for argument, and I will not have any more of it."

Slowly, keeping his eyes on Akamura, Narin reaches into a coat pocket and removes a sonic dart exploder. He raises it slowly to point at Akamura. His hand is shaking.

"Akamura-ji, I have to insist," he says. His voice is nervous. "We can't release the prisoners. Too much is at stake here."

"Are you withdrawing from the Freedom Movement?" asks Akamura.

"We *are* the Freedom Movement," says Narin, more confidently. "I hope you'll see it that way. If not, I'll have to fire, and we'll have the same result, won't we?"

Akamura looks at him, then, as if reaching for her lunch, opens a drawer and draws out a max gun.

"That doesn't change anything," says Narin. His nervousness is back. "The others will have the same position— Harma, Amin, Mina. And I have backup here."

"It doesn't *change* the situation, it *equalizes* it," clarifies Akamura. "What is it you New Bharatis say? There's nothing like drawing guns to see what a wallah is made of. We'll soon see what you're made of, Narin-san. I don't think you can do it."

"If I have to I will. I've killed people before." He moves in a little closer; the nozzle of the exploder is just a few inches from Akamura's forehead. Akamura's nose wrinkles.

"You don't have the guts to kill me."

"Damn it, you are always trying to change the terms of debate," yells Narin. "The issue is not whether I can shoot somebody. The issue is whether the Freedom Movement, once it's taken a clear, irreversible political action, mistakenly or not, should completely destroy its credibility by attempting to reverse itself."

Chattanji, meanwhile, has been trying to get Pramavi's attention. "I'm feeling a little outgunned here," he whispers. "How about letting me use your laser?"

"No way."

"Insect."

Chattanji looks at you.

You shake your head. "Sorry."

"I have got to get me one of those buccal plasmators," says Chattanji.

Akamura still looks unfazed. You think she's playing it awfully close to the line. "You can't threaten me with an exploder *and* argue with me," she points out. "Much as you'd like to. I think you're regretting it now, aren't you? But look at the situation you've got yourself into. You can't shoot me, but if you back down, you lose face."

Ooh, you think. That's not the way to talk him down.

"You're crazy," he says. "You're absolutely crazy."

"I just know what you can do."

"You don't know shit about what I can do," shouts Narin. He lowers the exploder abruptly.

After a moment, Akamura angles her max gun to the side, away from Narin. A minimal movement. She says nothing.

Narin turns round; there's an explosion and the crack of disintegrating bone; and Pramavi drops to the floor with a cry.

A sonic dart kills if it hits anywhere in the chest or head. Luckily, Pramavi's been shot in the arm, instantly liquefying his bone and muscle without breaking the skin. A few month's refetalization and he'll be good as new.

"Useless empty lizardskin!" says Narin. "If you hadn't brought that damned brother-in-law of a viper and his transmission, we wouldn't be in this mess!"

Narin is whistling a little tune as he saunters into the Static Faction headquarters.

"So," says Harma. "What's Akamura say?"

Narin looks at you meaningfully, then back at Harma.

"She was a little difficult," he says, with a shrug.

"I guess that explains it, then."

"Explains what?"

"Explains why she's called half a dozen members on detention detail and ordered Duress prisoners released. I see it now. She was being difficult."

"Well, shit, it got a little hairy," says Narin. "Akamura claimed that with Kumari out, the previous orders from Okura were countermanded. I was resisting that when Chattanji burst in. He'd overpowered Pramavi and was holding him with his own sonic dart exploder. I grabbed Morgan's pulse plasmator and there was a bit of a firefight. Pramavi got shot. I was about to waste Chattanji when Akamura came up from behind and shoved a max gun in my ribs. Then two more Duress Faction thugs showed up... We were lucky to get out of there alive. I'm pretty sure I got the two thugs."

Harma looks at you. Narin steps hard on your toes. "Ah, yeah," you say. "Ow."

"I'd have shot the bitch," says Harma.

Narin looks like a man who's set up a magnificent knight fork, only to have his opponent ram a queen across the board for an immediate mate.

"That would have been a good idea," he concedes.

Guns and ganaraj vindaloo

The Incatena has retained its offices in the colony ship—Port Rib 14, Deck 12— although the decks above and below have been largely dismantled for their metal and wiring. Its block of offices thus perches in the skeleton of the ship, fifty meters above the ground, amid a forest of girders, tubes, metal plates, and dangling wires. You pick your way through the debris to the elevator, climb upward through the metal jungle, and then step into the Incatena's office suite.

A security guard meets you. "Neut'al territ'y gun please," he intones.

"I don't have one," you tell him.

"Sorry bother you reg'lations," he explains. "Gun please."

"Look, man, I'm unarmed. Really. Left the damn thing at home."

The guard seems to look at you closely for the first time. It doesn't improve his disposition. "Shan!" he bawls out.

Another guard ambles over; by now the first guard has drawn a laser and is covering you as if there was nothing more dangerous than an unarmed perp.

"What's the matter, Beto?" asks Shan.

"Won't surrender arms."

Shan looks you over. "I understand and all," he tells you, in a good-cop voice. "But it's Incatena regulations— applies to everybody. It's neutral territory. We'll return them when you leave."

"I don't doubt it," you say. "The thing is that I don't have a gun. I'm unarmed."

"If you expect us to believe *that*," begins Beto, but Shan holds up a hand to stop him.

"If you'll permit me..." says Shan, advancing cautiously. He frisks you, expertly but thoroughly; then goes over you from head to toe with a handheld scanner. The scanner makes inquiring noises at various points, and Shan has to successively inspect your wallet, your pants zipper, your left ear, and your shoes.

"You're clean," Shan announces, finally, with an air of disappointment.

"I don't trust that piece of shit of a scanner," says Beto.

"Well, what do you want to do? Blow the vek away?"

Beto looks like he's considering the suggestion.

"I guess you don't get many unarmed visitors," you say, brightly.

"A few kids," admits Beto, sullenly.

"There was that religious vek," says Shan. "All in saffron robes, remember? Pong, or Panchi, or something. They don't believe in violence."

"Don't believe in violence? They walk around this planet with their eyes shut or something?"

The Incatena offices still look like they're a deck of an interstellar liner, with thick, burnished metal bulkheads, overhead wires and pipes, and controls and valves embedded in the walls. At first you worry that the Incatena on New Bharat is low on funds or on taste. Then you realize that, for a metal-poor, hardscrabble colony, it's actually an ostentatious display of power and wealth.

The local representative of humanity's glorious march to the stars must, of course, make itself hard to access. You yourself are almost certainly the highest ranking Incatena Agent on the planet— but till you get a 680 you're just another in the faceless mass of supplicants the interference personnel is paid to keep from bothering anyone farther inside. You take a number: 93. You look up at the readout on the wall; it says NOW SERVING ██, with a handwritten sign reading SYSTEM DOWN, and a scrap of paper with the number 32.

There's a small crowd in the waiting area— sitting, reading, talking, pacing back and forth, eating lunches, hunched over datanodes, comforting children. There's an angry mutter of conversation, suspended every few minutes as someone from the office replaces the number pasted on the wall. Detachments from the crowd waylay passing bureaucrats and attempt to make themselves heard. Disarming this crowd strikes you as an essential precaution.

You settle down next to an old woman carrying a enormous folder of documents. "Just sixty people ahead of me. Good timing, huh?" you tell her.

"Sixty?" The woman chuckles. "A hundred and sixty, you mean. They are one cycle behind."

"Shit. It doesn't look like there's that many people here, though."

"Some people are heading home for a day or two until they're farther along in the queue," the woman explains.

"What are you waiting for? Emigration?"

"Contraband permit."

"Contraband permit?"

"Importation of illegal substances— illegal in the Douane, I mean; perfectly legal here. It's a terrible mess. None of the office wallahs are knowing what department it falls under."

"Tell me about it," says another man, next to her. "I have been waiting six months just to get money which is owed to me. I don't have all the time to be sitting in this office all day; the riddlewasps will be getting into the cistern again."

You curse yourself. You are going about this all wrong.

"Neut'al territ'y gun please," says the guard.

It doesn't really matter what you say in response. "Nice monotone," you tell him.

"Sorry bother you reg'lations. Gun please."

"Steady on. Good work, Beto," you say, with an air of benevolent authority.

Beto looks at you closely, shakes his head. "I don't think I know you, do I?"

"You'll know me soon enough. I'll be your new boss. Ranking Agent Morgan," you say, extending a hand, which Beto shakes automatically. "Glad to meet you."

"Sergeant Beto Ramirez." He looks at you half-submissively, half-pugnaciously, caught in a classic fight or flight bind. "Are you, uh, expected?"

"Oh, no," you say, jovially. "I've been undercover. Listen, I'd like to meet the 405."

"Uh— no disrespect, but before I could do that—"

"You need a 680. Of course you do," you beam, as if at a prize student. "It's not just regulations, it's common sense."

Beto calls Shan over.

Shan is a little more on the ball than Beto. "Hey, isn't this the vek from this morning without a gun?"

"Shan, isn't it?" you say, extending a hand.

Shan nods, shaking your hand gingerly.

"Ranking Agent Morgan," you say. "Beto here was just getting a 680 together for me."

"Yes. Yes, of course," says Shan.

"But he can't leave his post," you point out. *Here is a problem! For you to solve!*

Shan looks at Beto, Beto looks at you, you look at Shan. With an almost sarcastic air of pointing out the obvious, you indicate the inner door, the door in the wall labeled STAFF NO ADMITTANCE. "Shall we?"

At any point Beto or Shan could balk, decide you're crazy, decide you're someone else's problem; but with every moment they do not, every moment they fail to protest the role that you've confidently assumed, protest becomes more difficult.

Shan smiles wanly at you and leads the way to the door. He opens it with a thumb print, then stops.

"Uh, did Beto get your weapon?"

"Agents on duty are permitted to carry sidearms in any Incatena facility," you remind him.

"I understand, Agent Morgan, but till we get that 680..."

"80," you say. This time you've brought a plasmator, and you hand it over. "Take good care of it."

"Um, of course," says Shan, and leads you inside. You get a glimpse of the crowded waiting room: dozens of faces turned toward you in hatred. You smile at them magnanimously.

You're handed off to a young woman— a pretty, petite thing, with an expensive Sihorian velvet blouse, earrings in the shape of frogs, and long blond hair that keeps getting in her face. She looks barely out of school— no more than fifty. She takes your retina scan and your picture, runs them through the datanode, and has you answer some questions for the station's AI.

"Cool," she says, finally. "It all checks out. I'll get your plasmator in two jiffs. Your 1038 is higher than the old man's! You want to meet him now or what?"

"Actually I'd like to meet Agent Beloman first," you say.

"That would be me," she says, with a giggle.

"The one who wrote the reports?"

"No other." She beams at the thought that someone was reading them; they must've been her first ones.

"Would it be rude to ask how old you are?"

"Very rude," Beloman tells you. "Fortunately, I'm very mature for my age, which is 49, so I can overlook your gaucherie."

You think back to when you were 49. Ah, the confusion, the trepidation, the lack of power and the scent of it, the exhilaration of late adolescence! You were on Tir Habitat. It was your first time far away from Sol, your first assignment as an Agent, your first salary, your first time firing a laser in the line of duty. Pity about that passerby.

Beloman takes you to her office. There's no room for an ergolounge; it's a tiny cabin from the ship which seems to be made all of corners. The ship designers did their best to make every rib, wiring conduit, and pipeline cross and criss-cross here. Beloman has tried to humanize the place by adding plants, brightly colored stickers, and toys.

You clear some take-out boxes and toy dinosaurs from a couple of large pipes that conveniently cross the room at knee level, and sit down. The dinosaurs walk around a bit, squeaking, seemingly disoriented, before settling down.

"I've always wanted to meet you, Morgan," says Beloman, settling into her chair in an anatomically improbable heap. "I've heard lots about you."

"You probably heard about the Garcheron trade treaty," you suggest.

"Wait a minute," she says. She concentrates, scrunching her eyes closed and putting her fingertips on her forehead. "Wasn't that Xiang?"

"No. Maybe you're thinking of the pirates of Pən'záč."

"The what?"

"The Empire and the chamber pot?"

"No, no, no. I know. There was this dinner at Areopolis when I was at the Academy, and you were the one that slipped on a puddle of spilled herring dip and knocked the boss into the swimming pool. That was *so* out of control!"

"It's always an honor to achieve renown in one's own life-time," you murmur.

"One of my professors talked about you, too. Said there was never a bigger— well, I mean, it was supposed to be inspir-ing, how far you've come. What about Okura? You've got to like tell me all about it. I mean, you really do, because I'm like an ana-lyst and all, but I want to know, too."

You oblige with a narration covering the first two hundred odd pages of the book.

"That's way cool— bringing down a dictator— I never did that," says Beloman.

You allow yourself to bask a little.

"Of course he wasn't really *down* till a few months after you left," she reflects. "If you hadn't got yourself nicked you might really have accomplished something, huh? ...You really like fell *hard* for this Ba, didn't you?"

You nod. An infinite sadness can be glimpsed, for a fleeting moment, in your eyes.

"You look hungry," suggests Beloman. "Should we order out?"

"Uh, sure. Nothing reptilian, if you don't mind."

She roots around the floor for the commaudio, sending the dinosaurs scurrying about again, and places an order for ganaraj vindaloo, with samosa and masala tea.

"Why did you become an Agent?" she asks you.

"So I could do things like this," you say.

"What, sit on a pipe in a dinky little office on a two-bit col-ony planet?"

"No, live in the unknown. Just about everything else in human space has been codified and understood and reduced to a set of formulas. If you want to run a society, grow it, shrink it, mold it like putty, make it jump upside down, we know exactly what to do. We've got three thousand years of data on it. But the rare events— the catastrophes, the innovations, the revolutions, are infrequent enough that all we have is heuristics, suggestions. Don't you feel any of that?"

"Kind of," she says. "I just wanted to get outsystem, you know? My parents are such leeches. They wanted like the whole total once-in-a-half-millennium child-raising experience, so they *both* quit their jobs and sat around all day staring at me. I love them both to pieces, but it's like there's no *way*, you know what I'm saying?"

The food arrives. There's chunks of rather crunchy meat in a spicy sauce, indigo in color, on a bed of basmati, and then the samosa, fried tetrahedrons filled with potato. You eat happily.

"It's not bad, huh?"

"Yeah. What's ganaraj?" you ask.

"It's a kind of desert beetle. You said you didn't want reptiles, so..."

You pause in mid-chew. You have to think about this. Are you going to spew ganaraj all over the office just because it has insects in it? Are you going to choke on one unusual ingredient in your dinner as if you weren't four times the age of this debutante sitting next to you? Do they cook the beetles enough so that they're not likely to get up and walk around? How big do you suppose they are? Are they hairy, with hard nasty little black legs? Do they come dead, or does the cook have to whap their heads against the table or something before frying them?

Don't mix zoology with gastronomy, you tell yourself. It's meat. It tasted fine till you knew what was in it. Good sauce, too. Here, have some more samosa, wash everything down with masala tea, and get your mind on something else.

"Technically they're not *Earth* insects," Beloman informs you. "They have more legs, you know. Kind of gross if you see them climbing over your shoes or something. Also the carapace, that's like the outer covering—"

"You know, I really wanted to ask about the datamoot," you interpose.

"—it's *sticky*, so if you don't—"

"The datamoot," you suggest.

"Well, it's just like it sounds. The whole planet gets together for two or three days and decides things."

"The whole planet? I hope they have valet parking."

"It's in the Vee, gloopy. Anyway, this one should be pretty intense. Most veks think the big do is going to be like getting rid of Khunarg, or maybe the Freedom Movement will stage something, but that'll be a sideshow, I mean what can they *do* in the Vee? Shoot our avatars with virtual max guns? No, no, no. I think Ormant's going to like try to take over everything."

"You can't take over something that's in your back pocket."

"That's what everybody says, but that's like totally bogus! Rich people don't think like you or me. They don't have the *restraints* that make us normal people."

"Well, he's one of the richest veks in the Incatena, he owns a third of the NBCC, which virtually owns this planet, but he wants more. What's *more*? He wants *two* planets?"

"See, you're thinking horizontally," Beloman explains. "What my idea is, he's thinking vertically. He doesn't want more *stuff*, he wants more *control*. Things are in his way: AIs, stakeholder laws, employee democracy, profit negotiation algorithms, startup bubble expiration clauses, workstyle charters— all the socionomic stuff that makes sure development benefits society as a whole. But what if he could like get *rid* of all that? What if he could run his company like it was his own house, snarf all the profits for himself, bag the charters— and destroy anyone who cribbed about it? He would be so *there*, right?"

"He wants to go back to the twenty-first century!" you exclaim. "But no one's going to stand still for that. There's laws—"

"Ormant's bigger than the law on this planet," Beloman reminds you, quietly. "And if he can get rid of the last obstacles— the ICA and us— he *is* the law."

"He's flying in the face of socionomics," you object. "He may get more for himself, but he's going to impoverish the planet!"

"It's a young colony," she points out. "It's going to grow plenty, for centuries. Not as much as under good socionomic management, but there's a load and a half of credits to be made, and most of them will go to Ormant."

"What a creep," you say.

"A complete shark," agrees Beloman.

With your mind occupied with Ormant, you find that you can eat the ganaraj vindaloo with relish. Fortunately Beloman keeps a jar of relish in her office.

"He's an insect," continues Beloman, with emphasis. "A giant, crawling, articulated insect. It's like when you leave the refrigerator door open, and the next day skimperbugs are crawling all over the pot roast. That's what we've got here. Or like when nightworms eat through your boots, and if you're still in them they start on your feet..."

Your stomach clenches in sympathy. "Let me have some tea," you say, quickly.

You talk strategy for awhile. Beloman says she'll work on the datamoot; it seems best that you continue your infiltration of the Freedom Movement.

You head back to the Static Faction offices. You see new faces around— Akamura has insisted on a forceful reintegration of the two factions, and Duress factioneers intermingle uneasily with their Static counterparts.

One day, after a Political Council meeting, you find Chattanji sitting with a young man. Tall, nattily groomed, light-skinned, with a neat goatee, he doesn't look much like other New Bharatis. Okurinese, you realize, with a start.

The man notices you, smiles. "So glad to see you again." he tells you.

It's the huge-eyed young man from the quickship.

Leverage

Every time you see the young man from the ship your stomach churns, though nothing else seems to come of it. You just wish he wouldn't look at you with those strange eyes and that sly smile. It could be a guarded friendliness, you reflect. He's not a bad person— he helped you convalesce, didn't he? He didn't actually *do* anything to you, did he? Maybe he doesn't like his job. Maybe he's working to undermine the system from within. Maybe that smile is really a rueful admission of a wasted life, a sadness only one stop short of bitterness.

No, you think. Probably it really is malice.

He takes to sitting down next to you, listening to your conversations with Harma or Narin or Chattanji. He says little; when he does speak it's weighted little double entendres, like "I wonder what the *Incatena* would think about that?", or "What if a *spy* heard us talking?"

When he's around, which is almost continuously, it's impossible or inadvisable to probe a line of thought, or ask about plans, or even to deepen a relationship; and when he's not you worry about who he's with and what he's telling them.

It's what the Agent Directives call a blocking situation. The standard strategy in this situation is to remove the blocker at any cost, because you will certainly fail if it continues. You have to change the situation. Change is disruptive, but it's your only chance to regain control. You buttonhole the young man after a strategy and education session, and sit him down in a storage room.

"What's the story?" you ask, in Okurinese.

The young man's perpetual half-smile momentarily lengthens. "What do you mean, Morgan-san?"

"I think you know what I mean."

"*You* know what you mean," he points out, slyly. "And you think *I* know what you mean. But do you *know* that I know what you mean?"

"All right, fine, I *know* that you know what I mean."

248

"Of course, I know what I mean, and if you're correct, I know what you mean, and you know that, and because you're telling me— which may or may not be advisable— then I know that you know, as well."

"Uh, yes."

"So, if you know and I know, and we each know that the other knows, what is there to talk about?"

"I'm not sure that we've said anything at all so far," you complain.

"On the contrary— you've put it *very* plainly."

You don't feel that you can return the compliment. You switch gears.

"What you *don't* know is how much leverage you have over me. Leverage is a tricky thing; its effectiveness derives from the threat of use; but when you use it, it's gone."

"Do you *know* that to be the case?"

"Oh, don't start."

"What you're saying is that leverage doesn't exist," says the young man, stroking his goatee. "You present it as a sort of paradox. I'm not sure I agree. Hey, Harma!"

Harma, who's come in to root around in the weapons cache, waves, then comes by with two anti-photonic desecrators on her shoulders, still shedding packing foam.

"Think these babies might give Ormant a bad day?" she asks.

"No," says the young man. "Listen, Harma, did you ever look into why Morgan-ji was sent here from Okura?"

"Sure," says Harma. "Political exile."

"What were the charges exactly?"

"Fuck, who cares? We don't have time to do your antisepsis for you."

The young man has to die, you realize, suddenly. You've forced his hand, but now he's forcing yours. You don't have your plasmator, but Harma's is right there in its holster. She won't mind.

He's still talking, and you're still trying to think of a good story that would explain to Harma why you seized her weapon and vaporized the young man and a good deal of the Freedom Movement's office supplies, when the meaning of his words registers: "So you didn't know Morgan-ji was an Incatena Agent?"

The plasmator is within reach; unfortunately, it's also pointed at you.

"I should have known," snarls Harma. "You're working for Ormant, aren't you?" She spits out a wad of betel juice, for emphasis.

The young man smiles, like someone whose day trades have once again inched up, but says nothing.

"No!" you say. Then, feeling that this answer requires a little amplification, you add, "I mean, of course not. Why would I be working *for* Ormant?"

"Ormant/*Mars*. Incatena, Areopolis, *Mars*," she says.

"Come on, that's incredibly simplistic."

"Seems realistic to me. Besides—"

"Besides, he's lying!"

"Who, Ormant?"

"No, him!" you say, pointing at the young man.

She shakes her head. "Nope. No, sorry, Morgan-ji, that would've worked a moment ago, right after 'You're working for Ormant, aren't you?' But 'Why would I be working for Ormant?' worked pretty much as an admission for me. How about for you?" she asks the young man.

"For me too."

"I'm working *against* Ormant," you insist.

"If that were true," says the young man drily, "he was on the wrong planet."

"Look, it's just his word against mine," you say, lamely.

"That's true," says Harma. "Of course, he's Kenzo Haikoa, Akamura-ji's boss, and you— well, I like you, Morgan-ji, but in a revolutionary movement justice is defined by— oh, fuck, I don't have to explain it to you, I just have to kill you."

"Truth is, I've actually been working for *you*," you suggest. "Why, on Okura I—"

"Orchestrated the revolt against the Peace Party Directorate," the young man, Haikoa, fills in.

"Really?" asks Harma, lowering her plasmator a little. "Not fucking bad."

"I'm more valuable to you alive than dead," you offer.

"I don't see that at all," says Harma, raising the plasmator again.

This is not at all going as you had planned. You wish you could consult the Agent Directives— preferably photonically; access speed would really count right now.

"Morgan is right, actually," says Haikoa, imperturbably.

"What?" you and Harma say, simultaneously.

"An Incatena Agent falling into our hands is an incredible opportunity. It has to be used."

Harma considers this. She lowers her plasmator, looks at you, looks at Haikoa. She looks hard at Haikoa. Her eyes are smaller than his, but it's all in how you use them.

"Haikoa-ji, you're not on Okura any more," she says, finally. "We use our brains, here. And mine tells me that your plans didn't work out on Okura— thanks to this character here, looks like— and they may not work out here, either, you get me?"

"That's true enough," admits Haikoa, gracefully. "But we intend to pursue those plans in any case."

"Fine," says Harma. "What I'm saying is that I'll pursue mine too. If I see Morgan-ji around here again— I pull the trigger, you got it?"

"Certainly," says Haikoa.

And Harma is gone, leaving just a small pool of betel juice behind her.

"Did you want to finish your reflections on leverage?" Haikoa asks you.

"I was right," you comment. "Leverage is a tricky thing. But things didn't exactly go your way, did they?"

"Things are going exactly our way," replies the young man, with an extremely slappable smile.

Jaimunda

"We've just passed the southern perimeter," Haikoa informs you. "We should be there in another hour or so."

You nod, as if ranches the size of small countries were small beer where you come from. You look outside the volant window at Jaimunda's line of border defenses, which include trenches, Tajima fences, and antimatter projectors. This hostile display differs only in scale and means from any other New Bharati property. The first thing a new settler thinks of here, before shelter or planting, is a fence. It comes from the colonists' individualism, but even more so from the crowded conditions of their homeland: the colonists appropriate empty space with a sort of drunken glee.

The interior of Jaimunda thus differs from the rest of the continent mostly in having less fences cut across it. Mostly it's dry, tough desert, red and brown, dusted with straggly brownish vegetation. Elsewhere you'd also see lurid green patches of cultivated land, irrigated with water mined from the outer planets; but Jaimunda is almost entirely wilderness. Whatever else he does, Ormant doesn't care to play farmer.

You've had no luck drawing Haikoa out about his plans and how you fit into them; he simply smiles and says, "Later." You decide to try a more general approach.

"There's something I don't understand about Ormant," you say.

"If you and I understood Ormant," Haikoa responds, "we'd be interstellar tycoons too."

That's a point, though an annoying one. You persist: "He's incomprehensibly rich and powerful. Why does he want *more*? Is he aiming for *ineffably* rich and powerful?"

Haikoa throws you a pitying glance. "Is that really how he looks to you?"

It occurs to you that "Yep" wouldn't be a really effective answer. "That's the reading back at the Incatena Spire."

"I suppose you think Kumari was just after power, too?"

"Well, at some point, theoretically, he wanted neoteny."

252

Haikoa smiles. "You've heard that, at least. But it goes far beyond that."

"Right," you say. "Ormant and Kumari don't want absolute power and the end of the Incatena just out of greed. It's also a matter of principle."

"I find that really offensive," remarks Haikoa.

"What?"

"That sort of statement."

You look at him; for once he doesn't look amused.

"I'm not following you," you say.

"That sort of *partisan ridicule*," he says, slowly and with great disdain. "It may be *amusing* to you and to anyone else who doesn't understand our thinking and what we're trying to do. But I don't find it *amusing* at all."

He's gripping the steering bar so tightly that the volant jerks and twists in the air.

"I'm not trying to be offensive," you say, with the delicate tact that people who don't deserve it always seem to require. "Besides, aren't you forgetting the power roles here? I'm your prisoner, after all."

"Oh, yes, you *are* innocent," says Haikoa. "You only undid half a century of the Peace Party's work on Okura, and were about to do the same on New Bharat."

You should ask for permission to quote him on your half-century performance review. However, now is not the time to ask.

"Listen, Haikoa-san, I was just teasing," you say, cajolingly. "To some people it would seem that Ormant is just after power, but of course that's not true. He's a highly principled man."

"Of course he is," says Haikoa, sullenly.

"He's concerned— he thinks the world is off track morally."

"Exactly."

"From his point of view, what he's doing is merely common sense, and his opponents are perverse fools for not seeing it."

Haikoa has recovered his calm. "You *do* understand," he tells you.

"Of course," you reassure him. "Except for the part about what his point of view *is*."

"The world is a very evil place," Haikoa says.

"Ah," you say, as if this was news.

"Most people give in to it, or become victims of it. But what you have to do is oppose it. Now, what do you oppose evil with?"

This is one of those trick questions, you feel. "Good" is the obvious answer, but it's banal, and we're looking for something that distinguishes Ormant's worldview from everybody else's, aren't we? You have to think like an Ormantite. Peace? Force? A country-sized ranch? A really strong Home Ministry? Neoteny?

Fortunately, the question was rhetorical.

"Order," says Haikoa. "In the exterior world, you oppose evil with order. In the interior world, with discipline. We've lost that, and look at the state the world is in."

"New Bharat doesn't seem like a very ordered place."

"On the contrary. New Bharat is full of ordered *people*— self-disciplined, independent, moral people. When you have true order, you don't need the false order of your so-called socionomics. Moral people can be allowed to act as they wish, because their actions will be moral."

"Like Ormant's. And Okura?"

"Okura was already corrupted with false order and false consciousness," Haikoa explains. "Correct consciousness has to be *re-created* there. When it is, the intrusive aspects of the Directorate won't be necessary any more."

"And can be removed?"

"Removed or not removed. If you've trained a dog to heel, it doesn't matter if you have a leash or not."

"I'm not sure that the Okurinese really want to be trained dogs," you observe.

"Dogs and children need training," counters Haikoa. "Human beings and animals aren't disciplined by nature. You train them; if they resist, you break their will. Actually that metaphor is backwards. They start out with their will broken: undisciplined, corrupt, going nowhere. It's a crime to leave them like that— to coddle them. What you do is *fix* their will, make them disciplined and moral."

You think about this a bit.

"Have you considered therapy?" you ask.

"That's a rather offensive statement," complains Haikoa. "I thought you were on the verge of understanding, and you..."

"Just a little humor," you lie.

"You don't have to be so... *humorous*. But no matter. The point is, despite your cynical humor and corrupt alliances, you're the same way."

"I am? How do you figure?"

"What's Agent Training if not discipline? What's your role if not to restore order, as the Incatena sees it? You couldn't pick someone off the street to do what you do. They couldn't do it; they probably wouldn't *want* to. A corrupt society can't even count on generating people who are skilled at preserving it. You don't have the same values as we do, the *correct* values. But, order in the service of an incorrect morality is still order. You're halfway over to our side; that's why we can use you."

"And how is that?"

"We're here," says Haikoa.

Haikoa picks up the commaudio and talks to the air controllers at the ranch. "Don't fire," you hear them say. Ormant must have a very proactive policy toward cold callers.

You catch a glimpse of the central compound before you land: an enormous walled-in area, virtually a small city. Buildings, cranes, greenhouses, power generators, ground vehicles, volants, orbital shuttles, weapons, scurrying men in uniform. A tall fence looms ahead of you, its top crackling with an antimatter barrier. The volant slips in over it, and lands in a huge hangar.

Haikoa has you get out first. As you stand there blinking, trying to adjust your eyes to the relative darkness, Haikoa snaps his fingers. Two guards trot up, max guns at the ready. Haikoa walks toward an inside door; you follow. The guards follow behind you.

You're not sure what you expected to see at Ormant's ranch. A herd of Herefords, perhaps. Brick fireplaces, knotty-pine furniture. Instead, the place looks like the headquarters of a small army. The corridors are wide, brightly lit, and functional. People rush by, looking highly purposeful in their grey uniforms and crew cuts. Hardened chestplates with high padded collars protect the vital organs and cushion the neck; a helmet ensconces the head, and probably contains night scopes, commaudio, and an array of photonic helpers and displays. The visors are small Tajima screens, so that each person's eyes look like they've been blurred for anonymity, like the suspects in a true-police holo.

Farther in, you pass banks of datanodes, laboratories, studios, conference rooms, a gymnasium, a cafeteria. There are identity checks; Haikoa is always waved on. As you proceed, you see fewer soldiers, and more engineers, managers, and mecs. They carry datanodes and cups of caf instead of weapons, and wear orange jumpsuits rather than armor, but they seem just as rushed. Jaimunda, you reflect, doesn't look like the sort of workplace that offers flextime, on-site game rooms, and really good company parties.

At the last checkpoint you have to stop; the two of you are given over to an array of scanners, which snap and crackle with various sorts of undoubtedly carcinogenic radiation, and probe you both with the utmost of photonic curiosity. The guards retire, and you follow Haikoa through an airlock.

Now the place looks less like a military headquarters than like the interior of a vast hotel. The light is dim and the gravity is high— about Sihor level, you notice. There are plants, tasteful if generic oil paintings, indirect lighting, carpeting on the walls. The uniforms here are gold and black, and their owners seem to be in less of a hurry— they walk by noiselessly on the thick carpets— though they are no less purposeful. A few people are not in uniform, but in the bare feet and silk skirts of the Satyampuri: the men bearded, with braided hair; the women veiled and topless.

Haikoa consults with a woman at a console— Sihorian, looks like. The woman looks at you, looks back at Haikoa, checks her datanode, nods. You have to wait a few minutes— you've reached the end of Haikoa's immediate access. Then she presses a switch and a door unlocks.

The room is large, dark, and circular; it's like entering a cave, though most caves don't have tropical plants, velvet draperies, and piped-in Sihorian cyberpop. You approach a desk long enough to rent volants from. The only lights in the room are behind the desk, illuminating the honcho's visitors and leaving him in darkness.

He's tall, thin, as stiff and straight and deadly as the hunting autofletch displayed on the wall behind him. You can make out grey hair, a long nose, a carefully controlled goatee, a small scar.

There's an enormous insect on his lap, a sort of iridescent green beetle with wicked-looking mandibles. There's a bristly patch on its head, which he strokes while observing your approach. His eyes glint as he shifts a little in his chair.

You've only seen him in android form, but you'd recognize the Planetary Marshal anywhere.

The overlords

Haikoa leads you up to the Planetary Marshal's enormous desk, stopping well back, and stands there mildly, with the particular intrusiveness that only a look of total patience produces.

"Whatever the hell it is, I don't have time for it," Kumari says.

"This is Morgan—" says Haikoa.

"And *whoever* the hell it is. The datamoot starts in two hours."

"—Agent of the Incatena—"

"Haikoa—"

"—most recently on mission to Okura."

Kumari looks up for the first time, and looks you over. He strokes his beetle absently. Haikoa takes this as an invitation, and leads the two of you closer to the desk.

"We talked about Morgan," explains Haikoa, nervously. "Most recently, last Thursday. My action item was to—"

"*That* Morgan," says Kumari, in a tone that indicates that the mental file he has just retrieved is not labeled *People to Send Yearly Bottle of Tanaki to.*

"Yes, that Morgan," says Haikoa, beaming as if he expects an immediate promotion. "You'll remember that my proposal—"

Kumari shuts him up with a wave of his hand and faces you. You consider several expressions, including the innocent smile and the defiant scowl, before settling on calm gravity.

"Nice work," he tells you, "starting a goddamn nuclear war on my planet."

"I can't really take credit for that," you point out. "That was the Peace Army."

"The occasion arose for the Peace Army," says Kumari, "only after *you* showed up and started a goddamn revolution."

"All I really did was to find some stress points within—"

"I think what's clear about that and other parameters of the operation," interposes Haikoa, "is that Morgan-san is an unusually resourceful Agent, whose considerable skills would benefit our side as much as they've benefitted theirs."

Kumari faces you. "What do you think about that? You flip on the Incatena, why should I be so fucking stupid as to think you won't flip again on us?"

"There's technology for that," says Haikoa dismissively. "A little thalamic inhibitor, subsmart..."

"I don't trust those goddamn things."

"I don't blame you," you offer. "Inhibitors hobble so many brain functions they're no good for anything but minions—thugs, colonels, accountants. And you never know if the other side hasn't laid down a pathway that can't be found."

"What I like," says Kumari, "is a vek who'd chop off a finger for me. Kill his own children. Drink a glass of my urine. No goddamn neurimplant's going to produce *that*."

You peek over at Haikoa's hands. It looks like he's escaped the first of these loyalty tests, at least.

"Additive techniques are more reliable than subtractive," you suggest. "Now if I wanted to flip Haikoa-san, say, I'd convince him—preferably with AI help, or a neuroconversion layer— that the Incatena was the true embodiment of Peace Party ideals."

"Sounds good, but you forget I don't have the goddamn resources I had on Okura," grumbles Kumari.

"Sorry about that," you say, grandly. "I guess you could say that's my fault."

"*How's* that?"

"Don't flatter yourself," says Haikoa.

You look back and forth at the two of them, confused. "Didn't you—"

"Flee before the boot of the Incatena like a cockroach?" supplies Kumari, scornfully. "Certainly not. I've been here for two years. This is where the action is, isn't it, Kawaii-chan?"

Kawaii-chan is the insect, which he nuzzles affectionately. The mandibles look like they could sever his neck, or at least slice off an ear, but no luck; the thing only chitters a little.

"Not that you didn't cause some goddamn complications," he adds. "You couldn't have done any of that shit if I'd been there, and some balls are going to be extracted, you can bet on that. But Okura is a solved problem. New Bharat is where our efforts are most needed— and it's where they're going to bear fruit. Once we have New Bharat, we'll have something. And then on to Sihor."

"You're not going to get very far with the New Bharat Freedom Movement."

Kumari laughs, and Haikoa's habitual smile lengthens. "For Haikoa's sake, I hope you're joking about the Freedom Movement. It's a goddamn sideshow. But here... an entire planet, ripe for the taking, and still in the malleable stage—"

"A place you can *order*?" you suggest.

"Exactly," says Haikoa, with enthusiasm.

"And better yet, an *interstellar* moral order— something the Incatena hasn't even pretended to provide?"

"You see, Planetary Marshal. Morgan understands."

"Only too goddamn well," says Kumari. "I told you, you can't flip Incatena Agents. All you can do with them is whack 'em. Don't you think so, Kawaii?" He holds Kawaii up to his ear, stroking the underside of its abdomen. "Kawaii-chan agrees."

"August Director—" begins Haikoa. He turns to you. "Listen, give us five, would you?"

You are happy to agree.

You wander away from the desk, letting your captors, the Planetary Marshal and his lackey, confer. You can hear Haikoa's voice, high and agitated; Kumari's words are inaudible. Occasionally there's a high-pitched chitter.

You examine the office as well as you can in the darkness, moving along the circular perimeter. There are plaques and memorabilia on the walls and in glass cases. Most of them relate to Ormant's businesses on a dozen worlds, though Ormant turns out to be the sort who puts his junior high school sports trophies on display, and even a yearbook opened to his picture. (Label: "Most likely to *party!*")

A little constellation of pinpoint lights hovers in the air. A star map, the deluxe version of the one installed in the boss's office back in Areopolis. You find the controls and set the holographic display to slowly wobble back and forth— the only way for humans to absorb a three-dimensional display. Any projection into two-space— including a static view of a hologram— misleads. Not a few interstellar schemes have gone awry for being based on perceived close relationships that were artifacts of a projection.

The fifty-odd human colonies shine in bright yellow, occupying most of the model— the vast reaches of the immense galaxy are clipped. You amuse yourself finding Sol, ε Indi, β Hydri, and ζ Tucanae, without turning on the labels.

There's a memory button on the console; you press it, interested to see what the last user of the map might have seen. The display twists a bit, magnifies slightly. Several stars are highlighted in red, some in purple.

You identify the red stars: p Eridani, β Hydri, ε Indi, and ζ Tucanae: the suns of Maraille, Okura, Sihor, and New Bharat. The seeds of Ormant and Kumari's vision; the incipient schism of human space. It's not hard to interpret the purple as well: prospective new colonies, near the little zone of red stars but farther out from Sol.

Why? you wonder. Why does anyone need to break free of the agonizingly limited powers of the Incatena? Neoteny? Order? Whatever Haikoa and other underlings believe, you have no evidence that Kumari believes in either of these abstractions. His loyalty tests stick in your mind. This is a man motivated by power. The Incatena, weak as it is, holds him back, prevents him from exercising the control over men he feels he deserves. Ormant must be the same. And such as Haikoa are attracted to them, feeling no doubt that these men of power will fulfill their own dreams of order.

And what countervailing vision do you have to offer? Democracy, decency, muddling through? The spectacle of fifty stars glowing the same color on this tiny fraction of the galactic map? You remember Ba's questions. Who are you to decide the fate of worlds?

But the Agent Directives have anticipated this. *If the Agent fears or fails to act, initiative passes to those who feel no such fear.* And new things will not come from such men, the Ormants and Kumaris; only old things, very old things: the primate hierarchy, the desire for control— over others. It was all there in that photo of Dr. Zhou.

Haikoa summons you back; you return to the presence of the August Director.

"Well, what'll it be? Are we going to work together?" you ask, briskly, with a bright smile.

"It's no use," says Haikoa, in a sad strangled voice. "We've decided to eliminate you."

"Ah."

"There's just the question of method."

"Before we try something where there's no undo gesture," you say, thinking furiously, "have you considered—"

"Nope, no more discussion," says Haikoa, shaking his head vigorously. "The question is *closed*." He glances at Kumari with a prim pout.

"What sort of deaths do we have on hand for high-ranking Agents?" asks Kumari, smiling, leaning forward in his chair. "Tell Kawaii-chan and me about them."

"Well... we had a neat trick for that Sihorian embezzler. We lashed him down, just under a running laser on a servocircuit. The circuit was slaved to the stock market index, so the laser would point up or down, following the trades. As soon as the market descended below the day's starting average, it would burn through his brain."

"An economical approach!" says Kumari. "Charming! How long did it take?"

"Unfortunately, we had announced his capture, and the markets rose. That gave him time to cut his bonds with his pocket comb and escape."

"Foolproof, I want foolproof," Kumari mutters. "How hard is that to understand?"

"With that Ikkyū-jin last year," continues Haikoa, "we used the Data Death."

"What's that?"

"We hooked her up to a neural probe. Her individual neurons were slowly, successively replaced with simulations— using a destructive read. Then, once her consciousness was transferred to the machine, the memory space was given over to a dynamic process as a heap store, so that her consciousness would be slowly eaten away by allocations and reallocations."

"Virtual horror!" chuckles Kumari. "No physical screams, I suppose, which is a pity. But the psychic trauma must have been unbearable."

"Unfortunately the traitors in the Ikkyū-shima Peace Party backed up the memory space, and restored her into the mind of one of our own men who was undergoing a routine brain-cropping."

"The Vee is too damn slippery. What else have you got?"

"Insubordinate general. Hung him from a rope, which ran through a pulley, and held up a huge pile of donuts in his own orderly room. As his own staffers took the donuts one by one, unsuspecting, he was lowered into a pit of ravenous hailon-beasts."

"His own staff! Delightful! This one worked, I hope?"

"Turns out he grew up on a hailon-beast farm," says Haikoa, regretfully. "Calmed them down and escaped."

"It's hopeless," says Kumari. "Look, just shoot the *baka*, would you?"

To your alarm, Haikoa produces a small but deadly sonic thrasher. Once he presses the stud, a silent beam, undetectable by photonics, will induce a series of waves in the brain of the target— in the present case, that would be you— which will culminate after a few seconds in a messy explosion.

"Not here, you fool," says Kumari. "The carpets! Think about the carpets!"

"Yes, Director," says Haikoa.

Datamoot

Haikoa leads you, dejectedly, back the way you came. You trudge through the dimly lit corridors of the inner sanctum, and out into the bustling offices beyond. You blink in the sudden bright light.

"Want to catch something to eat before I carry out my orders like a good soldier?"

"Sure," you say, trying to think of dishes that take time to cook. "Peking duck, perhaps? Steamed slamfish? Marinated puercón?"

"Let's just stop at the cafeteria."

"Well, OK. Do you mind covering for me? I can pay you back tomorrow."

In your line of work you've often thought about what you'd like for your last meal. You never really pictured it as greasy saag gosht, overcooked rice, a cup of yogurt, and watery Masala tea.

The cafeteria is almost empty at this hour of the afternoon, but Haikoa sits down only a table away from a pair of the bare-breasted Satyampuri women. One of them has brazenly removed her veil to eat; the other demurely slips bits of her sandwich underneath hers to her mouth.

"Before I get rid of you," says Haikoa, with a little more cheer, "I thought we could talk about socionomics."

"Like what?"

"Well, you know that the Peace Party doesn't accept it. And yet the Incatena believes in it wholeheartedly. Why is that? What's the attraction?"

"It works, that's all," you say. "Why doesn't the Peace Party accept it?"

"It's a deterministic theory," Haikoa explains. "It denies free will. It limits human capabilities."

Disconcertingly, as he talks, he looks not at you but at the two Satyampuri women. They hurriedly finish up their meal and leave.

"Do you accept gravity? That limits the human capability to fly."

"Gravity can be controlled."

"To control it you have to know how it works— you have to accept the theory of quantum gravity."

Haikoa thinks a moment. "But how do you know that socionomics *works*?"

"Three thousand years of data."

Haikoa shakes his head. "But then you're a prisoner of those three thousand years of data. Even if socionomics explains that, you can't extrapolate into the future. We refuse to be limited by the past."

You sigh. All this is covered in the first weeks of high school socionomics, before the first simulation, before the teacher can recall everybody's name. "Look, it's not like you plug every last parameter into the datanode and it predicts what's going to happen for the next 30,000 years, down to what clothes you'll be wearing," you say, though this is actually a bad example; bureaucrats' clothing choices are highly predictable. "There's discontinuities— even chaotic periods like revolutions. But as soon as things settle down, we can predict and manage what happens."

"Because human nature is always the same," says Haikoa, with the air of a man preparing a trap.

"More or less."

"But human nature does change. Look at the way different nations behave— or how societies change over time. Are you telling me that socionomics can explain Okura in AD 4900 with the same equations as Mongolia in AD 900?"

"Parameter differences," you say, imperviously. "Do you think no one's ever thought about these things? Socionomics is all about how one parameter suite changes into another."

"But the human factor—"

"Got it covered. It's not just a part of socionomics, it *is* socionomics. Without the human factors all you have is economics— the pseudo-mathematics of the ancients."

"But some nations, like Gōsei, have a *dynamism* that others don't have. How can you reduce that to numbers?"

"Give us a static society and socionomics will tell you how to turn it *into* a dynamic one— what to teach the kids in school, what comic books to write, what family behaviors have to change, what sectors to encourage. Of course, a static society won't *like* those changes... that's why it stays static. No problem... back up a level; we can tell you what to do to generate a liking for them."

"Or you send in an Agent to make changes for them," says Haikoa.

"That's introducing a discontinuity. Generally you can accomplish the same thing without one— *if* you can wait a couple centuries. You try to muddle through without Agents if you can."

"But what if you're *wrong*?" insists Haikoa. "Don't you ever think of that? What if Okura doesn't want to play by socionomic rules?"

"Which one don't you like?" you counter. "The Scarcity Law? Have you invented a way to distribute limited goods to a larger population? The Principle of the Conservation of Anxiety? Gene/Sex Calculus? Language Logic? The Hierarchy Conversions? I don't think you've exactly got rid of the primate hierarchy on Okura..."

"You're just snowing me with technical terms," complains Haikoa. "What if I started talking about the Cardinal Principle of Kumari Thought, or the Five Peace Actions?"

"Harmony," you say, brightly. "And the actions are Listen, Love, Labor, Lead, and Liberate. Do you want to know the Director's birthplace?"

"So we're at a standoff. We don't accept your beliefs and you don't accept ours. And don't bother to indignantly object that *yours* are actually *correct*. We think the same thing about ours."

"No, I'll indignantly object that ours aren't *beliefs* at all. Somehow I doubt there's any testing procedure for Kumari Thought."

"So you'd expect that, given a few centuries, the Incatena, using socionomics, will develop faster than the Peace systems, using Kumari Thought."

"Yep."

"Why not just wait and see?"

"Because we're not fighting against Kumari Thought; we're fighting against a dictatorship. *Elect* Kumari head of a planet and we'll be glad to let you impoverish yourselves in your own way."

Haikoa looks at his watch. "We may be about to do just that. Let's go."

He stands. You look around, and notice that the cafeteria has emptied out; there isn't even anyone behind the counter. He leads you down one of the interminable corridors.

"What's the procedure?" you ask. "Do you have an open grave out back, or do you just use one of these little rooms and leave the body for the cleaning people, or what?"

"There's no need to be *sarcastic*," says Haikoa, in a hurt voice. "This *wasn't* my idea."

"I'll remember to be more polite with the next guy assigned to kill me."

"Actually, *if* you think you can wait, we'll take care of it later. It's time for the datamoot."

The corridors are nearly empty; the few people that remain are rushing like they forgot to turn off the basmati. Haikoa takes you to an office, which is so devoid of personal characteristics that you feel sure it's Haikoa's own. He locks the door, then sits down inside the ergolounge and points to the guest chair. He reaches into a drawer and takes out a couple of Vee inducers.

"This should interest you," he says, handing you one. "We'll worry about the, uh, antisepsis in an hour or two, when things calm down a little."

He turns on a Tajima screen between the two of you. Then he puts on his inducer, crosses his arms, and seems dead to the world.

You glance at the door, notice the fingerprint pad, and sigh. You sit down, slip the inducer under your head, snug against your visual cortex, and—

And New Bharat is in your head with you.

You're inside a huge sphere, about a kilometer across, looking out at a roiling, moving crowd. The sphere is lined with people.

You move up a bit and fly across the virtual landscape. Each person has a square meter of dataspace; there's obviously room in the sphere for every inhabitant of the planet.

Each person seems to self-present any way they choose. The default representation is a three-dimensional face, laying like the head of John the Baptist against the surface of the sphere, and hundreds of thousands have gone no farther than this. Others appear as full figures lying or sitting in their square meter, or as cartoons, or as animals, aliens, gods, or abstractions— anything at all, really. Not a few have chosen to present themselves as a giant penis, rising from their square meter to the allotted maximum like a thick tan mushroom. Fratboys, probably. Others have made their space into representations of their living quarters, with a tiny avatar that moves round the simulated space following its owner. One rather creepy space is decorated with little detached eyeballs, whose pupils follow you as you move above it. Another features a non-focal image, one that can be seen only in peripheral vision, and vanishes when you look at it directly.

Most of the avatars are moving, reflecting the expressions and commands of their owners, plugged into the Vee wherever they are in the planet. A few are motionless, signifying a citizen who hasn't shown up yet; but many of these spring to life as you watch.

You wonder whose territory you started from. Haikoa's, presumably. You drift back and indeed, there he is, or rather his big-eyed head, glaring like a hunter's trophy on the vast peoples-cape. He looks busy; indeed, you can hear him talking, in a low mumble— both within the Vee and next to you in the real world, incompletely suppressed by the inducer.

You wonder where Beloman is. Does Agent Beloman have an avatar here? As you think about her, you feel a prompting, like a tugging at your elbow; when you give in to it you find yourself soaring through the sphere at dizzying speed. You approach the opposite surface, toward a large territory, raised from the surrounding datascape like a mesa, with an enormous label reading THE HUMAN INCATENA.

This must be, you realize— see trap, steel, your mind being, op. cit.— the Incatena's portion of the datascene. The mesa has room for various displays— a holo of nearby space, for instance, much like the one in Ormant's office; informational displays; an interactive map of the Incatena offices in Colony Base (including a helpful display of the number currently being served); a tiny gallery of famous artworks from human worlds; an enormous animated representation of Inky, the Incatena Mascot; and of course avatars of Incatena personnel.

You have no trouble recognizing Beloman, though she's chosen to appear as a cartoon character— a warrior princess with enormous eyes, wearing an improbable combination of cumbersome armor and bare skin, pigtails and firearms. You circle near and say hello; she doesn't respond. You wave a hand, and when nothing waves you realize that you don't have an avatar yourself— you aren't visible to anyone.

All your carefully constructed avatars are on your own datanode, which you left on Ba's bedside table back on Okura, or on storage disks back home in Areopolis. That shouldn't matter; you can construct a new one through the inducer.

Only you can't. The usual mental gestures have no effect; the interfaces you can access have big blank spaces. Haikoa handed you a maimed inducer.

It's not time for despair yet. You explore. Maiming is usually done after product ship, by coders who'd rather be doing anything else in the world; it tends to have holes in it.

You can't speak, can't produce objects, can't get to mail, can't access the coding level. On the other hand, you can move around, and there were those eyeballs that followed you. Other dataspaces can detect and respond to *you*. What else can you do? You reach out and touch Beloman's avatar on the nose. She startles; the big eyes open even wider, and she looks around confusedly. That's good news as far as it goes— you can affect the Vee— but she obviously still can't *see* you.

You look closely at her space, but it's simply a representation of a stone wall, presumably part of the cartoon princess's milieu. You slap it with your palm and produce a muffled sound; Beloman doesn't seem to hear it. Indeed, she's looking away, seemingly not at anything in particular; most likely her attention is somewhere else on the datasphere.

You examine the spaces near her, looking for props. Someone's represented their office; you grab a pencil, but it doesn't leave any marks. Damned abstract representations. But wait; he also has a salt shaker, a salt shaker that works in the Vee— it has simulated salt in it.

You grab it; when you approach the edge of his dataspace there's a resistance, as if the salt shaker doesn't want to leave; then there's an audible pop and the object duplicates; one of them drifts back to its place and the other remains levitating in space, held in your invisible hand.

Triumphantly, you move back to Beloman's space, and poke her in the arm with the salt shaker. This time she notices, and follows the salt shaker with eyes that take up half the character's face. You carefully write her a message in salt:

BELOMAN!

"What the hell?" she says.

You begin a new message— KIDNAPPED BY PEACE PARTY AGENT HAIKOA HELD IN ORMANT'S OFFICE JAIMUNDA— but you don't get past the second word without running out of salt. Cursing, you try to re-use the salt from the previous message, shaping letters with virtual fingers. This proves to be rather difficult, not least because Beloman keeps trying to guess what you're saying, as if you're playing charades, which flusters you, and once the sleeve of her gauntlet brushes the stones and erases half your work. The stone surface soon looks like it's been visited by a light snowfall and a plague of rats.

"Why don't you just like *talk*?" asks Beloman, plaintively.

"Because you can't hear me," you say, in frustration, because she can't hear you.

A smile suddenly lights up the cartoon face. The salt and salt shaker disappear, and a keypad appears. (An archaism; normally you'd use your UI neurimplant. Probably somebody constructed it as a coding exercise, and of course whoever maimed the UI wasn't even aware of it.) You grab it and type: *Beloman! It's Mogran.* The words appear suspended in the air above the keypad. You notice the typo and reach up to switch the two little red letters.

"I should have known. What are you playing at?"

You explain, typing as quickly as you can. The air is soon filled with red lettering.

So, they're planning on killing me in an hour, you conclude, and then go back and stretch out the word "killing". *So if you could see your way to rescuing me...*

"From Jaimunda?" she says. "There's like no way. I don't have a private army or anything. Is there something you want me to get back to the boss?"

Yeah, if they kill me, tell him I quit.

She thinks a minute. The cartoon princess's forehead wrinkles.

"Oh wait, I know what to do," she says.

The soul of the datamoot

What can I do to help? you type.

"Get lost," suggests Beloman. "Scope out the datamoot. It's really kind of a trip."

You're about to protest, but she's already busy (the cartoon princess is scowling, with her tongue stuck out of the corner of her mouth), and you realize that interruptions and explanations are only going to get in the way of her saving your hide. So why not check out the datamoot? It's said to be kind of a trip.

A little scouting around produces some simulated documentation, which fortunately is hi-res enough to serve as real documentation.

The datamoot, you learn, is just what is looks it looks like— a planetwide town meeting. It's empowered to pass laws, elect officials and tell them what to do, set taxes, bring judgments. Every inhabitant of the planet can appear, vote, speak, propose motions or laws. The documentation shows you how to display a monitor which shows pending motions and their electoral status. There are over a thousand pending now, as well as an even higher number of discussions, opinion posts, news and analysis scenes, and a plethora of tools for surfing the information flow: googles, datamoles, bozos, grepmonsters, kiboizers, text plotters, cyber-hounds.

This strikes you as chaotic, till you understand how the display of motions works: the color and size of the motions scales to the number of proponents. Motions with one vote appear microscopically small; indeed, you need specialized search functions to find them. They grow brighter and bigger as they get more votes. Motions which have already received ten thousand votes are readily visible on the monitor; motions with a million votes are bright blue and an inch high. Once they pass a threshold— usually a simple majority, but some sorts of motions require a higher or lower number— they pass. An alarm rings and the motion is removed to a display of motions adopted.

Nay votes make a motion grow as well, but slowly turn it red instead of blue; if the threshold of nay votes is reached the now bright-red proposal is rejected.

Currently the top motions, with several hundred thousand votes each, are:

DIVIDE NBCC AND ESTABLISH PLANETARY TRADE COMMISSION

GET RID OF THAT BASTARD KHUNARG AND HIS ICA

GET RID OF THE DAMN INCATENA TOO

LOWER CAPITAL GAINS ASSESSMENT FOR HIGH-EMPLOYMENT CORPORATIONS

REQUIRE DATAMOOT MEMBERS TO BE ROARING DRUNK TO VOTE

HALVE SALARIES OF PLANETARY PARLIAMENTARIANS

CONSTRUCT A BIG FUCKING OCEAN ON THIS FUCKING DESERT PLANET

You can grab a motion as it scrolls by, put it off to one side, and watch it or interrogate it. You can read the text of the motion, of course, or see who proposed it. Looking at the first motion, for instance, you're not surprised to see it attributed to the planetary government, the ICA.

When you think about the ICA, your attention is nudged upward, and you see, about a third of the way across the sphere, another raised mesa— obviously, the ICA's representation in the datamoot. It's only about a kilometer away; you can make out some of its displays from here, including a map of New Bharat and an enormous face of Rama Khunarg— unfortunately not animated, or it might be registering a certain amount of dismay as the proposal to sack him gains ground over any of the ICA's own proposals.

Looking around, you see a few more mesas, the largest of which— a veritable plateau, filled with entertaining commercial displays and expertly designed though transparent propaganda— is the representation of NBCC. Other mesas belong to other corporations, training academies and universities, guilds, gangs, cities and colonies, religious or ethnic groups, sexual minorities, and so on. Even alien embassies have their own mesas— you find the Dzebyet, whose mesa is actually an anti-mesa, a pyramidal hollow like an enormous dimple in the datasphere, and the Garcheron, whose space is all mirrors, lights, and movement, a gaudy spectacle of inhuman tackiness. There's a space reserved for the Ogorodé, but it's empty.

The motion on reducing corporate taxes comes from the NBCC; all the other major motions— whatever their real origins— are attributed to individuals.

You check out a few discussion groups. The groups are miniature versions of the datasphere, with dozens or hundreds of avatars instead of millions. Conversation proceeds in both text and speech. You ask the interface to find high-rated comments.

Khunarg is an insufferable little prick. The sooner we get rid of him the better.

We are needing some sort of planetary government. Do you want Ormant and the NBCC to control everything?

So long as I have my laser and a finger to fire it with the NBCC can't tell me a thing.

Certainly, you ignorant son of an owl, so long as you are growing your own food, making your own air, making bricks out of the sand, stamping your own photonics, forging your own iron and making it into spaceships...

You think Khunarg is some sort of protector, that he's thinking about us? He's after power, pure and simple. The bigger the government we let him have, the bigger he is.

Khunarg is just a puppet of the Incatena. He says it himself—"The Incatena requires a planet to have an effective government." The Incatena wallahs can go to hell with their buggered rules. They don't live here, do they?

That's right. We will decide how to run things on our own damn planet.

You stupid defilers of cows, the problem is not Khunarg, it's the NBCC. Their assessment is risible, and they want to lower it? Those jackals are thinking they own this planet— and they do, despite all the swamp gas that comes from your mouths. A dull child could see what they're aiming for: squeeze every last credit out of this planet they own, and give it nothing in return.

You don't marry the snake to protect yourself from the tiger. Khunarg is still an opportunistic bastard brother-in-law and I'm voting to get rid of him and the ICA.

Not the ICA, just Khunarg.

It's not Khunarg, it's the ICA as an institution. It was created as an incipient planetary government. When you have a cancer you don't just remove the tumors; you send in a nanoscourge to rip it out by the roots.

What is there to worry about? Look at the damn monitor. Khunarg's proposal is already red. So's the NBCC's. Their own employees voted for it, but who the hell else is stupid enough to do so? By Shiva, the only people who are controlling New Bharat are New Bharatis. So bag Khunarg, bag the ICA, bag NBCC, and bag the Incatena.

And that, you suspect, is what the consensus of the datamoot will turn out to be. You run a text plotter to be sure; an AI sifts through thousands of discussions, reduces the chatter to points in semantic space, devises explanatory axes, and displays the results holographically.[1] Clouds form before you and slowly rotate: representations of opinion-space. Various sources and sinks are labeled: points of convergence with the opinion of the ICA, of the NBCC, of Satyampur, of various parliamentarians or commentators. There are bright clumps round each of these— core supporters— but the cloud as a whole recoils from the dot in opinion-space that represents Khunarg.

You have to admire Ormant and Kumari, in a way. It's not easy to oppress New Bharat directly. The datamoot won't vote themselves into a dictatorship— or even into a normal, legitimate planetary government— if they can see what's going on.

But they can be tricked. They can be persuaded to remove a hated leader and the fledgling federation which has been inflated into a vision of tyranny, and very possibly membership in the Incatena as well— and those are the only effective barriers to complete domination by the NBCC. Once all economic and physical power in the company's hands, datamoots can simply be ignored or shut down, and settlers' lasers laughed at.

You stare at the text plotter's output, as into the cloud of sparks from a fire, as if the response to Ormant's strategy can be found there. That's absurd, of course, but—

Something about the cloud looks different. Something has changed.

---

[1] The analysis tools all work; the coders aren't going to spend valuable minutes maiming the statistics.

You look closer, confused. You have the plotter play back the last quarter hour of data. The shape of the cloud definitely changes, but how exactly? The cloud is still recoiling from Khunarg, still skirting the NBCC. You toss some analyzers at it and wait, impatiently.

"Hey, Morgan!"

You start at the interruption. "Beloman?"

"What? Come on, get up."

It's Haikoa's voice; and, as he removes the inducer from behind your head, you see the shadowy form of Haikoa, hovering in front of you, large as life and the eyes even larger. Almost instinctively you mentally reach for the brightness controls, but they don't work— this is reality.

"Killing time already? Too bad, I was just on the track of something, too."

Haikoa smiles slightly, and ushers you out of his office. "Let's just say that that order is under review."

"What? You're defying Kumari?"

"No, Ormant is," says Haikoa. "Come on, we're going to see him."

Satyampur

You climb down out of the shuttle, and feel like you've gone back in time a few thousand years. The sprawling buildings of Satyampur are red brick, the same color as the ground; the roofs are made of some brown, spongy vegetable matter. The streets are unpaved and dusty, and the only vehicles are small, boxy ground transports with ceramic bodies. There's no volants in sight, no streetlights, no street datanodes, no photonics fixtures, no weapons, no glass or metal, no advertisements. What words are visible stay put like they're dead.

The archaic technology gives it an air of squalor; but on a closer look you see that it possesses its own sort of staid prosperity, like an anti-Tunisian space bubble. The buildings are neatly made; the streets are straight and unlittered; and the Satyampuris stride by with a calm purposefulness, pressing their palms together in a namaste as they pass each other.

When everyone around you, including the young, the old, and the ugly, is dressed in the Satyampuri style— wearing nothing but a silk skirt, the men bearded, the women veiled— you find that it's you who feel out of place. It's their home, after all.

"So what do you get for a bite around here?" you ask. "Locusts and wild honey?"

Haikoa's eyes are on the passersby. "I'm afraid it'll be breast, I mean best, to see Ormant first. He doesn't like to be kept waiting."

"He's certainly got split-second timing. If he'd called half an hour later..."

Haikoa looks at you quizzically. "Are you saying it wasn't *your* timing? I figured that was your rack. I mean hack."

"What hack?"

"Having the Incatena announce that you were in negotiations with us at Jaimunda. Made it inadvisable to tit— er, hit you."

Comes the dawn. Beloman's work. That was what the text plotter was trying to tell you: the news had affected the climate of opinion.

"It wasn't *exactly* my idea," you say, generously.

"No? So what the hell were you *doing* at the datamoot? Why do you think I let you in there?"

"You *wanted* me to communicate with the Incatena?"

"Maybe I've just grown fondle of you. I mean fond."

Not everyone is in uniform: you notice a few ordinary-looking citizens strolling around, with imagizers and loud clothes. That's generally the way it works: Fundamentalists in power are dangerous. Fundamentalists not in power are a tourist attraction.

You're not sure how Haikoa finds his way around; all the streets look the same, there are no landmarks, and there are no street signs. You can tell you've arrived, however; the building you head for looks the same as the others, but there are two armored goons on either side of the door.

Haikoa exchanges a few friendly words with them. It's always prudent to be on good terms with the hired heat.

You rather expect to be taken downstairs into a vast underground bunker; but the building is as simple inside as out: bare plastered walls, cane chairs, wooden doors, and cement floors with carpets.

Ormant is busy— it would hardly do for an interstellar tycoon, even one living in a cult compound, to see a visitor right away. You and Haikoa sit down to wait. You leaf through the magazines arrayed on a side table: *Satyampur Today*; *Truth!*; *Ram Awakes*.

There's nothing really hard to understand about these atavistic cults: quite a few people, contemplating the complicated chaos of modernity, have the impulse to retreat somewhere simpler and safer, and in an age of colonies, space bubbles, and micro-sovereignties, nothing stops you and a thousand or a million co-idealists from constructing your own version of utopia. The main variables are how much of the present you let in your bubble, and whether you prefer a tactical retreat, sleeping and relaxing in the more godly 13th or 19th or 38th century but working in the 50th, or as complete an exile as you can manage, complete with border guards and airlocks to keep the outside world at bay and the weaker brethren from temptation.

Often it ends in tears, or life support disasters— having strong opinions about how things should be doesn't make them that way. But there's a few, such as the Amish habitat Neu Lancaster, that have lasted over 1500 years.

The magazines are somewhat impenetrable, full of citations from unknown scriptures and rants against sin— they could use an unbelieving editor to trim some of the adjectives and explain the allusions. But you get a picture of life in the colony.

Satyampur is isolationist but not completely closed off; the colony is mostly self-sufficient, but selected individuals are allowed outside to trade or work or scout for converts. They believe in a sober, meditative, simple life. Their beliefs are not completely out of line for New Bharat, in that they are not communitarian, but divided into family units, each of which is supposed to earn a living in a disciplined fashion, without depending on or exploiting anyone else. A family can run a business, but discreetly. It cannot hire employees from outside the extended family. Children work on the family farm or business, and are married off early, in matches arranged by their elders.

They're not hostile to technology per se, but try to do without anything they can't make themselves. With 40,000 members, a fair amount can be done. Education is minimal, however, and communication with the outside world is restricted; there's only a local Vee. Entertainments include liturgical dance, four-hour worship services, scripture trivia, festive vegetarian meals, and spelling bees.

It doesn't sound like a happening place to be on a Saturday night.

There's no mention of the NBCC— indeed, precious little about "the domain of illusion", as the outside world is called— and certainly no explanation of why the elite sector of Jaimunda is staffed by cultists.

The door to Ormant's office opens, and two Garcheron come out. They're about a meter and a half tall, with brown, corrugated skin, patches of thick hair in various places, braided or adorned with jewelry, and gaudy clothes cut to let the sex organs

280 • Against Freedom

poke out— in other words, they're dressed like dudes in the Garcheron fashion. Their snouts are long and toothy, their compound eyes swivel about, taking everything in; from their shoulders sprout iridescent wings— tall and showy, but vestigial.

They stop in front of you. Their wings flutter a bit, a sign of active thought.

"You're new here," one of them tells you. "Do you need anything?" Its Modern Hindi is perfect. Despite their having no tongues, their command of human languages is always flawless, so much so that no humans have ever been able to learn anything about Garcheron languages.

You have to smile. They're no doubt here to negotiate some big deal with Ormant— a Garcheron would rather lose a limb (which it can always regenerate) than an opportunity to do more business.

"What have you been selling Ormant?" you ask, not expecting an answer.

"Weapons. But we are not limited to that— whatever you need, we can find it for you."

"I don't have any money."

"Everyone has something," says the other Garcheron. "Some knowledge, perhaps— some time— some energy— some organs you're not using at the moment."

"I'd better wait to see how many organs I've still got after seeing Ormant," you say.

They bow and laugh, and give you a relay-card for contacting them back at Colony Base. Their wings scrape the top of the doorway as they leave.

"I find that sort of supposedly *jocular* statement about Ormant highly offensive," says Haikoa.

"Shut up," you explain.

You recognize Ormant immediately. He looks exactly like the little holos of him that litter the financial districts of the Vee: a long, reddish face, jutting chin; a big beaky nose; wispy, sandy hair; a portly body dressed in a garish, bejeweled business suit, in the ostentatious Sihorian style. What you don't quite expect is to see four of him— four identical Ormants, arranged round a conference table, surrounded by papers, datanodes, minimecs, and caf. You wonder if this is some sort of holographic protection against assassination, but it's soon clear that all of these Ormants are present physically.

Then you notice something about the nearest Ormant's skin. There's something very slightly off about it— a dullness you would hardly notice if you couldn't compare it to the Ormant next to him. Three of the Ormants are androids, no doubt housing the AIs that form the second tier of command of Ormant/Mars.

There are no chairs on your side of the table. You and Haikoa stand and wait. All four Ormants look you over. None of them like what they see.

"Agent Morgan, that the nick?" asks one of them— the real one, so far as you can see. He speaks Sihorian Franca.

"Pleased to meet you," you say, in the same language.

"So we're negotiating, are we?"

"Uh— yes. Yes we are."

"So make us an offer," adds another Ormant. "And it better have fins and a good horn section."

"If I can interject a word, Ormant-san," says Haikoa, in Okurinese, "what I've proposed to the Planetary Marshal is that a competent, well-placed Agent, suitably turned, would be—"

"Can it, Ken," says one of the androids.

"Morgan isn't here as a prisoner, but as the ranking representative of the Incatena," says another.

"You're dribbling truth juice," says the real Ormant. "Probably here to grovel and plead for the life of their pimply little puppet Khunarg. Am I right?"

"Not at all," you say. "I thought the Incatena and NBCC could work together toward the elimination of Khunarg and the ICA."

Talking turkey with the big cheese

There's a long silence. You can almost hear the mental gears turning. This is what you live for as an Agent, really: a few words, calmly delivered, which stun and discomfit, which establish a casual mastery of a new situation, chosen and well understood by yourself, new and perilous to them. You fold your arms and gaze over the Ormants' heads, with a half smile, the pose of an aristocrat languidly serving the country in between meals at the club.

"What an idiot," mutters one of the Ormants.

"Falls right into our hands," says another.

A monocle is what you need. It's hard to pull the act off without it.

"Nonsense," says the third, more gratifyingly. "There's a logic to it. Wouldn't have thought the Incatena would stoop to it exactly, but— they've got to figure, why drown in the collapsing wormhole when the tear gas is flying?"

"You're not just peddling cornflakes," says the real Ormant. "I'd say every lizard in the desert's scooped off the grapevine that *that* dog won't race."

"I don't trust the Incatena farther than I can kick a piano," says the first Ormant.

"That's code off God's own system disk," agrees another.

"Listen, when the tide washes in a new paradigm, you get on board," insists the third Ormant. "The vek may be crazy as a peach-orchard boar or crazy like a Dzebyet, but that's our name up on the big board and the violins are humming. I say let's hit this circus full throttle."

"I got lost about three metaphors back," confesses Haikoa.

"It's simple enough," you explain. "Supporting the ICA has become a no-win situation. The mood of the datamoot is against it, and, frankly, it just gives you and Kumari a villain."

"And what do *you* scrape out of the ashtrays when the party's over?" one of the androids asks you.

"We lose the black hats and support a winner."

282

"And what's the price tag? You keep your bacon?"

"Ha, ha," you laugh. "You think you're *buying* me, plastic man?" You stride over, sit on the desk facing the android, and point a finger in his face. "I think you haven't quite grasped the situation here. Your plastic pal here had it right. I'm not here because *m'sö* Haikoa captured me. I'm here because I wanted to talk to *m'sö* Ormant. As I'm doing."

"Correct me if I'm not scanning the right horseflesh here," says the first android, "but two hours ago weren't you browsing a tapas menu of death scenarios with the Planetary Marshal?"

"Sometimes the shortest path through two points touches the bottom of the curve," you suggest.

"So," says the real Ormant, quietly, "what *is* the price?"

"*We'll* propose the removal of the ICA. And the NBCC supports the proposal."

"That's it?"

"And of course you cease your media campaign against the Incatena."

"What campaign is that?" asks the first android.

"Look, there's nothing clever about playing dumb," you say, contemptuously. "It just wastes time. Are we negotiating, or dancing the fandango?"

"Is that it?" asks Ormant.

"That's it."

There's a short silence. The Ormants look at you, look at each other; there's a complicated dance of frowns, raised eyebrows, slight hand movements.

"Put on your boots and wash the windows," says Ormant, finally. "We're gettin' married."

The cartoon princess's brows knit. "I hope you know what you're doing."

Beloman is still at the datamoot; the easiest way to talk to her is to join her in the Vee. This time you have an avatar of your own. You usually present as a duck— it has to do with your college nickname— but that doesn't quite seem to befit the ranking Agent on the planet, so your avatar is simply a version of yourself, with an aging and slowing filter applied— a dignified portrait, suitable for use on currency.

"Of course I do," you reassure her.

"We've been trying to build up the ICA as a planetary government for like fifty years now."

"The datamoot is about to throw it out," you point out.

"Maybe," she says. "The proposal hadn't passed."

"How close is it?"

"Pretty close," she admits. "But still, what you've basically done is like, keep the bad guys from shooting up the sheriff by firing your laser first."

"It puts us back in the game," you insist.

"Listen, you bluffed the hell out of them, but don't try it on me."

"I'm not."

"If you even managed *that*," she continues, woundingly. "How free are you, exactly? A gilded cage with a Satyampuri guard at the door, am I right?"

"No guards. Nice room, well-stocked minibar, Vee access, private bath, continental breakfast. No gravity controls or free holos though."

"Can you like get back to Colony Base?"

"I don't see why not. But this is where the action is."

And indeed it is, as the laserfire and explosions outside your window testify.

You hang up the inducer and run downstairs. The other guests are running to and fro— some panicking, some rushing to the windows to take pictures.

You push your way to a window, but there's nothing to see except the murky shadows of houses in the dark streets. For a moment there's silence; Satyampur is peaceful, as if it's in complete denial over the alarming noises of a moment back. Then there's another burst of gunfire, lighting up the sky like lightning.

You venture out and head in the direction of the laserfire— the direction of the spaceport, you realize. You walk slowly and keep to the shadows of the buildings. There are others in the streets, guests or Satyampuri, many of them armed, some running toward the excitement, most running away, some simply milling about in groups, getting in the way.

After awhile the gunfire stops. You haven't reached it, but you continue to follow the crowd, which seems possessed more by curiosity than by fear. Finally you reach the center of the disturbance. A group of Satyampuri soldiers is marching along, escorting a single prisoner— a bulky, black, armored figure, whose arms are tied and whose face, for some reason, is masked and gagged.

The figure and the body movement, however, are obviously those of Harma Rakashri.

Two trials

"Do you know what's going on?" you ask a Satyampuri man standing next to you.

"Not for sure, but it is certainly good entertainment," says the man. He's tall, pot-bellied, jovial-looking.

The woman next to him clucks. "*Rajiv*," she says, in a voice that works as a fair approximation of a gravity control. "Don't talk like that. Someone could have been hurt."

The man simply laughs.

The woman looks over at you. Her expression is hidden by her veil, but you can guess it from the stiffness of her bearing. She manages to look prissy and bloodless even while wearing nothing but a skirt and veil. "I *hope* you don't think *this sort of thing* is typical of Satyampur," she says.

"Not at all," you say. "I suppose you don't believe in violence?"

"Of course we do," she replies. "We have the right to defend against armed intrusion, such as those ICA infiltrators and this terrorist, don't we?"

"So you're for self-defense."

"We are warriors for *truth*," she clarifies. "We will fight as the army of Arjuna when we are called to do so, leaving destruction in our wake."

"Ah," you say. There's an awkward pause. You never know quite what to say to people who are pro-destruction.

Then you ask, "So what sort of a bad impression were you worried that I'd get?"

"We are people of peace," explains the woman.

"You should come to one of our services." says her husband. "Don't worry, they're not all four hours long! We have a visitor's service most mornings at the temple, with brunch afterwards. Tomorrow is a theme brunch— every dish is made of lentils, what do you think of that? Even dessert! You've seen the temple, I hope? It's really something."

"I haven't had the time yet. I'm here to see Ormant."

286

You're curious if they'll be impressed, or alarmed, or disdainful, but they simply smile and nod, as if Ormant was a respectable if unexciting tourist destination in his own right.

"If I may ask," you ask, "why do you work with Ormant? His elite guard at Jaimunda is all Satyampuri."

"He's *undelivered*," sniffs the woman. "But it may be that the Lord wills for deliverance to come to this planet, *despite* you, *from* us, *through* him."

"So you're hoping—"

"I don't *hope*," she says, sharply. "I already have *my* deliverance."

"Well, how exactly is the Lord going to work through Ormant?"

The man laughs. "He certainly doesn't tell *us*. I'm a grocer."

The woman looks like she's considering writing a strong letter to the gods on the subject of their management of karma.

You spend most of the next day at the datamoot. The proposal to oust Khunarg is forgotten— replaced by one which suggested that he be put on trial by the datamoot for abuse of power. The proposal passes in less than an hour, and the trial is underway an hour after that.

A datamoot trial is alarmingly simple. Two motions are floated: convict or acquit. Whichever gets the majority's vote passes— with no appeal. If a planet decides something, there is no higher authority.

Anyone can submit or corroborate evidence, which is accumulated in dedicated, self-organizing datascenes. The defendant, his lawyers, or other supporters can contradict, question the evidence, or submit counter-evidence. News organizations, scholars, lawyers, and others assess the investigate evidence; analysts and AIs create datascenes which display only those statements accepted as well-founded. The NBCC has an impressively large organization engaged in amassing evidence, all of it against Khunarg.

You watch the process with a sort of captivated dread. From the discussion groups, it seems that people pride themselves on looking not directly at the evidence, but at verified statements produced by evidence analysts. There's a mound of verified statements by now— but a statement can be true, and even sound quite bad, and not be relevant to the charges at hand. And how much can the analysts be trusted? Several popular verifiers are datascenes maintained by the NBCC.

Worse yet, most people aren't really voting based on the evidence at all, but on unexamined opinion or moral judgments.

The CONVICT motion grows larger and larger.

Was Beloman right? Are you accomplishing anything by putting the Incatena behind the overthrow of the ICA? It's like judo, you tell yourself. You use your opponent's strength and momentum against him. Only sometimes an opponent decides to use his strength and momentum to crush you like an insect. And then make you into vindaloo.

Was Ba right? Does it really matter to Mars or Sihor what a few benighted provincials do with their planets? Or even if it does, what if you do more harm than good by interfering?

Do Kumari and Ormant ever have these night thoughts? Do they ever worry that perhaps absolute power isn't a completely satisfying career goal? It can't be that pleasant, constantly fending off rivals, rebels, and Incatena Agents. Do they ever wonder if they'd be more happy with lives dedicated to woodworking, bluegrass, and a career in sales?

Not a moment. And that's as good a reason as any to keep on fighting. There's no use worrying about the morality of being an Agent. Worry about the wisdom of working with Ormant, instead.

Of course you're not really working with him; what you're really doing is depriving him of a weapon. Nor are you simply capitulating, as a foolishly superficial analysis might infer. You're replacing a blocked situation with a changed one, one in which the Incatena is no longer perceived as a villain. And in the vacuum after Khunarg all sort of things could happen. Apply some skill and they might even be good things.

Haikoa comes into your room. He wears his usual unreadable half-smile, as if you're doing exactly what he wanted. It's a pretty good smile to have, and you might want to try practicing it in front of a mirror.

"How are you doing?" he asks.

"Never better. You know, it's been a slice, but I think it's time for me to get back to Colony Base."

"You'll miss Harma's trial."

"Harma's going to be tried? By who?"

"By Ormant— starting this afternoon."

"Sorry. I'd really like to see it, but I've got things to do."

"I really have to insist."

"I understand— but no thanks."

"No, I really have to," he clarifies. "You're going to be tried with her."

An eloquent defense

The trial is held in the Temple, the one large and grandiose structure in Satyampur. It's a party for the eyes— a loud and raucous party of the sort sure to attract police attention. The decorators operated on the principle that wherever you couldn't fit a sculpture you could fit in a light bulb, and whatever couldn't fit a light bulb could be gilded.

Hundreds of New Bharatis, from Satyampur and elsewhere, crowd the seats. The stage has been turned into a courtroom, complete with armed guards, a two-storey-high judge's stand over which the four Ormants loom, and an impressive array of data recording, truth gauging, analysis, and broadcasting equipment.

You and Harma are seated at separate tables facing the judges. Haikoa is next to you, to give the illusion that you are being provided with counsel. Harma has a similar tablemate, and in addition two guards stand behind her, lasers drawn. Her mask has been removed, but she is still gagged.

The first Ormant clears his throat. "Let's get the starting gate on the road," he says.

"We call this special session of the Satyampur Judgment Court to order," says the second Ormant. "We're here, of course, to try in open court and justly convict the terrorist from the so-called Freedom Movement, Harma Rakashri, for the murder of twelve citizens of Satyampur, and the attempted murder of Jules Ormant, President of the New Bharat Colony Corporation."

"We'll also convict Agent Morgan of the Terran Incatena as her accomplice in murder," says the third Ormant. "We will show as well that this assassination attempt is only part of a wide-scale, large-bore conspiracy of destabilization engineered by this Martian Agent against the legitimate authorities of two planets."

"The penalty faced by both criminals is death." says the fourth Ormant. "We'll be back after these announcements."

You wonder how much audience share the trial will generate, since the datamoot is still on. It doesn't really matter, of course. Those who don't watch will hear about what's happening. It's pretty obvious what Ormant is doing. He's counting on the trial to portray the NBCC, and the planetary order, as under attack; and he's also attempting to regain whatever ground was lost by your own maneuver.

There's a way out of this, you're sure of it.

Looking round the room, you spot the grocer and his wife in the gallery. You wave. The man waves back, with a grin; his wife looks in your direction without, it appears, any sensation impinging on her retina.

There's got to be a way out.

You look at Haikoa next to you. He looks satisfied with himself, as usual. When he notices you looking at him, he gives you an embarrassed smile and shrugs.

Think. Think.

You look at the journalists and analysts, who take up the first three rows of the audience. They all have their datanodes out, but only a few of them are writing. Most of them, so far as you can tell from here, are logged onto the datamoot instead.

Is there a way out?

You look back at the line of Ormants, just as the third one begins speaking again. He's sweating under the hot holocast lights. "Dataviewers, welcome back; victims, witnesses, and spectators, come to order. Before we fire up the jets and start the ballet, I have a brief announcement from the datamoot. The motion to convict Rama Khunarg for abuses of power has just successfully passed."

A wave of applause bursts over the audience, with whistles and shouts. It's another five minutes before the Ormants can restore order.

"We share your satisfaction," says the third Ormant. "After all, who wants to live under a shaggy-dog dictator who sells out the honest-Joe citizens who tossed him his so-called laurels? And while I've got the gavel, let me announce that the New Bharat Colony Corporation, which is the legal predecessor of the discredited ICA government, will temporarily reassume its functions."

The audience applauds again, with a good deal less enthusiasm. You shake your head, and hope that the New Bharatis are not taken in by this sleight of hand. You wonder if you could bolt into the audience, seize a reporter's datanode, and ask Beloman to nuke the place.

"But now let's jet to the headline attraction which we've marshaled our forces to run up the flagpole," continues the fourth Ormant. "Last night this known terrorist invaded the peaceful religious colony of Satyampur with grievous intent to cause bodily harm to victims. The entire sordid drama was captured in all its virulence by our surveillance devices."

Several holos are shown. It's about as you surmised: a light shuttle touches down in a sports field in the middle of the colony; Harma bursts out and advances like a one-woman army of Arjuna, mowing down all opposition with her buccal plasmator and copious additional weaponry.

A Satyampuri official offers a narration and commentary, which strikes you as fairly superfluous. Even if it weren't a kangaroo court it wouldn't be easy to get Harma out of this one. "Mistaken identity" or "weapons short-circuit" just wouldn't fly. You'd be looking for some sort of trendy mental disease to blame it on.

You look over at her. You expect to see despair or defiance, but you see neither. Rather, there is alertness and calculation. She'd make a good Agent, you think. She keeps thinking she has one more ace up her sleeve, even when she doesn't.

The two of you have a chance to make opening statements. The woman sitting next to Harma stands and explains that she will make Harma's statement, as for the security of the courtroom Harma's restraints cannot be removed. She concedes that the evidence of the holos alone makes a strong case against the defendant— one which, prima facie, would suggest that applying the death penalty would be lenient. And the defense goes downhill from there. Apparently an insanity defense is going to be made; beyond that, the role of the counsel seems to be to quote from Freedom Movement literature in order to underline her dangerous radicalism.

There's no way out, you think.

Finally, Haikoa nudges you, and tells you you have five minutes to speak.

Harma looks at you— a piercing look, but then all of her looks are piercing.

Suddenly you put two and two together. They make four. You understand what you must say.

You address the row of Ormants directly, searching their faces. "*M'sö* Ormant, this is a show trial, and even if I'm allowed to mount a defense, it will obviously be of no avail. I will use my opening statement instead to address you directly— perhaps for the last time.

"I would like to remind you, *m'sö* Ormant— and the people of New Bharat as well— that you are not a citizen of this planet. You are a citizen of Sihor. More than that, *m'sö*, you are a product of Sihor. Your success and your wealth derive from Sihor and from Mars, and you are subject to the laws of those planets— and of the Incatena.

"You will be judged by those laws, *m'sö* Ormant— sooner than you think, perhaps. I am not the only Agent on this planet."

The audience murmurs theatrically. You ignore them, and scan the line of Ormants, carefully, analytically. All are staring at you contemptuously, but your words and the hot lights have had some effect; they are sweating and angry. It's down to two of them, you think.

The second Ormant stills the hubbub with a gesture. "You're a hot-out-of-the-box little loser," he pronounces, leaning forward. "Maybe we should have you gagged as well."

That gives you the clues you need. Something about the voice is off.

"I'm not talking to you," you say. "The androids are not our concern at the moment— only the real *m'sö* Ormant, sitting at the far right— Ormant number four, if you like."

The fourth Ormant stands up and points his finger at you, furiously.

And explodes in a brilliant roaring flash of light.

The heirs

You look over at Harma, and are horrified at what you see. She's blown off not only the gag but her own lips and teeth; the lower half of her face is a burnt, bloody ruin. Before another second goes by, a barrage of laserfire hits her, and she's dead.

But her expression is triumphant.

No one ever expects an assassination, except sometimes the principal, and when it happens he's not in any position to help. There's just no planning. More than once, cleaning up a carpet or a régime, you've felt that leaders should hold a drill— "Listen, what are you going to do if I'm dead? Let's try it out, just so you get familiar with the process. OK, get ready... Blaargghk (slam)!"

But this never happens. So you get a scene like this one— people bustling about, yammering, screaming, crying, interviewing each other, making commaudio calls, gawking at the corpses, trying to assert authority, getting in each others' way.

There is a tradition of shooting the assassin, of course, but that's already been accomplished, so no one stops you as you pick your way through the crowd, making for the door. A few of the guards look at you questioningly, but you smile in the relaxed way of someone who is just stretching their legs, certainly not making a getaway; and since they have no orders, they let you pass.

At the door you find the grocer and his wife.

"You've done your work, haven't you," she says, bitingly. "But don't think that you can outsmart Krishna. You can set back our plans, but you can't stop them— you can't foil the plans of a god. God is stronger than you. You push us down, and we will only rise up stronger than ever. One day we will triumph; and as for you, if I see you in your next life, I shall step on you like any other insect."

"Now, now, you're giving a bad impression," chides her husband. "At least you saw the temple, eh? You have to admit it's really something. I hope you'll come back to Satyampur when

294

things are a little more settled. Can I leave you with a little literature?"

You accept the little book he proffers (*Is it 'uncool' to follow the Way of Truth?*), smile, and step out. The sunshine surprises you, somehow. There ought to be dark, brooding clouds.

One of the androids is walking past purposefully. Seeing you, it stops and stares— rather coldly, it seems to you.

"You've certainly launched a blow that'll have your name on it," it declares.

You make a suggestion; the android responds only with a snort.

Beloman meets you at the Colony Base spaceport. She has a tiny, beat-up little volant; she tosses aside music dots (which squeal their little tunes in protest), dirty clothes, fast food cartons, and weaponry to clear a place for you to sit. She starts flying before you've even closed the door.

"I don't know whether to congratulate you, commiserate, or have you court-martialed," she says. "I mean, is there like *any* one of the plans we've been working on for twenty years you haven't made completely irrelevant? And now instead of that, we have what, exactly?"

"Well, Ormant's gone."

"*One* Ormant is gone," clarifies Beloman. "Who cares if the real one is dead, when his mindset is preserved in triplicate and still running things?"

"Well, about that, there may be—"

"And what is this assassination scene anyway? You *know* there's going to be like an internal audit and stuff. This isn't a holo. We can't solve all our problems just by offing someone. It's— it's self-indulgent."

"It's not like I did it myself."

"Don't declaim responsibility, it was your own damn plan. I mean, I *hope* it was a plan. I'd hate to think it was all some kind of improvisation."

Beloman's suspicion is uncomfortably on the nose. Fortunately, a bit of stupid chance intervenes to distract her: ahead on the road there's a roadblock.

Beloman tries to fly over it, but the roadblock is equipped with a gravity sink, and there's nothing to do but land. Two uni-

296 • Against Freedom

formed figures approach the volant, casually fingering their laser
rifles.

"Papers," says one of them.

Beloman cracks the window. "And who the hell are *you*
pricks?" she asks.

"We're with the Provisional City Government," the man
says, proudly.

"Yeah? Just how long has it been provisionally governing?"

"We're in the process of taking over strategic centers and
data hubs."

"So who's the new top dog?"

"Marshal Kumari," says the man.

He smiles, and then frowns and touches his gun, as if reminding himself of the proper power roles. "So, I need to see
your papers."

New Bharat Masala

"They're in my jacket," says Beloman. "Morgan, would you?"

They watch you as you scrounge in the back seat. She raises her left hand; there's a neural flash in it, aimed at the man at the window.

"Seen a neural flash before?" she asks, conversationally. "There's not many on this planet. It's fast and it's clean, and you won't even feel it shutting down your brain and all, like a few moments before you can even touch your lasers, you know what I'm saying? Morgan, did you find the dealie I wanted in the pack?"

You did; it's a compact plasmator.

"Drop the rifles and step back," orders Beloman.

The men look sullen.

"You're here to man a checkpoint, not a cemetary plot," she suggests. "So, on a count of three..."

The men drop their lasers and step back.

"You got a good line on the grav sink?" Beloman asks you.

"Just a moment."

You open the volant door and stick your head and gun arm outside. The gravity sink is a big black drum several meters across, connected to a smaller control box. You fire the plasmator at the control box. It vaporizes with a resounding boom. You destroy the laser rifles too, for good measure.

The two men stare forlornly at their eviscerated checkpoint.

"Our compliments to the Marshal," Beloman tells them.

"We can't solve all our problems just by blowing things up," you point out. "It's self-indulgent."

"The self-indulgent thing to do would have been to just like fly away," Beloman responds. "Leave the next person to deal with it, you know? It's better to clean stuff like that out."

"You've certainly adapted well to this planet," you remark.

297

298 • Against Freedom

"It's in the Agent Directives," she insists. "When a para-military situation develops, and you're better armed—"

"Yeah, yeah. So where are we headed? How about a bit of dinner? I'm starved."

"We're headed for the war room."

She flies the volant right into the *Atman is Brahman*; you enter the Incatena offices through a port on the underside of the deck. You don't have to take a number. You look down fifty meters at the next deck down, and wonder if a hanging deck in the middle of a gutted colony ship is a good place for a war room, especially if a little war might be in the offing.

In a few minutes you stride into the war room. There are already personnel on duty, who look very alert, monitoring monitors, though you notice one of them seems to be monitoring a game of Final Fantasy MCMXXXIII. You find a datanode, and in very little time, with some help from Beloman to negotiate unfamiliar bits of the interface, you succeed in ordering dinner.

And then it's time to examine the developing situation. The datamoot is still in session, though motions to adjourn are gaining strength. The Ormant androids have established firm control over NBCC. Kumari, blaming the assassination on the Incatena, has declared his Provisional City Government in Colony Base. This has barely registered with the datamoot, which is still preoccupied with Khunarg and the events in Satyampur, but it worries you. There's just one Incatena ship in orbit over New Bharat; judging by what you saw at Jaimunda, you are massively outgunned by Kumari.

"The sitrep is *much* better than before you came," mutters Beloman. "Not."

"It may not be that bad," you say. "Now how do I—"

"Not that bad? We've only given Kumari an excuse to declare martial law and effectively take over the planet."

"How do I make a motion in the datamoot?" you continue.

"How do you the fuck *what*?"

You look at her. She seems upset.

"You're upset, aren't you?" you ask. "Would you like to talk about your feelings?"

"I just want to know *what* you are frying your synapses with."

"So you feel I might be frying my synapses? How does that make you feel? Angry?"

"Of course I'm pissed. Do you know how many years we've been working on the situation here?"

"So you feel your work hasn't been validated? Do you feel hurt about that? I'd feel hurt."

Dinner arrives— eftlizard vindaloo, New Bharat masala, curry custard, nan, tamarind soda. It seems to have a calming effect on Beloman, and you're awfully glad to see it yourself. Satyampuri cuisine didn't do much for you; you've never really accepted the idea that eggplant can do the work of meat, or even eggs.

You write out the motion for the datamoot. Beloman's eyes open wide when she reads it, so that she looks rather like her Vee avatar. She helps you enter it. You don't attempt to hide its provenance; it's a bit of a risk, but you figure it needs the extra attention that support from a major player will give. You also have the Incatena do what it can to shine a spotlight on what Kumari is doing.

"Now what?" asks Beloman.

"We wait," you say.

"What? We could be attacked by Kumari here!"

"You're worried those two coders might have slipped a tracer on us?"

"No, I— shit, they might have, right? They could be attacking any minute. I was just like thinking in general terms— if I was Kumari I'd like reduce any bastions of resistance under cover of the datamoot. And you know how he feels about little old us. We're like totally vulnerable here, aren't we?"

"I doubt they did— they didn't seem to have much presence of mind," you say, calmly, nibbling at a leftover piece of nan. "In which case all Kumari knows is *someone* took offense at his checkpoint. On New Bharat, that could be anyone."

"True."

"As for whether he wants to get into a firefight," you continue, "if it was just a matter of killing people he'd do it, but he'd be destroying the single most commercially valuable property on New Bharat."

"So if he kills us property values take a hit. That's reassuring."

Just in case, you organize part of the staff for defense. If an attack comes, it's likely to be from a few dozen volants firing plasma and laser bursts, supported by a large number of ground troops. In theory the *Atman is Brahman*'s antimissile defenses are still working, and under Incatena control; of course no one's tried them out in a century and a half. More effective will be the anti-projectors and plasma cannons on the upper and lower deck; you send Shan and Beto and two other security people to man them. You also order the orbiting ship into position over Colony Base, for space support. For the ground troops the best defense will be boson homing constellations; with a few of those a handful of men can hold off a thousand moving targets, and the counter-measures aren't likely to be available on New Bharat.

Unless Ormant bought them from the Garcheron, you think. Oh well— if Kumari attacks with everything available at Jaimunda you're doomed. But mobilizing that whole base will take days; you're counting on him to have rushed over to the city with only a fraction of his forces.

Maybe you should just nuke Jaimunda now. Why not, you know? You'd feel better.

You check the datamoot. Your motion is getting bigger, but slowly, slowly. You watch it for awhile; not much happens. Three million people take an excruciating long time to make up their minds.

Around midnight things start to happen. The Incatena ship reports military movements around Colony Base. Your heart sinks as you see the pictures: not just dozens of volants, but hundreds, and jets and shuttles as well. NBCC *is* throwing in everything it's got. The forces take up positions in a circle surrounding the city, and start to move inward.

The colony ship is in the geographic center of the city.

You calculate that you'll have about three minutes' warning for a volant attack. Three minutes for the orbiter and the heavy weapons to destroy those volants. It's doable, so long as the NBCC is stupid enough to send the volants in waves of fifty, like in the holos.

"Why don't we just like nuke Jaimunda?" suggests Belo-man.

"Because we'd be nuked back, property values or no property values."

The forces advance. They're playing it close to their vest, you think. They have the firepower to blast the *Atman is Brahman* into slag; obviously they don't care to do so. Failing that, the best strategy would seem to be to surround the colony ship in overwhelming force and wait for you to surrender. But they're not doing that either; they seem to be simply advancing block by block through the city.

At 00:30 you begin to hear the explosions.

Blowup

You try to follow on fifteen monitors at once. It takes about fifteen more minutes for you to realize that they're not shooting at you.

"It worked," you breathe.

"What?" asks Beloman.

"Just watch."

And as you watch, through the orbiter's spy systems, through a myriad information sources in the Vee, the NBCC forces close in and overwhelm a smaller force. The Vee buzzes to figure out what is happening, but you're pretty sure you know.

"It's Kumari," says Beloman. "They're putting down Kumari. But why? Isn't he on their side?"

"'They'?"

"The NBCC."

"And who's the NBCC?"

"Ormant, of course."

"Ormant's dead."

"OK, the Ormant-bots. Three Ormants, working together."

"Working together?"

Beloman laughs. "I should have known. Three Ormants *can't* work together— at least, once the real Ormant they were slaved to is gone. So this is one Ormant crushing Kumari, or maybe Kumari plus another Ormant. You knew this would happen?"

"I gave it a little push," you confess, modestly. "I suggested to one of the Ormants, as I was leaving the Temple in Satyampur, that we knew that he was the most capable of the three androids, and that Kumari and the other two Ormants were going to be working together to do him in."

"How did you know he was the smartest?"

"I didn't."

"Nice," admits Beloman. "So now we're going to have like a civil war between the three Ormants?"

"No, they'll come to an agreement."

"An agreement? Just like that? Look what's happening on Okura! And with all the weapons and loonies on this planet..."

"The military action is over," you insist. "Kumari would continue it— but he's out of the picture, now. The Ormants don't have any reason to fight; it's bad for business."

As the night turns into morning, the Vee confirms your speculations. Kumari's Provisional City Government lasted less than twenty-four hours. Kumari himself is reported dead, and Haikoa was arrested as an "ideological bandit" by his own subordinate, Akamura. Kawaii-chan is still at large.

The destruction of a gravity sink at one of Kumari's checkpoints was noticed last night, and attributed to a New Bharati citizen aghast at such a totalitarian imposition. A few other such incidents occurred, and are quickly inflated into the myth of a citizens' uprising against the outworld dictator attempting to recreate his empire. *If only I weren't at the datamoot, I would have been fighting this insect myself,* thinks virtually every New Bharati. The fact that Kumari was actually defeated by a branch of NBCC's corporate security forces is relegated to footnotes.

As for the Ormants, it's announced mid-afternoon that Ormant/Mars, and the NBCC with it, will be divided into three separate, competing corporations.

And in the evening, the datamoot accepts your motion, and agrees to reconstitute itself as a constitutional assembly to create a new planetary government.

One freezer ride later

"It's not much of a lounge," complains the Dzebyet.

You look around. The view is spectacular enough: the ceiling and three walls of the lounge are transparent Tajima screens, looking out into the depths of space. It's still possible to see New Bharat as a tiny disc aftward, almost lost in the glare from ζ Tucanae. The lounge itself features sofas in artificial fabrics, a bar, a piano with a mec keyboardist, and a transparent plastic fountain rimmed with lights.

"I guess it is a little tacky," you allow.

"Tacky? I'm referring to the accommodations," she clarifies. "Why no ladders or platforms? Why no seat-specific gravity and temperature controls? Why no chem baths and sim wires? Did the designers think their only passengers would be humans?"

"Probably. But— well, it's mostly for show, anyway. We'll be going belowdecks to get frozen soon enough."

"Not me, I'll be staying awake."

You look over at the little blue alien, twirling the umbrella in her drink, and boggle. "You're not getting frozen?"

"No."

"It's a 28-year trip."

"A little free time," she explains. "Good to catch up on things, you know?"

You shake your head in puzzlement. "I could see a few months of that, sure. Organize my mail, learn *savate*, finally get through all of Agatha Christie and Christophe Ngdeke. But 28 years, with no one to talk to but imaginary friends? No thanks. I know what they all have to say already."

"The AIs stay awake, and they're by far the most interesting humans to talk to."

That's probably true, for a Dzebyet, but you find it a little untactful.

"So what will you do for all that time?"

"Catch up with mail, learn line dancing, read all of Christophe Ngdeke," she responds.

"Ah. So what you're saying is we're not so—"

"Sing everything by Mzoufgé, pray, do some simulation, study the Skweeoo proofs of atheism, remodel my genetic inheritance, prepare for a campaign on Bdelo Ojai, lay an egg, fictionalize my memoirs, build ladders and platforms in this lounge and contemplate the stars, journey into the spiritual realm, see what can be done with this thing you call soybeans."

"So you won't be bored. I guess that's reassuring. Sometimes I think that when we humans have solved all our problems, we'll be bored to death."

The Dzebyet chuckles— a high-pitched, screechy sound, coarticulated with a low-pitched throbbing. "You humans solve your problems? I think my fur won't be blue anymore when *that* happens."

"We're making progress."

"Your minds are a swamp," she remarks, tactlessly. "Why don't you improve them?"

"You mean genetically? It's been discussed, but the consensus is that it's too much of a can of worms."

"Busy little lower life forms, right? I understand how that could be a disturbing image," the Dzebyet remarks, with a pointed look in your direction.

"There's some existential dilemmas here," you point out. "If we modify our basic nature, are we really who we are anymore?"

"Who are you now?"

"Well, that's not easy to say. In a sense we've been trying to answer that question for 10,000 years—"

"If you don't know, there's no loss, then, is there?" she asks.

"Perhaps, but one thing we have found— one thing we have learned— is sometimes we tamper with nature at our peril. We are happier than the caveman, yes—"

"Not really," she says. "We took a look."

"—but not every bright idea turns out happily."

"Well, of course. Your first attempts are going to be catastrophes. Ours certainly were. So we tried again, and eventually got it right. What do you think we've been *doing* for the last 90,000 years?"

*

The terraforming of Mars is proceeding, in dribs and drabs. A few centuries ago, it wasn't possible, in this, the most important of fifty-odd human worlds, to stand outside on the planet's surface without a spacesuit. Now you can walk outside the spaceport, shiver in the ungodly cold, and hold a printout over your head against the drizzle.

While waiting for the railpod, you tap a news dot to upload its contents to your datanode, and on the way home you read the news from Okura. Okura is just 24 light years away, so you have four years of news to catch up on.

The war has been over for several years. There's a coalition government in Atami, which has renounced its empire over the planet— all ten nations are free. Mariko Hitori is the prime minister of Ikkyū-shima; the Master of the Kagedō Shadowmen is president. Xinqeng is still dominated by Gen. Hitsumi and his neoteny, but this doesn't bother you much. The Incatena isn't against social experimentation, unless it's mandated by force, or unless there's no way to opt out.

The Gōsei economy is depressed, as the elements of the coalition squabble over the direction of the country, dismantle the police state, and deal with those— a substantial number of Gōsei-jin— who miss the certainties and glories of the old order. Some of them, plus elements of the Oji, are even hanging on in enclaves in the mountains. Shr is in a constitutional crisis, and for some reason the economy of Kwaikok is crashing, though this is balanced by a boom in Kamandamaung.

In short, it's a normal planet again, to be managed by socionomics rather than by the derring-do of Incatena Agents. It'll muddle through.

You sigh. Well, soon enough, the boss will swivel around in that floating chair of his and send you off somewhere else. Some other trouble spot, some other tricky situation, perhaps another whirlwind romance that plays with your heart like a cat playing with a gopher.

You check the datanode thoroughly, but at this distance, of course, there's no news of Dr. Zhou, and nothing of Ba— unless you count the ads for Ba Sweat Soda, "The taste of light water and gorgeous fruit flavoring that jumps in your mouth, pichi-pichi, ha ha, we are enjoying ourselves now!" Your heart jumps at the mere sight of Ba's name.

Think about something else. How about the fifty years of mail you're going to have to catch up on? How about the fact that your half-century performance review was due twelve years ago? How about making an appointment to get a new explosive tooth installed? You sigh.

Your place is a mess, as usual. But it's your mess. You toss your shoes in a corner, throw your max gun on the couch, and head for your home datanode to check the mail.

You discover that something wet spilled on it, and Iqizi's eaten most of it. You can't get at your mail.

"Good boy," you say, patting him on his unmoving head. "Good trelentocynomorph."

What should you do with the next six months? *Savate*, you think. I should learn *savate*. Or watch every Agatha Christie holo ever made. Order a good Areopolis-style pizza.

Or remodel your DNA. Or see about soybeans.

There's also a place in the program for sleep.

It's a good plan, you think, and you put it into execution right away.

10780035R0

Made in the USA
Lexington, KY
22 August 2011